FURIES:

An Ancient Alexandrian Thriller

D.L. JOHNSTONE

Furies: An Ancient Alexandrian Thriller by D.L.Johnstone
© D.L.Johnstone 2012, All Rights Reserved

AUTHOR'S NOTE: This is a work of fiction. Excluding historical figures, any names, characters, places and incidents either are the product of the author's imagination or are used fictitiously. Any resemblance to actual persons, living or dead, business establishments, events or locales is entirely coincidental. Given that it's set in 36 CE, that shouldn't be a surprise to anyone.

ISBN: 978-148200290

Cover Design: Jeoren Ten Berge
www.jeroentenberge.com/

Map Design: Ryan Mason
relevant.email@gmail.com
www.machinesofbloodandbone.blogspot.com

Author Photo: Martin Cho

Interior layout: Linda Boulanger
www.treasurelinebooks.com/

Proof Editor: Karen Gold

www.dljohnstone.com
www.twitter.com/DLJohnstone1

Also available in eBook publication

Printed in the United States of America

FOR CATHY

It's Always Been For You

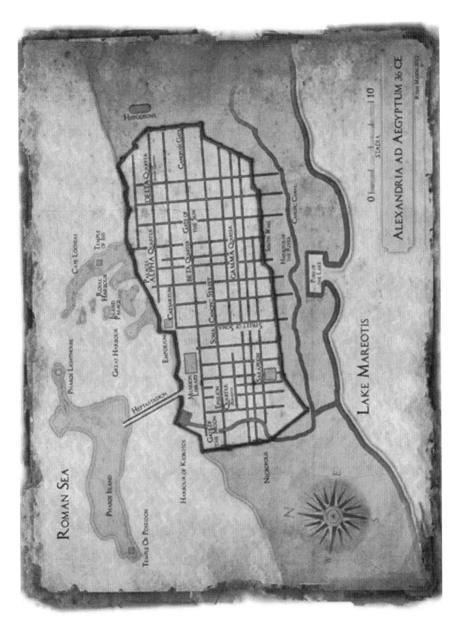

To see an enlarged copy of the Alexandria AD Aegyptum 36 CE map
and other background information on FURIES,
please visit D.L. Johnstone's blog at:
http://dljohnstone.com/furies/alexandria_map-final/

I shall not speak in riddles anymore.
Be witness that I smell out swiftly
The tracks of evil that have long been done.
There is a choir that never leaves this roof,
Unmusical, in concert, unholy.
And it has grown drunken and overbold
On human blood, it riots through this house,
Unriddable blood-cousins, the Furies.

Aescylus - The Oresteia - 458 BC

Dramatis Personae

Decimus Tarquitius Aculeo

Luculla Titiana – Aculeo's wife

Atellus – Aculeo and Titiana's son

Sekhet – Egyptian healer/funerary attendant

Merchants & Bankers

Vibius Herrenius Corvinus – Aculeo's business partner (deceased)

Marcellus Gurculio – Roman moneylender

Iovinus – Middleman for Corvinus and the moneylenders

Marcus Augendus Gellius – Aculeo's friend

Trogus – Gellius' partner

Bitucus – associate of Aculeo

Gaius Durio Pesach – friend of Iovinus, enslaved to a fullery

Lucius Albius Ralla – prominent banker in Alexandria

Posidippus of Cos – another middleman for Corvinus

Marcellus Flavianus – Roman investor

Hetairai & Pornes

Calisto

Neaera – porne at the Blue Bird, lover of Iovinus

Myrrhine – hetaira, friend of Calisto

Panthea – brothel keeper at the Blue Bird

Tyche – porne at the Blue Bird

Petras – cousin of Neaera

Philomena – street porne

Sophists at the Museion

Zeanthes of Araethyrea – friend of Calisto's

Epiphaneus of Cyrene – associate of Zeanthes

Hipparchus – guest at Ralla's symposium

Sostra of Nicaea – associate of Epiphaneus

Others

Xanthias – Aculeo's slave

Gnaeus, Viator & Vibius – Gurculio's freedman and slaves

Marcus Aquillius Capito – Junior Magistrate of Alexandria, friend of Aculeo

Apollonios – a recluse

Harpalus – brother of Apollonios

Idaia – ward of Calisto

Machon & Dryton – Public Order Officers

Avilius Flaccus– Roman Prefect of Egypt

Avilius Balbus – Son of the Roman Prefect

Callixenes – a freedman

Glossary of Terms

Objects & Places

Agora – the city's marketplace

As – a brass coin worth ¼ of a sesterce (NB. Egypt, after falling under Roman rule, operated using Roman currency)

Emporion – a warehouse area used for storage and trade

Heptastadion – A causeway built to connect the Island of Pharos with the mainland; it was seven stades in length, hence the name (*hepta=7)*

Hermes posts – wooden or stone mile-posts carved in the shape of erect penises (don't ask)

Hippodrome – a horse-racing stadium on the eastern edge of the city

Library – the forerunner to our modern libraries, the Library of Alexandria was said to house every written work known to man. Lost to fire and the actions of religious zealots.

Mollosus dog – a now-extinct breed of dog common in the Greek and Roman times, and an ancestor of today's Mastiffs

Museion – home to the scholars and those who came to Alexndria for academic pursuits

Necropolis – City of the Dead, where the remains of citizens were mummified or cremated

Pharos – the Lighthouse, one of the Seven Wonders of the ancient world

Sarapeion – the main temple of Sarapis

Sesterce – (may also be spelled sestertius) currency worth 4 asses. Higher denominations include denarii, aureii and talents; for simplicity sake, and based on readings of the time, I've used sesterces as the common measure

Soma – mausoleum which housed the remains of Alexander the Great, the Ptolemies and their spouses, found in the centre of the city

Stade – a unit of measure, approximately 100 yards in length (root of the modern word stadium, which is, of course, 100 yards long)

The Five Districts of Alexandria

Alpha – the Palace district, which housed the Ptolemeic palaces and assorted government buildings, said to house

Beta – known to exist but unclear what part of the city it occupied; I too poetic license and placed it just below Alpha as a wealthy but non-aristocratic area

Gamma – as with Beta, it was known to exist but without more specific information I chose to place it beteen Beta district and the southern edge of the city on the shores of Lake Mareotis and the Canopic Canal

Delta – the Jewish district, at the eastern section of the city. The Jews were believed to make up about 20% of the city's population at their peak and, unlike most cities in the Roman Empire, were permitted to be citizens of Alexandria with all the rights and prviliges that went along with it (partly courtesy of a substantial head-tax they paid every year)

Epsilon – otherwise known as Rhakotis, the original fishing village around which Alexandria was founded; home of the substantial native Egyptian population

Gods

Anubis – Egyptian god of the dead (the jackal-headed god)

The Furies – Greek/Roman goddesses of the Underworld, responsible for avenging murder victims

Hades (Pluto) – Greek (Roman) god of the Underworld

Harpocrates – the Egyptian hawk-headed god, and child of Isis and Osiris

Isis – the Egyptian goddess of fertility; Isis Pharia is the status of Isis on the island of Pharos

Janus – the two-faced god, god of gateways and root of the month Januarius (looking forward to year ahead and back to prior year)

Poseidon (Neptune) – god of the Sea

Sarapis – Alexandria's patron god of the city, created by the Ptolemies to centralize the citizens' worship; very popular god at the time so it looks like it worked

Zeus (Jupiter) – Greek (Roman) god, led the other gods; Zeus-Soter is the name of the statue of Zeus at the top of the lighthouse as it was commissioned by Ptolemy-Soter

People

Fellahin – the native Egyptian population; typically treated as second class citizens, somewhere between slaves and Romans; over the centuries, intermarriage made such divisions harder to distinguish

Hetairai – high-class courtesans

Murmillone – a type of gladiator, typically matched vs a retarius

Negotiatore – a middle-man who would represent the business interests of investor, either locally or from elewhere in the Empire

Porne – a prostitute; of a lower 'rank' than hetarii

Praegenarii – a clown who would be used to entertain the audiences between gladiatorial contests; often they were dwarves

The Ptolemies – the Royal dynasty that ruled Egypt, from (Alexander the Great's general) Ptolemy-Soter in 331 BCE to Cleopatra VII Philopater in 30 BC. The last true Ptolemy would have been Caesarion, son of Julius Caesar and Cleopatra, who murdered by Augustus Caesar after Rome's victory in Egypt, thus consolidating any would-be claims to the throne

Thrattia – a derogatory term for a bar maid – means 'of Thrace'

CHAPTER I

ALEXANDRIA AD AEGYPTUM
THE 1ST DAY OF JANUARIUS, 36 CE

Decimus Tarquitius Aculeo gazed bleakly about his stylish multi-level villa. It looked so desolate now with the crates and chests filled with every last stitch and stick of the family's fine belongings, now stacked up in the vestibulum and along the main hallway like vegetables heading off to market. Most of the furniture was already gone while that which remained was covered in sheets of canvas, ready to be taken. The moneylender's slaves walked back into the house, marching right through the front gate bold as could be, their sandals caked with dust from the street, ready to heft the next load into the wagon. Aculeo clenched his jaw as he watched them, wanting for all the world to kick them out into the street, but holding his tongue. Gnaeus, the toad-like little freedman, strutted about the villa, chest puffed out, touching everything with his grubby hands, barking out orders on what should be taken next.

Titiana watched from the edge of the tablinum, her lovely face expressionless, a plain woollen travelling cloak wrapped tightly around her graceful shoulders. Her hair, gleaming and black, an elegant contrast to her alabaster skin, was tied back in a simple Cypriot braid beneath her veil. Her hands lay on the shoulders of little Atellus who sat at her side on a pretty couch, the one with the ivory legs and mother-of-pearl inlaid like flower petals along the arms, which they had bought only last summer. So long ago, last summer. Back when the world itself seemed to lay at their feet.

"Titiana …" Aculeo started.

She turned away, gazing out the window, her perfect lips pressed tight together, the very picture of decorum. Titiana would never have risked saying something that would embarrass the family, even in front of slaves. Not even now. He couldn't help but recall the way her eyes had shined with delight the first day they'd wandered through the atrium, when? Only two years ago? Was that possible? The way she'd clutched his arm in excitement as they'd strolled for the first time through its Aswan marble halls to the garden colonnade with its fine statuary, elegant box hedges and sparkling fish ponds. Oh, and the exceptional view of the city from the rear atrium – she'd actually gasped at the sight. Truly it was the finest home in all Alexandria. Now to be auctioned off to the highest bidder like some wretched old fellahin shack. It was all too much!

Viator, the bald slave, snatched up the Etruscan amphora set in a central nook of the wall, clearly a place of honour. Titiana flinched, her cheeks flushed, but she held her silence.

"Put that down," Aculeo snapped.

"My master told us to take it all," Viator said.

"Your master can get buggered by a radish." Atellus looked up at his father, his eyes wide in surprise, but remained silent as his mother. "That was never part of it."

Gnaeus appeared, took the amphora from Viator, smearing the splendid black and red surface of the double-handled amphora with his greasy fingerprints. "It's not worth much anyway," he said, pursing his lips. "Two hundred sesterces perhaps."

"It's a classic piece, worth twenty times that," Aculeo seethed.

Gnaeus scratched at his beard - probably swarming with fleas, Aculeo thought. "Three hundred at most," the freedman said with a shrug.

"Just put it …"

"Oh what does it matter?" Titiana said irritably. "I'm surprised you didn't pawn it as well."

"I could never have done that," Aculeo said. "I gave it to you on our first anniversary."

She sighed and turned to Gnaeus. "Five hundred."

"Titiana, no …"

"Is it mine or not, Aculeo?"

"Of course, but …"

"It's a long journey to Rome and we need silver more than an old amphora." She turned her attention back to the freedman. "Five hundred.

No more haggling, I'm not a fishwife in the Agora."

Gnaeus smirked and counted out the coins, then passed the amphora to Viator. "Box it up with the rest."

"Back to work, leeches," the old slave Xanthias snapped, herding them out of the tablinum. "Leave the Master and Mistress be!"

The moneylenders' slaves returned to stripping the contents out of the villa, stacking the fauces with more crates, tables, chairs, tapestries unhooked from the walls, preparing to load it all into the mule wagons parked outside the gates.

"Titiana, if you'd only just listen to me," Aculeo whispered, kneeling on the floor at her feet, trying to take her small hand in his. She gently but firmly pulled it from his grasp.

Little Atellus beamed at his father. "Why you on the floor, Poppa?" he asked.

Aculeo felt his heart break at the child's sweet beauty, his plump, rosy cheeks and lips, thick chestnut curls and oh, his mother's golden-brown eyes. "I'm just tired," he said, smiling at the boy.

Atellus raised his hands, sticky from the honeyed dates he'd been eating, and chirped, "Poppa, come play!" Aculeo laughed and snatched him up, tossing him in the air. Atellus squealed in delight and Aculeo tried to kiss his cheek but the boy was too full of energy. He squirmed out of his father's arms and ran down the marble hallway towards the atrium.

"Ah, he's heading to the garden again. I'll fetch him," Xanthias said, leaving them alone at last.

"Titiana, it's not the season to travel," Aculeo pleaded. "By the Gods, we just lost two fleets! Why don't you wait until spring at least, or summer?"

"Perhaps you should have picked a better time to lose everything," she said. The softness of her tone did little to reduce the words' sting.

"A few months at most and we'll be back on our feet."

"Don't be a fool, Aculeo."

"Titiana, you have to trust me ..."

"Trust you?" she cried, tears in her dark, lovely eyes for the first time since he'd broken the news of their bankruptcy ten days ago. "Why didn't you trust me enough to even discuss things before you threw everything away on Corvinus' foolishness?"

"It was an investment. An investment like any other ..."

"An investment that required you to put up our house as security? Our entire estate? Even my dowry?"

"Titiana ..."

"My dowry, Aculeo, not yours to do with what you will. But that wasn't enough, was it? No, you had to tangle up some of our dearest friends in your *investment*, ruining them as well for the sake of that stupid, stupid man!"

"We owed our entire fortune to Corvinus."

"Where is that fortune now, husband? And where is the man? Both just ashes on the pyre."

She's twisting it, Aculeo thought, though he held his tongue. How could I have predicted what would happen? How could anyone? Storms off Portus had sunk not just the primary but also the secondary of the company's great fleets of grain freighters. And when Aculeo had called on Corvinus and discovered the villa empty, his patron's pale, bloated body floating in the bath, the blood from his open veins staining the bathwater, flies already crawling across his forehead …

"Corvinus was like my own father! How could I have said no?"

She fixed him with a withering glare. "How could you have said yes? And borrowing from a man like Gurculio!" She spat out the name as though she had a mouthful of lye.

The moneylender's slaves stumped into the room opposite. Vibius approached the death masks of the illustrious Tarquitius ancestors hanging on the wall in their ashwood frames and plucked one off, examining it in puzzlement. "What about these?" he asked, passing it to Gnaeus.

"Put that down, fool," Aculeo hissed.

"I can get a good price for them if you like," Gnaeus offered. "New men are always trying to gild their pasts." Aculeo glowered in response, seething. "Fine, dusty old things anyway," the freedman said, tossing it carelessly onto a table. The masks seemed to gaze across the room at Aculeo, silently casting their unanimous judgement.

Xanthias returned with Atellus in hand, the boy's tunic smeared with dirt. "Can you not stay clean for five minutes?" Titiana sighed.

"I'm sorry Mistress, he was too quick for me," the slave said.

"You too old," the child proclaimed.

Titiana allowed a small smile, laying her hand gently on the slave's cheek. "Thank you, Xanthias. It's hardly your fault, he's quite wilful. Come, Atellus," she said, holding out her hand for her son. The boy stuck out his lower lip and hugged Xanthias, turning away from his mother.

"Perhaps he's hungry," Xanthias said. "I'll have the cook make him something."

"He just ate. I don't want him to get sick. He can eat again once we're aboard."

"Titiana, I beg you not to go," Aculeo said.

Titiana closed her eyes. "Please don't make it more difficult than it already is."

He took her in his arms, holding on tight. "I can't bear to lose the two of you," he whispered.

"Oh my love, don't you see? You already have."

Aculeo felt actual pain at her words, like a knife stabbing in his heart. "Titiana, I give you my oath," he said, his throat so tight he could barely speak, "I'll get it all back. This is just a temporary setback. We'll build a palace, anything you could ever want ..."

She looked up at him, her dark, lovely eyes glistening with tears. "It's not about our money, our home, our things. I love you in spite of all that. I always shall."

"Lucullus then?" he asked bitterly. Titiana's father, Lucullus, had been tepid about the marriage from the very start, especially given that it had involved his beloved daughter moving from Rome across the sea to Alexandria.

"I don't care what my father thinks," she said, stroking her fingers back through his hair, sweeping the stray curls off his forehead. "It's about Atellus."

Aculeo felt a lump swell in his throat as he gazed down at their perfect little boy running about the aulos. "Atellus? He's just a child. By the time we're back on top he'll not even remember this."

"Oh won't you face the truth for once? You've ruined your family's good name with this horrid mess. You've thrown away your honour. That's bad enough for you. For me. But I can't allow that for Atellus. I won't."

"But ... what will I do without you," he whispered.

"Oh my love," she said. He could have faced her anger or resentment, he'd grown used to it over the past few weeks, but not the pity that now lay like heavy stones in her eyes. He looked away, wishing he could crawl into a deep, dark hole in the ground. She wrapped her arms around his shoulders, held him close, kissed his cheek with her soft, warm lips. He tried to kiss her back, to embrace her but someone made a small coughing sound behind them. Titiana's slave stood in the hallway, pointedly avoiding Aculeo's gaze. Even the damned slaves won't look at me, he thought bitterly.

"The wagon is ready, Mistress," the slave said. "We need to hurry or the ship will leave without us."

"Come then," Titiana said firmly, breaking away from Aculeo. Too soon, too soon. Atellus put his head down and went to her at last. She took the boy by the hand and led him down the hallway, past the stacks of

D.L. Johnstone

boxes and furnishings towards the gates and then into the hired wagon. They're leaving, Aculeo thought, they're actually leaving. He followed them.

"You come too, Poppa?" Atellus asked as Aculeo tried to step into the wagon.

Titiana held up her hand. "No. You shouldn't show your face in public yet," she said. "It's too soon." She looked towards Xanthias. "You're to take care of him."

"Yes, Mistress," the old slave said, tears running down his deeply lined cheeks.

"Why Poppa and Xanfas not come?" the boy asked, sensing something was amiss.

"You're taking a special trip to Rome just with your Mamma, remember?"Aculeo said, forcing a smile, though his eyes were burning. "I'll come as soon as I can."

Titiana paused before handing him a small packet wrapped in linen. "What's this?" he asked. She said nothing. He looked at her for a moment, then reluctantly unwrapped the bundle. It was her emerald necklace with the matching earrings – his wedding present to her. They suddenly felt heavy as a millstone in his hands. "Titiana, no ..."

"They'll only get stolen when we get onboard," she said.

"Oh, of course," he said at last. "I'll ... I'll keep them here for you then."

"Aculeo ..."

"I'll keep them safe for you. I'll come for you once I've found my feet again. By summer at the latest. My oath."

Titiana held his gaze for just a moment, unsmiling now, unreachable. "If you truly love us you'll let us be," she said. She nodded to the driver and the wagon rattled off along the creamy paving-stone street towards the city, the winter breeze cold and damp off the Egyptian Sea.

"I should stop them," Aculeo said hoarsely. "I... I should do something."

Xanthias shook his head. "No, Master. The mistress is right. Let them go."

Gnaeus appeared next to him in the doorway, scratching at his beard. "When are you leaving?"

"The agreement was midnight," Xanthias snapped.

"The auction's first thing in the morning. Gurculio's orders ..."

"Oh shove Gurculio's orders and let the man be!" The freedman scowled but slumped away. Xanthias turned to Aculeo and said gently, "How about some wine, Master? There's an amphora of aged Tameotic

6

I've been holding back. An excellent vintage. Or so I'm told."

"No, nothing," Aculeo said, and wandered back through the villa. It had been so full of life only a moment ago. Now it was just the echoes of his sandals slapping against the stone, the empty chatter of the slaves as they packed everything up. The back wall had been removed last summer to reveal an extraordinary view of the city down below, the vast gridwork of red clay tile roofs and bone-white buildings, temples and palaces that lay beyond. To the north, ships bobbed in the Great Harbour of the wine-dark Egyptian Sea. There in the harbour the great Pharos soared, dove grey in the early morning light, a billowing trail of smoke and glint of yellow firelight spilling forth from the lighthouse mouth, and Rome itself a lifetime away.

Aculeo thought he heard the sound of distant horns and drums, a joyous festival in the city, and realized it was the first day of Januarius. Already? He watched a flock of brown and grey birds pass overhead from left to right before they turned as one and wheeled out to the darkening sea.

He couldn't recall if the omen was good or bad.

CHAPTER II

THE 15TH DAY OF APRILIS

Aculeo awoke to the sounds of the street below and squinted about his little bedroom, which was hardly big enough to hold his simple, narrow pallet. Rays of morning light scratched across the cracked plaster ceiling. The crumbling walls were etched with graffiti from previous occupants, stained with soot and sweat and the gods knew what else. And the smell, a rank, musty odour that seemed to have penetrated the very walls. He'd hoped when he and Xanthias had moved here a month ago that the stench would eventually fade but it had only gotten worse over time, as though something had died, a prior resident even, and been plastered into the walls themselves.

He closed his eyes again. Nights were the worst – long hours spent staring at the ceiling waiting for dawn to come. He'd fallen into a dull routine of late, drinking himself into a stupor every night as hope slipped through his fingertips like water. Never mind, it's morning now. I only have to get through the oppressive weight of yet another day.

His head throbbed, the taste of sour wine like paste on his tongue. I don't even remember coming home last night, he muddled, though I suppose I must have. What day is it anyway? The twelfth? Thirteenth? I'm losing track. No, it's the fifteenth, the Ides. Which makes it three-and-a-half months since Titiana and Atellus returned to Rome. Three-and-a-half months. Is that all it's been? Still, it's better they aren't here to witness this. Or, even worse, be part of it.

As the ripples of financial disaster had spread and the other investors began to experience the full effects of their own ruin, rumours had sparked and fanned – that perhaps it had all been a scam, with Corvinus and Aculeo themselves at the root of it. Aculeo must have hidden the money away somewhere and was even now preparing to flee the city! And like a beautiful, elaborate knot severed by a blunt sword, he'd run out of both willing hosts and most of his remaining funds. These simple lodgings, a two-room flat above a marble worker's shop, had to suffice for now.

A line of silverfish emerged from the window's cracked edge, scuttled across the wall and slipped behind the wooden frame of his father's funerary mask – which had apparently become their new nest. *I should have sold you to the damned moneylender after all, Father, it would have given you a better view of the world at least.*

"Ah, there you are. I thought for certain you'd been murdered in an alley somewhere," a bitter voice pronounced. Xanthias was standing in the doorway staring down at him, shaking his bald, freckled head.

"You seem disappointed I wasn't," Aculeo grumbled.

"Not at all, Master. My soul dances at the prospect of another day basking in your presence."

"Shut up and leave me be."

"Of course, Master," Xanthias said with a deep, mocking bow. He snatched up the tunic Aculeo had dropped in a heap on the floor and held it up against the morning light, a sour look on his face. "Are these blood or wine stains?"

"How should I know?"

"As you wore it, Master, I had hoped you may have been able to shed some light upon the matter. It's scraping the top off an empty measure, I know …"

"Oh by the gods, just let me sleep in peace!" Aculeo snapped and tugged the woollen blanket back over his head, hoping the room would stop whirling about long enough to let sleep overtake him again. *I'll get back on my feet soon enough,* he thought. *And Corvinus will rise up from his scattered ashes, our broken fleets will lift from the bottom of the sea, the money will flow once again, my debts will disappear, Titiana and Atellus will return to my arms, she'll beg for my forgiveness, as will our so-called friends, I'll buy back our villa and then … then the world will be restored to sanity.*

A pleasant dream to cling to at least.

Aculeo was just drifting back into the dark, subsuming tide of sleep when the silence of his bedroom was shattered by an ear-splitting din of hammering and chiselling, followed by laughter and a stream of fellahin chatter. It was the damned marble workers from the shop below, who'd just begun their day's work. He could already taste the chalky marble dust on the back of his tongue.

"Pluto's stinking hole," he grumbled. There was no chance of sleep now. He crawled out of the bed, his feet found the cool floor, and he pulled a tunic from the chest. He held it up to the light. It was cheap linen fabric, so plain and such a provincial design he despised it but there was little choice. He gave it a cautious sniff, made a face at the off-smell, then slipped it on anyway.

"Where are you going?" Xanthias asked as he emerged from the cubicle of a bedroom.

"To the Agora, then the baths."

"The baths?" the slave said in a tone that made Aculeo feel like a wayward child.

"It's been days since I last went. I can barely stand my own smell."

"A wiser man would simply be thankful he still has a nose with which to smell his own stink. We've not a crumb of food in the pantry and our rent is due."

"I've got business prospects still," Aculeo said irritably. "I'll take care of it."

"Business prospects!" Xanthias cried. "Haven't you already tossed away what little money we had left on dice and wine?"

"You're a slave. You know nothing of business."

"I know something about a fool and his silver though."

"I'll be back in a few hours with some money and tonight we'll eat and drink like Caesar himself."

"A flawless plan, Master. Then tomorrow we can go back to starving like Tantalus."

Aculeo watched the pawnbroker turn the emerald earrings about between his stubby fingers, holding them up to the dusty light. "You should've brought 'em to me at the same time as the necklace," the man said. "I could have given a better price."

"I wasn't planning to sell them at all," Aculeo said dully. He'd pawned the necklace over a month ago, and the coins he'd gotten for it had flowed through his fingers like water.

"No one ever does," the pawnbroker said with a dusty laugh. He laid the pretty baubles out on the counter, giving them a weary appraisal. "Eighty."

"Eighty sesterces? That's outrageous, I paid over a thousand …"

"I don't care what you paid, I care what I can get for them. We're hardly in the Painted Stoa here after all." The man pursed his lips distastefully. "A hundred, but that's it."

"Three hundred or …" The pawnbroker snorted. "Two?" The man slid the earrings back towards him. "Fine. A hundred."

It's alright, Aculeo told himself hollowly as he watched the pawnbroker tuck the earrings away and set a small stack of coins out on the counter. It's fine, I'll buy them back and more when things are right again.

The Street of the Pawnbrokers was little more than a rutted back alley that reeked of piss and old vomit, its tight walls echoing with the dusty clink of mallets from the workers inside the countless shops along its length. It was part of the close-packed artisans' ghetto, tucked in amidst the Street of the Goldsmiths, the Street of Textiles, the Booksellers Street and all the rest. The upper balconies of the surrounding tenements huddled together, practically touching one another, blocking all but a sliver of blue sky overhead.

The day was early still, pedestrians meandering into the shops were a scattered few. Aculeo's mind wandered as he headed towards the baths, his joints aching as he walked over the cracked, uneven paving stones, feeling aged beyond his years.

"Aculeo?" a chipper voice cried. "Aculeo, is that you?" Aculeo reluctantly turned around and saw a plump, finely dressed young man with a large port-stain birthmark across his right cheek approaching him. Fundibus Varus – of all people to run into down here. The gods do enjoy shitting on mortal men.

Aculeo forced a tight-lipped smile. "Varus. What a pleasant surprise."

Varus' eyes flitted over Aculeo's patched, plain tunic, a joke compared to his own pure white linen finery embroidered with glittering gold, blue and scarlet thread. Varus tore his gaze away in an effort to appear not to notice. "Well, well, I haven't seen you in months. How've you been?"

"Never better. What are you doing down here?"

Varus gave a theatrical sigh. "Shopping for a new fountain of all things. My lovely young wife, Aelia, is anxious to decorate the new villa in the very latest fashion."

"You have a new villa?"

"Oh yes, you know, Valentinus' old place. I picked it up at auction earlier this year. And dirt cheap, too, I never thought ... oh," Varus said, putting a manicured hand to his mouth, looking mortified.

Valentinus, Aculeo recalled, his stomach churning. Valentinus, Montaus, Protus, Bitucus, Gellius ... and how many other of our friends lost their homes, their fortunes? He'd given up counting. He hadn't been able to watch the auction of his own villa, though Xanthias had heard it had sold for just three hundred fifty thousand sesterces – a sickening plunge from what he'd paid only two years prior. That was what happened when too many fine homes went on auction all at once and the mortgage-holders were anxious to unload.

Aculeo managed a tight smile. "Don't worry. I'd likely have done the same given the chance. You and Aelia are happy there I trust?"

"Oh yes, very. Still, I must do my utmost to keep her in the manner to which she is accustomed. You know women," he said with a knowing wink. "What of Titiana and your son ... Atellus isn't it? How are they?"

Will the torture never end? Aculeo thought, his head ringing with the man's inane chatter. "Never better."

"Did I hear they were back in Rome?" Varus asked, trying to sound nonchalant.

"Yes, actually, visiting family." Aculeo's mouth ached from holding his rictus smile. He'd heard word from mutual acquaintances that while the divorce was not yet final, there'd already been numerous inquiries to her father, Lucullus, from potential suitors. He glanced sideways at the other man. The rotten prick – he probably knows this already! Gossip spreads faster than thistles!

"Family is important, but Rome's so dreary this time of year. Ah well," Varus sighed. "Shall we get something to eat perhaps? It will give us a chance to catch up properly."

"Thanks, but no," Aculeo said. "I'm far too busy today. You know how it is."

"Oh, oh yes, of course," Varus said, clearly disappointed. "Too bad though. I was planning to head to the Hippodrome."

"Just as well, I've already dropped enough silver on the races this week, so..."

"I know that feeling. Still I've a tip about one running today." Varus gave a wink. "From a very reliable source."

Aculeo considered the man with renewed interest. "Oh? How reliable?"

The street leading to the Hippodrome's main entrance gates was lined with beggars and weary-looking pornes loitering in the shade of the palm and acacia groves, awaiting emerging patrons to help them either spend their winnings or drown their sorrows with whatever coins they might still possess. The building itself was a vast, oval-shaped structure, six stories high and the length of three stadia, elegant and lovely creamy limestone framed against the dusty blue Egyptian sky. Grandiose rose-veined marble gates marked the main entrance, wide enough to allow four chariots riding abreast to pass within, and twice again as tall.

Outside the gates, three young Roman soldiers gave offering at the Shrine of Bucephalus, Alexander's loyal mount during his successful twelve-year campaign to conquer the world four centuries ago. It was said that upon the beast's death in battle, a grieving Alexander had spent a staggering fifty talents on his funeral in addition to establishing the namesake city of Bucephala on the banks of the Hydapses. The conqueror's further plans to build a series of grandiose monuments throughout the empire commemorating his stallion, however, expired when he himself did on the battlefield in Babylon. This alabaster shrine – a place of worship for all lovers of horse and chariot races, evidenced by the number of votive offerings littered about the statue's hooves – had to suffice.

"Say, isn't that Gellius?" Varus said. "Gellius!"

Caught off guard, Aculeo glanced towards the gates where Varus was looking. The man standing there was thinner than he recalled Gellius ever being, and pale as milk, his chin badly in need of a shave, his hair an unruly brown mop atop his head, but it was certainly him. Aculeo was seized with a sudden, stark panic. He tried to look away but caught the other man's furious glare of recognition. Aculeo stammered and began to sweat. He tried to think of something to say but Gellius turned and left without a word.

"What's with him I wonder?" Varus asked as they continued down the mosaic-tiled corridor. "Ah well, I suppose it has something to do with that Corvinus nonsense, it quite ruined him ..." He glanced at Aculeo, eyes wide, and bit his bottom lip. "Ah, by Hera, there I go again, I didn't mean that ..."

"My own losses were minimal," Aculeo lied again, offering what he hoped resembled a carefree smile.

"Well, that's good. It's part of doing business, I suppose," he said, giving Aculeo a quick, sidelong glance.

They passed through the gates, the marble archway overhead carved with an elaborate frieze of a chariot race. The stench of rancid sweat from the crowds within, straw, manure and spilled beer all proved a challenge to his unsettled stomach and throbbing head. The heat inside the Hippodrome was relentless, the viewing area where most of the crowd stood unprotected from the strong Egyptian sun. Slaves walked around the inner ring of the track between races carrying large buckets of sparsiones, perfumed water which they sprayed as a mist over the welcoming crowd, providing them with some relief from both the heat and oppressive smell.

Betting brokers wove their way through the throngs, offering their odds, taking patrons' bets and silver. Aculeo watched the next group of race horses being led in from the back stables towards the red clay dirt track ring within.

"Place a wager, sir?" one of the brokers asked him. "Four to one on Heracles' Fury."

"That's the one," Varus whispered eagerly.

Aculeo, still brooding over his encounter with Gellius, watched the other patrons standing nearby appraising the animals and their riders, touching them, saying a prayer, spitting out a curse, anything to gain an edge in the upcoming race. "Which one is she?"

"See there, in the green colours with the white blaze on her forehead?" the broker said. "An auspicious sign, sir."

She is a fine looking beast, Aculeo thought, sleek black coat, fine long legs, fire in her eye.

"Five to one," Varus proposed.

"Ah, sir, too steep," the broker said, scratching at his beard. "I could do nine to two."

"Done," said Varus. Aculeo was thoughtful for a moment and gave a silent prayer to the gods before he counted out his silver and took the betting slip from the broker. The two men climbed the staircase to the second level to find some seats.

Aculeo looked down at the oval track as the horses were led into their stalls, their gleaming noses peering over the starting gate, anxious to begin. The red flag was dropped and the horses thundered out of the starting gate and the crowds roared in delight. The horses rounded the first corner, their bare-chested riders driving them, the crowds cheering them on. Varus cheered loudly for Heracles' Fury, slapping his hands against the rail.

A familiar face caught Aculeo's eye, moving through the crowd on the level below. Isn't that Iovinus? he thought, his blood practically chilling within his veins. It can't be. He moved closer to the rail, leaning over as far as he could. The same bony frame, stilt-legged walk, big ears, deeply receding hairline … it was surely him. The man licked his lips and gave a nervous look about, as though he was aware he was being watched. Iovinus, who had been Corvinus' and Aculeo's negotiatore, working as the conduit between the investors and the moneylenders to arrange the loans for the fleets, including for the final cursed voyages. He'd even sailed aboard the flagship of the second fleet to complete the exchange of goods on the other side. So what in the name of the blessed fucking Apollo is he doing here instead of at the bottom of the Roman Sea where the fish could pick his bones clean?

He watched Iovinus push his way through the cheering throngs towards the exit. Aculeo bolted towards the stairway – it was all he could do to keep from screaming. The horses thundered around the track below, clouds of red dust flying in the air beneath their hooves, their riders dressed in leather kilts switching them across their haunches, driving them on, the crowds roaring for their favourites.

"Where are you going?" Varus cried. "The race isn't done!"

Aculeo raced down the steps, trying not to lose the man. Iovinus. Iovinus! How could that wretched, miserable bastard possibly still be alive while everything I had is gone? He reached the bottom level and elbowed through the spectators, including a pair of angry soldiers, drawing as close as he could as Iovinus neared the exit, almost close enough to grab the leather satchel slung about the man's bony shoulder.

Someone shoved into him hard, almost knocking him down. "Where do you think you're going?" a man's voice cried, trembling with rage. Aculeo spun around in surprise – Gellius.

Iovinus had gained a few steps now and was almost through the exit. "Not now, Gellius," Aculeo growled, trying to push past the man, but Gellius grabbed the hem of his tunic. Iovinus had almost reached the street. "Will you just …"

"I don't think so!" Aculeo glanced down and paused. Gellius was pointing a shard of broken roof tile at him in a shaky hand. "I want to talk to you."

The crowds roared again as Heracles' Fury pulled a full length ahead of the rest, pounding along the track towards the finish. The impressive lead was quickly undone however when the horse stumbled a few lengths from the finish line and rolled into the dust. The crowd cried out in anguish as the horses that followed stumbled as well, tripped by the first horse's upturned legs, all except the last, who managed to avoid the chaos

D.L. Johnstone

and surge forward, her nose alone across the finish line.

"Gellius, I've got to go!" Iovinus was on the street now, slipping into the crowd.

"No!"

Aculeo pulled out of the man's grasp to head to the gates when a hot streak of pain sliced across his upper arm. "Fuck!" he cried and punched Gellius square in the face. Gellius' eyes went wide with shock as he fell awkwardly to the ground, hand to his face, blood streaming through his fingers. He sat there blubbering like a child. Aculeo broke away, looking around desperately for Iovinus.

The agonized whinnies of the fallen horses filled the Hippodrome, the poor beasts in obvious distress as they struggled to stand on their shattered legs, while slaves hurried out onto the track to dispatch them.

And Iovinus was gone.

CHAPTER III

Aculeo and Gellius threaded their way through the crowded laneways of the Agora. The market was alive with the raucous chaos of flute and drum from streetside musicians begging for spare coins, the bellowing cries of the merchants trying to entice any potential customers and the shrieks of street children playing tag amongst the stalls. A man took his life in his hands walking at mid-day down these narrow, twisting streets as pedestrians competed with chariots, mule carts, cattle and oxen. A pungent clash of smells hung in the air of rich spices from the Indes, fresh caught fish, roasted chickpeas, baking bread, barley beer and fresh garlic, mixed with the ripe, sweaty smell of the people themselves, gossiping, bartering, eating, drinking as they went.

"I should have left you there to rot," Aculeo said, his wounded arm bound in a makeshift, blood-stained bandage.

"I'm surprised you didn't," Gellius said with a sniff. "You already stole our fortune, you thieving prick!"

"I've told you a thousand times already, I didn't steal anything from anyone."

"Say it a thousand more and I'll still not believe you!"

"Then don't. Where are you living?"

"The Little Eagle in Delta."

"A tavern?"

"It's just a temporary arrangement," Gellius said.

Aculeo made no reply. Before the shipwrecks, Gellius lived in a fabulous villa with his partner Trogus just outside the palace district in Beta, an elegant showcase of a home where they'd hosted countless spectacular affairs, bolstered by a cellar stocked with the finest wines.

17

Now look at him, limping along the street, gaunt, broken, his cheeks wan and unshaven, dark shadows like thumbprints pressed beneath his eyes. His tunic was a fine weave but frayed and greasy with wear, and now further marred by bloodstains down the front. His nose had stopped leaking at least, though it was swollen and dark as a fig.

"You there, sir," a merchant cried, "yes that's it, come in, come here. Tell me, have you ever seen such a beautiful carpet as this one? Straight from Babylon, not one of those Assyrian shitrags like they sell at the stalls down the way, I wouldn't even let my wife's mother wipe her buttocks with one of those. Look at this, look at the craftsmanship, I tell you there's not another one like this in the world. Your wife would be the envy of her friends, believe me."

"Just got a fine selection of new slaves in, my dear sir, you're in luck," exhorted another merchant. "You're the first to see them, so you get first pick. This one, she's a Thrattian, not so pretty I agree, a bit old and yes her teeth are not the best but she's a hard worker and if you bring her home then perhaps your wife would forgive you for buying this lovely little one over here as well ..."

"Fish?" another grinning vendor cried. "Come here. Look here, shark, tunny, oh, and Canopic eels – you'll dine like Caesar himself. These were still swimming about in the sea this morning, they'll be on your dinner plate tonight, come now, sir ..."

"I do miss eels," Gellius said softly. "Our old cook used to wrap them in beet leaves, cook them over some coals, serve them with some Antylla wine, sweet as plums ..."

Aculeo's own stomach ached at the memories of fine meals and evenings filled with wine and music and careless joy. Enough. "Let's just get you home."

"I haven't a home anymore, thanks to you," Gellius snapped, though he let himself be helped all the same.

A weathered sign painted with the image of a tattered birdlike creature swung over the door. This must be the Little Eagle, Aculeo mused. It was situated on a dingy little side street. It had a small dining area with a few mismatched tables and chairs and no place to recline – which was likely just as well, one wouldn't want to get too comfortable here. Freedmen, pornes and clusters of sailors sat at the tables jabbering away in their foreign tongues, sizing up the new arrivals. Aculeo reluctantly followed Gellius inside.

The owner, a bald, dark-skinned man with hooded eyes and damp circles staining the armpits of his tunic, stood sweating behind a long, scarred marble counter. The length of the counter was interrupted every few feet by the purple-stained mouth of a large clay wine jar set into its surface. At the end of it was a charcoal brazier that filled the little tavern with eye-stinging smoke. The grill sizzled with chunks of meat and a simmering pot of water, the wall behind it charred with soot. Overhead, an arbour tangled with a few withered grape vines provided scant shade.

"Ah, Silo," Gellius called in a friendly manner to the capo. "Could I trouble you for a cup of wine? It's not bad actually," he told Aculeo. "A bit ordinary but ..."

"Show me the money first," the capo snapped.

Gellius glanced towards Aculeo, then looked away, not wanting to speak the obvious. "Some bread and meat as well," Aculeo said reluctantly, flashing the capo some brass. They took a table in the corner facing the door and a serving girl delivered plates of gritty-looking bread, a shallow bowl of opson, some pickled radishes and a platter heaped with chunks of charred, gristly pork (at least he hoped it was pork) plucked from the brazier. The harsh wine burned Aculeo's throat and made the backs of his eyes ache. The surface was swimming with little stems. He wisely put his cup down. Gellius ate hungrily, eyes closed, savouring each bite as though it were broiled peacock.

"Where's Trogus?" Aculeo asked.

"Staying here with me of course. He's gone out with Bitucus somewhere I imagine."

Aculeo squirmed a little in discomfort. "Bitucus was caught up in things as well?"

"Of course," Gellius scoffed. "Them and dozens more. Are you actually surprised?"

"I know it well enough."

"You're not a very popular man down here you know. Ah, here they come now."

A pair of men approached the table. Trogus was squat, thick through the body with short, powerful arms and a dense, knotted brow that almost touched the crest of bristling black hair. Bitucus was his physical opposite, tall and slender, watery blue eyes in his long, moony face, his fair hair greying at the temples, long and unkempt now. Both men were badly in need of a shave, a bath and a haircut.

"What's he doing here?" Trogus growled as he stared at Aculeo, his fists clenching at his sides, his face twisted in sheer loathing.

19

"Ah, Trogus, look who I met at the Hippodrome," Gellius said brightly. "Aculeo broke my nose."

"He what?" Trogus demanded, shoulders tensed like a big dog ready to attack. He started to cough rather violently then, his face turning reddish purple, eyes bulging from his face with every cough.

"It was a simple misunderstanding," Aculeo said after the man had finally caught his breath. "I brought him back here afterwards." Gellius shrugged unhelpfully, saying nothing in his defence. "Please, join us." Bitucus eyed the food and drink hungrily, licking his lips.

"Yes, join us," Gellius said, slapping the tabletop. "We're still Roman after all, are we not?"

Trogus stood back in disbelief. "I'd sooner starve to death than sit with the likes of this thieving bastard!" Aculeo saw the man's fine tunic had a poorly mended tear near the hip. His sandals were cheap and badly worn, and he had an infected-looking ulcer on his left shin.

"I think I should go," Aculeo said, rising from his chair.

"But we just got here," Trogus said, shoving him roughly back. "We never even had a chance to talk about what you did with our money!"

"I did nothing. I never actually touched it. And now I'm as broke as you. Whatever happened, I'm as much a victim of it as ..."

"You're a liar!" Trogus cried, then started coughing again.

"Trogus, please," Gellius said soothingly.

Trogus knocked his partner's hand angrily away. "I can scarcely believe I was duped by the likes of you," he said, his voice shaking, tears welling in his dark brown eyes. "We lost everything, him and I. Everything! We've been reduced ... to this!" he cried, sweeping his hand about in disgust. A few patrons at the neighbouring tables looked up, shrugged and returned to their own conversations.

"Trogus, look at me," Aculeo said. "Do I truly look like I'm living well?"

The other man moved in close, his breath hot and foul. "You're still breathing aren't you? That's more than you deserve."

Bitucus suddenly sat down and scooped some food onto an empty plate. Trogus looked at him in disbelief. "What do you think you're doing?" he demanded.

"What's it look like?" Bitucus asked, swiping a crust of bread through the meat juices and popping it into his mouth, chewing noisily.

"It looks like you're betraying everything we stand for, you stupid shit."

Bitucus shrugged and poured a cup of wine. "I'd betray every one of my honoured ancestors if it means a full stomach for a change."

"Stupid son of a bitch." Trogus glowered at Aculeo one last time before limping out of the tavern.

"Give him a chance to cool his head," Gellius said, filling his plate with more food. "He's a proud man. This whole mess hit him hard. It's hit all of us, of course, but him most of all I think."

"Your wife left you I heard," Bitucus said abruptly, more a statement of fact than a question.

Aculeo shrugged and nodded. "She took Atellus back to Rome for a while."

"My wife and daughter went to Antioch to stay with her sister," Bitucus said, chewing thoughtfully. "I'm planning to join them as soon as I have the passage money. Say, you wouldn't happen to …?" Bitucus gave him a pleading look.

"Hardly," Aculeo said.

Bitucus sighed. "I feel like I'm going mad these days, living here like this. After my family left, Gellius and Trogus kindly took me in. We hoped to climb out of this mess together."

"More like drowning men clutching onto one another in a storm," Gellius said. "We'll likely all drag one another down in the end."

"An unfortunate analogy under the circumstances," Bitucus mused.

"Tell us what you know," Gellius said, putting a hand on Aculeo's arm. "Please."

And so he did.

Aculeo had joined up with Corvinus over a decade ago after his father's death. A former associate of his father, some had intimated that the man had only wanted to use Aculeo's family name and status to further himself, for Corvinus was only of the equestrian class after all, but it had mattered little at the time. Aculeo's father may have been of more noble blood but the inheritance he'd left behind was barely enough to cover his funeral. So Corvinus had stepped in and extended a hand, lifting Aculeo from that mess, teaching him the grain business, encouraging him, helping him invest in his own small fleet.

Corvinus, a rotund little man with a sparkle in his eyes, a rapid patter, ready laugh and a thousand filthy jokes to tell, always made anything seem possible. And so it had been for well over a decade. Over the years they'd financed many of the great ships that transported grain shipments to Rome to fill the permanently gawping mouths of the always growing empire. The tremendous returns on their investments had swelled everyone's purses.

They'd started with half a dozen two-sailed vessels and done quite well even before they were awarded a prized annona contract to Rome.

That had led to rapid expansion, building a fleet that included a pair of massive freighters, each over 100 cubits in length and capable of carrying over 120,000 modii of grain in their vast holds. In just eight years, Aculeo had managed to turn father's inheritance of a handful of tarnished brass into something truly phenomenal, spinning grain into a mountain of gold.

Not that they weren't always looking for private investors to fund the expansion of the fleet, anything to keep it growing and out of the hands of the bankers and grasping moneylenders like Gurculio. What did we have to lose? Nothing. Nothing at all. It was easy money ... or so it always seemed. You could trust Vibius Herrenius Corvinus after all.

And so, of course, when Corvinus came asking that last, fateful time, Aculeo could hardly have said no. He'd borrowed the necessary cash as had many of the other investors. Iovinus, their negotiatore, had arranged everything, borrowing from various moneylenders, Gurculio foremost among them. And while Aculeo had to mortgage virtually everything to cover the loan, he'd done so with only minor hesitation, even at the Roman's exorbitant rate of interest – twelve percent per week.

Still, the interest rate had seemed of little consequence in the greater scheme of things as the loan was only for a short term, a few weeks at most. Besides, hadn't the opportunity been even grander than ever before? After the first storm at Portus, the subsequent demand for grain had soared, prices could be doubled, trebled, the difference pure profit ...

Until the gods had sunk the second fleet as well, taking Iovinus and the ships' crews down with it. Everything had been lost, Iovinus had drowned, Corvinus was dead – a loss Aculeo still couldn't fully fathom. All gone, their lives and fortunes with it ...

"Or so I thought," Aculeo said.

"What do you mean?" Bitucus asked.

"I saw Iovinus at the Hippodrome this morning."

"What?" Gellius asked, almost choking on a mouthful of the wretched wine.

"I saw him with my own eyes."

"Iovinus is still alive?" asked Bitucus.

"I don't believe in ghosts."

"What do you think happened?" Gellius asked.

"A good question. Steered the ships to another port, sold the grain there most likely."

"I never liked that little shit," Bitucus said.

"We have to find him then," Gellius pronounced.

"A brilliant revelation, how did you possibly think of it?" Bitucus said acidly.

"I would have had him this morning if you hadn't stabbed me," Aculeo said, wincing as he touched his wounded shoulder.

"You stabbed Aculeo?" Bitucus asked.

"Never mind that," Gellius said. "Don't you get what this means? There's still hope!"

"What are you talking about?" Aculeo asked.

"Think about it! Sunken ships are one thing, but stolen ships are something else entirely."

Damn. He's right, Aculeo realized. He felt a thin, warm wedge of hope invade his heart for the first time in months. "Perhaps. But it will only help us if we can find him. Who else knows Iovinus? Does he have any family or friends?"

They thought in silence for a moment. Iovinus was a different sort of fellow, brilliant at numbers and the like but not the sort of person who gathered friends easily.

"There's Pesach," Bitucus suggested.

"Yes," Gellius said. "If Pesach was friends with anyone it was Iovinus."

Aculeo recalled Pesach dimly, a small-time investor that he'd met at a dinner once. An annoying little fellow, boorish, constantly pestering himself and Corvinus about details of the business instead of socializing like a civilized person. "Where might we find him?"

"I heard he was sold into slavery when he couldn't pay his debts," said Bitucus. "Someone mentioned they'd spotted him fetching pisspots from a public latrine."

"A fuller's slave?" Gellius asked in horror. Bitucus shrugged.

Aculeo shuddered at the thought, While he barely knew Pesach and disliked what little he knew, the very idea of a Roman citizen being sold into slavery was atrocious. And to a fuller? The poor wretch would be lucky to survive the year.

"I'd have killed myself before letting that happen," Gellius said with a shudder.

"Do you know where he is?" Aculeo asked.

"Near the fabric makers' macellum in Gamma is all I know," Bitucus said.

"It's a start," Aculeo said. He dropped a few coins on the table and stood to leave.

"Wait, where are you going?" Gellius asked.

"To find Pesach," Aculeo said. "Then I'll find Iovinus and get my money back."

"Our money you mean," Bitucus said sharply.

"Yes, Aculeo, our money," Gellius said, almost desperately. Aculeo looked at the other men with their haunted eyes, gaunt, unshaven cheeks, so utterly broken from the fellows he'd known. And so like himself.

"Of course," Aculeo agreed. "Our money."

CHAPTER IV

Aculeo threaded his way through the market stalls in the Agora, mingling with the crowds. A wooden marionette jerked about in a funny dance near one of the stalls as the merchant pulled its cords. A little monkey leaped up onto the merchant's arm, clambering up to sit on his shoulder. A pretty little girl, perhaps seven years old, stood nearby watching the monkey in fascination.

The merchant's cart was stacked with marionettes, painted balls, hoops, tops and carved wooden soldiers. Aculeo watched as the girl slipped one of the colourful tops from the tray and tucked it under her belt when the merchant's back was turned – clever little thief, he thought with a smile. She noticed Aculeo watching her and darted back to a nearby stall where two women, one with dark hair, the other fair, stood like exotic, beautiful birds as they examined bolts of gleaming Cosian silk. The women laughed and chatted with one another, pretending not to notice the countless men who watched them, captivated. Hetairai, Aculeo thought. The little girl attended to the dark-haired woman, holding a cloth parasol over her veiled head.

Aculeo picked up one of the soldiers from the cart. The horse was painted bright yellow and had thick brown horse hair for its mane. The soldier's arm moved easily, lifting his little sword up and down, and a silver shield fixed across his chest. "Wonderful craftsmanship," said the vendor. "Only three asses." Aculeo felt a pang of loneliness well deep inside like a hollow drumbeat as he thought of Atellus.

He bought the toy. I'll give it to you soon enough, he thought. I just need to find that cursed Iovinus and my troubles will be done with. He watched as the hetairai and the girl walked towards a litter and stepped within. The dark-haired one, gazing through the litter's window, caught Aculeo's eye for a moment, smiled, then the curtains closed and the enormous Nubian slaves lifted the litter and carried them away.

The attendant at the public latrine near the fabric makers macellum readily told Aculeo the name of the fullery that had contracted to buy their waste. There was stiff competition for the golden liquid, as fullers, dye-makers, fruit-growers, even gold and silversmiths all found good use for it in their busy little shops.

The fullery in question was only a few blocks away, tucked in the rear of a narrow alley off the main street. A painted owl stared down at him from the wooden plaque hanging over the doorway. The symbol of Minerva, Aculeo recalled, the fuller guild's protective goddess. The fullery's taberna was unattended so he walked down the short corridor into a bustling atrium. The fetid pong of ammonia mixed with rotting eggs was enough to make him cover his nose. Cone-shaped wooden drying frames wrapped with freshly laundered tunics and togas were set in rows about the fullery's atrium, suspended over pits of smouldering sulphur fires to bleach the cloth. Clusters of slaves were hard at work in the nearby laundering pits.

A toothless crone with a sweat-stained cloth knotted about her head spotted him and approached, offering a subservient, gap-toothed smile. "Help you, sir?" she asked in broken Greek.

"I'm looking for a man named Pesach," Aculeo said, gazing about the atrium, his eyes burning from the pungent air.

"A man?" the crone asked in puzzlement.

"A slave," he said, the words curdling in his mouth even as he spoke them.

The woman nodded towards a slave walking carefully through the yard, barely balancing a broad wooden yoke with bulging skins of stale urine slung from either end across his bony shoulders. Aculeo would normally have ignored such a wretched creature, but he recognized Pesach's familiar features beneath the scruff of whiskers and greasy, greying hair. He was decidedly small and weak for such an onerous task, staggering under the weight of the yoke, trying not to spill the skins as he shuffled barefoot towards a pair of slaves working the treading vat in the corner. The slaves unhitched the skins from the yoke and poured their contents into a nearby pot to boil. Pesach climbed wearily into the treading vat.

Aculeo threaded his way carefully around the drying hoops towards the slaves. "Pesach?" he called tentatively.

The slave looked up. His bushy grey eyebrows lifted in recognition, then his expression darkened into a scowl. "Aculeo. What do you want?"

"I need to talk to you."

"Well I'm clearly occupied here, aren't I? It's very exacting work you know – one wrong step and they make you start all over again." Aculeo felt his skin crawl when he noticed the man's red, scabrous hands and dead, yellowed eyes, his ribs in stark relief amidst the shadows of his cheap, soiled tunic.

"A minute alone. Please."

Pesach considered him for a long moment, then glanced at his co-workers. "Is it alright with you gentlemen? I hate to leave our conversation just as things are getting interesting."

"What'd he say?" the old slave asked. The other slave shrugged.

Pesach climbed out of the treading vat, feet dripping with urine, and walked barefoot across the atrium to a stuffy little storage area where a number of gleaming white tunics and togas had been hung, awaiting pickup. Aculeo took a closer look at the man, who scratched every few seconds at the raw pink patches of skin on his arms, bare shoulders and shins.

A fat, bearded man lay snoring on floor. "The master fuller," Pesach explained. "He shouldn't wake for another hour or two. Good man, keen eye for talent. He made me assistant velicus, you know. See, only eight weeks in and I'm already making my way back. You can't keep a good Roman down for long."

"What happened to you?"

"What do you think happened? I lost everything because of you and that asshole you called a partner. Well, that and a few unfortunate gambling debts, I suppose. I got in too deep to that moneylender Marcellus Cocksucking Gurculio and so here I am."

"I'm sorry, Pesach ..."

"You're sorry?" Pesach sneered. "Well then, as long as you're sorry! Did you know they sold me to this drunken boob for eight hundred sesterces? I'm a Roman fucking citizen! At least I was. I ran my own business, and a highly successful one I might add! At the very least he could have sold me to a decent place for ten thousand at the snap of a finger and covered my debt. But no, they went out of their way to sell me here at a loss. Just to fuck me over!"

The fuller gave a rumbling snore. Pesach placed his filthy, urine-stained toes on the man's whiskered cheek and pushed, turning his face the other way. The man smacked his lips and belched but remained fast asleep.

"I'll find a way to help you, Pesach, I give you my oath," Aculeo said.

"Stick your oath up your festering hole and leave me be," Pesach said, turning to leave.

"Wait, that's not the only reason I came."

"You didn't come to borrow money I hope. I'm a little short right now."

"You were friends with Iovinus," Aculeo said.

"There's another one. It's a bit late for him though, isn't it? He was lost at sea."

"I thought so too, until I saw him at the Hippodrome this morning."

"What?" Pesach said, looking at him in surprise. "Good swimmer is he? Survived the shipwreck and swam all the way back to Alexandria?"

"Apparently."

"What was he doing alive and at the Hippodrome?"

"Good question," said Aculeo.

Pesach's face darkened, he shook his head in dismay. "Fuck. Fuck!"

"Any idea where I might find him?"

"Hm? Oh, how should I know? I was friendly enough with the man once upon a time but I've no idea where he lived."

"He lived with Corvinus' family," Aculeo said. "They treated him like a son."

"So much for filial loyalty," Pesach said, scratching at his red, scaly legs and arms again, which began to bleed. Aculeo tried not to shudder. "He got himself involved with a porne a while back, I recall."

"How involved?"

"He talked of buying her freedom outright, even marrying her. Fool that he was."

"Do you remember her name?" Aculeo asked.

Pesach thought for a moment, itching his arms and shoulders. "Neaera, I think. She worked in a brothel in the Venus District. The Blue Bird I think it was called. Pricey little place but quite pleasant. Pretty young girls."

The fuller started to stir. Pesach considered him for a moment, then horked loudly and spat a wad of phlegm on the man's head. The fuller absently ran his fingers back through his hair, blinked up at the two men in vacant surprise, then closed his eyes and started snoring again.

"Ah well," Pesach sighed, "enough fun for now. I'd better get back to work. I've many important responsibilities to take care of, you know."

The Venus District lay in the western edge of the city tucked in behind the Gates of Selene near the Harbour of Kibotos. It was already late in the day by the time Aculeo finally stepped onto its narrow streets. A rank stench rose from the yellow-brown sludge that spilled into the Eunostos Canal from the nearby tanneries, swirling at the water's edge. Ornate marble tombs and funerary monuments lined the main road that led out through the gates. The covered benches of the tombs, which by day provided shade and respite to mourning family members, served by night as relatively private meeting places for those in search of more carnal comforts. As long as the pornes and pimps continued paying the city their fees for use of the area however, no one troubled them much.

It was a dangerous time of day as the narrow laneways filled in with shadows, the day's crowds had thinned, new groups emerged. What had been quaint, quiet corners by day had turned into sullen meeting places filled with grunts of passion from the couplings in the shadows. The she-wolves slinked along the city's outer walls, their faces painted, pale breasts barely covered, calling to the men, chanting in singsong voices about the services they'd provide, no matter what the danger, he supposed, for who knew what their lovers had in mind for them? And the rent boys, scared, scruffy little fellows, their eyes devoid of any joy in life.

"Hey lover, where you headed?" a veiled porne called out. Aculeo looked up and saw her smile at him. Her dark brown eyes had a flinty prettiness to them.

"I'm looking for a brothel," he said.

"Why pay extra to a harbour master when you can bring your great ship to port right here?" the porne said with a laugh.

Aculeo held out a brass coin. "It's called the Blue Bird. Do you know of it?"

"I know a place we could go," she said, appraising the coin with a scowl. "You'll need more than that, though."

"And worth every as, I'm sure, but I'm looking for the Blue Bird."

"There's a thousand birds in the sky, should I know each one by name?" she asked, pressing her body against him, her slender hand stroking his thigh, caressing him, smelling cloyingly of amber mixed with sweat and body odour. "You should see the things I'll do to you for a single sesterce. Come on, let's see your silver, lover." Aculeo felt her fingers grasping for the purse tied about his neck and pushed her hand away. The porne thrust her knee up hard into his groin. Aculeo dropped to the pavement, writhing in agony.

"Why don't you go fuck yourself then," she said sourly, plucking the coin from his outstretched hand, then moved on to find her next mark.

Aculeo made his way to his feet after the aching waves of nausea passed. He watched as drunken clots of men and their rented lovers staggered together through the streets that stank of countless years of piss, spilled beer and sour sweat, wandering from tavern to tavern, the loud revelry, flute and lyre and roaring laughter from behind the mud-brick walls. The porne was right, he thought, there's hundreds of brothels about the city. How am I to find this one, running about the Tannery like a fool? Pornes of all ages, sizes, shapes, sexes, colours ... One's choice is practically without limit in this city.

He was about to enter a nearby tavern when a porne brushed past him, weaving drunkenly into the street. He glanced down at the paving stones, dimly lit from the torches near the entrance. And there, where her sandaled feet had just touched the ground, the blue inked image of a little bird with its wings folded in against its breast. Pornes often put ink blocks with the name of the brothel they work for into their sandal heels so that when they walked about the city men might know where to find them later.

"Hold up a moment, pretty one," Aculeo called, taking the porne by the arm. "Come on, I'll buy you another jar."

The building he sought was a few blocks southwest of the Tannery, down the dismal Street of the Dye-Makers. It was a dingy little building, its darkened doorway painted what may have once been a cheery shade of blue, now scarred and peeling. Over the lintel was a small painted placard of a blue bird.

A slave, a thick-shouldered brute with a harelip, answered the door, eyeing Aculeo warily before finally permitting him within. The slave led him down a dim hallway lined with half a dozen doors decorated with paintings of men and women in various sexual positions and in multiple combinations. Whether they were for decoration or simply advertised the services available behind the doors wasn't entirely clear. At the end of the hall was a large open courtyard, leading to a small colonnade overlooking a verdant forest at the edge of a moonlit pool. A naked woman stood next to a rectangular reflecting pool, pink and blue seashells at her feet. When Aculeo entered the atrium he saw it was only a plaster statue, the pool, colonnade, forest and sea just a painted mural on the wall.

There were several small tables and chairs set up about the atrium, most of them occupied by pornes and their clients, the young girls' diaphanous chitons clinging to their bodies, their pretty faces blushed with rouge, wine and laughter. The thick smell of incense hung in the air like an invisible veil. The space was filled with a soft, warm light from the oil lamps sconced into the pale plaster walls. On one wall was a mosaic of Venus on the back of a white goat, soaring through the sky between day and night towards the moon, the sun resting on her heels. In a room off the atrium, partially hidden by thick curtains, sat several empty looms, the girls' daytime occupations no doubt. The brothel keepers saw little value from idle hands by day or night.

A middle-aged woman approached, her hair flaming red, her narrow face painted with white lead and bright ochre accenting her cheeks and lips. She offered Aculeo a practised smile. "Welcome, sir, welcome. I'm Panthea, the owner of the Blue Bird. Let's fetch you some wine and a pretty friend."

"A friend of mine is a frequent guest here," Aculeo said. "Iovinus. I'm sure you know him?"

"Of course," Panthea said. She wore a gold ring with a ruby-eyed snakehead, which she twisted around and around on her finger as she considered him.

"How long since you saw him?"

"A few months at least. Where's he then? Not with you tonight?"

"He's been away," Aculeo said in disappointment, and glanced about the atrium at the other tables. "There's one girl in particular he recommended to me. Neaera."

"Of course. She's a lovely, talented girl. She's already been taken tonight, though," Panthea said. "I do have a new girl. Ethiopian, only sixteen years, and even more talented than Neaera. She was just brought in the other day. I promise you won't be disappointed."

"I'm happy to wait for Neaera," Aculeo said, offering up a coin – silver this time.

"As I said, she's taken for the night." Panthea eyed the coin and traced her fingertips across his shoulder, giving his arm an inviting squeeze. "Why don't we find you another friend for the evening."

"It has to be Neaera. I'll come back tomorrow then. Thanks for your help."

"Of course, sir. My sincere pleasure," Panthea said graciously. Her smile hardened though as she watched him leave and she summoned the harelip slave.

Aculeo walked towards the main street of the Tannery. A wasted trip, he thought in annoyance. No sign of Iovinus in months? Now what will I do? He paused a moment, listening, thinking he'd heard the echo of sandals against the pavement behind him. He looked around. Nothing. He continued walking then heard it again, the soft footfall of someone who did not want to be heard. Thieves, he thought bleakly, why not? He felt his palms begin to sweat, his heart throb in his throat. Am I to be murdered in this dismal maze at the end of a pointless day?

A face appeared like a vision from the shadows. It was just a girl, fourteen at most, with dark braided hair, long, lovely lashes and a round pale face. She was one of the girls from the Blue Bird, he realized. He'd seen her flirting with a client in the courtyard. She came a few paces towards him, keeping her distance from him though, her pretty cheeks marked with small circles of pink.

"Did you want something?" Aculeo asked.

"I … overheard you talking with my mistress," the girl said, her head bowed shyly. "You're looking for Neaera."

"Yes. Why? Do you know something about that?"

"I don't … I …" Her voice cracked with emotion, her ebony eyes glistened with tears. She tottered, ready to faint.

Aculeo barely caught her in time. "Take a deep breath. What's your name?"

"Tyche," she said weakly.

"Do you need to sit down, Tyche?" The girl shook her head. "Tell me about Neaera. When did you last see her?"

"She disappeared two days ago."

"Oh? Why did your mistress lie?" The girl shrugged, looking desolate. "Did she live in the brothel with you?"

"No, not anymore. She lived in a tenement next to the Kapeleion of Menon. Her flat was paid for by her patron."

"You mean Iovinus?" he asked hopefully.

The girl nodded. Aculeo tried not to smile. At last some progress, he thought. "She's still owned by Panthea though. Panthea was furious when she learned Neaera was missing. Panthea thinks she ran away. She beat me because she thought I might know where she went," the girl said, unconsciously touching a purplish bruise on her cheek.

"And do you know?"

"Neaera didn't run away. She would have told me if she was going to do that, I know it. She … she promised to take me with her when she left. She gave me money a few days ago, told me to be ready … and that was the last time I saw her."

"Have you checked her flat?" Aculeo asked.

"I can't, they watch my every move."

"I can check it then."

The girl dropped to her knees on the pavement before Aculeo, pressing his hands to her lips. "I pray to the sacred Venus to bless you sir! I've been so afraid."

"Afraid? Why?"

"There's stories," the girl said, still gripping his hands, her lovely eyes haunted.

"What stories?"

"Of demons that prey on women. Of rites they're taken to and never return from."

Demon tales, Aculeo thought, the sort children tell one another when they lie in bed at night, trying to frighten one another. He helped her to stand. "Don't worry yourself."

The girl had put herself in danger coming after him like this, risking a beating or worse. She looked up at him, clutched his hands again like a drowning child might cling to a scrap of wood. "You'll tell me if you find anything? Please? Please?"

"If there's anything to tell, of course," he said. Though I think the only demon here is that bastard Iovinus.

The flat was in a rickety, five story tenement in the outer edge of the Tannery. A small votive statue of Venus had been placed in a niche next to the building's lintel, the white plaster stained with soot from years of long forgotten prayers. The landlady, a furtive little woman with brightly hennaed hair, claimed not to have seen her tenant in days but was vague on further details.

"Show me Neaera's room," Aculeo said.

"Who are you to her?" the woman demanded.

"Her brother." She clearly didn't believe him, but grudgingly allowed him into the building. He followed her up to the second floor. A pretty young woman wearing a traditional Egyptian braided black wig and a translucent chiton smiled at him as she passed him in the hallway, her lingering perfume smelling of jasmine. He could hear moaning and rhythmic thumping behind some of the doorways they passed. The landlady seemed oblivious to it all and led him to the far end of the hallway to the last flat. She opened the door and stood aside to let him enter.

It was a small, cramped little closet of a room with a small open window cut near the ceiling, letting a dim grey light from the streets below seep in. There was a small wooden table set against the wall with a terracotta basin and matching jug, a threadbare rug on the floor, a few cheerfully coloured Persian pillows and a tortoise shell lyre in the corner. A reed birdcage stood beneath the window. No sign of a bird though, the door was open, the water dish was dry, empty husks of seed lay scattered about the floor. On the wall hung a papyrus painting of three women standing near Pharos, the sort tourists have made for themselves by street artists, finely done though.

The first girl was fairly attractive with dark brown eyes, long, light brown curls that framed her round face and draped over her shoulders, a birthmark on her upper lip. The second looked familiar somehow, tall with high cheekbones and a sharp nose – he couldn't recall where he'd seen her. The third had a spark of mischief in her dark eyes, a hint of a smile on her lips, as though she was about to laugh. She wore an elegant cameo necklace around her pale neck. Aculeo untacked the papyrus from the wall.

The cubiculum was barely more than a closet with a narrow bed, a soft red woollen blanket tucked up to the edge. A large wooden chest sat in the corner. Aculeo opened it – it contained a fine, ivory chiton and a smaller wooden box filled with jewellery, cheap gilt-terracotta bric-a-brac, nothing of any value. And no cameo necklace. He put everything back, then stripped the blanket off the bed. A rough hemp cloth mattress, stuffed with straw. He lifted the mattress to reveal a simple wood frame with thick leather strapping to hold up the mattress. He glanced under the bed. Nothing …

Someone coughed behind him. The landlady stood in the doorway of the bedroom, her suspicions of Aculeo's unsavoury intentions apparently confirmed. He laid out the portrait of the three women on the table. "Which one's Neaera?"

The landlady shot him an accusatory look. "I thought you were her brother."

"We grew apart. Just tell me which one's her?" The woman reluctantly jabbed a crooked fingertip on the woman with the cameo. "Who are the other two?"

"How should I know?"

"You never saw them here before?"

"No," she scowled.

"What about a man named Iovinus? He would have paid her rent."

The woman sniffed and shook her head. "She paid the rent herself. Except for this month – she's two weeks late. My oath I'll throw her pretty little ass out on the street if she makes me wait another day!"

Your whore disappears around the time you return from the dead, Aculeo thought as he left the dismal place. What are you up to, Iovinus? And where did you go? With Neaera or in search of her...?

Pah, what does it even matter? he thought bitterly. Either way, their trail is cold and I'm just as fucked as I was before I began.

CHAPTER V

THE 19TH DAY OF APRILIS

The Sarapeion, the city's main temple to Alexandria's patron god Sarapis, stood on the acropolis, the highest point in the city. Aculeo turned eastwards down the street leading to the temple. Ancient statues pillaged from the banks of the Upper Nile – sphinxes, long forgotten pharaohs and animal-headed gods – decorated the streetside along its length while towering stands of date palms rasped overhead in the warm morning breeze off the sea. Not the most private place to commit a murder, he thought.

His hurried breakfast of fermented fish paste, a heel of bread and a cup of flat beer sloshed about in his stomach like lumps of wet paste. He'd woken only half an hour before to snatches of Xanthias' inane gossip picked up in the Agora that morning, including mention of a dead woman found in the temple at the feet of the god Sarapis himself. Aculeo had tried to get back to sleep until the potential meaning of the discovery had slowly bubbled into his sodden brain and he had dragged himself from bed.

Perhaps a dozen murders of citizens took place in Alexandria in a given year, typically triggered by lovers' quarrels, retribution for various misdeeds, drunken brawls that went too far, disputes between the various collegia or citizens of warring nations that had been carried over here. Countless other murders occurred as well of course, of slaves or other members of the city's teeming underclass of freedmen, actors, pimps and pornes, but those were usually of little concern unless a respected citizen or official happened to be involved somehow. The possibility of the dead woman being Neaera was remote at best, but Aculeo could hardly ignore it. He hoped it wasn't, of course – as long as Iovinus' porne was alive, so was the chance she could lead Aculeo to her elusive patron.

Despite the early hour, the streets leading to the Sarapeion were already filling up with worshippers, young and old, healthy and invalid, Greek and fellahin, all moving up the steep slope to seek Sarapis' renowned healing powers. A low wall lined the long, empty street leading to the great temple, topped with small, elegant sculptures of panthers, bees, peacocks and goats, with an occasional sphinx to break the decorative motif.

Aculeo looked with dismay up the hundred steps that led from the street to the temple, a vast compound encompassing most of the hilltop, then joined the dozen or so worshippers in the gruelling climb, grunting and cursing with the rest of them towards the summit. He paused halfway up to catch his breath, work out the kinks and look back over the city. Thick knots of dark cloud unspooled across the sea horizon, coupled with a throaty rumble of thunder, promising a heavy spring rain.

When at last he reached the top step of the temple, his legs and lungs were burning, his heart pounding in his chest. He leaned against a cool stone pillar to catch his breath. It had been years since he'd bothered to even come up here. The temple compound was enormous, fully two stades in length by one in width. An outer colonnade circuited the area with elegant porticoes leading to the living quarters for the priests along with a large and outstanding library. The compound itself housed a vast mazework of pillared corridors and shrines for the pantheon of Roman and Egyptian gods. The narrow stalls that lined the temple's main promenade were manned by the merchants and moneylenders to deal with the worshippers.

He walked across the ceremonial dromos, the only sound the echoes of his own sandals scuffing along the marble tiles, until he reached the temple's outer courtyard, then into the Hall of Appearance. An inner colonnade led from the hall across a walkway to a square red granite and porphyry sanctuary at the far end. Sarapis was enthroned within the sanctuary. A trick of the architects made him seem even larger and grander than he actually was, for the floor rose gradually as the ceiling lowered between the entrance and the sanctuary. Aculeo continued along the Path between Light and Twilight, across the Hall of Offering and just beyond that into the Sanctuary itself. A thin morning drizzle started to spatter across the marble floor as a rumble of thunder rolled through the darkening sky.

The god sat on his throne in the centre of the room, his seated height taller than that of two men standing atop one another, his broad, handsome gold-leaf face framed with a flowing mane of ivory hair and thickly curled beard, a look of warm paternal concern on his face and on his head a sacred measuring basket symbolic of the fruits of harvest. A temple attendant poured morning libations into the golden bowl near the god's great feet, while another whispered into his ivory ear to awaken him. Sarapis' jewelled eyes sparkled in the morning light.

The story was three centuries ago Sarapis had visited the old emperor Ptolemy Soter in a dream and informed him that he would be the patron god of the new Egyptian Empire. Also that his cult statue, a creation of ivory, fragrant wood and precious metals, could be discovered in Sinope, a city on the distant shores of the Black Sea. So it was, and after a suitable compensation had been paid to the people of Sinope, the god had been freed from his temple there and resurrected in his new place of worship in Alexandria. Bought and delivered – the perfect object of worship for a city of merchants.

A handful of curious onlookers stood about near the entrance to the stoa, trying to get a peek within. Their view was blocked by several men dressed in the scarlet-edged tunics of city officials. The Office of Public Order dealt with the city's most serious public issues, those being virtually anything that might somehow slow the wheels of trade. Typically that meant merely ensuring merchants in the Agora had paid their requisite bribes, that the street cleaners were clearing dung properly from the rutted city streets and so on. While the Sarapeion had no role in the city's trade, contamination of Alexandria's main temples with the blood of a dead woman would hardly be well received by the priests or city officials.

Aculeo spotted what looked like a pile of rags heaped behind Sarapis' glittering throne. The murdered woman, he thought. Another onlooker trying to take too close a look was angrily shoved away by one of the officers. The unfortunate fellow tripped, knocking over a merchant's barrow, spilling a load of charms and small replicas of Sarapis on the floor. There were cries of outrage as the merchant beat the poor fellow about the head and several of the man's friends rushed to his aid. The remaining officers swarmed in, trying to break up the tussle.

Aculeo slipped past the scrum and into the stoa, stepping behind the throne. The body was partially covered with a red cloak, faded red, threadbare, patched and filthy. He took an edge of the cloak and lifted it.

The woman was likely no more than twenty years old, with a plain, thin face, chestnut-brown skin, wide cheekbones and thick dark lips. One arm was bent awkwardly over her head, the other folded neatly across her chest. Her dark, almond-shaped eyes were still open, unblinking, no spark of life behind them. Her dull black hair was cropped short and uneven, patches of skin on the scalp, neck and arms were mottled with pink bumps. Clearly not Neaera, he thought with relief. A fellahin perhaps.

Her tunic was torn and stained with blood under her right arm. A deep-looking cut ran from her wrist halfway down her forearm. Aculeo noticed a glint of something clutched in her fist and gently pried her stiff fingers open. It was an earring. A pretty thing, like a cluster of tiny gold grapes with leaves of what looked like jasper. It was fine work, and expensive. He glanced at her ears. No sign of its mate.

"Hey, what are you doing?" A pair of very large Public Order officers loomed over him, scowling.

"Apologies," Aculeo said. "I meant no harm."

One of the officers snorted and circled a thumb and forefinger against his lips, jabbing his tongue through the opening. The other man roared in laughter.

Aculeo scowled and left the stoa. He spotted a familiar looking man in the purple-bordered toga of a nobleman in conversation with one of the priests just outside the sanctuary. Marcus Aquillius Capito the younger, Aculeo mused. The youngest son of the senior and very wealthy Marcus Aquillius Capito the elder, he'd been shipped to Alexandria two years back to gain experience in public office. That had been at the apex of Sejanus' tyranny, of course, when a man never knew which end of the sword he might end up on. Aculeo recalled Capito as being a fairly typical young noble, bright, eloquent, arrogant, not to mention painfully ambitious. Still, they'd gotten along well enough in the few social meetings they'd had. What's he doing here?

"Capito," Aculeo called, hand raised in greeting.

Capito looked over and gave a puzzled smile. "An odd place to run into you, Aculeo," he said, coming over to greet him. A retinue of four Roman soldiers followed, keeping only a few steps away.

"Are they with you?" Aculeo asked.

The other man offered a sphinx-like smile. "My personal guard. I'm Junior Magistrate now."

"Oh? Very impressive."

"Well father's pleased at least. What about you? Why are you here?"

"I'm looking for a woman who's gone missing. I heard a dead woman had been discovered here this morning and came in case it was her."

"And?"

"She's not the one I'm looking for," Aculeo said.

Capito considered the dead woman thoughtfully. "A street porne perhaps, or a runaway slave."

"The she-wolves often try to bring their men here at night," a priest said as he looked down at the corpse with a look of revulsion. "Fornicating in the shadows, defiling the sanctuary."

"So what does a City Magistrate care about a dead porne?" Aculeo asked, ignoring the priest.

Capito gazed over Aculeo's shoulder. "That's why." An obese priest clad in a pure white tunic and silk scarlet himation was waddling towards them, face flushed with anger, half a dozen priests in his wake.

"Why is the whore still here?" the High Priest seethed. "The desecration continues every moment her blood pollutes our sanctuary!"

"My deepest sympathies for this terrible outrage to the temple, Eminence," Capito said.

"Your sympathy," the other man spat. "What do you intend to do about it, Magistrate?"

"I'll be leading the investigation of course."

"Well get on with it. You can start by getting the body out of here!"

"Of course, Eminence," Capito said calmly.

"I'm sure the potential impact of the desecration on the temple's daily revenue has nothing to do with his dismay," Aculeo said as they watched the priests walk back to their private offices. The rainstorm began in earnest then, fat, warm drops splashing down around them through the open roof of the temple.

"If she'd been murdered in the street it would have caused little issue," Capito said as he and Aculeo moved towards a sheltered part of the sanctuary. "But here in the Sarapeion ... well it's another matter altogether."

"Very thoughtless of her," Aculeo said.

Two temple priests approached Capito. "This is him," the older priest said, pushing forward the other man. He looked barely out of his boyhood, his chin covered with a wispy beard. "The acolyte Leto. He was on duty here last night."

The youth looked down at his feet, avoiding their gaze. "So? What happened here last night?" Capito asked.

"A supplicant came to the temple very late," Leto said, biting his lower lip.

Not surprising, Aculeo thought. Worshippers came from around the world to the temple seeking healing for whatever it was that afflicted them – sleeping in the sanctuary overnight in order to receive instructive dreams from Sarapis, or even paying the priests to dream on their behalf.

"And?" Capito said impatiently.

"I accepted his votive offering, brought him some wine and a lamp and let him be."

"You were supposed to stay with him," the priest said angrily, striking the youth on the head.

"He asked to be left alone so that he might receive his vision," the acolyte cried, wincing from the blow.

"So what did you do?" Aculeo asked.

"I … I fell asleep in one of the chapels," Leto admitted. "I awoke when I heard the supplicant cry for help."

"Fool," the priest growled, striking him again

"You know, it's rather challenging for a man to talk when you keep hitting them on the head," Capito said in annoyance. "Why did the supplicant cry for help?"

"He claimed he'd been attacked by a madman in the Sanctuary," said the youth.

"There was a madman?" Aculeo asked.

"I never actually saw him, sir. I came as quickly as I could, but the madman must have already escaped. The supplicant was most upset. I tried to calm him down but he was inconsolable, claimed he'd been attacked by this man. Then … then I saw her," the boy said, glancing towards the body. "I summoned the priests and told them what I'd found."

"You neglected your sacred duties and the Sarapeion was desecrated!" the priest cried, striking him again. "When the High Priest learns of this …"

"Discipline him later, please, it's quite distracting," Capito said irritably. "What of the supplicant? Did he say anything about the murdered girl?"

"No Magistrate," the boy said. "He left soon afterwards."

"What was his name?"

"Cleon, sir. Cleon of Athens."

"Any idea where we can find him?"

"No, I'm sorry," Leto sniffled, wiping the tears from his eyes.

"If Cleon shows up again, send word to my offices," Capito said. The youth gave a sullen nod.

A pair of temple slaves carried in basins of washing soda and horsehair brushes to scrub the blood off the stoa floor. Other slaves approached the dead woman and laid out a sheet of canvas on the floor, carefully lifting the body onto it before carrying it down the mosaic-tiled corridor towards the temple doors.

"I need to talk with the Public Order officers before I leave," Capito said. "I trust next time we meet it's under more pleasant circumstances, Aculeo." With that, the Magistrate walked away.

Clotted clouds of pink-brown blood swirled in the rain puddles on the marble tiles as the temple slaves tried to erase any remnant of what had gone on here the prior night. Aculeo looked at the earring he'd found in the dead woman's final grasp, with its perfect little golden grapes and finely carved jasper leaves. A pretty piece for a street porne to be carrying, he thought. The whole thing didn't add up somehow. What did happen here last night?

Ah well, it really is none of my concern, and it brings me no closer to finding Iovinus. Every day that passes, the trail grows colder. The man's like a ghost. Did I truly see him at the Hippodrome that morning? His head was throbbing again – he wondered if the priests kept any sacrificial wine about.

Aculeo made his way out of the temple and down the hundred steps. When he reached the bottom he noticed a small white shrine in the shadows, all but obscured behind a thick tangle of thorn bushes. The sculpture on the shrine was of three hideous old women with knotted hair, roaring mouths and bulging eyes. The Furies, the goddesses who sought vengeance for victims of murder. The deities stared back at him, their painted eyes unblinking. Something caught his eye in the shadows of the shrine, a stain of some sort, he thought. He crouched next to it, carefully pulling the branches of the bush aside to get a closer look. Not just a stain but a painted symbol – like a bodiless stick figure man with bent arms and splayed legs protruding from where its neck should have been.

He scraped at the mark with his fingernail, then rubbed the scrapings between fingertip and thumb – they softened into a chalky paste as they mixed with the oils on his skin. He smelled his fingertips – the distinctive, metallic tang of blood.

CHAPTER VI

THE 20TH DAY OF APRILIS

The villa was as it had been, all their fine furniture, beautiful artworks and splendid tapestries in their proper places once more. Aculeo walked down the dark marble hallway. It was odd – he could hear the sounds of people bustling about and talking to one another, but he couldn't actually see anyone. In fact, every room he came to was empty yet still echoed with voices. Where is everyone?

When he reached the garden wall at the rear of the villa he stepped through the Himmatean marble archway. The air was warm and sweet, tinged with the spicy perfume of the hyacinths and mock orange trees that bordered the impluvium. There he saw Titiana standing next to the fountain. He ran forward to take her in his arms. She didn't move. He pulled back slightly at the hardness of her cheek pressing against his, her lips cold and unyielding as he tried to kiss them.

He took her hands in his anyway, squeezed them tight. "I've missed you so much," he said. "Did you just arrive?"

Titiana gave no response, though Aculeo sensed she did not want to be there at all. "Everything will be better now, on my oath. We're together again. Where's Atellus?"

Titiana remained silent and still as a statue, but she was clearly troubled. Something was amiss. Aculeo called for the boy. He could hear nothing but the breeze and birdsongs in the trees.

"You didn't leave him back in Rome, did you?" But he knew even as he asked that wasn't the answer. "Titiana, you're worrying me. Where's our son?"

Titiana's unsettling gaze fixed upon a narrow path at the far end of the garden leading deep into the flowered shrubs. Aculeo released her hands and stepped onto the path. The path quickly narrowed with overgrown foliage. "Atellus?" he called. Still no answer. He pushed the branches aside, ignoring the thorns that pricked at his arms and legs, moving deeper and deeper into the untamed shrubbery until at last he reached the garden's back wall.

There was no sign of the boy. The ground suddenly rolled and fell like a great wave beneath his feet. Aculeo clutched at the wall to catch himself and felt the bricks start to crumble and come apart beneath his fingers. He stepped back just as the wall gave way and watched the bricks and the pathway's paving stones topple down a sheer cliff that led to the sea far below, where waves pounded and crashed against a wild shore.

And then he spotted a small figure tumbling down the cliff's face as well, breaking into pieces as it tumbled to the sea ...No!

"You're not an easy man to find," said a man's voice.

Aculeo awoke with a start. Two figures stood in shadow at the foot of his bed. He blinked up at them, utterly disoriented. Gellius and Bitucus, he realized. They appeared almost amused.

"My friends can still find me easily enough," he muttered. His head was throbbing, still clouded with wine, his mouth dry as sand.

"I'm surprised you have any friends left," Gellius said.

"I've all I need. Though I could use a new slave. The current one seems too willing to let any riffraff cross my doorstep."

"I tried to stop them, Master," Xanthias said from the doorstep.

"Don't go blaming the poor fellow," Gellius chided. "We didn't give him much choice."

"Nice place," Bitucus said, looking about the cramped, dingy little closet of a room.

"We could schedule a tour if you'd like," Aculeo said. "It might occupy a full thirty seconds if we took the scenic route."

"Another time."

"Where's Trogus?"

"Waiting in the street," Gellius said. "Any luck finding Iovinus?"

"Not really." Aculeo told them of his disturbing encounter with Pesach at the fullery the prior day.

"It's worse even than I could have imagined," Gellius said, clearly upset. "To think that a former associate, a fellow Roman, could have fallen so desperately far. Poor, poor fellow."

"He did tell me about a porne Iovinus used to patronize," Aculeo said. "The trouble is no one's seen her in days. We've reached a dead end I'm afraid."

"Perhaps not," Bitucus said with a sly grin. "We know where Iovinus is."

"What? How?"

"Unlike you, we still have friends," said Gellius. "We put the word out the other day. Most of them were all too willing to help us find that bastard. They didn't seem too keen on you either, mind you. Anyway, someone spotted him at a tavern in Delta last night. Apparently he rents out a room there."

The oppressive shroud of Aculeo's dream immediately dissipated, the prospect of regaining his fortune so real he could almost taste it! "What are we waiting for? Let's go!"

Delta, the city's Jewish Quarter, was quite unlike the rest of Alexandria. There were few images of any god there, no statues, shrines or plaques marking the boundaries of any divine presence or influence. The Jews' prohibitive customs of food and worship had kept them distinct and apart from the rest of the city's diverse populace. Even so, as citizens of Alexandria they'd certainly been successful enough – it was said there were now more of them in this city alone than all those who'd followed their prophet Moses out of Egypt.

Aculeo watched Trogus limp ahead of them. His cough had grown worse and he looked even more ill than he had the day before – gaunt and flushed and the ulcer on his leg looked puffy and seeped a trickle of clear pus. It was painful to even look at. "You should see a healer," Aculeo said.

"Why don't you take that long nose of yours and stick it up your ass," Trogus growled.

"Don't worry," Gellius said quietly, "he'll be fine once we find Iovinus."

"We all will," Bitucus agreed. Trogus said nothing, just put a clenched fist to his mouth to smother another racking cough.

"I can hardly wait," Gellius said. "We'll have ourselves a feast for all our friends – the finest food, the very best wine, music …"

"It will be as though none of this ever happened, as if it were simply a bad dream," said Bitucus.

Gellius clapped a friendly hand on Aculeo's shoulder. "What of you, Aculeo? What will you do once we recover our fortunes?"

"Take the first ship to Rome," Aculeo said without hesitation. "I'll take my wife and son back, we'll buy the finest villa in the Seven Hills and never look back on this fucking city again."

"An excellent plan," Bitucus said with a grin.

"You're idiots, all of you," Trogus growled, wincing as he limped along the street.

"Why do you have to talk like that?" Gellius asked, sounding hurt.

"Oh use your head, damn you. If Iovinus is so fatted on our stolen fortunes, why's he living in a room above some horrid little tavern in Delta?"

The others glanced at one another in sudden realization, but held their tongues for the rest of the journey.

The tavern was a small, seedy little dive in a dark corner of Delta with a handful of patrons, even at this early hour. The thrattia was pouring a jug of black wine from the swollen cowhide hanging on the back wall, siphoning it through a hole cut in one of the animal's hooves. She glanced at the newcomers. "Find yourselves a table. Something to drink?"

"We're not here for that," Aculeo said. "We're looking for a Roman named Iovinus, skinny fellow, big ears, late twenties." The thrattia held his gaze, an eyebrow raised, saying nothing.

"Pay her something, fool," Trogus growled. Aculeo handed her a bronze as. The woman wrinkled her nose. Aculeo reluctantly found a mate to the first coin.

"Upstairs," she said with a shrug, and returned to her duties.

The men walked carefully to the bottom of a narrow staircase and looked at one another. "So what do we do now? Just burst in on him?" Gellius asked.

"Someone should wait in the alley in case he tries to escape," Bitucus said.

"I'll do it. Just try not to fuck things up too badly," Trogus grumbled, and limped to the back door. The others headed up the stairs. The only room with a door was at the end of a short hallway. The door hung crookedly in the frame, its boiled leather hinges cracked and peeling.

Gellius knocked. No answer. "Maybe he's out."

"To hell with it," Aculeo said and put his foot to it. The door flew open with a crash against the wall. The room was dimly lit, a narrow pallet of a bed the only furniture, and smelled of must and sour body odour.

A creaking noise sounded near the window. A figure hiding in the shadows turned slowly to face them. Aculeo recognized the outline of the man's face. "Iovinus," he whispered, scarcely able to believe it.

"He's going to jump!" Gellius cried. The three men raced forward to grab Iovinus before he could escape through the window to the alley below. But he only turned about slowly with a shuddery creak. By the dim light of morning they could see the way Iovinus' eyes and tongue bulged from his bloated purple face and the rope that led from the rafters knotted about his broken neck.

"Hephaestus' crooked cock," Trogus growled as they lay Iovinus' corpse out on the thin straw mattress. Trogus started coughing again, long, painful hacks that seemed to shred his lungs.

The tavern-keeper, a fat little Illyrian, kept running his stubby fingertips back through his thin, greasy hair. "This is bad luck, very, very bad luck," he muttered almost to himself. "Why did he have to kill himself in my tavern of all places?"

"Where are his belongings?" Aculeo asked.

"What belongings?"

"He was carrying a satchel when I saw him at the Hippodrome. Where is it?"

"How should I know?"

"You must have stolen it," Bitucus said.

"I never did such a thing!" the Illyrian cried. "I'm a man of the very greatest virtue!"

"He searched the room when your man went out yesterday," the thrattia said helpfully. "He didn't find anything worth stealing though, just a few wax tablets."

"Filthy whore! I did nothing of the sort!"

"He lies," she said indifferently.

The tavern-keeper cuffed the back of her head. She then pounced on the man, knocking him to the floor, striking him about the face with a flurry of fists. Skinny and raw-boned, she likely would have beaten the man to death if the others hadn't pulled her off of him.

"Enough!" Aculeo said. "Where are the tablets now?"

"I don't know," the tavern-keeper wheedled. "I swear! I noticed them only by accident when I came to clean his room, a service we gladly provide all out guests. I never touched them though, my most sacred oath!"

"For what that's worth. What was written on them?"

"I have no …"

"Some numbers and such, he told me," the thrattia said. "He wouldn't know anything else. He can't read." The tavern-keeper fell into a sulk, not daring to say another word.

Aculeo reluctantly searched Iovinus' corpse – hardly a pleasant task. He found a few sesterces in the coin purse and a small, round silver box tucked in a small pocket behind the belt. The box lid was engraved with a mythological scene, Perseus perhaps, and inlaid with mother-of-pearl – fine work, rather expensive looking. Aculeo flipped open the lid. There were three small waxy spheres within, each the size of his thumb tip and coated with tiny black seeds, glistening with an oily residue. He smelled them – incense. An odd thing for a man to carry about.

They made their way into the narrow hallway to get what passed for fresh air in the foul little tavern.

"Such a tragedy to lose a dear friend," the tavern-keeper said, breaking the silence. "My deepest condolences. If you gentlemen like, for a modest fee I would be pleased arrange his funerary services."

"What – so you can pocket our money while you toss him in a ditch outside the western gates?" Trogus growled, then started coughing again.

"If you're that lucky," the thrattia said with a bitter laugh. "A man tastes much like pork if he's prepared right. Or so they say."

"An outrageous lie!" the tavern-keeper howled, raising a hand to strike her again, only to drop it when she shot him a look, daring him to try. Aculeo glanced down at the smoking brazier below, the sizzling chunks of meat being tended to by a slave. He and Gellius glanced uncomfortably at one another as they recalled their meal at the Little Eagle the other day.

"What now?" Bitucus asked.

"Now nothing," Trogus said after his coughing fit ended. "Whatever Iovinus was up to is lost with the man himself."

"But what about…?" Gellius whined.

"Enough! Any dreams of recovering our stolen fortunes are just that! Foolish dreams for halfwit children. Think about it, Gellius! If Iovinus had stolen our fortunes, why would he have returned to the city only to take his sad excuse of a life in a shithole like this?"

"Shithole?" the tavern-keeper protested. "I'll have you know …"

"Oh shut up!"

"We should take his body to the Necropolis," Gellius said at last.

"A noble thought. And who'll pay for his funeral?" Aculeo said.

"Who d'you think?" Trogus said.

Aculeo glared at him. "And why should I do that?"

"What would you suggest we do instead? Dump him outside the city walls with the dead slaves and street scrapings for the jackals to dispose of?"

"Of course not," Gellius said firmly. "Thief or not, Iovinus was still a Roman. He still deserves some semblance of virtue on his final journey."

Aculeo glowered at the other men. "Fine!" he cried at last. Even in death Iovinus had found a way to cut his purse.

CHAPTER VII

Rhakotis, a ragged sprawling district of the city built across the barren delta behind the shipyards in Epsilon, was the original fishing village around which Alexandria had been built three centuries ago. The native fellahin still comprised the majority of the quarter's population. The clean, even gridlines and pristine colonnades of the city's broad boulevards were replaced here by cart paths, heavily rutted, thick with weeds and clods of animal dung. The air hung with the sweet, pervasive smell of baking bread and fermenting barley from the little breweries that dotted the area. Bronze-skinned fellahin men and women sat cross-legged on reed mats in what shade there was, pots and cups, idols and other crafts laid out before them for sale. They met Aculeo with guarded stares as he followed the hired slave pushing the barrow with Iovinus' shrouded corpse along the hot, dusty street – Romans coming to their part of town rarely meant anything good.

The Necropolis lay outside the Gates of the Moon where the Eunostos Canal branched from the Egyptian Sea. Aculeo followed the slave down the road that led from the gates to a row of simple houses on the edge of a marshy section of the canal. The houses there, made of plastered mud-brick with small pens out back for their animals, had been built on high ground well above the floodplain amidst a grove of palms.

"How much further is it?" Aculeo asked irritably.

"We're almost there," the slave replied, steering the barrow down a narrow laneway towards the fellahin buildings. He finally turned up a walkway towards a single-storied hovel with a small ivory carving of Isis framed by a few Egyptian pictograms set in a niche over the doorway. The slave slapped his open hand against the door a few times. The door opened with a creak a moment later and an old woman stuck her head through the crack, scowling at them.

"Greetings, Sekhet," the slave said in Greek, bowing his head in deference.

"What d'you want?" she replied in the same language, her accent thick and guttural.

"We need to arrange funeral services," Aculeo said.

"Hm." The woman glanced down at the body and furrowed her brow. "Greek, fellahin or Jew?"

"Roman."

The woman looked him boldly up and down with her sharp black eyes, her face brown and creased as a tattered old purse. "And who are you?"

"Tarquitius Aculeo," he said, irritated by the crone's presumptuous tone.

"Another of our humble city's great Roman overlords? I should feel honoured," she said, though her sour tone hardly matched her words. She nodded towards the body. "Cremation then. Ten sesterces."

Aculeo almost laughed. "Ten sesterces? You're joking."

"Do it yourself then," Sekhet said with a shrug. "There's a clearing you could use down near the canal. Just gather a few sticks into a pyre, throw on a shovelful of pitch, he'll be done in no time. I trust you don't mind his shade dogging your steps throughout eternity for the sake of a few pieces of silver." She moved to close the door in his face.

"Wait," Aculeo said, stopping the door with his foot. I hope you rot in hell, Iovinus, he thought, counting out the precious coins.

The crone quickly tucked them away, then stepped forward and lifted a corner of the old blanket to reveal Iovinus' corpse, already beginning to stiffen in the barrow. She bent down and pinched Iovinus' chin between her fingers, turning it slowly side to side, humming to herself. Aculeo turned away, feeling ill. Was there any clearer example of fellahin barbarism than their fascination with handling the dead?

"What do you think happened to him?" she finally asked.

"I know exactly what happened to him," Aculeo said. "He hung himself."

"Hm. And why would he do that?" Sekhet asked, arching an eyebrow.

"Remorse? Guilt? Cowardice? I've no idea, nor do I care – I've wasted enough time on him as it is. Not to mention money. Just deal with his remains."

The old woman narrowed her eyes at Aculeo then garbled something in her native tongue to someone inside the little house. A heavyset fellahin man came outside and helped the slave wheel Iovinus' body back up the laneway to the dusty street. That's it then, Aculeo thought, and turned to leave. He felt a tug on his sleeve.

"Come," Sekhet said, pulling him into the doorway.

"What? Why?"

The woman didn't bother to reply, she simply stepped back into the house. What an irritating old woman, he thought. He had half a mind to simply turn around and go, yet he found himself following her into the house all the same.

She led him down a narrow passageway to the back rooms. "Wait there," she said, then disappeared into the back of the house.

There was only one place to wait, in a small, low-hung room, the only light leeching in from a small window cut near the ceiling. Mud-brick benches lined the walls, all three of which were fully occupied – by runny-nosed children, a feeble old man with white-cast eyes, a woman heavy with child, another holding a crying baby on her lap, a third with a hideous brown tumour sprouting over one eye. Most of them were fellahin, although there were a handful of Nubians and a couple of impoverished looking Greeks or Romans. Aculeo leaned against the wall. What am I doing here? he thought impatiently. I can't believe I actually listened to her.

A few minutes later he heard a scream of agony from one of the back rooms. No one else seemed to notice. Aculeo hesitated a moment before finally walking over to investigate. A slave stood within a doorless chamber grinding medicines in a mortar, the walls behind him lined with wooden racks containing dozens of small glass vials and papyrus packets. The slave was paying no attention to the heart-wrenching wails from the adjacent room.

Sekhet stuck her head out from behind the door. "Panebkhonis!" she cried. The slave ducked behind a bench. Sekhet muttered something nasty-sounding in fellahin, then spotted Aculeo. "Roman. Come here," she said. And though she was only a fellahin, and a woman at that, her tone left little room for debate.

A young man sat on a bench in the small room, gingerly holding his arm. His hand was puffy and purple, the fingers swollen and bruised beneath the nails.

"He broke his arm two weeks ago," Sekhet said irritably. "Yet instead of paying a few asses to see a proper healer, he buys tonics from some low market rootcutter. He'll be lucky if he even keeps it."

The man groaned in agony, his face pale and slick with sweat. The woman gave him a piece of dark wood to chew on. "Mandrake bark," she said. "It helps dull the pain and induce sleep before the procedure."

"What procedure?" Aculeo asked. "What kind of games are you …?"

"Shhh. Come on," she said, "wrap your arms around him, that's it, under the shoulders. Hold him tighter, I'm sure you're stronger than that. Tighter – good. And, now…" Sekhet twisted the patient's forearm with surprising strength. The man gave an agonized screech of pain, then fainted in Aculeo's arms. Aculeo held him for a moment before laying him awkwardly down on the bench.

"Alright," Sekhet said, turning to mix some powder and water in a large bowl.
She dipped thick linen rags into the gypsum sludge and carefully wrapped them across the man's forearm. "Don't drop him – hold him still."

"Are you a funerary attendant or a healer?" Aculeo asked.

"Depends on the patient." Sekhet smoothed the white sludge of the cast with her hands, her knuckles swollen and distorted like knots of rope. Her patient was slowly returning to consciousness. She felt his forehead, greasy with sweat, looked into his groggy eyes and gave an encouraging smile. "See, that wasn't so bad. Let's stand you up. Come on now, don't get all weak-kneed on me. There you are. Feeling better?"

"No," the man mumbled.

"You will in time." She handed him a small pouch. "Take a pinch of these herbs as a tea four times a day. It will clear the poisons from your body. And don't stray too far from a chamber pot."

"Don't I need to be bled?" the man asked weakly.

The healer made a face. "Pah! Of course not, just shut up and listen for a moment. Eat only thin, hot soup and absolutely no wine." She tapped her fingertips against the cast, saw that it was dry enough, then wrapped a clean cloth sling over the patient's shoulder and under his arm. "Be careful with that, don't let it get wet or I'll break your other arm, understand? And I won't be so gentle next time. Give an offering to Isis every day for the next four days and pray for your recovery."

"What of Sarapis?"

"Hm? Oh, him too if you like, why not? But Isis before all others," Sekhet said as she sent him back outside and closed the door behind him and gave a deep sigh. "He waited too long to seek proper help, but sometimes all we can do is try and pray it's enough. So," she said, washing the sludge off her hands in a broad clay bowl. "Let's talk about your friend's passing."

"He was hardly a friend," Aculeo snapped. "He was a thief and a liar and he hung himself in the back room of a tavern. I've done more for him than he deserves bringing him here in the first place, much less paying for his damned cremation."

"And who are you to him?" she asked.

"I was his employer. And a victim of his thievery."

"Hmm," Sekhet mused. "Were you aware he was severely beaten shortly before his death?"

He looked at her in surprise. "What?"

"You see, even in death he still has secrets left to tell you," Sekhet said with a smile, then she opened the door and held it for him. "Wait outside a few minutes then we'll deal with it."

"I've waited long enough. If you have something to tell me then do it now."

"My deepest apologies, but the almighty Roman overlord will just have to be tolerant until the humble fellahin healer has finished with her living patients," Sekhet said.

Aculeo scowled – she truly was an annoying old woman. "Fine, I'll wait a few minutes then," he grumbled.

She reached up and took his chin between her fingertips, examining his face intently with her deep, dark eyes. Aculeo pulled away – her manner was unnerving. "You eat poorly, sleep hardly at all and drink far too much wine," she said with a disapproving cluck of her tongue. "You need to realign your humours. One cup of cucumber juice three times per day. Water your wine one to four, no less. Eat no red meat, only fish, and try to get more sleep," she said, then pushed him through the doorway.

The portly attendant grinding medicines in the room next door gave Sekhet a sheepish look. She scowled at him. "Panebkhounis, you've been chewing on lotus root again, haven't you? Don't lie to me, I can see the stains still on your lips. Now send in the next patient and stop being so lazy or I'll have to beat you and I won't even bother to treat you afterwards, I promise you."

A warm, fragrant breeze swept along the dusty streets as Aculeo followed Sekhet through the outskirts at the western edge of Rhakotis, relieved at being out of that stuffy little house and into fresh air at last. Sekhet had taken forever seeing the rest of her patients – there seemed to be an endless supply – before she finally appeared and instructed him to accompany her. Once again, her tone had left little room for debate. She moved at a surprisingly brisk pace for an old woman, torch in hand, humming to herself as she followed a well-travelled path down a rugged slope toward the caves.

After several minutes walk the path came to an end at a craggy rock wall. An entranceway had been carved into the face of the wall. Sekhet passed through it without a second glance. Aculeo hesitated at the entrance a moment, peering within at a high vaulted ceiling overhanging a steep shadowed staircase leading down into the Necropolis. He glanced up at the open sky one last time before reluctantly following the healer down the steps into the realm of the Egyptian gods of old.

At the bottom of the staircase Sekhet hurried along a narrow passageway cut into the rock, leading off into the darkness. Something about confined spaces always disturbed Aculeo. The walls felt like they were ready to swallow him, steal his air, bury him alive. He felt his chest grow tight, his breathing rapid, shallow, his head spinning. He closed his eyes, forced himself to breathe slowly.

"What's wrong with you?" Sekhet asked.

"Nothing," Aculeo lied.

"Hurry up then," she said snapped. "Praise Isis, it's like walking with a hobbled mule."

They walked through the interconnected tunnels for several minutes until at last they reached a large chamber, cool and still and smelling vaguely of death. Four doors had been hewn into the rough rock walls, a crescent moon carved in the pediments above each of them. A hole had been carved into the ceiling, through which a splash of sunlight spilled, though it had travelled from a very long way up. How deep into the ground have we gone, he wondered, cold sweat prickling his face and neck.

One of the doorways was partly open, dimly lit with torchlight. Sekhet walked towards it and threw open the door. A body draped in a linen shroud had been laid out on a stone funerary table. The table was carved in the form of two lions facing forward with the corpse's head fitting into a basin between the lions' tails, a drainage channel running down the centre and feeding into the basin. Sekhet set her torch in a wall sconce and pulled back the shroud.

And there lay Iovinus. His face was grey in pallor and slightly bloated now. The scent of rot and the noisy buzz of flies filled the airless little room.

"Bring the torch closer." The flickering torchlight highlighted the gauntness of Iovinus' face, the sharp edges of his cheekbones. The purplish tip of his tongue protruded partially from his mouth. As Aculeo took a queasy closer look, he noticed the right cheek was indeed shadowed with bruising, while the left side of his jaw was quite swollen. "See now?" she said. "His jaw was fractured. His left cheekbone as well I think."

"That could have happened when we cut him down. He fell on the floor. And one of my associates may have kicked him once or twice."

"Then his injuries wouldn't be so apparent. As it is, he had barely enough time to swell and bruise before his death. It doesn't happen afterwards. Do you know who might have done this to him?"

"Yes. I'd have beaten him myself if I'd had the chance." Still, Aculeo was puzzled by this news.

"Hm," Sekhet said. She took a sharp knife from her satchel and cut open Iovinus' tunic. His ribs were edged in shadows, his belly distended, tinted greenish yellow. She probed her fingers around his abdomen, eyes closed, humming to herself. "He was ill. Wasting disease."

"Oh?"

His groin was bound with strips of cloth dark with congealed blood. Sekhet cut them off and delicately peeled them off the man's skin. "Ah," she said when she was done. "He was castrated recently."

"Castrated?" Aculeo asked, feeling ill.

Sekhet said nothing as she reached her gnarled fingers beneath the back of Iovinus' long, skinny neck, probing, then turned his lifeless head side to side with her other hand. "His neck's not broken, so death by hanging would have been from strangulation." She said it quite easily, as though she were discussing the weather. "Were his hands bound?"

"No," Aculeo said, turning away – he felt like he'd be sick any moment. Like most civilized men, he'd never understood the fellahins' obsession with death. Sekhet eased Iovinus' eyelids open with her thumbs and made another tsk tsk sound.

"What?" Aculeo asked.

"Tell me what you see."

He glanced reluctantly into Iovinus' eyes. "What should I be looking for?"

"When someone is strangled, the tiny vessels in their eyes will burst like flooded dams and they will appear shot with blood. That's not the case with you, though, is it Roman?" Iovinus' lifeless eyes remained open, unseeing, like the painted eyes of a statue. "This tells us he was already dead before the rope was slung around his neck. Which means that hanging himself would have been quite an impressive feat."

"You're saying that someone castrated him, then beat him to death and finally hanged him?" Aculeo asked dubiously. Sekhet nodded. "But why hang a man who's already dead?"

"I know not. From what you told me, the man had his enemies."

"More of them than friends these days."

"Hm. Was anything stolen from him?"

"Some tablets. I don't know what else. Oh, we found this on him." Aculeo dug around in his satchel for the little silver box and handed it to her. "Incense."

Sekhet opened the box, carefully sniffed the contents, then pinched off a bit and touched it to her tongue. She made a bitter face. "It's not incense, it's opium."

"What?"

"Opium. It's made from the sap of Persian poppies. It's used to bring pleasure and sleep, and relieve pain. It's also extraordinarily expensive."

"Why leave it on him then? Even if the murderer didn't know the value of the contents, the box alone would have fetched a few sesterces."

"Robbery of that sort may not have been the goal," the healer said with a shrug. "I should also be curious where your friend may have gotten the opium from in the first place. It's not an easy thing to acquire." She pulled the shroud back up to Iovinus' chin. "So, I think he's told us all he can. More questions than answers I'm afraid, but that can't be helped. Would you care to say your last farewells?"

Aculeo gazed into the dead man's eyes one last time, open wide as though in wonder, then shook his head. "I've nothing to say that might give him rest. The truth of what happened died with him." He hesitated before placing an as for Charon in Iovinus' mouth.

As they made their way back into the main chamber, Aculeo paused outside the open door of a room where a number of other bodies had been laid out on wooden tables, covered in canvas shrouds. "It's a common chamber," the healer said. "It contains the bodies brought here for ordinary funerals over the past few days."

"A woman was found murdered in the Sarapeion yesterday."

"Oh? You seem better acquainted with our newest residents than I am. Shall we examine her as well?"

"She was just some nameless porne. Let's go."

But Sekhet had already headed into the carved stone chamber. Aculeo reluctantly followed. As anxious as he was to leave this wretched place, he wasn't about to head back through the dark passageways on his own.

Sekhet used her torch to light the oil lamps set about the room then approached the nearest table and flipped back the canvas shroud. It was an old man, his skin sallow, ripe with the stench of death. The next body was a fellahin youth with bluish-tinged lips. "Drowning," she muttered. Then a woman, her face contorted in pain. "Breech birth."

Then she pulled back the shroud of the next table. "That's her," Aculeo said. Sekhet eased the shroud off the woman's body. Her skin was the colour of tallow and her belly had already begun to bloat. Tiny black flies crawled around her eyes, mouth and nostrils. Aculeo shuddered, looking away.

Sekhet stroked the girl's cheek. "Poor thing," she said. "How did you come across her?"

"Iovinus had patronized a porne named Neaera. I'd hoped she could tell me his whereabouts through her but she disappeared a few days ago. When I heard a dead woman had been found in the Sarapeion I'd thought it might be her."

"And?" Aculeo shook his head. The old woman pursed her lips, then took her knife and carefully cut away the girl's soiled chiton, exposing her naked body, thin and malnourished, with lean, ropey muscles and breasts small as figs. She examined the cut that ran the length of her forearm. "Fairly shallow, just enough to break the skin," she mused. "And done just prior to her death, barely enough time to scab."

A thin braid of frayed yellow jute cord was knotted around one of the girl's wrists. "Someone tied her up," Aculeo said.

The old woman examined the girl's wrists, both of which were marked with the dim red imprint of rope, then took the cord firmly in her hands and yanked – it snapped easily. "Yes. Not with this though." She inspected the girl's face, looked in her eyes, her ears, her nose. "The side of her face is bruised, she was struck recently." She opened her mouth then, prying open the jaws. "Her teeth are worn flat along the surfaces. Common in the poorer classes – all the sand and mill-grist that gets into cheap bread. Bring that lamp closer."

A gaping wound ran down the side of her abdomen beneath the ribs, caked with dark blood. The girl's hips were narrow as an adolescent boy's, her legs long and skinny. Her body was still locked in the pose it had been in when they'd found her, with one arm raised over her head as if to ward off a blow, the other crooked before her, her hand covering the dark triangle between her legs, giving the impression of modesty.

"Pour some water into that basin," Sekhet said. Aculeo did so and watched as the healer dabbed a wet rag at the blood encrusted wound on the girl's abdomen. "So deep!" she said, pressing along the edges of the gash with a long metal instrument. "The wound's too short for a knife, too wide for a javelin. A sword perhaps." Sekhet carefully rolled the body onto its stomach, waving away the little flies that rose in an angry, buzzing cloud.

Several raised, pinkish scars criss-crossed the girl's back and shoulders. "Whip marks – not recent." The healer rolled her onto her back again, examined her hands which were caked in pinkish-grey dirt and blood. She began to clean them. Her nails were broken to the quick, her fingertips covered in tiny cuts. As though she'd been clawing at something, Aculeo thought. Or someone. "Perhaps she was defending herself from her attacker," he said.

"No," Sekhet mused. "If she was that close to her attacker there would be cuts and bruises on her hands or arms as well. Yet only her fingertips are injured. She was digging at the earth with her bare hands."

Aculeo looked away again as the healer examined the girl's pelvis. "She was raped recently," she said with a sigh. "She shows no signs of the diseases pornes tend to get." She examined the girl's legs, clicking her tongue. Her buttocks and the backs of her thighs were covered with purplish-yellow bruises, her calves and ankles streaked with dried pinkish-grey mud. "An unusual colour," she mused. "Not from around here." Sekhet washed the girl's calves, running a fingertip along a pale ridge that ran half the length of one leg. "Guinea worm. It lives in the shallows of rivers and lays its eggs in small cuts in the feet and toes. It's a common enough thing with river slaves." The soles of the girl's feet were like thick sandal leather, the toenails brown, cracked and broken, the tops of the toes cut and raw.

"You think she was a porne?"

"More likely a working slave. And yet she was murdered near the Sarapeion in the middle of the night, when the only other visitors are supplicants and pornes."

"I found this in her hand," Aculeo recalled, taking the tiny gold earring from his coin purse and handing it to the healer.

Sekhet turned it over in her hand, pensive. "Hardly the sort of thing to be worn by a river slave. She must have stolen it. You'll know more about her if you learn who she stole it from. So, the more we know, the more questions we have. What shall we do with her body?"

"The slaves who brought her must have given you money for her burial."

"If she's in the common room then we got barely enough to cover her with a shovelful of bitumite and dropped in a pit," Sekhet said with a weary sigh, stroking the girl's small, pale face. "I suppose little more could be expected for a nameless slave. Murdered and tossed aside like garbage, her death unmarked, her soul unable to reach the afterlife. A shame, when for just one more sesterce we could take care of her properly."

"You are a thieving old crone, aren't you? Here," Aculeo said, tossing her the coin. The girl's shade won't linger in the Harbour of Souls to haunt me at least, he thought irritably.

D.L. Johnstone

Sekhet nodded and placed a twisted hand over the girl's eyes, then closed her own. "We will shed our sorrows and put away our mourning, O Isis, and by your foresight you will enclose our days with wholesome health and beneficial wealth. On this day, and whatever days shall be born from this night hence, we shall direct our troubled thoughts to your commands alone."

CHAPTER VIII

THE 21ST DAY OF APRILIS

Gellius answered the door, blinking in the dim morning light, eyes caked with sleep. "Aculeo," he said in surprise. "Is everything alright?"

"Yes."

"You took care of Iovinus?"

"Yes, I ..."

"What does he want?" Trogus growled from the shadows, then began coughing, a wretched interminable sound. Gellius put his hands over his ears and closed his eyes. It was painful to witness Trogus in this state, especially given he'd always been such a hale, cheerful man. To see him now so bitter and sickly was truly dreadful.

"There's a healer I know of ..." Aculeo offered.

"Don't you get it yet?" Trogus cried between coughs. "I want nothing ... nothing to do with you, you ... son-of-a-bitch ... just leave me be!"

Aculeo held up a round loaf of fresh hard bread, an amphora of wine, a small block of fresh cheese and a few dried plums. He said nothing as he handed it to Gellius. "I'll leave this here for when you're hungry."

"D'you expect gratitude for your charity now?" Trogus said angrily.

"It's not necessary ..."

"Nor is it deserved. Though I'm sure it lessens the guilt poisoning your heart."

"What guilt? It's hardly my fault you're here. I've fallen almost as far as you, as have dozens of others."

"And whose fault is it?" Trogus said, trying to restrain a cough. "Iovinus'?"

"Perhaps."

"Blame a dead man, why not? Just do me a favour, Aculeo – stay out of my sight. I detest your sympathy and I don't really need the reminder of all I've left behind. Just leave us alone." With that, the man pulled his blanket up over his shoulders and rolled to face the wall, his shoulders hitching up and down with each wretched cough.

Gellius touched Aculeo's shoulder. "Come on," he said quietly. "Let's go for a walk."

The two men threaded their way through the morning crowds that thronged and chattered along the Canopic Way. The eastern harbour had a fine view of the magnificent palace grounds, nestled within the Royal Harbour where elegant skiffs and great triremes sat at anchor. Treacherous shoals blocked all but one entrance, but the harbour was deep enough to allow large ships to moor right up against the palace steps. Beta, the palace district, sprawled across close to a quarter of the city with its winding porticoes, lush groves, and grandiose public buildings. Once home to the great Greek kings and queens of Egypt, from Ptolemy Soter to Cleopatra VII herself, the magnificent old buildings now served as the headquarters for the Roman Prefect Flaccus and the various officials who ran the city, as well as the Library, the Museion and the Gymnasion.

The grounds of the Museion were just ahead. The heavy fragrance of flowering acacia hung in the air, along with the softly clattering sound of leaves from a grove of date palms growing outside the walls. A colossal pair of Aswan marble statues of some ancient Egyptian kings and queens stood solemn-faced on either side of a towering marble archway.

"Everything else may have been taken from us, but we can still appreciate beauty," Gellius said gently, taking a seat on a marble bench beneath a shaded portico. "This truly is the loveliest place in the entire city. It seems so different now, though I suppose it's really me who's different. I can reflect on what I once had at least."

"You sound like you've already given up," Aculeo said, sitting next to his old friend.

Gellius said nothing for a while. Then he turned to Aculeo, taking his hands in his, squeezing tight. "I pray you forgive dear Trogus. The moneylenders are after us, you see. We're so terribly in debt, I fear we can never be free again. Yet Trogus is far too proud to ask anyone for help. And I can't go against his wishes. I won't."

"But what will you do?"

"We want to go back to Rome but we can barely afford food and a roof over our heads much less ship's passage."

"You know I'd help you if I could," Aculeo said. "It's just …"

"What would be the point?" Gellius said. "Leave here so we could be paupers in another place? No. Besides, Trogus is too ill to travel."

"And yet he refuses to see a healer."

"I'll try to get him to see reason. In the meantime we'll just hide as long as we can, as long as we can afford the rent, which isn't much longer I fear."

"Stay with me then," Aculeo said. "What little room I have is yours."

Gellius smiled. "Thank you, but I doubt Trogus would accept your gracious hospitality, however well intended. No, we'll just stick it out where we are and try to leave once he's feeling better. In the meantime, there's still a chance we can recover something of what Iovinus stole from us."

"A fading chance I fear," Aculeo said. "I've some bad news. Iovinus didn't take his own life. He was murdered."

Gellius gave a sharp intake of breath and his eyes narrowed warily. "What are you talking about?" And Aculeo recounted what he'd learned from his visit to Sekhet. Gellius slumped down in the marble bench, pounding his fists against his head. "Why? Who would have done such a thing?"

"I can think of several names off the top of my head who would have gladly done the deed once the word got out of where to find him."

"This is a disaster! What shall we do? What of his porne, Neaera? Any luck finding her?"

"Not yet. I doubt it was a coincidence she disappeared within days of Iovinus' murder though."

"Perhaps not." Aculeo pulled the portrait of the three women near Pharos and unrolled it on the bench between them. "What's that?" Gellius asked.

"I took it from Neaera's flat." He pointed to the woman in the middle of the portrait with the cameo necklace about her pale throat. "This is Neaera."

"She's lovely," Gellius said.

"Do you recognize the other two?"

Gellius examined the portrait more thoroughly, then tapped the dark-haired woman standing to Neaera's right. "This one I know," he said, stroking her cheek, a smile curving his lips. "Calisto. I'm sure of it. It's rather a fine likeness."

"Who is she? Another porne?"

"Hardly. She's a hetaira, and an expensive one at that. She entertains at only the finest symposia. I don't attend those much myself these days. My social life is rather limited of late."

"As is mine," Aculeo said. "Where could I find her?"

Dotted about the Beta Quarter, like seeds on a crust of bread, were a number of exclusive little demes where the city's wealthiest citizens resided, including Aculeo and his family only a few months before – it felt so terribly long ago to him now. The winding streets of Olympia were carved into a hill above the central city area. From the top of the hill one could see the Sarapeion to the southwest and the Lighthouse in the northern harbour.

The Street of Lagos was lush with ornamental acacia, fig trees and date palms and a long stretch of pretty white garden walls, the tops of which were blanketed with fragrant pink blossomed boughs. And there, the Shrine of Ares – across from it stood a particularly beautiful villa just as Gellius had described it. Two lush plum trees stood on either side of the entrance, their branches drooping down, heavy with purple-red fruit. No drab little flat near the Tannery for this one, Aculeo mused. Sweat trickled down his brow and back from the exertion of the walk. He wiped his brow with the back of his hand as he approached the gates.

Someone within was playing an aulos, the sound like the melodious buzzing of wasps haunting the air. He knocked at the gatehouse and the music ended. A child, perhaps seven or eight years old, darted to the gate, her feet bare, her eyes wide when she saw Aculeo standing there. It was the little thief from the Agora who'd stolen the wooden top from the merchant's cart. He realized where he'd seen Calisto before – she was one of the hetairai he'd seen in the Agora that same day.

"Greetings," Aculeo said. "I'd like to talk to your mistress. Please tell her I'm a friend of Gellius' and come at his recommendation." The girl stared at him, unmoving. He smiled. "I believe I may have seen a little girl who looked just like you steal a red top in the Agora two mornings ago. Are you enjoying it?"

The girl gaped at him in astonishment, then turned and ran back inside. Several moments later a very large, intimidating looking Nubian appeared and opened the heavy gates. The slave silently escorted Aculeo through the auleios that led to an inner courtyard. Peacocks strutted across the grounds, fanning out their tail feathers in proud display, and an ivory ibis strode about stilt-legged in a garden pond, spearing fish that splashed and darted around its feet. The little girl was standing at the edge of the courtyard, watching him. He gave her a small wave. She smiled shyly then disappeared into the garden. The Nubian stood off to the side, silent, watching.

Aculeo heard a swish of sandals across the mosaic floor behind him. The birds looked up from their preening. He turned and saw a young woman walking towards him. Calisto. She was tall and slender and wore a loose ivory chiton pinned at the shoulder with an exquisite gold fibula. She had a pale olive complexion and rich, amber-coloured eyes, but her features were too sharp and angular, her nose too thin, her mouth too serious to be considered beautiful. *I could find a dozen prettier pornes walking down any street in the Tannery, and at a fraction of the price for the lot of them, no doubt. What's so special about her then?*

"Greetings," she said. "I'm Calisto." Her voice had a slight dusky accent, the origin difficult to pinpoint.

"Greetings, I'm Decimus Tarquitius Aculeo. I hope I'm not disturbing you."

"Not at all. You said you were a friend of Gellius."

"I am," he said. "He sends his greetings."

"Please give him my regards," she said graciously. "How may I help you?"

"I was hoping you might know a woman named Neaera," Aculeo said.

Calisto looked at him, caught off guard. "Yes, of course ... but why do you ask?"

Aculeo retrieved the portrait he'd taken from Neaera's flat from his satchel and laid it out on the little table between them.

"Where did you find that?" she asked.

"I took it from Neaera's flat in Delta."

"But I don't understand – what's this all about?"

"Neaera disappeared a few days ago."

"Disappeared?" Calisto said, her voice trailing to a wisp. "I don't ..."

"I'm a colleague of her patron, Iovinus."

"Yes, of course, I know him well. But I still don't understand."

"I'm afraid Iovinus was murdered yesterday morning."

"Oh ... that's terrible." Calisto's face went pale.

"Are you alright?"

"Yes. Yes. I'm just … I'd heard he'd drowned months ago. How could he have only just …?"

"I'm trying to answer the same question, frankly. That's why I was looking for Neaera. I hoped she'd be able to help me."

Calisto looked as though she might faint. Aculeo took her by the hand, helping her to sit and poured her a cup of water. She appeared younger and less certain of herself than she had initially. How old is she, I wonder – twenty-three or so?" This is very upsetting. I don't know what to say. What … did something happen to Neaera?"

"I've no idea. I thought she might have run away, but she left her jewellery, lyre and some clothing behind at her flat in Delta." And an unkept promise of helping the little porne, Tyche, escape the Blue Bird, Aculeo thought.

"Did she ever say anything to you about wanting to leave Alexandria?"

"No, no nothing. She … she was ..." Calisto's voice trailed to a wisp and she began to cry. Aculeo waited until she finally managed to regain her composure. "It's all so terrible."

"I fear Iovinus' murder and Neaera's disappearance are linked somehow," he said. "When did you see her last?"

"I don't know. Five or six days ago perhaps, I can't recall exactly. She came here for a visit. We had a … a lovely afternoon." Calisto's voice caught with emotion.

"Did she say anything to you? About any troubles she'd been having? Anything about Iovinus?"

"No, nothing. She was happy, happy and calm as I'd ever seen her."

"Was there a mention of some tablets that Iovinus possessed?"

"Tablets?" Calisto asked, confused.

"Never mind." Aculeo indicated the portrait once again. "What about the third woman? Who's she?"

Calisto glanced down. "That's Petras. Neaera's cousin."

"Is she a porne as well?"

"A hetaira," Calisto corrected him.

"Of course. Where can I find her?"

"I haven't seen Petras in some time. I never really knew her all that well."

All these women running off, Aculeo thought irritably – are they running from or to something I wonder. "I'm sorry to have brought you such unwelcome news," he said. He could hear the sound of a child playing and laughing in the garden, singing a song in a strange tongue.

"I … appreciate knowing at least," Calisto said, then started to weep again. "I'm sorry, it's just …"

"I understand."

She took a deep, quavering breath, and dabbed at her eyes with a square of linen. "It's late. I'm supposed to be getting ready. I've a symposium to attend this evening."

"Of course," Aculeo said, and stood to leave

"This is madness," Calisto said. "The last thing I want to do is go out tonight and entertain while I'm worrying about Neaera. I doubt the host would understand if I didn't come though."

"We don't always get to choose such things. May I ask who the host is?"

"Marcellus Gurculio," she said. "Do you know him?"

"I do," Aculeo said, forcing a smile. Is this what fate dictates for me now? he thought bitterly. Scraping about in the streets like a beggar selling my wife's wedding jewels for food and rent while moneylenders host symposia with my stolen wealth? Curse the gods!

"Are you not well?" she asked with sudden concern.

"I'm fine. Again, my condolences."

Calisto stepped closer to him, touching his arm with her soft cool hand. Her touch, the closeness of her body, the scent of her, wild flowers mixed with sweet wine. "I'm indebted to you. Please, if you find out anything else, anything at all, you'll let me know."

"I will indeed."

She stood back then, managing a small smile. "Fortune be with you, Aculeo."

"And you, Calisto."

"What do you think that man wanted?" little Idaia asked Myrrhine. They sat in a cloistered area at the bottom of the garden, watching Aculeo walk back up the path towards the outer gates.

"I don't know, little bee," the fair-haired hetaira replied, returning her attention to her small silver mirror as she applied dark grey galena to her upper eyelids with a flat stick of ivory.

"I like him, he has a nice smile."

"That's a silly reason to like someone."

"Don't you like him?" Idaia asked. Myrrhine shrugged. "Do you think Calisto likes him?"

D.L. Johnstone

"Idaia, please, enough with all your nonsense!" Myrrhine said, picking up a jar of green malachite which she began to apply to her lower eyelids, complementing her golden hair in such a fetching manner.

"Let me try it," Idaia said, reaching for the jar.

Myrrhine held it out of her reach. "Not until you're older."

"I'm old enough now."

"You're still a child. You need to be thirteen at least. Old enough to marry."

Idaia sighed and sat back down. "Will you marry someday?"

"I don't know."

"Can I come live with you if you do?"

"I suppose, if my husband lets you."

"You'll have to make him," Idaia said. "I should like to be a hetaira when I grow up."

Myrrhine hesitated a moment, then continued applying her makeup. "You don't know what you're talking about."

"Yes I do. You get to dress up pretty, you wear nice jewellery, you go to parties all the time, and men give you beautiful presents …"

"Men would want to do things to you too."

"What kind of things?" Idaia asked.

Myrrhine sighed. "Never mind."

Idaia watched a peacock bobbing its head along the garden path, pausing to preen its long tail feathers. "I remember home."

"Really? You must have been a baby when you left."

"I can still remember. I remember a tree outside the house where I played, I remember my mother who'd sing me songs."

"You don't remember your mother," Myrrhine scoffed.

"I do too!" Idaia said, tears welling in her eyes.

"Oh stop crying!" Myrrhine said, then glanced at the child's reflection in the mirror. "What's that you're playing with?"

Idaia hid her hands behind her back. "Nothing."

Myrrhine held out a hand until Idaia finally surrendered the top. "You stole that."

"I did not! One of the slaves made it for me!"

"Which slave?"

"I don't remember."

Myrrhine shook her head. "I told you not to steal things anymore, you'll get into trouble. They'll cut off your hands."

Idaia burst into tears. "But I didn't steal anything!"

"Stop crying."

"I … I'm n-n-not crying," she sniffed. After a while she said, "Tell me

68

what you remember about your home."

"I don't want to. This is my home now. And yours as well."

"I know."

Myrrhine smiled at her, then pulled her into a hug, tickling her until she laughed, and kissed her cheek. "Don't worry, little bee, we have one another now, right? Where we'll both be safe and sound."

It had grown dark as the hours stretched late into the evening. Aculeo was tired of waiting in the shadows of the street outside Gurculio's villa. A villa that used to belong to dear old Nigellus before he too lost everything when the damned fleet sank, he thought miserably. If the damned fleet sank that is, he thought, correcting himself. More likely stolen by Iovinus and whoever he was working with.

So the moneylender lives here now, does he? Why not? A vast marble fountain stood outside the villa's ornate iron gates, and the tops of its high garden walls were alight with coloured lanterns. He could hear music from behind the walls, the sound of flutes and lyres, laughter echoing into the evening airs. He watched as half a dozen slaves carried heavy amphorae in through the back entrance. Another slave stood at the front gates dressed as a satyr, complete with a long wooden phallus strapped to his waist and the ears and tail of a donkey, greeting guests as they arrived in their elegant litters, pretty young women accompanied by much older men.

Aculeo recalled all too well the endless evenings he himself had either hosted or attended in the old days, hours filled with music, rich food, fine wine, entertaining talk, lovely dancers – a feast for the mind and the senses. The days before everything had utterly fallen apart. It seemed a lifetime ago. Could it actually be measured in mere months?

Three young men arrived then, two slender and dark, one a fat, moon-faced boy who looked oddly familiar. Where have I seen him before? he wondered. A number of sophists from the Museion, among them a short, balding, barrel-chested man with a grey-streaked beard who stood back from the fray, smiling, taking everything and everyone in. How much actual philosophy will be talked tonight? And there, the host of the evening's festivities, the moneylender, with his crudely cut features and chunky gold rings that flashed and sparkled on his thick fingers, displaying his ill-gotten wealth for the world to see. A tangle of purple veins branched across his nose and cheeks, the inspiration for his cognomen, Gurculio – Latin for mealworm. He appeared quite inebriated already, laughing uproariously as he bellowed greetings to the new arrivals.

Aculeo watched another litter being carried down the street and pressed his back flat against the wall, deep in the shadows. The Nubian litter bearers arrived at the gates and eased the elegant structure to the ground. Calisto emerged, wearing a bright red peplos with a matching, diaphanous veil over her head. She looked quite lovely, far more entrancing than she had at the villa. She's in her element here, he thought. Next to step from the litter was the fair-haired hetaira he'd seen with her in the Agora the day prior. She was dressed in a tight coral chiton, without a veil this time though, her hair the colour of wild honey, with a garland of tiny flowers woven through it. She had a pretty face, with a large birthmark that marked her upper lip.

Another figure emerged from a splendid looking litter – a balding, weak-jawed man in his forties, with a rounded belly and skinny limbs. Lucius Albius Ralla, Aculeo realized in surprise. Ralla was a very wealthy banker, not to mention confidante of the Roman Prefect Flaccus himself. What's a man of his rank doing at a moneylender's symposium? He was warmly greeted by Gurculio and the two of them fell to whispering with one another, laughing at some private joke. Aculeo felt his skin crawl. So the moneylender has enough money and influence to climb so high in society as this?

Ralla approached Calisto, took her hands in his, leaned in close and kissed her on the lips. She accepted it graciously enough, then politely disengaged. Ralla then grabbed the fair-haired hetaira by the wrist, pulling her tight against him, kissing her on the neck as he grabbed one of her breasts. Half a dozen pretty young flute girls dressed as Maenads with fawn skins and wreathed in ivy emerged giggling from behind the garden gates and moved in amongst the guests. Ralla, distracted, turned to them with a drunken grin and released the hetaira as the Maenads crowned the guests with garlands, anointed them with scented oils and led them inside. The gates closed behind them then. Aculeo decided there was little to do but leave.

"Hey, I've been waiting for you." The recluse was sitting there in the doorway of the empty shop again, staring at the porne.

Philomena's head was spinning. A belly full of beer and little else, she'd had scant sleep in days, but the night was still young. "Ay, it's been a busy night."

"Busy, yes, a busy night," the recluse said with a shy smile. He moved over to make room for her to sit with him in the doorstep and passed over his jar of palm wine. He's sweet enough, she thought, poor fellow. She took a long drink from the jar, shuddering at the harsh brackishness of the stuff. The night was filled with a dour yellow glow.

"My Eurydice," he said softly.

She laughed. "Call me anything you like I suppose. What shall I call you?"

"Orpheus."

"Alright, Orpheus, you've been waiting for me again, have you? How long this time?"

He hesitated, blinking rapidly, and scratched his beard. "I can't recall. A long time I think."

"You've been okay then? Got enough to eat?"

"Eat?" he said, licking his lips. "Yesterday.....yesterday, I think I ate, but.... I can't recall."

"Here," Philomena said, and gave him some hard bread and figs she'd been keeping for later in her pouch. He looked at them, mystified for a moment, then gobbled them down. Poor thing, she thought, he's like a stray dog, just sticks and hide, not even a cloak, and she could see his jutting ribs beneath his dirty chiton. "What happened to your old cloak?"

He looked down at himself, mystified. "I don't know."

"Aren't you chilled?"

"I'm kept warm by the love of Sarapis," he said simply, as though the answer was obvious. His beard and hair were filthy as well, still, he'd probably not been bad looking once. Save for the knotted pink scar that twisted like rope across his face from ear to cheek, curving in cruelly across his lips to his chin.

"Well listen," she said, "I should ..."

"Do you know of the grace of Sarapis?" he asked suddenly, then closed his eyes, muttering, "may others learn to worship you as I so humbly do and offer you your rightful tributes throughout eternity."

"What? Oh, sure, I suppose."

"He rules over all that is good and light," the recluse said fervently.

"That's nice."

He wouldn't stop staring at her – it was unsettling. She took another draw from the jar before passing it back to him. "Well, I suppose I should go."

"Go? Where shall we go?"

"I don't know where you're going, but I have to meet some people. I've business to do," she said, standing up, staggering a bit from the beer and sheer exhaustion.

"Wait. Wait. Would you like something pretty?" he said, his eyes lit with a strange light.

"Silver and bronze are as pretty as they get these days."

The recluse wiped his mouth with the back of his hand, watching her, drawing closer. She could feel the heat from his body, and that awful smell, he probably hadn't been to the baths in years. Which baths would even admit him? She watched him fumble in his dirty tunic, then he held his closed fist out to her. A thin braid of yellow twine was tied around his filthy wrist, she noticed, like a makeshift bracelet. "Guess what I have here."

"I don't know, darling. Really, I have to..."

"Here, see, I brought it for you," he said, sliding closer to her, close enough to touch her, his breathing hard and ragged. He licked his lips, still staring at her with his eerie, unblinking eyes. She looked at his clenched fist, wondering what it held, until finally curiosity got the better of her. She held out her hand. He was frighteningly fast the way he seized her wrist.

"Ow, stop it," she gasped, trying to pull away, but he twisted her wrist, forcing it around, then opened his fist and dropped something into her open, trembling hand before finally releasing her.

She looked into her open palm cautiously, raising her eyebrows in surprise. "Is it real?"

He stroked her hair awkwardly, breathing hard, pulled her close, tried to kiss her on the lips, his breath foul, his teeth rotting and brown as old apples. "Eurydice," he whispered.

She pushed him away in revulsion. "Oh no, please." She looked in her hand, then up at him and she sighed. "Not here at least."

CHAPTER IX

THE 22ND DAY OF APRILIS

The skies were a tattered grey from the morning rains, but the sun was at last beginning to peek through near the horizon, the husk of clouds peeling back to reveal great blue swaths beneath. The air smelled of copper from the rain. Decius liked to watch the pink worms wriggling on the paving stones as they tried to escape the morning light. His teacher's house was just up ahead, he could see the peaked roof above the tops of the date palms. School was always so boring, so many lines to memorize, music to learn, and the teacher smelled of garlic. How much better would it be to run about and play instead? Why do grownups insist on making life so dreary?

"You've memorized your Phocylides?" the slave Scato wheezed, limping along the road after him.

"Umhm," Decius said, profoundly disinterested in the whole matter. He looked at the little woven reed boat he'd made, turning it to and fro in his hands. A master shipbuilder couldn't have done better, he thought.

"Put that silly thing down and pay attention," Scato said.

"Do you think it will float this time?"

"How should I know? You have your music today as well. Your teacher said you weren't paying attention last class, that he had to flog you before you'd listen."

Decius shrugged. "He likes to flog boys. He's odd that way."

"So you were paying attention?"

"What?" Decius asked, barely restraining a smirk.

"Don't test me, boy." The child could be such a challenge sometimes. Still, Scato regularly thanked the gods for granting him the brains to be permitted to serve as the child's pedagogue and not one of the normal household slaves. He was getting on fifty after all – he doubted his old body could have taken the sheer physical drudgery of that sort of work anymore. "Ah, let's slow it down a bit, my hip is stiff."

"But I want to try out my boat."

"On the way home we shall."

"You always say that, we never have time."

"Decius…"

"I'll tell father you stopped off to drink wine with your friends again and made me late for school."

"Tell him what you like, little Master, but if you don't slow down I'll take the rod to you myself and tell your father how rude you've been."

"I'll just be a minute," the boy said, and ran ahead towards the banks of the canal. Scato yelled after him, of course, but there was no chance of the old slave catching him. The canal wound through the city before feeding back down to the tributaries that led from the Nile. Whitewashed, single-story buildings rose on either side of the banks, their red-tile roofs crisp against the morning sky. Decius ran through the little gardens that lined the banks, the plants still wet from the rain, then kicked off his sandals and slid barefoot down the muddy banks to the water. He could hear Scato cursing behind him, though his thin voice was growing fainter.

Decius set his little boat in the water and let it go, watching it move steadily along in the gentle current, light as a feather, twisting and turning in the eddies before finally getting tangled in the reeds. The boy stepped into the murky water, up to his calves, almost slipped in the stinking black muck, and pushed the boat free. The reeds were high, almost up to his chin, the soft hum of insects skimming along the surface, ducks paddling lazily about. The sun appeared for a moment from behind the clouds, turning the water surface a soft hazy gold. Decius looked up – the boat was caught in a current, almost tipping over before righting itself, then it turned straight and floated well down the way, like a tiny trireme.

"Decius, what in the name of the gracious Isis are you DOING?" Scato cried from the banks. "You got mud on your good chiton! You come back up here right now!"

"But I have to get my boat," Decius said as he waded along the shore.

"Oh leave it be, you're in enough trouble as it is."

"Just a second." The ducks, startled, quacked in protest and beat their wings noisily along the water surface before rising up and over the bank. The little reed boat was just ahead, caught amongst some yellow palm fronds. Decius waded out towards it, the water up to his knees now.

"There are crocodiles in there, child! Just leave the cursed thing alone!"

"I almost have it," said the boy. He grabbed a palm frond floating nearby and lowered it towards the boat. The boat bobbed about beneath the sodden and dripping leaves but remained caught in the reeds. Decius waded in further, the water up to his waist almost.

"If I have to come down there …"

The boy carefully moved the reeds aside, prodding the boat, which finally disentangled itself from the debris and floated free. Something moved in the silent darkness of the water towards him from the debris.

"Oh!" Decius moved back with a start, his feet slipping in the black mud as he moved, his heart pounding in his chest.

"Decius, get out of there now! Decius!"

The boy tried to get away but the mud sucked at his feet, holding him back. He lost his balance and slipped, falling backwards into the debris. The slave cried out in horror. The thing rose to the surface just beside the boy, a pale orb bobbing towards him. The thing had gaping eyes, straggling dark hair across its pale face, puffy grey lips and a ragged slash across its pale throat.

Decius screamed.

Sekhet looked down at the woman's corpse, her expression grim. Aculeo stood back, closing his aching eyes against the bright morning sunlight, his stomach sour. Rumour in the Agora about a dead woman being pulled from the canal had proven all too true. So far, Aculeo and Sekhet were the only ones on the scene save for a handful of curious onlookers and some dirty-faced children hovering behind them, watching her work.

The woman's throat had been viciously slashed, almost decapitating her. Her face, breasts and thighs had been cut several times as well, the wounds raw, grey and puffy from the water. She looked to be in her early twenties, slender of body, with strands of short dark hair strung across her water-logged cheeks. Her face was streaked with white makeup, her arched eyebrows and long lashes still dark with antimony, a dark beauty mark on the corner of her upper lip. Blue lines were etched along her arms, neck and chest to mimic veins beneath the skin to suggest pellucidity, the goal of every woman these days it seemed.

"The wounds are fairly even," Sekhet said, kneeling down beside the victim. "Short, slashing cuts. From a knife I'd guess. Her body was dumped in the canal after she was murdered."

"You, get away from there!" a voice called from behind them. Aculeo turned around and saw a pair of Roman soldiers walking along the muddy bank towards them. The Junior Magistrate Capito was right behind them.

Capito frowned when he spotted Aculeo. "How is it that you seem to appear wherever a dead woman is found?"

"A peculiar hobby, I admit," Aculeo said.

Capito didn't smile. "Is this your missing hetaira then?"

"I'm not sure yet." Aculeo took the portrait from his satchel and carefully unrolled it out on the stony ground.

"What's that?"

"I found it in Neaera's flat. What do you think?" Aculeo asked, indicating the image of Neaera. Capito gave the portrait a quizzical look and shrugged.

"It's not her," Sekhet said. "The face is too long and narrow, and the eyes aren't right, her eyes are brown, not green, see?" Aculeo nodded, somewhat relieved. Although this brought him no closer to finding Neaera, at least there was still a chance of her turning up alive.

"Who is that woman?" Capito asked, indicating Sekhet.

"She's a healer from the Necropolis," Aculeo said.

"A healer? Why would we need a healer?"

"She has a unique skill in getting the dead to talk." Capito gave them both a wary look.

Sekhet delicately touched the birthmark on the dead woman's cheek, then peeled it off, revealing a rose-coloured pox scar the size of a small fingernail beneath. She ran her bony fingers through the girl's weed-strewn hair and pulled out a few long strands that had been woven in, the colour of wild honey. "She wore a German wig."

The other hetaira at Gurculio's symposium had fair hair, Aculeo recalled. Could it be her, I wonder?

Sekhet held up the woman's wrist – a thin braid of yellow jute rope was knotted about it just below her hand so tightly it dug deeply into the flesh. "There's no bruising. The blood had already stopped circulating when it was tied onto her wrist. Whoever killed her must have done it after she died."

"Why would they do that?"

"Like the river slave," Aculeo mused.

"What river slave?"

"The murdered slave in the Sarapeion had a yellow braid tied about her wrist as well."

"She did?" An expression of profound unease marred Capito's noble young face. "What are you suggesting? That the murders are connected somehow?"

"It's simply an observation."

Sekhet eased open the dead woman's mouth – the jaw was quite stiff. "Two of her front teeth were broken recently – during her attack most likely. Ah. There's something in here." She reached her fingers between the stumps of broken teeth and extracted a small linen pouch. She opened it and emptied the contents out on her palm – six small white pellets. "Seeds. Pomegranate I think."

"What does it mean?" Aculeo asked.

"I've no idea." She tried with some difficulty to move the girl's limbs. "She's still quite stiff, not too bloated yet, her colour is fine, just a bit pale from being in the water. She was murdered six to ten hours ago, I'd say."

Capito queasily considered the dead woman's wounds for a moment, then turned away and faced Aculeo instead. "I have a feeling you know something about this, don't you?"

"She's a hetaira. I saw her at a symposium last night."

"Whose symposium?"

"Gurculio's."

"The moneylender?" Capito asked.

"Yes. It seems he's moved up in the world of late. Albius Ralla was in attendance as well."

Capito cursed under his breath, considering the dead woman more carefully now. No doubt calculating the implications of this incident to his career, Aculeo thought. It wasn't some nameless Tannery porne this time but a hetaira who'd purportedly last been seen attending an event also attended by one of the most powerful men in Egypt. "You're sure of this?"

"Sure enough."

"What were you doing at Gurculio's symposium in the first place?"

"I didn't attend. I happened to be in the area last night and saw her. She's a hetaira."

"You just happened to be there," Capito said dubiously. "And that's all you know, is it?"

I could tell him about Iovinus' murder as well, Aculeo thought, but it would be a dangerous game for all concerned. Gurculio's connection to both the murders and the likes of Albius Ralla was most disturbing of all. A powerful man and his powerful friends was not someone to be trifled with based on pure conjecture. Especially if it were true. Aculeo held his tongue. "That's it."

Capito sighed. "Fine. I'll leave them to help you if you need," he said, nodding towards the soldiers. "But I expect you to come to me first if you learn anything else though. Is that clear?"

"Of course, Magistrate."

"You never were a very good liar," Capito said. He gave his orders to the soldiers then made his exit back up the muddy river bank to the street.

Sekhet knelt down next to the dead woman, placing her gnarled hand over the eyes while closing her own. "We will shed our sorrows and put away our mourning, O Isis, and by your foresight you will enclose our days with wholesome health and beneficial wealth," she said solemnly, reciting the entire prayer before finally climbing stiffly to her feet.

"You!" she snapped at the soldiers, who looked up at her in surprise – they weren't used to being spoken to in such a manner by a mere fellahin woman. "Fetch a wagon."

"A wagon? Why?" one of the soldiers demanded.

"Would you prefer to carry the body all the way to Rhakotis?"

They looked to Aculeo, who shrugged. "You heard the Magistrate, do as she says."

CHAPTER X

The litter bobbed back and forth as the occupants were carried along the road. Idaia could hear the grunts of exertion from the litter-bearers as they walked. The little girl pulled back the curtain of her window and watched their muscles strain against the weight, their dark skin gleaming in sweat. She smiled at one of them, who responded with a weary smile of his own.

They had entered a poorer part of town, she saw, the fellahin part. The red-tiled houses and public buildings had given way to simple mud-brick dwellings that were much smaller than what she was used to in Beta, with narrow criss-crossing streets that adjoined the rank-smelling canal. A group of street children came running alongside them, calling out, laughing. She waved at them, wishing she could go out and play with them, they seemed to be having so much more fun than she was.

"Idaia, please sit back," Calisto said in a hushed voice. "And close the curtain – the air is bad in this part of town. You don't want to get sick do you?" Calisto had been extremely upset ever since the little street urchin had arrived that morning with a message requesting she come to this place. Still she did her best to maintain her composure. Idaia didn't want to add to her worry if she could avoid it.

They stopped some time later. Calisto sat back, her eyes closed for a moment before at last she stepped from the litter. Idaia tried to follow but Calisto shook her head. "No. Stay here please," she said.

Idaia peeked out from behind the curtains and saw they were near the canal, a long azure ribbon that stretched through the city, sparkling beneath the morning sun. And there was the man who'd come to visit Calisto the other day, the handsome one with the nice smile. Aculeo, she recalled. He looked very solemn now as he stepped forward to meet Calisto, taking her by the arm, leading her towards a mud-brick structure.

Idaia slipped out of the litter and headed towards the little building. She peeked around the doorway, watching. Aculeo stood next to Calisto. Standing beside them at a long table was an old fellahin woman who was touching something on the table covered in a plain canvas cloth – what is it? The woman pulled back the cloth. Idaia wasn't sure what to think at first. It looked like a woman's naked body, like a statue, or a big wooden doll, save that her pale flesh was marred with ghastly wounds. Oh, but she's real, the child realized … and she's dead. Idaia felt chilled all of a sudden, despite the morning heat.

Calisto's face turned pale. "No!" she cried in anguish, falling to her knees on the earthen floor.

Idaia took a closer look at the dead woman's face and gasped, unable to process what she was seeing. It looks like … Myrrhine. But no. It can't be her.

It can't!

Aculeo helped Calisto to her feet. "What … what happened?" she managed to ask.

"She was murdered," he said. "Her body was retrieved from a canal in Gamma this morning."

"Oh … oh no. I don't understand, I was with her just last night," she whispered, as if somehow that simple fact should have made the difference.

"Myrrhine was with you at Gurculio's symposium?" Aculeo asked, as if he didn't already know the answer.

"Yes," Calisto said softly, her face ashen, and wrapped herself tightly in her himation, hugging herself, though the crowded little shed was quite warm and stuffy. "She left early though, she said she had another event to attend."

"What event?" Aculeo asked.

"She didn't say."

"Did she leave with anyone?"

"No … I don't know. She didn't return home last night, but I … I …" Calisto gazed down at the dead girl, then sobbed and turned away. Aculeo looked at her awkwardly, unsure what to say in the face of her grief. She regained her composure and turned to Aculeo. "Could there be a connection with Iovinus' murder?"

"I've no idea. It's as tangled as a ball of knots," Aculeo said, rubbing his eyes, his exhaustion and hangover rebounding on him at last.

"If you like, I can see to your loved one's final journey," Sekhet offered gently.

"Oh please, yes," Calisto said, her eyes glistening with emotion. "I want you to do anything you can to bring her comfort."

"I shall treat her with the utmost reverence," Sekhet said with a small bow.

Calisto took out her purse and counted out five gold coins, her fingers trembling. "This should cover things, I pray."

"Exactly enough," the healer said, accepting the coins.

Calisto turned to Aculeo, put a hand on his arm. "Walk me to the litter please."

They left the little building, walking in silence for a moment. She took a deep breath. He sensed she was trying to recover her poise, not wanting to appear upset in front of Idaia, who had climbed back into the litter and now watched their approach from behind the partially raised curtain. She was clearly shaken, pale and trembling.

"Myrrhine had words with her patron last night," she said at last.

"Who is her patron?"

"Albius Ralla. I overheard them arguing about something at the symposium. I'm not sure what it was about."

"Do you think it's possible …?" Aculeo paused, not daring to speak the words.

"No, no, I realize it makes no sense," Calisto said and glanced towards the litter, shaking her head. "Please, if you learn anything, anything at all about what happened to Myrrhine, you'll come and tell me," she said with soft urgency. "I have to know."

"Yes, of course."

"Thank you. For all you've done." Calisto kissed him on the cheek, her perfume rich and dense, her lips warm and soft against his skin, then climbed into the litter. Idaia lifted a corner of the curtain and smiled tentatively at Aculeo.

Sekhet sniffed as the Nubians hoisted the litter up and carried it away. "The slave carrying the front left corner of her litter has a bad left hip. He looks far too old for this sort of work if you ask me, but at least his mistress will save getting a blister on her pretty feet."

"Perhaps she should carry him instead?" Aculeo asked.

"It might be a pleasant change." She gave Aculeo a critical look. "Are you drinking your cucumber juice?"

"Of course," he said, his head throbbing.

"Really? Because you look like shit. I say that as a healer, you understand, not as a lowly old fellahin woman to one of her omnipotent Roman overlords."

A slave escorted Aculeo into the Blue Bird's atrium. Most of the little tables scattered about the courtyard were occupied by men and pretty young women. Sunlight streamed in from the compluvium, scattering in the rippling water of the rectangular pool beneath it. A dark skinned beauty approached him with a lovely smile and a cup of wine.

"Welcome, my name's Sabina," the girl cooed, snaking her arm around his and pressed her body against him.

"I'm looking for Tyche," Aculeo said, and politely disengaged from the girl, who shrugged and returned to one of the rooms off the atrium. A moment later, Tyche emerged, a wary smile fixed on her face. Her eyes brightened when she saw Aculeo. "Can we go someplace private?" he asked.

She signalled a slave, who approached the table. "Two sesterces for fifteen minutes," the slave announced. Aculeo handed him the coins. "Third room."

Tyche took Aculeo's hand in hers and led him down the dark hallway to a room. There was a small, crude painting of a threesome on the wall outside the doorway. Tyche opened the wooden door and they stepped into the tiny cubiculum, hardly big enough to hold the narrow pallet.

She turned around and pressed his hand to her lips. "I'm grateful to see you again."

"And I you," he said. "How've you been?"

"Well enough," Tyche said, though her eyes were far too burdened for one so young. "Please, sit."

"I only came to talk with you."

"Just do as I ask," she whispered anxiously.

Aculeo sat on the pallet and Tyche knelt on the floor before him. She unstrapped his sandals and pulled a basin of water from beneath the bed and started to wash his feet.

"Don't," he whispered, taking the sponge from her hands. "Listen to me a minute. Iovinus was murdered."

"What?"

"I went to Neaera's flat as you told me. There was no sign of her there. She hasn't been seen in days. She left all her possessions behind though. I fear something may have happened to her as well."

"Oh!" Tyche cried, her face crumpling in grief as she stifled a sob.

The door rattled in the frame and opened a crack. Tyche climbed onto the pallet next to Aculeo, placing a hand on his thigh as she kissed him hard on the mouth. The door closed again as the watcher moved on.

"They watch everything here," she whispered, clinging to him, her tears wetting his shoulder.

"I'm sorry," he said. "I wish I had better news."

"It's as I feared, I only hoped I was wrong."

"A woman was murdered last night. A hetaira named Myrrhine."

"Who?" Tyche asked.

"You didn't know her?" Aculeo asked.

"No. What happened?"

"She attended a symposium last night. Her body was dumped in a canal in Gamma. She'd been stabbed to death."

Tyche bowed her head, her shoulders trembling. I shouldn't have come here, he thought, she can't help me, I'm only adding to her worries. He decided to change tack. "Did Neaera ever mention Albius Ralla or Marcellus Gurculio?"

"Of course. Ralla used to own her," she whispered hoarsely.

"Oh?" Aculeo asked in surprise. "But I thought Iovinus …?"

"Yes, but first it was Ralla. He was … a very cruel man," she said. "Neaera told me how he liked to bind and beat her before forcing himself on her. She wanted a way out, any way she could, even death. He finally tired of her and sold her back to Panthea perhaps six months ago. That's when she met Iovinus. She was so happy, she'd finally found a way out. She was wrong, there is no way," Tyche wept, burying her face into his shoulder, clinging to him as though she were drowning.

There was a rap on the doorframe. "Two minutes," the slave called.

"Did you know a hetaira named Petras?" Aculeo whispered.

"Neaera's cousin?" Tyche asked. "I've met her, yes, but I haven't seen her in months."

"Any idea where she went?"

"No. We all prayed she'd simply run away."

Aculeo strapped his sandals back on as Tyche huddled in the corner of the bed, hugging her knees to her chest. She tried to smile but faltered, her haunted eyes filled with tears and she looked away. He put his hand on Tyche's, so small, so fragile, and squeezed it tight, promising himself at that moment that someday he would take her from this wretched place, that he would find a way to change her fate. He didn't dare speak the words aloud though – she'd had enough broken promises already in her young life.

"Time," called the slave.

CHAPTER XI

THE 23RD DAY OF APRILIS

Aculeo awoke drenched with sweat, his heart pounding in his chest, his head spinning. He rolled onto his back and stared at the ceiling, watching shadows flit across its cracked surface. He thought of Iovinus, the sound the rope made as his corpse had swung back and forth in the backroom of that foul little tavern. Someone murdered him, stole his tablets, tried to make it look like suicide. His porne, Neaera, fell off the face of the earth. Myrrhine's body pulled from the canal after an evening at Gurculio's symposium. And a random river slave is murdered in the Sarapeion. What was the sense of it all?

He climbed out of bed and pulled on a tunic, trying not to wake Xanthias as he slipped out the door. He walked along the streets, the torches that lined the lime-paved streets making them appear as bright as daytime. A pair of soldiers from the Night Guard watched him curiously as he passed but didn't bother challenging him. Clots of drunken men stumbled out of the many taverns that lined the streets, arms thrown about one another's shoulders, singing and laughing in joyous camaraderie.

He made his way to the Little Eagle in Gamma. It was still busy enough, the crowd consisting of a rough-looking group of sailors and some itinerant merchants, all of them deep in their cups. Aculeo took a torch from the wall and headed upstairs to Gellius' and Trogus' room. He knocked on the door. The door creaked open, the room was in darkness.

"Gellius? Trogus?" he called quietly as he stepped inside, his torch casting a flickering glow. The room was empty, all their meagre possessions gone, though the stench of illness and unwashed bodies lingered. Perhaps they'd found the money to leave the city after all. Or had something happened to them?

He headed back downstairs and spotted Bitucus sitting at a corner table, looking much like his old self, surprisingly enough – clean-shaven, hair trimmed, and wearing a fine new tunic, though his pale eyes were glassy from drink. Aculeo approached the table.

Bitucus blinked at him in surprise. "Aculeo."

"I thought you'd all left. Where are Trogus and Gellius?"

"Is that who I think it is?" a cheerful voice boomed from behind him. He glanced over his shoulder – Theopompus, an Icarian merchant, met him with a huge grin, clapped him on the back and dropped down in the chair across from Bitucus.

"Theopompus, it's been awhile," Aculeo said.

"Indeed it has, old friend. Why don't you join us?" Theopompus said and called to the thrattia for another cup and some more wine. Bitucus looked away, holding his tongue. Aculeo warily sat down – he had a bad feeling all of a sudden.

Theopompus, with his flashy clothing, jewelled rings on every stubby finger and chunky gold and silver bracelets covering both forearms, had always seemed friendly enough, like any good merchant, but Aculeo had always thought him a bit of a snake. "I'd heard you'd gone back to Rome," the Icarian said with an easy smile, though his hooded eyes, rimmed black with kohl, watched everything.

"My family did. I'm staying here for now."

"For now, that's the thing!" the man barked as he poured Aculeo a generous cup. "There's not much left of this fruit for most of us but the husk, is there?"

"You, uh, haven't seen Gellius about, have you Aculeo?" Bitucus asked.

The two men seemed too watchful, too interested in what he might say. What game are they playing? And on whose behalf? "I haven't a clue. I know they were planning to leave the city. As you said, there's little left here but husk."

"Come on Aculeo," Bitucus said, feigning jocularity, and doing a poor job of it. Aculeo glowered at the man, who faltered and looked away. The Icarian laughed again, though his darkened eyes hardened, unblinking.

"Why are you looking for him?" Aculeo asked.

"We've a business opportunity for him," Theopompus said.

"Oh? What sort?"

The merchant didn't bother to reply as he counted out ten silver sesterces and slid them across the table, the coins gleaming in the lamplight. "Just let us know if you run into him, will you?"

Aculeo's general unease was replaced with a sense of dread, though he tried not to show it. The Icarian stood to leave. Bitucus stood as well but Aculeo stopped him. "Before you go, a moment in private please. I trust you don't mind, Theopompus."

The Icarian nodded. "I'll wait outside then. Good to see you again, Aculeo."

They watched him leave. Bitucus gave a nervous smile. "Aculeo, I …"

Aculeo grabbed the man by the front of his tunic, clutching at the soft linen, exquisitely embroidered with gold and purple thread. "What's going on here, Bitucus?"

"Wha … what d'you mean?" the man stammered, unable to look him in the eye.

"What do you want with Gellius?"

Bitucus pulled away, absently straightening out the front of his tunic. "This doesn't involve you, Aculeo."

"You found Iovinus' tablets, didn't you!"

"It's nothing like that!"

"And why just Gellius? Where's Trogus?"

"Come on, Aculeo, you have to understand …"

Aculeo glanced down at the coins glinting on the tabletop. Everything came horribly clear. "Your loyalty to your friends comes cheap. You turned him in to Gurculio, didn't you?"

"Should I betray my family instead?" Bitucus cried.

"The first defence of a traitor."

"At least I'm not a fool who refuses to see the tide's turned until it's too damned late!"

Aculeo swept the coins off the table. They rang and rolled across the floor and a few other patrons scrambled to retrieve them. Bitucus tried to escape and Aculeo shoved him to the floor.

He looked up at Aculeo in surprise and hurt. "What's gotten into you?"

"You'd better get out of here before I cut your damned throat."

"You were always a reasonable man."

"Fuck your reason, Bitucus! I'm a Roman, damn you, as I thought you were. What about virtue?"

86

"Where's virtue gotten either of us, you pompous prick?" Bitucus demanded as he struggled to his feet. Aculeo started towards him. The other man's face showed a flash of fear and he scuttled quickly towards the door. "Come find me when you come to your senses!"

Aculeo waited a minute, watching Bitucus and the Icarian through the window, engaged in a heated discussion. The Icarian threw up his hands and walked away. Bitucus followed reluctantly, shoulders slumped. Aculeo stepped outside, following the two men from a safe distance along the darkened streets. Where are they going? They led him deep into Beta along the winding, lovely streets. They came at last to Gurculio's villa, still lit up in the depth of night, and the guards let them inside.

So I was right, they're working on the moneylender's behalf, collecting on his loans. They probably have Trogus in there right now. He heard the sickening sound of Gurculio's braying laughter and resisted the urge to storm the gates and face the man. What would I say exactly? Bitucus may be a fool and a traitor, but he's not wrong – the tides have changed. The question is, can they change back?

The guards looked towards where he stood. Aculeo stepped back into the shadows, helpless, exposed and furious at himself for being that way.

Aculeo turned south onto the broad Street of the Soma, the Great Crossroads, where the golden-domed Tomb of Alexander shimmered in the noonday sun, well behind him now, and headed up towards Olympia. The crowds had begun to thin at last as he moved away from the marketplace, leaving the tangled noises and smells of the streets behind. Here the air smelled of hyacinth and jasmine and he could hear birds singing in the acacia trees.

His head was throbbing. He'd slept late after staying up drinking almost until the break of dawn, rolling his shrinking options around and around in his head like loaded dice. Meeting with Calisto again and asking her what she knew of Gurculio's involvement with Iovinus was a longshot at best. Then again, it did give him a reason to see her again.

As he neared the villa he spotted the little girl playing just inside the gates, feeding bits of bread to a flock of geese. Aculeo whistled to her. The girl looked up in surprise, then beamed at him. "Hello."

"Hi," Aculeo said with a smile. "Is your mistress at home?"

"Yes," she said. The towering Nubian guarding the gate met Aculeo with a stolid glare. "It's alright. Go fetch the mistress." The man bowed and opened the gate for Aculeo, then disappeared into the house.

"Come," she said, and skipped just ahead of him as they made their way along the creamy marble hallway towards the atrium. There were half a dozen fine marble statues and some splendid tapestries on the walls, softening the sounds of their footfalls. They could hear the clatter of slaves working and chatting in distant sections of the villa. Aculeo's heart was filled with a sudden sense of nostalgia at the scene – he half expected to see Atellus running down the fauces to greet him.

"Have you found the man who killed Myrrhine yet?" the little girl asked, breaking the spell.

"No, not yet. Did you know her well?"

"Oh yes, of course, she was very nice, so pretty and such a lovely voice. I'll miss her terribly." Idaia was quiet for a moment. "Do you have children?"

"Yes. A son."

"How old is he?"

"Three. He lives in Rome with his mother though."

"Oh." The girl stopped skipping then and fell into step with him. "Why?"

"His mother didn't want to live here anymore, so she returned to Rome and took my son with her."

"Do you miss them?"

"Yes I do. Very much."

"I'm sorry." She slipped her little hand into Aculeo's, surprising him. He'd forgotten the simple joy of holding a child's hand as he walked. "Are you Roman?"

"Yes."

"Have you ever met Caesar?"

"No I haven't."

"I met the Prefect once and he's a friend of Caesar's," the girl chattered. "He was at a party we went to. I go to lots of parties, Calisto lets me come sometimes. Do you like parties?"

"I used to, but not anymore," Aculeo said.

"I do. All the food and music and singing … Do you like Calisto?"

"She seems very nice."

"A lot of men like Calisto."

"I would imagine so."

"She goes to parties all the time. She's not only beautiful but terribly talented and clever as well."

A peacock gave a haunting trill, bobbing its head back and forth as it hurried along the marble tiles just ahead of them, as though to warn its mistress. The girl slipped her hand from his and chased it down the hall. Calisto was standing in the midst of the sun-filled atrium. The way the sun lit her face, Aculeo saw how truly beautiful her eyes were, a deep honeyed amber, with an exotic, Persian slant to them.

She came towards him, took his hands in hers and kissed his cheek, the scent of her perfume multi-layered, evocative. "Aculeo! What a lovely surprise."

"Your pretty little slave let me in," he said.

"Idaia's not a slave," Calisto said, taking his arm and escorting him deeper into the atrium, her hand soft and cool against his skin. "I freed her the same day I purchased her. She comes from Phrygia, which is my homeland as well."

"She's quite fortunate then, to have found such a kind benefactress."

"I'm fortunate as well – she provides me a great deal of pleasure," Calisto said, gazing after the girl as she disappeared behind the garden wall at the rear of the atrium.

Two men were sitting and talking animatedly with one another beneath a white cloth awning, one of them spare and balding, his hair and beard streaked with silver, the other heavy-set with a thatch of stony grey hair atop his head and a gloomy expression on his florid face.

The balding one glanced up at Aculeo and smiled. "Ah, who's this?" he asked, his dark eyes piqued with curiosity.

"This is the gentleman I was telling you about," Calisto said. "Decimus Tarquitius Aculeo, these are my dear friends Zeanthes of Araethyrea and Epiphaneus of Cyrene."

"A great pleasure to meet you, sir," Zeanthes said warmly Epiphaneus mumbled incomprehensibly into his cup. Judging by the bleariness of his eyes, he'd already drained it several times that day.

"The pleasure's mine," Aculeo replied.

"Zeanthes and Epiphaneus are sophists at the Museion," Calisto said.

"What field of study?"

"I follow the teachings of Pyrrho of Elis the Skeptic," Zeanthes said.

"The braggart and the fool!" Epiphaneus blurted, slapping the flat of his hand down on the table, clattering the cups and dishes. "It's been over a century since Pyrrho assigned what passed for knowledge to paper yet his thoughts are more muddled now than ever."

"Must we do this now?" Zeanthes sighed.

The other sophist looked disconsolately at his empty cup. "Are we out of wine?" A slave scurried over to remedy the matter.

"Aculeo is trying to learn who murdered Myrrhine and what might have happened to dear Neaera," Calisto said.

"Ah yes, Calisto told us what happened," Zeanthes said with a pained expression. "Most distressing."

"You knew them?" Aculeo said.

"I never met Neaera but I knew Myrrhine, of course. To think that she could have been murdered. A lovely girl."

"Lovely," Epiphaneus mumbled, almost to himself, fixing his piggish eyes on Aculeo for a moment before returning his attention to his cup.

Zeanthes cleared his throat and smiled politely. "So, good sir, how is it that you're involved in such a dreadful business?"

"I was an associate of Neaera's patron Iovinus."

"Was?"

"He was murdered earlier this week."

"Oh my!" Zeanthes said, his face drawn suddenly. "But ... what happened?"

Aculeo explained as delicately as he could, leaving out the matter of Iovinus' embezzlement and the disappearance of the tablets he'd been carrying. The sophist listened in rapt attention to every word. "How utterly dreadful!" the sophist said at last.

"I've been looking into Neaera's disappearance, hoping she could shed some insight. I've had little luck though."

"He fears Myrrhine's murder may be connected," Calisto said.

"Well I wish you good fortune and a swift resolution to your endeavour," Zeanthes said solemnly, then raised a cup.

"Hear, hear!" Epiphaneus slurred, raising his cup to drink.

"I only hope it's not too late for dear Neaera."

"Perhaps we could talk of more pleasant things for a while," Calisto said with forced cheerfulness.

"Of course, my dear," Zeanthes said. "You know, man's true nature is to pursue pleasure after all, not merely to do his work, whatever it might be. He takes joy in good wine perhaps, or the love of a beautiful woman. What of Tarquitius Aculeo? How does he find his pleasure?"

"I've given little thought to pleasure lately. It's all I can do to simply try and live my life, such that it is."

"Pah!" Epiphaneus said sourly. "You sound like a damned Epicurist, pursuing pleasure through the avoidance of pain."

"Oh? And what pain do you imagine I seek to avoid?"

"Why, the pain we all face, of course," Epiphaneus said hoarsely, his bloodshot eyes suddenly filled with a profound sadness as they gazed into some indeterminate place far removed from the courtyard. "The pain of the void." Tears slipped down his sagging cheeks and he began to cry.

"I think you've had enough for now," Zeanthes said, signalling one of the slaves. "Perhaps Kushu can find you a couch where you can sleep it off."

The other sophist was still sobbing as the slave helped him to his unsteady feet and led him into one of the adjoining rooms.

"You'll have to forgive Epiphaneus, he spoke without thought," Zeanthes said. "We should have watered down his wine a bit more."

"Of course."

"Come," Calisto said with a smile. "I'm sure you're both famished."

Servants brought forth platters of food, far too much for the three of them to eat on their own. There were exotic fruits, cheeses, cold meats and bread, and a large silver platter overflowing with succulent, milky-pink shrimp and a delicious Tameotic wine as fine as any Aculeo had ever tasted – certainly far better fare than he'd had in months. He had to consciously keep from making an ass of himself and devouring everything in sight like some starving dog.

Calisto summoned Idaia partway through the meal and asked her to perform a dance while Calisto herself played the aulos, the same haunting melody he'd heard that first day they'd met. Aculeo sat back and watched her play, her fingertips dancing along the twin ivory flutes, her dark hair glistening in the soft rays of the afternoon sun as Idaia danced and twirled in the courtyard. There was something captivating in Calisto's manner, her elegance, her grace ...

It was over too soon. Zeanthes led the applause, which Aculeo quickly joined. Idaia beamed, out of breath, her face flushed.

"Such beauty and talent combined, truly a wonder," Zeanthes said, sipping his wine, his eyes twinkling as he regarded Aculeo.

"A pleasure to behold," Aculeo agreed.

"You're both exceptionally kind," Calisto said graciously.

"Calisto, I wonder if we might talk in private for a moment?"

"Certainly. I trust you'll be alright here for a moment, Zeanthes. Idaia will be happy to entertain you."

"Yes, yes, of course my dear," the sophist said with a smile.

Calisto led Aculeo along a path of crushed red stone and box hedge that wound from the courtyard towards a chest-high wall housing a lovely inner garden, filled with lush tropical plants, great colourful and fragrant flowers and pretty little birds that flitted about the grounds through the trees, chirping their intricate melodies.

"Zeanthes is an interesting man," Aculeo said.

"And a brilliant scholar," she said. "I'm pleased you got a chance to meet one another."

"You mentioned that Myrrhine lived here with you," Aculeo said.

"Yes," Calisto said. "Why?"

"Can you show me her room? I'm hoping I can find some clue of what happened to her among her belongings."

"Of course. Come, I'll take you there now."

She led him past a sparkling fountain in the centre of the garden with a beautiful statue of a woman in a chariot being drawn by a pair of lions. At the edge of the garden stood a statue of a handsome youth sitting on a tree trunk, two nubs of horns sprouting from his forehead, a wreath of grape and ivy wrapped in his thick stone curls, a flute in his hand. Two doors faced the garden. Calisto opened one of the doors to reveal a large, elegant sitting chamber. Half of it was filled with sunlight that streamed in from a rectangular window cut near the ceiling, while the other half remained in shadows. An exquisitely carved wooden chair and table with ivory legs stood against the far wall just beneath a small silver mirror. On the table was an empty copper bowl, a water jug, an assortment of cosmetics – white lead, malachite, antimony – ivory application sticks and several small clay jars. Aculeo lifted the lid from one of the jars and smelled it.

"They're unguents," Calisto said. "Frankincense, myrrh and the like."

On the floor next to the table was an ivory board game shaped like a coiled snake. The pieces looked expensive, precious wood inlaid with mother of pearl. "What is this?" he asked.

"It's called menet," she said. "A fellahin game. The players move their pieces around the board until one of them reaches the end – the hole in the snake's mouth. The secret of life, they say. Myrrhine's bedroom is in here."

In the adjoining room was a wooden bed with bedclothes neatly folded over the mattress. Next to the bed sat a wooden chest. Aculeo opened it. A blue silk chiton. A white linen tunic. A breastband. Two girdles. Some ivory combs. He took out the chiton, ran the cool, soft silk between his fingers, held it to his nose and smelled it. There was a faint perfume – hyacinth, he thought. Calisto gave him a curious look.

A small ceramic jar sat at the bottom of the chest. Aculeo picked it up and lifted the black enamelled lid, which was engraved with a silver profile of a naked nymph walking alongside a panther. A few dried flowers with broad, faded red petals and pale yellow centres lay within. Aculeo smelled one of the flowers – it had the faint, dusky scent of incense. He passed the jar to her. Calisto sat on the bed and opened it up, looking with puzzlement at the fragrant flower petals within. She smelled them, then handed the jar back to him. "What are they?"

"Persian opium. Or the flowers anyway."

"But why would she have them?"

Aculeo smiled ruefully. "I was hoping you could tell me."

"I've no idea."

"Did she have any kind of connection to the moneylender, Gurculio?"

"That horrid moneylender? No. Why?"

"I think it likely he was involved in Iovinus' murder. He also seems to have a connection to Myrrhine's former patron, Albius Ralla."

"Ralla?"

"You told me they'd argued at the symposium that night. Someone else mentioned he treated Neaera cruelly when he was her patron. Apparently he took pleasure in beating and tying her up before taking her."

Calisto's lips were pale, pressed tightly together, her fists clenched in her lap She was visibly upset at the prospect, but held her pretty tongue.

"Are you alright?" he asked.

She gave a small, tentative nod. "It's just … everything seems so mad lately. Do you think Neaera could still be alive?"

"I've stopped looking for her," Aculeo said.

Calisto gazed up at him from the bed, her eyes searching his, the crisp sound of a fountain burbling from the garden outside the room. He could sense the warmth of her body so close to him, could smell the rich, dense perfume of her skin. A thin, white scar ran from her ear down along her jaw line, flicking up near the tip of her chin, barely visible against her smooth olive skin, like a hairline crack on a sculpture's face. He found himself wondering what it would be like to push her back on the bed, to kiss those lips, that neck …

She cocked her head, regarding him. "What is it?"

"Nothing. Nothing at all."

Calisto gave a small, perfect smile. "You hold onto your thoughts without speech while Epiphaneus speaks without thought. I'm not sure which is preferable," she said, then stood up, smoothing the folds of her chiton. "We should get back. Zeanthes will be wondering what's taking us so long."

She took his arm and they walked back along the crushed gravel path towards the atrium. They could hear the sound of Idaia's laughter, followed by Zeanthes' feeble cry of protest. They found them sitting beneath the awning, while Epiphaneus sprawled in a chair next to them, eyes tightly closed, pinching the bridge of his fleshy nose between his thumb and forefinger. Zeanthes and the girl were in the midst of an intense game of Hounds and Jackals, which, judging by the dwindling array of pegs on the board in front of him, the illustrious sophist appeared to be getting routed.

"This young lady seems suspiciously brilliant at this game," Zeanthes said in mock anguish.

"You're not very good at it," Idaia proclaimed.

"So gracious of you to inform the world, gentle child," he said. He looked at Calisto with sudden concern. "Are you ill, my dear?"

"I'm just very tired all of a sudden."

"Do you need anything?"

"No, thank you. I just need some rest," Calisto said.

"Then my new friend Aculeo and I should gather up Epiphaneus and take our leave."

"Of course," Aculeo said.

"Please, feel free to stay," Calisto said.

"A good guest knows the perfect time to leave." Zeanthes nudged Epiphaneus.

"What d'you want, damn you!?" the other sophist whispered hoarsely, opening his eyes the smallest of cracks.

"Time to go." Epiphaneus gave a dramatic groan, then slowly climbed to his feet, leaning on the chair to keep himself steady. Zeanthes sighed. "Perhaps we'd best send you back by litter."

"Thank you so much for coming," Calisto said. "I apologize for being such a poor hostess."

"Not at all," Aculeo said.

She embraced Zeanthes, then Epiphaneus, and finally Aculeo. "Tell me if you learn anything," she whispered in his ear, then she was gone, Idaia close on her heels in a swirl of coloured silks.

Zeanthes took Aculeo's arm as they headed towards the Agora, walking amidst the throng of pedestrians along the narrow, dusty streets, tumbled blocks of whitewashed, red-tiled buildings rising on either side of them. The streets were a cacophony of sound, a mad procession of merchants bellowing out their offerings to passersby, drovers herding their bleating sheep and goats to market, street performers singing and tumbling through open squares, actors standing on corners, sonorously reciting fragments of recent plays and poetry.

"Where do you hail from, Aculeo?" Zeanthes asked.

"Rome, originally," Aculeo said. "Though I've lived in Alexandria since I was a boy."

"Really? For what reason may I ask?"

"My father was posted here to work in the Office of the Annona, contracting agents to secure grain for Rome. I carried on that work after his death."

Marble columns and tall, fragrant bay trees lined the public walk that circuited the quadrangle of the Museion. In the centre was an enormous and ancient plane tree, its thick, trunk-like branches sweeping gracefully down and back along the ground like a great living fountain. It had been imported from the copse in Plato's Academy itself in Athens centuries prior at an astounding price, and not altogether legitimately, it was said. The promenade ended in a lush garden with black and white veined marble benches and small shrines to the Twelve Gods scattered amongst the groves.

"The gardens here are said to contain flowers, plants and trees from every part of the world," Zeanthes said. "A library of life one might say. See there? Orange trees from Phoenecia, fig trees from Asia Minor, olives from Attica, those great red flowers are from the forests beyond Upper Egypt. The animals and birds as well," he said, pointing towards the calm man-made ponds amongst the gardens, where pink flamingos waded on their yellow stick-like legs and monkeys rattled about and shrieked in their cages. In the distance he saw a camel-leopard, a strange, long-necked creature, nibbling leaves from a towering tree.

"There used to be some great cats here as well, I understand, but they didn't do as well as the other beasts unfortunately. Inside, of course, there are even more wonders. The bones of the Titans that fought Zeus for Olympus. A mermaid. A cow with two heads, a pig born without any head at all, even a young girl with two faces, like the God Janus himself. All of these things give us a chance to enhance our understanding of life, its mechanism, the forces that guide it."

They passed a group of young sophists sitting in the shade of the plane tree, listening to an older man speak about the nature of virtue. Zeanthes smiled. "It's such a great gift and honour to be part of this vast pool of knowledge and diversity of thought with the world's greatest works and most learned men at your disposal. I feel that we are on the cusp of reaching another plane of reality, a breakthrough in human understanding."

The man was pleasant enough but his voice droned on and on and Aculeo's hangover afforded him little patience. "I should probably go now. My apologies, but I've a number of things I need to attend to."

"Forgive me, I get carried away. I have so enjoyed talking with you, Aculeo. I hope we have occasion to talk again."

"I look forward to it. A pleasure to have met you."

The sophist put his hand on Aculeo's arm, holding him back for a moment. "If I might say, these murders must be very distressing for you. It's sometimes challenging to understand the will of the gods."

"What are you talking about?"

"The gods affect our every move. They occupy every common and private space in our lives. As in Plato's cave, we mortals can only grasp at the shadows of reality."

"Whatever gods might have willed such things to happen are of no consequence to me," Aculeo said stiffly.

"You challenge the Fates themselves when you speak that way," Zeanthes replied. Other sophists were watching them now, drawn to the harsh tone of the discussion. "I imagine you must blame yourself for the recent events."

"Why should I blame myself?"

"You shouldn't, of course, yet we can't always choose the things we feel. Your friend Iovinus was murdered, and you assigned yourself the task of finding his murderer."

"With all due respect, sir, you've no idea what you're talking about."

"Come, come. The lovely Neaera is still missing while Myrrhine lies dead, her young life cut short," Zeanthes said. "If you truly think the will of the gods has so little bearing, then who else could you blame for this turn of events but yourself? You weren't forced to do this task, you chose it. Therefore you must also bear the blame for the destination, knowing now that if you had succeeded, you could even have helped Myrrhine escape a dreadful fate. Whoever has murdered these people may not be finished. Yet you are no closer to stopping them, are you?"

Aculeo stared at the other man. He felt like he'd just been kicked in the stomach. "I ... I don't ..." he said, his voice rough and weak amidst the sweet songs of the birds in the gardens that surrounded them.

The sophist put a hand on the other man's arm, his eyes filled with a soft inner peace. "The will of the gods is real, dear Aculeo, as real as you and I standing here right now, and it cannot be ignored however much you try."

CHAPTER XII

THE 24TH DAY OF APRILIS

Aculeo approached the entrance to the Magistrates' offices in the outskirts of the Palace Quarter. Statues of Isis and Apollo stood overlooking the square of the Court of Justice, their impassive faces dappled with light and shadow from the morning sunlight falling through the leaves of the acacias and sweet sycamore. A slave had appeared at Aculeo's door at the crack of dawn bearing a message from Capito summoning him to his offices. And while Aculeo half considered sending a reply to the Magistrate as to where he could stick his summons he decided to accompany the slave instead.

He was escorted into the inner chambers of the Magistrate's luxurious chambers where he saw Capito already hard at work with his scribe, dictating something about land transfers and owed tariffs while the slave scratched the words out on a tablet. The Magistrate spotted Aculeo out of the corner of his eye. "Aculeo," he said. "Please have a seat."

"I'd rather you just got to the point," Aculeo said irritably. "What is it you want, Capito?"

"I thought you'd be interested in helping me question a certain Athenian."

"Not particularly, I've ..." Aculeo paused a moment. "What Athenian?"

"Cleon of Athens," Capito said with a smile. "You recall the name, I trust. The purported witness to the slave's murder at the Sarapeion."

Aculeo considered him for a moment. The river slave – he'd almost forgotten about her. "I'd be pleased to join you."

"I thought you might be," Capito said, dismissing the scribe with a wave of his hand. "What of your murdered hetaira? Any news?"

"Not really," Aculeo said.

"Well, let's worry about that later, shall we? Come on. The day's half over already."

The crisp, even lines of the Harbor of Eleusis wrapped around a desolate stretch of beach along the eastern edge of the Egyptian Sea before tapering off into a rocky shore and a golden-brown, grassy ridge that extended far into the distance. In high season, Eleusis was renowned as an exclusive retreat for wealthy citizens and tourists who enjoyed its warm shallow waters, health spas, countless kapeleions, readily available male and female companions, and the infamously debauched festivities that took place along its sandy shores.

The Sanatorium of Asclepius By the Sea itself had a somewhat less refined appearance than its name implied, for it was little more than a collection of rundown waterfront shacks built along a bleak stretch of the shore. Yet it was to this desolate spot that Cleon of Athens, the only witness to the river slave's murder, had decamped, according to the information provided by the remorseful acolyte Leto. The supplicant had returned to the Sarapeion again the prior evening, still seeking to be healed, and Leto, true to his word, had sent word to the office of the Magistrate Capito.

The sanatorium's outer wall had a sun-bleached fresco of Poseidon and Hapi, father of all Egyptian gods, surrounded by faded seahorses, octopi, silvery fish and garish seashells. A damp breeze gusted off the sea, skittering sand and debris across the mosaic floor, patterned in pale blue tiles like curling waves. A slave busied himself sweeping the floor with such resigned demeanour it seemed he might have occupied himself with little else all day. He said not a word when Capito asked for Cleon, but silently led the two Romans through a garden gone to seed, past algaic fishponds and trickling waterfalls to one of the little bone-white mud-brick cottages. The waves crashed ceaselessly against the craggy grey rocks that lined the beachfront. A flock of dirty white seabirds wheeled overhead, their wingtips catching the brisk, briny-smelling wind as they glided further down the shore.

They came around a waist-high garden wall, drooping with ragged, sun-scorched rhododendrons, and there on a little patio balcony overlooking the sea sat a grossly overweight young man, busily shovelling food into his fleshy face. Before him was a banquet of eggs, winecake, bread, roast chicken, fruits and cheeses. Aculeo guessed that what the sanctuary lacked in guests, this single occupant made up for in sheer quantity of food devoured.

"Are you Cleon?" Capito asked.

"Ah, at last," Cleon groaned, dropping his half-eaten chicken leg on his plate with a damp thud. "I had another dreadful sleep last night. For all the money I'm paying to stay at this fleapit I would think at least I'd get some decent rest."

"You're feeling better I hope?" Aculeo asked. "Recovering from your injuries?"

"Oh I suppose, still a little tender of course, but still, praise Sarapis," Cleon said, quaffing a long swallow of wine.

"I've had more than my fill of Sarapis, thanks," Aculeo said, taking a seat at the table and, to Cleon's astonishment, helping himself to some wine.

"I understand you were at the Sarapeion a week ago where you witnessed a murder," Capito said, taking the seat next to Aculeo.

Cleon almost choked on his food. "I'm sorry, who, ah, who did you say were again?" he asked, still gasping.

"Magistrate Marcus Aquillius Capito. And my associate Tarquitius Aculeo."

"Oh?" Cleon said warily, wiping his mouth with the back of his greasy hand. "A Magistrate you say?"

"Indeed. I deal with any capital crimes committed in Alexandria."

"Capital crimes?" Cleon said, sweat trickling down his fleshy, troubled face. "But what do you want of me?"

"We just need to ask you a few answers and we'll be on our way," Aculeo said.

"Well, I, uh, I'd be happy to help you normally, of course," the florid young man stammered, "but in fact I'm rather busy right now. Perhaps another day, next week even?"

"It will only take a few minutes," said Capito. "Tell us about the slave's murder."

"I'm still trying to forget it," Cleon said, mopping his profusely sweating brow as he stuffed some cake in his mouth, washing it down with a hurried swallow of wine, half of which spilled down his chin, staining his tunic.

D.L. Johnstone

"You have the rest of your life to do that," Aculeo said. "Think about it for just a few more minutes first."

"Please, I came here to be healed, instead I must bear witness to some horrible murder," the young man said, his eyes welling up, his mouth full, his voice quavering. "I simply want to be left alone."

"When did you arrive in the city?" Capito asked.

"Just last week. The same day as the cursed murder."

"Attend any symposia while you've been here?" Aculeo asked. Capito gave him a puzzled glance.

"What? No. Why do you ask?"

He seemed an unlikely killer, Aculeo mused. Still .... "Tell us exactly what you saw that night in the Sarapeion."

"I don't know what to tell you, really," Cleon said. "I'd just finished my prayers to Sarapis as the priest instructed me and entered the sanctuary to rest and receive my visions when I noticed someone skulking about in the shadows. I came closer and saw it was a man in the midst of assaulting that poor woman, before my very eyes. I called on him to stop, but then he turned on me! It's a wonder I wasn't slain myself."

"This man attacked you?" Capito asked.

"More demon than man. He threw me to the ground as he made his escape," Cleon said, his voice catching with emotion. He held up for examination a plump elbow, which had a small yellowish bruise on the tip and a smaller scrape along the side. "There was a great deal of blood. It was quite dreadful."

"What did the killer look like?" asked Aculeo.

"He was a brute of a man. Broad shouldered, powerful. A lunatic's face."

"Describe his face," said Capito.

"I don't know. Filthy, for one thing, rotten teeth, his hair and beard unkempt, matted. And a nasty scar running down the length of it."

"A scar?" Capito said sharply.

"Yes. He was wholly disreputable looking," Cleon continued.

"You know the man he's describing?" Aculeo asked Capito.

"Yes, I believe I may," Capito said. "A vagrant by the name of Apollonios."

"Then why is such a monster still running around in the street?" Capito cried. "Why aren't you doing your job? I was certain he was going to murder me as well."

"You seem to have survived alright. Anything else you can tell us?"

"Only that I hope for everyone's sake you catch him, and quickly." Cleon closed his eyes, putting a limp hand to his sweaty forehead. "Now

100

if it's all the same to you, I've a pounding headache. Mother was right – I never should have come to this cursed city!"

The merchant Harpalus' pottery factory was a small, windowless building in the Ceramicus, tucked in a squalid section behind the harbour's edge southeast of Lochias. The still, dry heat from the kiln fire inside the shop was unbearable. A dozen or so exhausted looking slaves were hard at work at narrow wooden benches, their naked backs gleaming with sweat, some of them spinning wet clay on the potters' wheels at one long table, others etching elegant glazed patterns and designs onto the pretty reed-green faience vases and deep brown urns stacked on the tables. The designs were all of a consistent theme – women and impressively endowed mythical beasts copulating with one another in anatomically unlikely positions, a popular item for the tourists, apparently. A number of ancient looking stone icons were stacked against the wall.

Harpalus was in the midst of haggling with a couple over a knee-high pink granite Egyptian sphinx. He tried his best to ignore the arrival of Aculeo and Capito.

"We need to talk," Capito said.

"Magistrate Capito, my dear friend, such an honour to see you!" Harpalus gushed. "I'll be with you in one moment. These lovely people and I were just ..."

"Where's Apollonios?" Aculeo demanded.

The merchant grinned fiercely at him. "I'm sure I don't know what you're talking about, but if you could just ... oh!" Capito had tipped one of the vases off the table, letting it tumble and smash on the floor. "Please, be careful, Magistrate! Not to worry," he said, smiling at the customers.

"I'm sure he already told you these pieces are all forgeries," Capito said to the customers. "Probably made only a year or so ago, then chipped and buried in lye-soaked earth to add a millennium or so of wear. Decent enough quality – I'm sure your friends at home won't be able to tell the difference."

"A preposterous accusation!" Harpalus cried. "I'm the most honest and scrupulous of men, I love my customers, I ... wait!" The would-be patrons had slipped out the door as quickly as they could. The merchant stared after them, crestfallen. "They were just about to buy."

Capito shoved him up against the wall, making the nearby tables stacked with pottery rattle. "I hear your brother's back in Alexandria. I need to talk to him."

"Apollonios? But ..."

"He's murdered two women, damn you! Now where is he?"

The slaves' activity at their benches had slowed to a crawl, though they didn't dare look up at their master. Harpalus glared at them. "Get back to work." He turned to his visitors. "Let's go somewhere and talk. Eupolis, you're in charge until I return. No slacking or I'll beat you all, I swear!"

Harpalus escaped into his office, fell into a chair and poured himself a cup of undiluted wine, which he quickly drank and followed up with a second.

"When did he get back to town?" Capito demanded.

"Really, Magistrate, Apollonios never ..." Harpalus caught a warning glance from the man and slumped back in his chair. "A few months back. He promised he'd stay for a few days only, a week at most, but then he simply ... stayed on. What could I do?"

"He murdered a hetaira," Aculeo said. "Dumped her body like a piece of trash in the canal. Not to mention a slave he murdered in the Sarapeion."

Harpalus stared at the men, eyes wide. "I don't believe it. Not my brother."

"Oh stop it!" Capito snapped. "What of the porne he attacked last year? You remember her, don't you? He'd have killed her too if those Assyrian sailors hadn't come along."

Harpalus sat in silence for a moment, gazing at the unfiltered debris that swirled on the surface of his wine, his mind a thousand miles and many years away. "He's a war hero, fought in the Battle of Teutoburg, honoured by Tiberius himself."

"Spinning tales of Teutoburg doesn't make a man a hero," Aculeo said. Barely a handful of men were said to have even survived the battle, yet countless old veterans begging for coins on Alexandria's streets claimed to have been heroes on its blood-soaked battlefields.

"He's my brother."

"He's also a murderer," Capito growled. "Now, where is he?"

"I don't know," the merchant cried, tearing at his tunic. "My oath. I haven't seen him in days. We had an argument and he hasn't been back."

"If I find out you've been lying to me, Harpalus, I swear you'll never ..."

Something on Harpalus' wrist caught Aculeo's eye. "Where did you get that?"

"This?" the merchant asked, holding up the piece of yellow twine tied around his wrist. "Apollonios asked me to wear it – something about a symbol of Sarapis' love or some such nonsense. Why? What does it matter?"

"Show us where he sleeps."

Harpalus reluctantly led them to the backroom of the shop. "Down there," he said, nodding glumly to a stairwell leading down to the basement.

Aculeo took up an oil lamp and headed down the stairs, Capito right behind him. The ceiling was low and the walls stacked with various figurines, pottery wheels covered in dust and cobwebs and soon-to-be-antique icons. There was little room to move. There, at the far end of the cramped, windowless room, a filthy-looking mattress and some blankets lay on top of the dirt floor. He squatted down beside the mattress, lifted up the blankets. Nothing. He turned over the mattress. Again, nothing. He didn't know what he might have found, but ... The soil was soft in one spot beneath where the mattress had been. Aculeo dug the soft, sandy dirt with his hands. Something wrapped in wax cloth. He removed it from the ground and unwrapped the musty-smelling cloth.

A knife handle missing its blade.

A small dead bird, dry as dust, clumsily wrapped in papyrus.

A trio of mismatched earrings.

A gold fibula, embedded with glittering semi-precious stones.

A small piece of torn blue linen ... stained with blood.

"What is it?" Harpalus whispered.

"Your brother's death sentence," Aculeo said.

"What pieces am I missing, Aculeo? What is it you're not telling me?" Capito demanded as the capo brought a jug of wine to their table. Capito was smiling, but it was clear he wasn't playing about.

"Please trust me," Aculeo said. "It's better left unsaid until I know more."

The Magistrate swirled the wine about in his cup. "It's well within the privileges of my position to arrest you, even torture you if I thought you had information important to operation of the Empire."

"Are you planning to torture me, Magistrate?" Aculeo asked irritably.

"I was hoping for a gentler approach to start."

Aculeo drank some wine – it was terrible stuff, but his thirst got the better of his palate. He wanted to tell someone, anyone, what was going on – the whole thing was driving him mad, but it was terribly risky. The Magistrate was an influential man with good connections, he could be useful up against men like Ralla and Gurculio. But that was part of the problem too. Any inquiries that his office might make could scare them off, force them to cover up, and that would be the end of his chance to learn what had happened to Iovinus. No, it was better to be quiet for now, to stay beneath their notice.

He smiled at Capito. "Better you stay out of this for now. You don't want the wrong sort people taking an interest in the Junior Magistrate of Alexandria's fledgling career."

"Why don't you let me decide that," Capito said stiffly.

"You're too virtuous a man. You wouldn't be able to let it go. Wait till I have some proof first."

Capito said nothing for a while, weighing Aculeo's words as he sipped his wine, reluctantly swishing it about on his palate. Finally he swallowed. "Fine. But I want your oath you'll involve me when you're closer. When you have your proof."

Aculeo held out his hand. "You have my oath."

Capito smiled and gripped Aculeo's hand. "We'll hold off on the torture a little longer then."

Xanthias was perched at the door when Aculeo returned at the end of the day, exhausted. "Not a word, Xanthias, I just want to sleep," Aculeo said.

"Yes, Master," the old slave said without another word, critical or otherwise.

Aculeo looked at him suspiciously. "What's the matter?"

"You've received mail," Xanthias blurted, nodding towards to the scarred wooden table where a cylindrical leather case sat.

Aculeo felt a chill descend. "Oh?"

"From Rome, the courier said."

Aculeo sat at the table and picked up the case, turning it slowly in his hands before carefully opening it. A thin scroll slid onto the table, its red wax seal marked with the initials of the family Lucullus. "It's from Titiana, I imagine," he mused.

"I believe so, Master," the slave whispered hoarsely, watching his master carefully, his lower lip trembling.

Aculeo looked sharply up at him. "Have you read it already?"

"The seal remains unbroken, does it not?" Xanthias asked, a thin varnish of defiance coating his anguish.

Aculeo picked the scroll up, weighing it in his hand for a moment. The paper felt cool and heavy, smooth, the finest quality. He took a knife and slit the seal open, unrolling the document. His hands started to shake and he felt a pang in his heart when he saw the elegant handwriting, something he had not seen in the longest time. The air was sucked from his lungs as he read through the letter, then let it fall on the table. "She's divorced me."

"Oh, Master!" Xanthias wept.

"She'll be getting remarried in a month's time to someone by the name of Spurius Lartius Carnifex. A senator's son, apparently, and a dear friend of her father's, she says. She requests that I permit him to adopt Atellus as well."

Xanthias made a broken, wordless sound.

"So that's it, it's over. Carnifex is a good man, no doubt. A man of privilege and honour. The gods know I'm a long way from being that again."

"Master, I ..."

Aculeo stood up suddenly and headed to the door. Xanthias, brave Xanthias blocked the door with his crooked old body. "Out of my way."

"Where are you going?" the slave demanded.

"If I had the coin, I'd take the first ship to Rome to cut off Carnifex's balls and feed them to him. As it is I can barely afford to get blinding drunk. Any objections?"

Xanthias sighed and stood aside. "No, Master. None at all."

CHAPTER XIII

THE 25TH DAY OF APRILIS

Aculeo was pulled from the dark shroud of sleep when he hit the floor. He looked up, head swirling with thick starbursts of pain. "What the …?" he mumbled, thick-tongued and muddle-headed.

Two dark figures loomed over him. "Get up!" one of them growled, punctuating his order with a sharp kick to the ribs.

Aculeo cried out in pain. "What's this about?"

"I said get up!" Aculeo curled in on himself, tensing against the coming blow.

"Give him a chance, will you?" a familiar voice pleaded.

The second kick never came. Aculeo looked up from his place on the floor and saw Viator and Vibius, Gurculio's slaves, glowering down at him. Bitucus stood just behind them in the doorway. In my bedroom, he realized dimly, I'm in my bedroom. "What's going on?" he gasped, trying to catch his breath.

"Please, Aculeo, you need to come with us," Bitucus said in an apologetic tone.

"I already told you I don't know where Gellius is, now …"

Viator kicked him again, this time in the side of his stomach. Aculeo felt like he was going to retch.

"Stop it, stop!" Xanthias cried. Vibius lashed out at the old man, striking him across the face.

"Leave him be," Aculeo said, rolling onto his back, panting. "Just leave him be."

"Come on, Aculeo," Bitucus said. "Gurculio just wants to talk to you."

"About what?"

"I … I'm not sure."

"So you've gone from Roman to beggar to Gurculio's messenger boy now, is that it?" Aculeo asked.

"I'm sorry, Aculeo, truly."

"Not as sorry as you will be, Bitucus. I give you my oath."

The three men escorted him through the crowded noonday streets. Aculeo felt nauseous, his head throbbed, his ribs ached where he'd been kicked with every breath. He wouldn't have been surprised if he'd broken something. It was almost noon, the sun high in the sky and hot enough to cause a sour sweat to drip down his ashen cheeks. The previous night was a blur. He recalled reading the letter from Titiana, which was followed by an undetermined number of kraters of undiluted quaff in some nameless back alley tavern. And then this.

"Is this how you took Trogus?" he asked Bitucus.

"Aculeo, it's not like that," the man replied.

"Isn't it? You led Gurculio's goons to me as you did him. Now you're taking me to your master like any good slave might do."

"I'm no one's slave, damn you!"

"Oh? You had me fooled."

"Just shut up and walk," Bitucus said bitterly.

The Great Harbour was thick with flax-sailed skiffs and barges sliding up to the jetties near the Emporion, loaded down with grain, amphorae of wine and other tradewares. A dirty white cloud of seabirds kited across in the early morning sky, drawn by the ripe, briny stench of the arriving fishing boats, their shrill cries clawing at Aculeo's aching skull.

He looked past the warehouses that littered the harbour, following the even lines that webbed across the city, broken only by the Canopic Canal twisting like a blue umbilicus around the eastern edge of the city before turning southwards to empty into the inland harbour where they now walked. A billowing trail of smoke and a glint of yellow firelight spilled forth from the mouth of the Lighthouse, shining out over the sea. Zeus-

Soter stood atop the peak, welcoming all travellers and prospective citizens to this cruel and joyless city. Mocking him, it seemed.

The wooden amphitheatre stood just ahead. Aculeo could hear the roar of the noonday crowds erupt from within as they approached the gates. "Is this where we're going?" he asked.

"Gurculio's hosting some friends here," Bitucus explained.

"Your master's tastes are so refined." Bitucus ignored the jibe. Built decades ago to host gladiatorial games, one of the Roman conquerors' favourite pastimes, the amphitheatre never lacked for attendance. Personally, Aculeo despised them – the idea of watching men attempt to slaughter one another on blood-soaked sand wasn't his idea of an afternoon well spent.

They led him through the noisome, stinking crowds and up the steps to the second level. Aculeo spotted the moneylender settled into one of the smaller boxes beneath a grey canvas awning. Look at him sitting there, he thought, like a spider in his web, for all the world to see. Half a dozen men, merchants and bankers, Aculeo recognized, all of them already boisterous and drunk – sat next to the moneylender amidst a flock of pretty young girls who fawned over them all.

Anger churned under his skin like poison as he watched Gurculio laugh and talk to his associates. The man stole everything from me, he tore my family apart, orchestrated the downfall of dozens of my friends, twisted Iovinus against me then murdered him, and here I am, unable to do anything but stand here at his command. What's wrong with me? His heart felt lodged in his throat all of a sudden. He felt massively unprepared, foolish and weak. What does he want of me now?

A flash of scarlet hair caught his eye – Panthea herself was sitting next to one of the men, laughing politely at whatever banality he'd uttered. The girls were all pornes from the Blue Bird, he realized. He scanned the group but saw no sign of Tyche. Panthea caught his eye – there was a flash of recognition, then she turned back to her seat mate, placing her hand on his thigh and squeezing. Aculeo watched as another of the guests grinned wolfishly at a dark-skinned girl and took her by the wrist, pulling her into one of the small canvas tents set up just behind them. Sabina, Aculeo recalled.

In the stadium below, a pair of dwarf praegenarii strode through the gates to the raucous welcoming cheers of the crowd. The praegenarii raised their small wooden swords overhead in salute, then turned to face one another. A trumpet sounded and the little gladiators charged towards one another, accompanied by a great clash of cymbals from the orchestra. The crowd roared in delight as the mock battle carried on, trumpets and cymbals erupting with every blow to mimic the sound of steel on steel.

Bitucus squeezed his way past the other guests and whispered in Gurculio's ear. The moneylender finally deigned to notice Aculeo. He smiled, giving him an imperious wave to take the vacant seat next to him. Aculeo reluctantly complied. Gurculio was heavier than he recalled, the thick slabs of muscle that ran across his back and shoulders gone to fat since his rise from the gutters not so long ago, but he was still a dangerous, powerful looking man. His liberal use of unguents provided but a thin floral skein over his foul body odour. Sour sweat ran down his cheeks, darkening the neck and armpits of his tunic. The wormlike veins that branched across his cheeks were an angry violet.

"I'm so glad you could join me," he said magnanimously. "Bitucus, fetch our friend some wine." Bitucus gave him a look as though he'd just been slapped in the face, but went all the same to do as he was told.

"Your men hardly gave me a choice but to come," Aculeo said.

Gurculio laughed. "My apologies. But would you have come otherwise?"

The dwarfs made wild swings of their wooden swords at one another, turning somersaults in the sand to the clash of cymbals. The audience howled in laughter at their act.

"Do you enjoy the Games?" the moneylender asked, popping a handful of snails into his mouth with a crunch. He was behaving like a noble Roman, or his image of one at least. He wiped his greasy fingers off on a crust of bread which he tossed to a dog that lay at his feet.

"No more than I enjoy your company," Aculeo said. Gurculio shot him a dark look. Clearly the man had grown fat on flattery of those seeking his favours.

The gates opened and out drove a tiny chariot driven by a monkey, pulled by a team of goats. The monkey brandished a javelin and drove the chariot straight towards the combatants, who turned and ran into one another in another ringing clash of cymbals before somersaulting into the sand and running from the arena, the little chariot in hot pursuit. The audience roared its approval.

"I don't know what it is you want," Aculeo said. "I already told your dogs I know nothing about Gellius."

"Word is Gellius already left the city," Gurculio said. "I've no need of him anymore anyway. Trogus already settled their debt."

Aculeo felt a chill descend despite the stifling heat. "Settled it how?" he asked. "With a knife across his throat? Or did you just sell him to the fullery as you did to poor Pesach?"

"Don't be so dramatic," Gurculio said, shifting in his seat which groaned beneath his heavy frame.

"What of Iovinus? Did you murder him too?"

The moneylender smiled. "Word was he drowned months ago."

"You know very well he did nothing of the kind. What was the deal the two of you made? Whatever it was, it couldn't keep him alive, could it?"

"You really are a fool," Gurculio laughed. "Men like you, Gellius, Trogus, Pesach … your days are done. You need to adjust to that new reality as Bitucus has done if you mean to survive."

Aculeo's blood was boiling now at the audacity of the man, a mere moneylender daring to talk to him like that!

The gates opened once more and through them stumbled a full-sized gladiator, a murmillone, a sea fish glinting on the crest of his silver helmet, chain mail covering his sword arm. He carried a gladius in one hand and a short, oblong shield in the other. Skinny and stumbling, and having trouble even lifting his sword, the murmillone looked around at the crowd in confusion. The man was likely a nexus, a convicted criminal they often tossed into the Stadium for quick sport. Next through the gates strode a retiarius, a fisherman, a giant of a man, nearly twice the size of the poor murmillone. He carried a trident and net, with armour extending from the left side of the chest and length of his arm to the shoulder, while a metal shoulder shield covered his neck and the lower section of his face. The crowd buzzed in anticipation.

The little dog which had climbed into Gurculio's lap began to yap, startled by the noise. "Hush, Felix, hush," the Roman cooed, stroking its ears. "Did you know my grandfather was born into slavery? And yet he died a free and wealthy man."

"You had family? I'd always assumed you'd been squeezed out of a pig's ass one cursed morning."

The moneylender's eyes flashed with irritation. "Watch your tongue, ceveo."

"Call me that again and you'll join your ancestors soon enough," Aculeo growled.

Gurculio ignored him. "My grandfather always said to make sure you cover your own ass, because nobody will do it for you. Especially now."

"What's that supposed to mean?"

In the stadium below, the retiarius raised his trident over his head as he swung his net, getting ready to cast it. The murmillone stumbled backwards to stay out of reach, then tripped over his own feet and fell in the dust. His helmet slid forward, covering his eyes as the net sailed over his head. The crowd cheered – this contest was even funnier than the dwarfs! The murmillone scuttled away like a crab, struggling to right his helmet.

"I heard you were sniffing about after Calisto. Even went to her villa the other day," Gurculio said, looking sideways at Aculeo with his tiny, pebble-like eyes. "Why?"

"What business is it of yours who I visit?" Aculeo demanded, though in truth he was caught off guard. How could he have known?

The retiarius, picking up on the crowd's mood, decided to draw things out and have some fun with his opponent. He slammed his trident hard into the murmillone's shield, piercing the thick wooden plank, then tore it from the man's shaking hands. The murmillone wheeled backwards in a panic as the retiarius kicked the shield off his trident and advanced.

"Calisto's not just some Tannery toe-toucher."

"You think I don't know that?"

"You might well know it, but you clearly don't understand its significance," Gurculio said, then shoved a piece of black winecake in his mouth. "She's a companion to men of wealth, power, influence. You're none of those things. Not anymore. Understand me? That means when men of any import piss upon your noble-born head, you're to thank them and tell them that it smells of myrrh."

"Fuck you, moneylender," Aculeo spat, barely managing to hold his temper.

"Hold up, I'm not through with you yet," Gurculio said.

"I'm not going to sit here listening to whatever nonsense dribbles out of your lips."

"You're well out of your depth on this one. Do you even know who her fucking patron is?"

"I couldn't care less," Aculeo said.

"I trust you know who Lucius Albius Ralla is."

Ralla? Aculeo thought in surprise. Calisto belongs to Ralla? The thought of him lying in her bed, touching her, fucking her ... Enough, he thought, trying not to expose himself. It's hardly my concern. "What of it?"

"Ralla's not a man to cross. He's not likely to be all that appreciative of someone like you showing an interest in his rightful property. Now do you understand?"

"I'll bear it in mind."

"You'll need to do a lot more than that if you want to keep that empty head atop your shoulders!" Gurculio snapped.

"If this is the only reason you summoned me..." Aculeo said, rising from his seat.

"Don't be in such a hurry. I've a proposition for you. You remember Posidippus of Cos, I trust?"

Aculeo was caught off guard a second time. He knew the Cosian slightly, a low-level grain merchant who operated well outside the usual channels. He'd never trusted the man personally, though he recalled Corvinus had mentioned him as someone who got things done. "I know of him," he said cautiously. "Why?"

The retiarius caught his net on the fish-shaped crest on the murmillone's helmet and pulled. The other man cried out and fell to his knees, dropping his sword in the sand. The crowd roared and stomped their feet against the walls of the amphitheatre.

"He disappeared two weeks ago," Gurculio said, "and no one knows where he is. Not his business associates, not his friends, not his family. I need to find him."

"What do you expect me to do? I barely know the man," Aculeo said.

"He used to work with your old patron, Corvinus, didn't he?"

"And Corvinus died months ago. Any connection I would have had to Posidippus died with him."

Gurculio raised an eyebrow. "Don't devalue your connections. It's the only thing you have left in your favour. There's a price on Posidippus' head. One thousand sesterces if you find him for me."

The offer represented a small fortune, at least in terms of Aculeo's current circumstances, and Gurculio surely knew it. But it made no sense – why offer such a price for a middling merchant like Posidippus of Cos?" And what will you do with him once you find him?" Aculeo asked. "Sell him to the fullery? Or just murder him like you did with Trogus?"

"Don't be such a spineless cunt," Gurculio said irritably, fanning himself as the sweat filled the crevices between his fleshy chins. "I never murdered anyone. Besides, I already settled matters with Trogus. He's a free man now."

The retiarius advanced on his fallen opponent. The crowd stood on their feet, swept up in blood lust, screaming for gore. The murmillone fumbled in the sand for his weapon.

Aculeo looked at the moneylender in surprise. "Why didn't you tell me that before?"

"My business is my own. Yours is to do what I tell you, which right now is to find Posidippus. Understand?"

The man's arrogance was astounding. "Find him yourself, moneylender. I've better things to do."

"Wait," Gurculio said, pointing into the stadium, "you should really watch this first."

"So I can witness a man getting slaughtered like a staked goat?"

"He's found his sword at least."

Aculeo glanced down into the stadium in spite of himself and saw the poor murmillone had indeed managed to find his sword. He held it trembling before him, for it seemed to weighed heavy in his hands. The retiarius made a side-to-side dodging move as though wary of approaching a dangerous beast, making the crowd laugh. As he did so, the retiarius tripped over his own feet and stumbled. The murmillone took a reluctant check swing with his sword, catching his opponent's right calf.

"There, he's had it," someone cried and the crowd started chanting the words, laughing at the great sport. The retiarius looked down at his shallow wound in surprise, then simply stepped in and stabbed the other man in the midsection with his trident. The murmillone cried out, a sound of agony woven tight with surrender as blood spilled from his wounds. The retiarius put his boot on the man's chest and shoved him off, tearing his trident free. The murmillone stared down at the fresh gore of his guts spilling from his body and tried in vain to hold them in.

"Enough," Aculeo said, turning to go, nauseated by the gory spectacle.

"Not quite," Gurculio said. The retiarius grabbed the murmillone by the helmet and stripped it off, throwing it with an empty clatter to the blood-soaked sand. Aculeo looked at the mortally wounded man's face.

"No," he whispered. It was Trogus kneeling there in the sand, eyes glazed, pink foam bubbling from his lips. Aculeo glanced at Bitucus in disbelief. Bitucus' cheeks were drained, his eyes wide with shock. If he knew, he wore the cloak of innocence well. The retiarius grabbed Trogus by the hair and arched his head back, placing a dagger to his pale throat. He gazed up into the stands to the Games' Editor, blinking in the glaring afternoon sun. The crowd was mixed – some jabbed their thumbs towards their hearts in a call for death, others pinching thumbs and forefingers together to ask that the man be spared. The Editor glanced towards Gurculio, who paused a long moment.

"What are you waiting for?" Aculeo demanded. "Spare him! Spare him!"

Gurculio casually pointed his thumb towards his chest.

"No, damn you!" Aculeo cried, then leapt to his feet. "Spare him! Spare him!"

The Editor copied Gurculio's gesture. The retiarius complied, slitting Trogus' throat before letting him fall, his lifeblood spilling dark upon the sand, then turned and walked away.

Aculeo stared at Gurculio in horror. "You told me you'd freed him."

"I did. He merely needed to make his way out of the stadium today," Gurculio said calmly, leaning back in his seat, a smile spread across his fleshy face. "Sadly that didn't happen. I hope you learn from this, Ceveo. Now stop be such an idiot and find the Cosian, understand?" The Roman turned his attention back to the stadium as they dragged Trogus' lifeless body away.

Viator and Vibius moved closer to them, looming over Aculeo, waiting for him to act.

"This isn't over. I promise you," Aculeo choked, then tore himself away, pushing his way past Bitucus and the other slaves.

"Aculeo," Bitucus whispered, pleading. "I didn't know, I swear ..."

Aculeo shoved the man into the churning, sweating crowds. As he headed towards the steps, the flap of one of the privacy tents lifted and Tyche emerged, blinking in the sudden harsh daylight. She seemed to stagger and held out her hand against a post to catch herself. Her cheek was bright red as though she'd just been struck, her upper lip was puffy and bleeding, her peplos torn at the shoulder. A man emerged from the tent right after her, narrow-shouldered, weak-jawed, receding hairline, watery brown eyes. Lucius Albius Ralla. He gave a vague, satisfied smile and adjusted his toga as he moved towards Gurculio's box to join the others. Tyche spotted Aculeo out of the corner of her eye and looked away, touching her bruised cheek with her fingertips. Ralla took the seat Aculeo has just vacated next to Gurculio, leaned over and whispered something to the moneylender, who roared in laughter.

CHAPTER XIV

Aculeo followed the gridwork of streets outside the city walls, the image of Trogus' horrendous public spectacle execution like an indelible stain in his mind. He found his way into a tavern where a weathered wooden sign cut in the shape of a wagon wheel hung over the door, the sound of music and talk rising from behind the garden walls, the evening air thick with the smell of frying fish, spices and sharp tang of palm wine. He took a quiet table in the corner and ordered a pitcher of palm wine. He downed a cup, then another, barely tasting the unfiltered, pale yellow swill that passed his lips. *I was unable to lift so much as a finger for him,* he thought angrily. *Or Gellius, wherever he is. Or Pesach. Not even Tyche.*

Ah, Tyche – how her eyes burned into me when she'd saw me standing there, both of us powerless, filled with shame. It's as Zeanthes said, I can bring only pain and misery to others of late. Even Titiana and Atellus have abandoned me. He splashed more wine into his cup.

And what of Ralla? Why didn't Calisto tell me he was her patron too? To protect him? More likely herself. Can I blame her? She's terrified of the man. Ralla, who'd sat next to Gurculio at the Games, jesting with him after abusing poor Tyche. Aculeo poured himself another cup of wine, spilling a good portion of it on the table. *What do they want with the Cosian? Could he be connected to this tangled mess somehow?*

Any successful business required a vast network, not all of it so reputable. Least of all men like Posidippus of Cos, but Corvinus had always taken care of such matters. The Cosian was well enough known in the Agora – a feral little man, often seen accompanied by a ragged retinue about the marketplace, striking some deal or other. And the Cosian had spun his own web of contacts and lesser investors to form a loose partnership with Corvinus, giving him access to small, ready transport ships, opening the grain market into Assyria and beyond. Disreputable, perhaps, but he and his ilk had their place. He must have known Iovinus at least – could he be connected somehow to his murder? Could he have stolen the tablets as well?

Aculeo pushed himself away from the table, dizzy with drink and exhaustion. Well worth looking into at least.

The deme of Berenike was built into a low sloping crest overlooking the Port of the Lake, the main mercantile port for shipments from the chora in Upper Egypt. Silty grey waves sloshed against the square-sailed ships anchored at the dock, the twilight echoing with the mournful lowing of the cattle in the stockyards and the shouts and curses of the merchant sailors as they loaded and unloaded their cargoes, rushing to finish as darkness fell. Sacks of grain from Upper Egypt, the fertile Nile Valley, were stored in granaries, waiting to be stacked onto barges to be transported to the main harbour in the morning and thence to the Roman Empire to feed its insatiable hunger. On Rome's requirements alone fortunes could be made.

Or lost.

And there, he thought, eyeing the dark, derelict building across the street, stood Posidippus of Cos' warehouse. A dog's bark echoed through the empty streets. The lock on the door, a simple row of grooves above the bolt, snapped readily under the blade of his knife. Inside, the building was as it had appeared from the outside – abandoned.

There were basic living quarters inside the front entrance. A chair lay tipped over on the floor. A bowl of apricots on the table had gone rotten, the fruit flesh now brown and sickly sweet, the air dotted with fruit flies. Something dark and sticky had spilled across the desk and dripped onto the floor. Aculeo smelled it warily – it was just wine. There was a skittering sound in the corner that disappeared into the darkness.

A table in the corner was covered with scrolls and scraps of papyrus. He scanned through a few of them. Business documents, legal papers, purchase agreements, inventories of ships' cargoes. Another set of scrolls sat tucked on a shelf above the desk, coated in a thick layer of dust. He unfurled a few of them – accounting ledgers. He tucked what he could into his satchel.

The warehouse area itself was cavernous. Judging by what little he could see in the torchlight, it looked well picked over. All that remained were a few amphorae of rancid olive oil, some rusted swords, moth-eaten bolts of cloth, an amphora of wine turned to vinegar and a handful of broken Egyptian statues of Anubis, Isis and sphinxes of assorted sizes – either counterfeit or stolen from some Upper Egyptian temple he guessed. Rats, startled by the sound of his footsteps, scrabbled deeper into the darkness, their yellow eyes glinting from the shadows as they watched him.

Aculeo was about to leave when he felt the wooden floorboards give beneath his feet. He knelt down and tapped the floor. It sounded solid enough ... except for one spot. He wedged the torch into a sconce then took up one of the rusted swords, sliding the blade between two of the floorboards and carefully prying one up. He held the torch over the area. Empty – whatever had been hidden there was gone now. He reached in and felt around – his hand brushed over something dry and papery. He shone the torch over it – a dried flower with large, dull red petals. The same sort he'd found in Neaera's little flat and Myrrhine's room – petals from the opium flower.

For whatever reason, the Cosian had left this place in a hurry before falling off the edge of the world, Aculeo mused as he headed back. Much like Neaera. And Petras. And what of Myrrhine who started her evening at an exclusive symposium and ended it dumped in a canal with her throat slashed? And the damned river slave in the Sarapeion.

No matter how many more cups of wine he drank that night, the puzzle never seemed to clear beyond a great, amorphous muddle.

Philomena walked along the paved street, through the crowds, a group of men spilling out of the kapeleions followed her a ways, calling to her. "Hai hai, over here love," one of the men cried. "I've got something for you."

"Too small by far to see in this dim light I'm afraid," she replied. The man's friends all laughed.

"Well, on a highway that's been driven as much as the Street of the Soma, even a chariot might look small," the man said.

"So it might seem to a man used to pulling his own little wagon. Maybe you should stick with that and keep off the roads tonight."

The man split off from his friends, put his hand around her waist and pulled her close. "Such a mouth on you," he said, kissing her roughly on the cheek.

Philomena pushed the man away, giggling. "Don't be brash. I don't even know your name."

"Cleobis. Want some company?"

"Buy me a drink, then we'll see."

They sat in a local tavern, drank a few jars of beer, eating bread and opson as the music played around them, flutes, jangling tambourines and pounding drums, laughing with the crowd over the bawdy songs they all sang. Cleobis' hands were all over her. She felt she was getting drunk but stayed clear headed enough to remember her business. They settled quickly on a price.

"Where to then, darling?" he asked.

"The Western Walls near the monuments. The neighbours are quiet there – they never make a peep."

"I should hope not," he said, spitting on the ground to ward off any evil spirits that might be lurking about. They walked along the dark street, weaving and laughing, holding each other up as they walked, singing what lines they could remember from the songs they'd heard that night. Shadows followed, a whisper on the street, flitting through the alleyways. Cleobis pulled her close to him, planting a sloppy kiss on the neck. Philomena squawked and slapped his hands away.

"Come on, in here," she said, pulling him into the darkness beneath the arch of a monument. She kissed him hard on the mouth, holding him close. There was a wind off the water, damp and cool in the night, sounds like whispers scratching against the stone. She felt goosebumps rise on her skin.

Cleobis pushed her up against the archway, kissing her on the mouth. He grabbed the backs of her knees and lifted them, stroking the soft, warm skin of her legs as they wrapped around him, squeezing. "Ah, wait," he gasped.

"Wait for what? Come on then."

"No, really, I have to take a piss, all that beer."

"Gah, such timing. Why not just keep your thing in your hand when you're done and finish yourself off then."

"Such a mouth on you," Cleobis laughed. He stepped out from the archway, leaned against the stone structure, weaving and wobbling, holding himself up with one hand as he tried to relieve himself with the other but nothing seemed to flow.

"Whore," the wind whispered.

"Wha's that?" he said. "Ah, now, here we go."

A blinding pain exploded in the back of his head. He stumbled forward, his face smashed against the stone, breaking his nose and chipping a tooth, then slumped to the ground. Another blow fell, then another. "Stop, stop, by the Gods, please stop!" Cleobis bellowed in pain, holding his hands over his head in protection.

The blows stopped at last. He had just managed to catch his breath when he heard a woman's scream. Everything was going black. He shook his head, trying to stay conscious. He heard the woman scream again, but it was cut off this time. He staggered unsteadily to his feet and stepped into the shadows of the archway.

A dark figure crouched in the shadows over where Philomena lay, straddling her, a bracelet of yellow cord tied around his wrist. "You bitch," gasped a demon's voice. "You whore!"

Cleobis fell on the figure, wrapped his arm around the other's throat from behind, locked his arm with his free hand and squeezed as hard as he could. Philomena pulled her fibula from her torn chiton and stabbed it into her attacker's neck. The man screamed in pain and fury, arching backwards with the fierce strength of a crazed animal, and swung his fist like a club back into Cleobis' groin. A nauseating wave of pain washed over Cleobis as he fell to his knees. The man pushed away and scrambled off.

Philomena lay curled up on the ground, coughing and weeping. Cleobis squatted down beside her, managed to get her to sit up at last. "Hey, he's gone. Shhh, don't worry. You alright?" She nodded, trying to catch her breath. "Did you see his face?"

"Yes ... I ... I think I know him."

CHAPTER XV

THE 26TH DAY OF APRILIS

Aculeo emptied his satchel out on the table, trying his best to ignore Xanthias' mutterings about the great mess some people liked to make first thing in the morning before they'd even had a sip of wine or a bite of bread, still stinking of the streets from the previous night no less. He unrolled the accounting scrolls he'd gathered from Posidippus' office and scanned through them.

Corvinus had rarely discussed his dealings with the Cosian. Aculeo had met the man on a few occasions, but hadn't realized how tightly Posidippus had become involved in the company's business over time. For the most part Aculeo had let himself to drift away from the day-to-day details of the company's business. There were detailed entries in the Cosian's documents on no less than eighteen ships in the company fleet in the year leading up to Corvinus' suicide. According to the documents, Posidippus had worked closely with Iovinus to broker the supply for the annona from several middlemen, cobbling them together into shipments on half a dozen occasions. He appeared organized enough, for the earliest entries had been written methodically in a tight, cramped hand. More recent entries however, starting about six or seven months ago, seemed to have been written by an entirely different man. The handwriting more of a scrawl, the entries less frequent, the transactions themselves significantly less detailed. Posidippus had started buying from a middleman by the name of Goranus starting about six months ago. There were several entries for such transactions, totalling a significant amount of money over time, close to half a talent's worth. Yet there was nothing in the records of him reselling the product. What had he done with it all? Stockpiled it? The warehouse was empty though. It made no sense.

A knock sounded on the door. Xanthias grumbled irritably as he went to answer.

One document indicated that the Cosian's warehouse and another property known only by its title number had been offered as surety for a shipment on the tenth of Januarius, two weeks following the sinking of the second fleet, Aculeo thought. There was no record of any further inventory being bought or sold since November, five months ago. Another document noted that he'd been borrowing money from several sources, the only one called out by name being the negotiatore Shimon-Petrus. There was no record of repayments made since the eighth of December. The entries grew even more erratic as time went on, until at last they stopped two months ago. What then? Aculeo wondered. Had Posidippus stopped keeping records? Or was there nothing left to record? Whatever happened, according to the documents he'd owed double the money he'd possessed just a year ago. It was enough to make any man want to flee. And enough to make his lenders nervous, and perhaps in search of retribution. Was Gurculio among them? Or just Shimon-Petrus? In the end, he was missing and Iovinus was murdered. It couldn't be a coincidence.

"Excuse me, Master, if you're not too busy turning our kitchen into a complete disaster," Xanthias said.

"Can't you see I'm busy," Aculeo snapped. He leaned back in his seat and rubbed his eyes. Too many documents, too many cursed questions, and no time to find the answers. What if the Cosian...?

"Alas, Master, I'm but a simple-minded slave after all, it's difficult for me to comprehend the many complex demands placed upon a master's shoulders. But there's a fellahin boy outside who claims that someone named Sekhet wants to see you as soon as possible. I would have – wait, where do you think you're going? Master, you haven't even eaten yet! Fine, go," the old slave muttered. "Down into the gutter, yes, that's where civilization is going, straight down into the gutter."

The morning air in Rhakotis hung with the heavy, yeasty smell of fermenting beer, baking bread and the rich spice of the foods being peddled by the bellowing street vendors. Sleepy-looking merchants crouched at the sides of the road beside large reed baskets, offering goods for sale – linen clothing, leather bags, sandals, crockery, glass amulets and figurines, cones of salt, dried fish, ox hides - watching Aculeo curiously as he passed.

The healer herself answered her door. She took one look at him, then clicked her tongue and shook her head in disapproval, a shock of grey hair straying across her deeply etched face. "A porne was attacked last night near the western walls," she said.

"Is she still alive?"

"Yes, praise Isis, she managed to fight her attacker off."

"You think it's connected to the murders?"

"No, I simply missed seeing your cheerful face." Sekhet stabbed a crooked finger sharply into his chest, her dark eyes hard as flint. "Be gentle with her, understand me, Roman? She's been through quite enough already."She led him past the room filled with waiting patients into her back office. A figure lay beneath a blanket on the daybed in the corner of the room, facing the wall, asleep.

"Is she alright?" he asked.

"She will be. Philomena," the healer said gently. "Are you awake, dear?" The girl reluctantly turned to face them. She was young, no more than twenty. Her left eye was red and swollen almost shut, the other bloodshot, her lower lip split and puffy, her neck bruised black and blue. Her good eye widened when she saw Aculeo. She began to cry and turned away to face the wall. Sekhet sat beside her on the bed, stroking her head. Philomena flinched. "Shhh, don't worry. He's a friend of mine."

"Leave me alone," the girl pleaded, her voice muffled by the blanket.

"He's here to help, dear one. His name is Aculeo. He only wants to find the man who did this to you."

Philomena turned over in the bed and looked at him with her one good eye. "Why?"

"Just tell us what happened," Sekhet said, stroking her hair.

The girl took a deep, trembling breath, then told them her story of how she'd been attacked and almost murdered near the funerary monuments. Her voice trembled at first, uncertain, frightened, but she gained confidence as she went, until, near the end, she was sitting up in bed, more angry than anything.

"You're lucky to be alive I think," Sekhet said, squeezing her hand.

"You said you knew the man who attacked you," Aculeo said.

"I … I think so."

"Did he tell you his name?"

"Orpheus."

Damn, he thought. "How'd you know him then?"

"I used to see him sitting on the steps of a little tavern in Epsilon. He'd sit there almost every night, waiting for me, wanting to talk. It's on my route, see?"

"He hired you?"

"Once," the girl admitted, blushing.

"Did he hurt you that time?"

"No." She closed her good eye, thinking. "I mean, yes. I … I didn't think he meant to do it, he always seemed so harmless."

"What did he do to you that time?"

"He grabbed my arm was all," she said, touching her fingers to her throat.

"So what was different this time? Why did he attack you?" Aculeo asked.

"Maybe he was jealous. I don't know. I was with another man. He's a different sort, you know? Maybe he was confused, thought just because we'd been together that one time."

"You said you always saw him sitting in the same place," Sekhet said. "Where was that?"

"In Epsilon Quarter at the Tavern of Sefu. He'd sit on the steps there and wait for me."

Such attacks are likely common enough, he thought. It's possible that the attack is linked somehow to the murders, but for that matter so could a dozen other assaults that take place on any given night. "Sekhet, I don't know…" he began.

"Show him your wrists," the healer told the girl.

Philomena looked at her oddly, then pulled her hands out of the blanket and held them up in the dim lamplight. She wore a number of bracelets on both wrists made of silver and copper and bronze. On the left wrist, she also wore a bracelet of yellow twine.

Aculeo felt his heart pound in his chest. "You worship Sarapis?"

"What?"

"That yellow cord tied about your wrist – that's part of your worship of Sarapis, isn't it?"

She looked at her wrist and bit her lower lip, puzzled. "I'd forgotten about it. He gave it to me that first time. He may have said something about Sarapis, I can't remember really …"

"What does this Orpheus look like?"

"Very skinny, his hair and fingernails are filthy, and he has a big scar across his face, running across his lips and down his chin. Must have almost split his head open whatever made that."

Apollonios, Aculeo thought, his heart pounding. It had to be. "And you're sure his name was Orpheus?"

"He called himself that. Kept calling me Eurydice. I thought he was being sweet," she said, her voice trailing off. "You know all I could think of when he attacked me? That this is what must have happened to those poor girls who disappeared. That I'd be the next one. Just another missing porne that everyone forgets about in a day or so."

Aculeo stared at the girl – more stories of missing pornes like the ones that frightened Tyche, or is there some truth in it? "Do you know who Gurculio is?" he asked.

"Who?" the girl said, a look of confusion on her face.

"Gurculio the moneylender. Did he ever hire you for any private parties?"

"No," she said, her lower lip trembling.

"Aculeo," Sekhet said.

"What about Ralla? No? Iovinus? Think, damn you!"

"No! No no no no no no!" Philomena held her fists tight against her temple, her arms tucked tight to her breast and curled against the wall, sobbing like a child.

"Hush, you're fine now," Sekhet said, stroking the girl's head. She glanced at Aculeo, her expression more troubled than her tone implied. "That's enough for now. You just close your eyes and rest."

Sekhet led Aculeo out of the room and closed the door. "I told you not to upset her. The poor child was attacked once already today," the healer seethed.

"I had to see if she was hiding anything." Sekhet shot him a withering look. "I'm sorry."

"And what did you learn?"

"Apollonios is the one who attacked her."

Sekhet raised a puzzled brow. "She said his name was Orpheus."

"And he called her his Eurydice," Aculeo said, rubbing his eyes in exhaustion. "It's from schoolboy stories. Orpheus was a Thracian king, Eurydice his wife. She went out walking in the valley one morning, whereupon she was raped and murdered. Orpheus followed her shade down into Tartarus where he tried to convince Hades to allow him to bring her back to the land of the living. Hades relented on one condition – when Orpheus led his wife's shade from Tartarus, he must not look back at her until they reached the safety of the sun. They set out at once, and as soon as Orpheus felt the sun on his own face again he was overjoyed and turned to kiss Eurydice's lips – but part of her was still in shadow. She disappeared as soon as his eyes touched hers, losing her forever."

"So perhaps in his madness he thought he was trying to save this woman," Sekhet mused. "From the streets. From that life."

"And when he couldn't, he tried to kill her instead," Aculeo said. "Her, Myrrhine, the river slave, Neaera. It's been him behind these murders all the while. The question is whether he acted alone."

"We can only guess."

They almost missed him. Drawn by the sweet scent of bread, spices and grilling meat and the friendly chatter of the customers, Apollonios wandered past the courtyard of the white-washed little tavern in Epsilon later that afternoon, hoping for handouts. He hardly looked dangerous as he shambled barefoot along the crowded street, weaving his way amongst the other pedestrians, favouring one leg. He was skinny as a beggar, his beard and hair unkempt, likely crawling with vermin. His chiton was as filthy as the rest of him.

A cold rage coursed through Aculeo as he watched the man, his mind filled with the horrific images of the poor women raped and murdered, their savaged bodies left behind like garbage. Could a wretch like him be working on Gurculio and Ralla's behalf? Why not hire a mad dog to commit a mad crime? He nodded to Capito, who considered Apollonios for a moment, then signalled the two soldiers to move in. The recluse squatted down outside the tavern, picked up a scrap of food he saw on the ground, sniffed it, tasted it before tossing it aside.

The soldiers drew closer, only fifteen cubits from him. Ten. Apollonios scratched an armpit and stretched, watching the people walking by. Capito nodded to the lead soldier, who headed straight for their quarry. Apollonios suddenly stood up and slipped quietly into the back alley. The soldiers followed, Capito and Aculeo right behind them.

As they entered the back door of the building, Aculeo saw the recluse waiting for them with a steaming copper kettle in hand. "No!" he cried, but too late. The lead soldier screamed in agony as the boiling water poured over him, scalding his face and outstretched hands. The recluse threw the kettle at the others and bolted through the back kitchen, knocking over a table of food and plates behind him where they smashed on the floor. The servants and patrons looked up in amazement as the three furious men came crashing into the dining room, then burst through the door out onto the street behind their quarry.

They spotted him just ahead, limping at a furious pace down the street, weaving his way through the crowd. Aculeo, Capito and the remaining soldier chased after him, knocking aside any pedestrians that got in the way. Ah, there now, he's turned up a blind alley. But as they rounded the corner, they saw he'd managed somehow to squeeze himself through an impossible spot between two buildings. They could only watch as Apollonios scrambled up over a wall and into another side street.

"What are you waiting for, let's go!" Capito cried, and kicked in the back door to one of the buildings then charged inside, the soldier right on his heels. Aculeo turned back and ran down the alley out to the street. He pushed his way through the crowds again, trying to see where Apollonios had come out from the alley.

We can't have lost him! So many people, how in Pluto's name are we going to … ah, there. Apollonios was walking slowly along the street, head down, trying to blend into the crowd. Aculeo pushed through the pedestrians, trying to get closer. He was approaching the Agora now. The recluse glanced back over his shoulder just then, saw his pursuer drawing nearer, and ran.

The man was like a silverfish the way he slipped through the crowds, never missing a step. "Hoi, stop him!" Aculeo cried in vain. Apollonios veered to the right suddenly. He's heading to the canal – he crosses that and he's into Rhakotis, a cursed maze – we'll never find him there! Aculeo sprinted after him, heart pounding, lungs burning. The recluse slipped down onto the dry mud bank and plunged feet first into the canal, wading across, the water up to his chest in a hurry, his filthy chiton billowing out behind him. Aculeo stood back on the bank, ready to plunge in after him, when he saw Capito and the soldier appear on the other side of the canal. They must have crossed at the bridge down the way, he thought, then he jumped into the water, bellowing at the top of his lungs to drive Apollonios forward.

They seized the recluse as he climbed dripping onto the opposite bank. He roared in fury as they held him down, wept in despair as they bound him hand and foot. "What do you want with me?" he cried. "What did I do? Sarapis, Benefactor of all that is good, protect me! Get your hands off me!"

"Just gag him while you're at it," Aculeo gasped, collapsing in exhaustion on the bank of the canal.

CHAPTER XVI

The stairway leading down to the underground cells was rank with the stench of human waste and death. They could hear rats scrabbling about in the darkness, startled by the sudden influx of torchlight. The prisoners cried out in a dozen different languages, begging for food, water, freedom as Aculeo and Capito passed their cells.

Apollonios' cell was in a distant corner of the complex. The man lay curled up in a pile of fetid straw on a mud-brick platform, his breathing harsh, laboured. The guard opened the cell door. Aculeo held up his sputtering torch, stinking of sulphur and pitch.

Capito sent the guard away. "Get up," he growled. Apollonios didn't stir. Capito grabbed him by his dirty hair and dragged him onto the cold stone floor. The recluse cried out in pain as he looked up blearily at the two men. In the dim, sickly light of the cell, they could see his jaw was swollen, likely broken, his upper lip split and caked in blood. It seemed the guards had had some sport with him.

Apollonios touched his mouth with a trembling hand. "Hail Sarapis, who weighs the lives of men, know that your sacred place in my heart ..." he whispered, barely audible. He began coughing, then resumed his fervent, mumbling rant.

"Your brother told us you fought at Teutoburg," Aculeo said. "Decorated by Caesar himself – is that right?" Apollonios made no reply but stopped his wretched mumbling at least. "They say the waters there were still dark with blood a year after the battle was done. How could a man like you have survived?"

"Hail ... Zeus-Soter, God of All Men," the recluse stammered, "may you protect these men who know not your love, may you teach them."

"So the Gods saved you?" Capito asked.

"I serve only Sarapis, ruler over all that is good and light, may others learn to worship you as I so humbly do and offer you your rightful tributes throughout eternity." Apollonios blinked and looked up, as though noticing the two men for the first time. "Who are you?"

"Don't you remember me, recluse?"

A light of recognition filled the prisoner's bruised eyes. "Hail to Hades, Lord of Shadows, may you curse this lover of his own mother!" he snarled and spat a thick wad of phlegm on the floor.

"He seems to remember you well enough," Aculeo said.

"And do you still remember the porne you attacked last year before you fled the city?" Capito asked.

"Let him drink of the waters of the white cypress of Lethe so he loses his mind in the eternal fire of your foul and hideous realm!" Apollonios muttered, turning to face the wall.

"We know what happened at the Sarapeion," Aculeo said. "You murdered a slave there."

"A cursed lie!" the recluse cried. "Hail Sarapis, who weighs the lives of men, know this wretched man before me is unworthy of your sacred love. May you strike him down with your beneficent fire and bring him to his knees, even as you cast this loathsome city into the sea!"

"A witness saw you attack that slave. You murdered her, covered her with your cloak."

"She … she was already dying," Apollonios said, his fury abated, muttering feverishly under his breath. "Already dead. Hail Sarapis!"

"Enough with your cursed Sarapis!"

"So pretty, such a pretty thing," Apollonios whispered to himself. "She'd like it, wouldn't she?"

Aculeo felt a chill run down his back. "What would she like? What would the pretty girl like?"

"Hold me," the recluse said softly. "Please."

"You murdered her then and there. And Myrrhine, whose throat you cut before you dumped her body in the canal. And what of Neaera?"

"I need to get out of here," Apollonios said, covering his ears, rocking back and forth in his mud-brick bed. "Please, Sarapis, save me!"

"We know you murdered those women, damn you!" Aculeo snarled, grabbing the man by his soiled chiton. "Why did Gurculio want them dead?"

"What are you talking about?" Capito hissed under his breath. Aculeo ignored him.

The recluse covered his ears and curled up on the floor, hugging his knees to his chest like a frightened child. "Please, I couldn't. He would never kill."

"Come on, Apollonios," Aculeo said. "You must have killed a hundred men to survive Teutoburg. What's a few girls to that?"

"Why am I cursed with this miserable existence, O Great One?"

"Tell me about Gurculio, damn you, or I swear I'll beat you to death here and now!"

Apollonios turned and grabbed Aculeo by the wrist with surprising strength. "Take my life then, Roman! Take it! Take it! Take it! Take it!"

"Unhand me!"

Capito moved in to separate them.

The recluse suddenly released Aculeo and dropped to his knees on the stone floor, raising his wasted arms to the shadows overhead, the yellow cord bracelet slipping to halfway down his filthy forearm. "O Great One, have I not stood on every street corner of this wretched city, spreading the word of your divine purpose, invoking your sacred will? Have I not dedicated my very life to you?"

"Let's get out of here," Capito said. "We could have a clearer conversation with the rats that nest in his bedding."

"Fine," Aculeo said, rubbing his now aching wrist, his heart pounding. Capito called for the guard to let them out again.

"Hail Sarapis, hail Isis, hail Harpocrates, your divine child," Apollonios whispered in a feverish rush. "Please, please, please, won't someone save me from this wretched vision?"

The walls of the tavern glowed with the soft yellow lamplight, shadows shifting across a mural of a priapic Pan and a group of nymphs dancing deep within a bucolic forest. The sound of slurred song and mindless laughter from the other patrons floated about as slaves carried forth jugs of wine and platters of food.

"The Library must be closed for the night," Capito sniffed, glancing about the place, "all the great sophists have gathered here instead."

"I felt like strangling the man," Aculeo said.

"It's your own damned fault. Everyone knows you should avoid the gaze of a murderer, lest you become infected with a murderous rage yourself."

Aculeo said nothing, gazing deep into his krater of cheap palm wine, swirling the debris about. Capito reached across and gave him a clap on the shoulder. "Come on, Aculeo. Let's celebrate. We caught the murderer today."

"You believe Apollonios murdered them, don't you?" Aculeo asked.

"Eh? Yes, of course he did, of course."

"Myrrhine? The river slave? Neaera perhaps?"

"Yes, and who knows how many others?" Capito gave him a puzzled look. "What game are you playing at, Aculeo? You yourself convinced me of it."

"I know it."

"So what were you going on about, asking him about the moneylender?"

"Something doesn't fit," Aculeo said and went to refill his cup from the small amphora.

Capito snatched his cup away, sloshing wine on the table. He was smiling still, but his eyes were steely. "Are you going to tell me what this is all about or not?"

"Let go of my wine," Aculeo said, meeting the other man's gaze.

Capito put the cup down. "Why did you ask the recluse about Gurculio? What were you fishing for exactly?"

"I'm not sure myself. It's a tough thing to fish when your net's as tangled as this one."

"When we found the murdered hetaira by the canal, you said you'd seen her at Ralla's symposium. You saw Gurculio there too, if I recall correctly. You think the two of them are connected to these murders as well?"

Aculeo held his tongue. The Magistrate drummed his fingers on the tabletop, his mouth tightened into a narrow slit. Aculeo looked away. Part of him wanted to reveal what he knew to his friend, but the rest of him held back. *What do I know, exactly? One hetaira is missing, while another is murdered along with some random river slave. And their murders are connected somehow by a length of yellow thread. And I'm still no closer to finding who murdered Iovinus and stole my fortune than I was before.*

"It's just foolishness," he said at last, forcing a smile.

"I'm invited to a symposium at Ralla's villa tomorrow evening, so if you're truly expecting him to start murdering his guests I'd like to know beforehand so I don't get my best tunic soiled."

"It was nothing. It was the recluse that murdered these women. End of story."

"Doubt can nag at you like an old woman, eating away at the edges of any brief joy a man may feel," Capito said. "Just let the murder court do its job now. The Archipegaron will try Apollonios, convict him and execute him. As for us, we'll be done with it. Ah! I must be getting drunk. This fellahin piss is actually starting to taste good. Come on, let's find some decent wine and women to match so we can forget about this scabrous world at least 'til morning."

"Not tonight."

"You're certain?"

"Quite."

"Fine, sit and muse amongst your fellow sophists then. Good night. And try to find yourself a little pleasure, will you." With that Capito stood a little unsteadily, braced himself, then walked out the door and into the street.

The evening breeze had picked up outside, whistling through the unmortared bricks of the kapeleion walls, rattling the door in its frame, the dry palm fronds that made up the roof rustling restlessly overhead.

Aculeo's thoughts returned to the missing merchant Posidippus of Cos. What happened to him, I wonder. And what's the moneylender's interest in him? A thousand sesterces' worth. With a merchant, there's always money to guide you, as surely as the river leads to the sea. And at the head of this river – the moneylender Shimon-Petrus, who'd loaned the Cosian a small fortune, none of it repaid according to the documents. Was it possible Shimon-Petrus was somehow involved in Posidippus' disappearance? And perhaps Iovinus' murder too? It was difficult to conceive of – the man had always seemed quite honourable in any encounters they'd had. Still, being owed vast sums of money could adversely affect a person's view of the world, as he himself well knew. Could he be connected to the rest of this somehow? If nothing else perhaps he can shed a little light.

Aculeo threw back his wine, his eyes watering as the harsh liquid seared his throat, and headed into the early evening streets towards the Agora.

Shimon-Petrus ran his enterprise from one of the high end shops along the Painted Stoa in an immaculate part of the Agora. The shops there were graceful and fashioned of heavy blocks of lime and marble instead of the mud brick used in poorer sections of town. A wind had picked up, sweeping in from the darkening sea, clattering the leaves of the date palms and sweet acacias that grew like weeds in tight groves along the Canopic Way. The early evening sky had turned a pale orangey-pink, like the inside lip of a seashell, ready to wink out on the horizon to the west, a warm fresh breeze blowing in from the harbour.

Shimon-Petrus was a negotiatore, not a moneylender of Gurculio's sort but an investor in legitimate businesses, working on his own behalf and that of wealthy backers. He'd been an associate of Corvinus' for many years, even partnered with him on occasional mutual opportunities. While Aculeo knew the man socially, he'd dealt with him directly only once. As they'd sought out bridge investors for the second fleet, Aculeo himself had approached Shimon-Petrus. The old man had listened but politely declined the opportunity, stating the deal was just too risky for his comfort. He'd also strongly encouraged Aculeo to reconsider his support of the deal for the same reason, but hubris had prevailed. And if I'd listened to the man, what then? My life would have continued along quite a different course.

Shimon-Petrus' shop, it turned out, was closed for the evening. A neighbouring shop owner informed him it was the Jewish Sabbath and that the old man had already headed off to temple to worship. To Delta then, Aculeo thought.

The columns outside the Great Synagogue in Delta had been lit with oil lamps, making the entire area almost as bright as day. While there were numerous Jewish temples scattered about the city, Israel's Glory was something else entirely. An enormous, oblong building of pale limestone quarried from distant lands, it rested within an exquisite double colonnade as a golden yolk lays within an egg's shell. Broad marble steps led up from a garden to a pair of great bronze doors, a gold-gilded Star of David gleaming above the entrance, facing Jerusalem far to the east. The granite plaques on the walls next to the doors proclaimed that Augustus Caesar himself had been a patron of the temple, along with his wife Livia and eventually his successor, Tiberius Caesar. The worshippers slowly filed up the steps into the temple to join their brethren, the mournful sound of a gong echoing through the streets, summoning them to worship.

Aculeo covered his head and stepped inside with the other worshippers, the soot-stained walls dimly lit with torches. The interior of the temple was a vast hall, which quickly filled with worshippers, each standing amongst their own, goldsmiths with goldsmiths, bankers with bankers, blacksmiths with blacksmiths. Along the collonaded sides of the huge central hall, men often continued to conduct business and socialize during service.

In the centre of the temple sat seventy-one golden chairs arranged in a ring within which were seated the elders with their oiled white beards, fine tunics and himations. One of them, an elegant looking man with a neatly trimmed white beard, was Shimon-Petrus. A Jewish priest climbed atop a wooden platform in the centre of the ring and called the worshippers to prayer. The temple was so vast that as he read from the book of prayers a second priest would wave a red flag so the worshippers in the most distant sections would know when to answer for each blessing.

Aculeo listened to the worship, his head bowed, his eyes closed, hypnotic threads of solemn prayer and cries of Amen rising up through the windows cut near the temple ceiling, spilling against the darkening sky.

When at last the worship ended, Aculeo followed Shimon-Petrus and a small group of men out into the street as they chatted good naturedly with one another. He approached him with a friendly wave.

"Shimon-Petrus?" Aculeo said. "My apologies for the interruption."

The man looked up, his pale brown eyes clouded with cataracts, squinted at him then gave a puzzled smile. "Tarquitius Aculeo. Well, well, such a pleasant surprise."

"Kind of you to remember me, sir. I was hoping to speak with you about something."

A young man looked warily at Aculeo and took Shimon-Petrus by the elbow. "This is my son, Eli. We need to get home for our dinner. Come, Aculeo, we can talk as we walk. You've been well I trust?"

"Well enough," Aculeo said as they headed down the well-lit street. "I would have fared better had I listened to you about my last investment."

"You had a bad turn, I know." Shimon-Petrus placed a hand on his shoulder. "I was sad to learn of the deaths of Corvinus and his lovely wife. A terrible loss. I considered them dear friends."

"Corvinus was like a father to me. This is an unrelated matter though. At least, I think it is. I understand you had business dealings with Posidippus of Cos."

"Yes?" the old man said, puzzled.

"He's disappeared."

Shimon-Petrus paused for a moment, his smile slipped off his face. "Is this true?"

"Quite true."

The man looked shaken. He shook his head and tapped his son's arm. "Let's keep walking, Eli. Ah, this is not good news. Not good at all. Any idea where he might be?"

"No. By the looks of his warehouse, he left quite quickly, either on his own or against his will. I understand he owed you quite a bit of money."

"He did indeed. But how did you know that?"

"He left some documents behind."

"And so you're wondering if I might be involved somehow in Posidippus' disappearance?"

Aculeo glanced at the elderly man walking beside him at his son's arm, frail, gentle, his vision failing. Any suspicion he might have had suddenly dissipated like smoke, leaving him with nothing. "Nothing like that. I'm simply trying to find him. I was hoping with your connections you may have heard something."

"I've heard nothing at all I'm afraid. Posidippus did indeed owe me money. I let it carry on too long. I should have been more careful, but he'd always been a fair man to deal with, a little rough about the edges perhaps but a shrewd businessman." Shimon-Petrus paused, deep in thought. "He missed a repayment of his loan five months back and came to me for further investment. A bottomry loan. I declined until he could give me a better sense I'd ever be repaid. Posidippus is not an easy man to say no to, but I had little choice. He got quite angry but he finally went elsewhere."

"Do you know where?"

"I had heard he received funding from the Concessionary Bank of Arsinoe the Consummator."

It wasn't unusual, of course, Aculeo thought. Unlike the Imperial banks, which were dedicated solely to the always thriving business of tax collection, the Empire licensed out a small number of concessionary banks responsible for greasing the other parts of the machine required for a successful marketplace, including bottomry loans to ship-owners, loans against land holdings and tax farming. The Bank of Arsinoe the Consummator was one of the largest of these. "Do you know who at the bank he might have dealt with?"

"Ah, well, a loan in the amount he was looking for, twenty thousand sesterces if I recall correctly, he would have had to deal with the principle owner directly. Ralla, that is."

Aculeo stared at the other man. "Albius Ralla?" he said, trying to hide his shock.

"Yes. I'm not sure whether or not the venture was even successful, although Posidippus has yet to settle his debt to me. I have doubts now he ever will."

They had arrived at the gatehouse of a lovely home in Delta, the rich smell of broiling fish wafting through the air. "We should go in now, Father," Eli said. "You should eat."

"I'll come in a moment, you go ahead."

"But Father ..."

"Do as I say." Shimon-Petrus smiled as the young man turned and entered the gates of the home. "He worries about me too much."

"He's a good son who honours his father," Aculeo said. "Do you know Ralla well?"

"Well enough," the old man said.

"Do you think he could be involved in the Cosian's disappearance?"

Shimon-Petrus looked directly at Aculeo with his milky eyes and reached his hand out to touch his arm. "You should take more care with your words when it comes to men like Ralla, my friend. Wealth and influence are everything in Alexandria, and he has a great deal of both."

"I'm merely asking questions," Aculeo said.

"Well, I doubt a man of Ralla's stature could be involved in such a sordid thing. And even if he were ..." The old man shook his head in dismay.

"Did you ever have any dealings with Iovinus?"

"Your negotiatore? Of course, on several occasions. Why do you ask?"

"Did he ever approach you directly seeking investment? Since Corvinus' death I mean."

Shimon-Petrus gave him a look of genuine surprise. "Did he not drown when your fleet sank?"

"That's what we all believed, until he returned to Alexandria a week or so ago and was found murdered."

"Oh?" The old man's cheeks turned pale. "That is most troubling news. Are these things connected?"

"I don't know. I think they must be somehow, but ..."

"Father," called a voice. Eli stood in the entranceway of their home, his jaw clenched as he glared at Aculeo.

"My family is expecting me," Shimon-Petrus said. "Please, join us for dinner."

"Thank you, but no. I appreciate your counsel."

Shimon-Petrus patted his arm. "Troubling times. I wish you good fortune. But a word of advice from an old man. Take care with the questions you ask. Some words can turn to poison before they even leave your mouth."

CHAPTER XVII

THE 27TH DAY OF APRILIS

The sun was beginning to set over the western harbour, the ships bobbing in the golden waters, the Lighthouse towering above, its fiery eye gleaming like a second sun in the sky. Capito was dressed in a splendid tunic of a coppery sheen and a splendid ivory toga that Aculeo could only envy, for his own tunic, albeit his best one, was fraying at the edges while his toga had been repaired three times already – and Xanthias' fingers were not as nimble as they had once been. The prospect of standing out like a country peasant at Ralla's symposium was disconcerting to say the least.

"Aculeo," Capito said, greeting him with the slightest of nods.

"I'm pleased you were able to extend an invitation, Magistrate. You have my gratitude."

"Keep it. I've enormous doubt about the wisdom of my assent, given your obsessions about this evening's host."

"Can a man not simply seek a night of socializing?"

The Magistrate rolled his eyes towards the heavens. "It's bad enough for you to strain the limits of what influence I might have without you treating me like a pot-headed fool. Tell me what you suspect at least or I'll leave you on your own to explain your attendance to Ralla."

Aculeo hesitated at first. He'd been as vague as he could in his note to Capito about why he wanted to accompany him to the symposium that evening but clearly the man's patience had run out. And so as they made their way along the still busy Canopic Way past the crossroads at the Street of the Soma, the palm trees rustling in the evening breeze that swept along the broad and picturesque colonnade, Aculeo revealed what little he knew and what more he suspected. The evening air smelled of the Egyptian Sea, an evocative mix of brine and sweet acacia.

When he was done, he felt a knot of doubt twist in the pit of his stomach. Capito kept his silence.

"Those tablets Iovinus had," Capito said at last. "Any idea what might be on them?"

"No. Something important though – enough to draw him out of hiding. And get him murdered. Do you think me deranged then?"

"Worse," Capito sighed. "I fear you might be right. Which makes my bringing you here tonight an even stupider idea than it seemed before."

"I'm not about to confront the man in his own home."

"See that you don't, or may Jupiter squeeze himself between your hairy cheeks."

They followed the winding street into Lagos, the exclusive deme where Ralla lived. It offered a fine view, the Lighthouse on Pharos, the Brucheion palaces and the neat, glistening gridwork of seemingly endless white-washed buildings that stretched toward the sea, awash in the orange-red glow of a dying sunset.

They came at last to Ralla's villa. The high garden walls were lit with glowing lanterns covered with pink, green and blue cloth. The evening air was laced with the smell of roasting lamb and strains of lyre music, pounding drums, jangling cymbals, singing and laughter. The pathway beyond the gatehouse circuited the front garden, leading towards a wide entrance hall bordered by tall columns of white and grey-veined Himmatean marble. They could hear the whisper of laughter from deep within the garden, the shadows of people moving along the many tributary pathways that branched away from the main path.

Lucius Albius Ralla, dressed in an exquisite black tunic and silver-bordered toga, greeted his guests as they arrived, his face already flushed with drink. "Magistrate Capito," he said, "you do me honour, sir."

"Such a gracious invitation, Ralla, it is my sincere pleasure," Capito said, embracing the other man, kissing his cheek. Could he truly be behind it all then? Aculeo wondered. Ralla looked an ordinary enough man, almost frail with his pale, slender limbs, rounded belly and watery brown eyes. Could he have ordered Iovinus' murder? And what of Myrrhine? Or Neaera?

"You know Tarquitius Aculeo I trust," Capito continued. "I hope you don't mind me extending the invitation to him."

The banker's eyes flashed towards Aculeo, measuring the man. "Of course," Ralla said. "Aculeo, a pleasant surprise to see you again."

"The pleasure's mine," Aculeo said with a forced smile. "I'm looking forward to a splendid evening."

"And I hope to surpass your expectations. Please make your way inside. Ah, Vestorius, you do me honour sir," Ralla said, moving away to greet another guest.

Capito and Aculeo walked down the elaborate fauces towards a set of broad marble steps leading up into the triclinium. "Satisfied?" Aculeo asked.

"The evening's only just begun."

A pair of pretty young girls approached them bearing garlands of myrtle entwined with white narcissus. They were dressed as traditional Egyptian dancing girls, with translucent linen kilts, their pubescent breasts barely covered with elaborate necklaces, their eyes painted with kohl, and plaited black wigs atop their heads, crowned with fragrant perfume cones. They draped the sweet-smelling garlands around the men's necks. A third girl, lovely with dark skin and almond-shaped eyes, anointed the two guests with perfumed oil, touching a drop of it on their foreheads while a fourth girl washed their feet with scented water.

The triclinium was a spacious room with a dozen finely crafted couches placed in a squared-off circle around the perimeter on a low platform, with a swill-channel running down the middle. The room, lit with coloured lanterns and a smoking hearth fire, had a compluvium cut into the high ceiling where the smoke spiralled up to escape into the starry sky. The decorations were outrageously gaudy, the walls covered in garish murals of what appeared to be the heroic exploits of Aeneas and his men. Many of the couches were already occupied by other guests. Aculeo spotted a pair of familiar faces – the sophists Zeanthes and Epiphaneus.

Zeanthes smiled warmly. "Aculeo, my dear friend," the sophist said. "What a delightful surprise to see you again. Come join us."

Aculeo and Capito settled on a pair of empty couches next to the sophist. "I must admit, Ralla's symposia are always among the finest in Alexandria. Still, you'll both be a breath of fresh air amongst all the stuffy types that usually attend this sort of thing. Such as Epiphaneus and myself."

The other sophist sniffed in annoyance. He looked relatively well-groomed and sober compared to the last time Aculeo had seen him. The haunting sound of aulos, the double-reeded flutes, filled the air, played with admirable skill by pretty young girls who wandered between the couches. A few handsome youths wandered through the room as well, playing their lyres. In front of each couch were small wooden tables filled with platters of food – figs, cold roasted swan, broiled eel and great reed baskets of bread.

Two young men entered the andron. Aculeo recognized them from outside the gates of Ralla's symposium – a plump, moon-faced boy dressed in an expensive looking pale blue tunic and a thick rope of gold chain about his neck, and a small, rodent-like man who seemed to laugh uproariously at everything the portly one said. They were much younger than the other guests, in their early twenties at most. The moon-faced boy gazed at Aculeo, then turned away, bored.

"Who are they?" Aculeo asked.

"The little one is Asinius Camillus, I believe," Capito said. "The other is Avilius Balbus."

"Avilius? As in the Prefect Avilius Flaccus?"

"His son, yes."

The youth Camillus grabbed a passing flute girl by the wrist and pulled her close, interrupting her play. The girl looked frightened, uncertain what to do. Flaccus the younger brayed in laughter as the other guests did their best to ignore the situation and carry forth with their conversations.

Gurculio arrived then, along with his retinue of Viator and Vibius. The moneylender, dressed in a garish yellow tunic and scarlet-edged toga, scanned the triclinium, widening his eyes slightly when he spotted Aculeo, then took an empty couch near Capito.

"Let us offer a libation for the health of the Emperor Tiberius, may he bestow honour and pleasure on our evening together," Ralla proclaimed, his voice grating as stones clattering on a clay-tile roof as a slave brought forth an amphora and set it in the centre of the mensa. Ralla poured some of the unmixed heavy black wine into a cup, drank from it then passed the cup to one of the flute girls, who brought it to each of the guests in turn.

Aculeo tasted it, thick and sweet, and passed the cup back to the girl. She was quite pretty and wore a peplos of a silvery gauze, revealing the shadows of her young breasts and the slenderness of her waist beneath. She glanced at him in recognition, then bowed her head. Tyche, he realized – her lip still swollen, her cheek still discoloured beneath her makeup. And there was Panthea standing at the edge of the triclinium, watching. Her harelipped slave stood a few steps away from her. He briefly caught Aculeo's eye, then looked away.

After the food was done, slaves moved in to take away the tables and sweep the floor of bones, shells and discarded fruit. They brought forth large bowls of warm, fragrant water and fine cotton towels for the guests to wash their faces and hands. Ralla then signalled one of his slaves and a large amphora was carried out to the middle of the chamber.

"A fine fragrant wine of Lesbos," Ralla announced, "aged in my cellars for many seasons, in honour of our honoured guest, the esteemed sophist Zeanthes of Araethyrea."

"Also aged for many seasons," a young poet named Hipparchus said to much laughter. The poet's face was painted with white lead, his lips and cheeks rouged like a woman's.

"Make sure you mix it well this time, if you will," grumbled Epiphaneus. "It was far too thick last time, gave me a raging headache for days."

"Much like Hipparchus," Zeanthes rejoined.

Aculeo watched Ralla carefully as the man settled onto the central couch. A slave girl poured the amphora into a deep ceramic krater, then added a measure of water, swirling the mixture around before pouring it into a jug. Tyche carried the jug around the circle, pouring wine into each man's cup. The other girl continued to mix kraters of wine until there were five in all.

"Five kraters, Ralla?" one of the guests howled in surprise. "Are you trying to kill us all?" Ralla laughed, waving off the man's complaint as he downed his first cup and held it out for more.

The first of a dizzying number of delicacies to be brought forth that evening, a gold platter of pheasants stuffed with sugared grapes and olives, accompanied by a silver platter of peppercakes and beestings pudding, made from the milk of new mother cows. The slaves brought the platters to each diner's small tables in turn, then went back to ready the next course.

"Did anyone attend this morning's lecture by that Skeptic fellow, Varialus?" Epiphaneus asked.

"The fellow with a big mole on his chin?" Hipparchus said with a frown. "I thought he was Neo-Platonic."

"No, definitely Skeptic. And he's from Crete of all places."

"Now that's a hideous place, bad wine, lots of flies and no culture at all."

"How in the world could Skepticism have become so popular of late, and fools like Varialus be received with such acclaim?" Epiphaneus grumbled.

"Ah, there you go," Hipparchus said archly. "Always wondering when you'll be cast out of the Museion like nightsoil from an overflowing chamber pot."

"If I am, so be it. At worst I shall have to return to teaching some backwards merchant's squawling little brats in Phaleron or some such blightful place. There as here I'll serve no master except my own ideas. The rest of you can rot in Tartarus for all I care."

"And what is it that you … do?" Hipparchus asked Aculeo.

"Grain export."

"Truly?" the sophist said with a melodramatic shudder.

"Oh? And how is it any lesser than what you do? Instead of grain, you sell your words and ideas. Few men die from an empty head. An empty belly is another matter."

"Some do quite well with empty heads in fact," Epiphaneus muttered.

"Another cup of wine for my friend Aculeo," Zeanthes laughed. "A speaker of truth, thus a rare and curious man indeed."

"What truth is there in discounting the philosopher's worth?" Hipparchus asked. "Did Plato himself not proclaim that man has progressed through the five stages of evolution, and at its zenith is the philosopher, who pursues wisdom in and of itself?"

"And so, according to you, mankind's zenith consists of buying expensive clothes and dallying about the baths with pretty young men?" said Epiphaneus.

"Of course, what else? If I'd wanted to experience boredom and ugly fashion I'd have stayed in Cyrene."

"Then maybe the rest of us could have experienced a pleasant evening for once."

The slaves returned with the next course, a great filagreed cage constructed entirely of honeyed sweets and packed with live songbirds. The diners all applauded as the slaves broke open the cage, setting the birds loose to fly about the triclinium then out into the night, filling the air with their song.

"Ah, here she is," Zeanthes said. Aculeo glanced up toward the doorway and felt his breath catch – it was Calisto, her delicate red and gold peplos clinging to her slender body, her face lit with the soft light of the coloured lanterns. She seemed transformed by the context of night into an exotic and beautiful creature. I'm a fool – I never even thought she might be attending as well.

"Calisto!" Ralla called, clambering off his couch and almost falling on his face as he tottered towards her. He took her hand to kiss it. Calisto quickly scanned around the room, a smile dancing on her lips. Her smile faltered when she saw Aculeo, then she looked away. Ralla had turned his attentions to a passing flute girl, pulling her towards his couch to openly grope her amidst the derisive laughter of Balbus and Camillus. Calisto passed by without a word, engaging instead with the other guests.

"She does look lovely, doesn't she?" Zeanthes said.

"A vision," Capito agreed.

"Her skin is a bit dark," Hipparchus sniffed. "Is it only her tonight then?"

"Looks like."

"Myrrhine was murdered four nights ago," Epiphaneus blurted, his eyes puffy and sodden with drink.

"Is that true?" Hipparchus said in shock, his fey affectations forgotten for the moment. "What happened?"

"Her throat was slit and her body dumped in the Canopic Canal," Capito said.

"How absolutely ghastly," the sophist said, his face drained of colour. "We saw her just days ago, didn't we?"

"She was murdered that very night," Aculeo said, glancing towards the banker again. Capito gave a warning clearing of his throat. Aculeo ignored him. Ralla's eyes were already pink-rimmed and glassy. The flute girl had managed to slip from his clutches somehow and he had turned his attention to filling his belly instead.

"Why would anyone do such a thing?"

"And poor Neaera is missing as well," Zeanthes said. "She hasn't been seen in over a week."

"Neaera too? We'll pray to the gods she's alright," Hipparchus said.

"Is there any idea who may have murdered Myrrhine?" Zeanthes asked.

"We arrested a lunatic named Apollonios just yesterday," Capito said.

"Well then," Hipparchus said, then raised his cup in a toast. "Health and prosperity to you and your offices then, for clearing madmen off the streets. Perhaps you could turn your attention to the Museion next."

Aculeo watched Calisto out of the corner of his eye as she moved about the room, greeting others with a warm smile, an embrace and a kiss.

"Must one be mad to commit murder?" Epiphaneus asked.

"It depends on the circumstances," said Zeanthes. "A soldier in a battlefield kills to achieve a military goal."

"Also to guard his own life, and the lives of his comrades," Capito said.

"Spoken like a soldier, not a general," Hipparchus laughed.

"A man may also kill to steal another's property for himself," said Aculeo.

"Out of greed, yes, but to kill for lust?" Epiphaneus asked. "To put one's life and liberty in jeopardy for the sake of a moment's passion? Surely that is madness."

Calisto at last made her way to their section of the triclinium. "My dear, you look breathtaking," Zeanthes said. "Feeling better than the other day I trust?"

"Much better, thank you," Calisto said, lowering her eyes. She wore a garland of violets and lotus and stood a mere hair's breadth from Aculeo, such that he could feel the heat from her body, her smell intoxicating.

Hipparchus smiled at her, then looked to the skylight where the moon had just disappeared behind a cloud. "You see, even Diana hides her face when Calisto appears, so envious is she of her charms."

"Now who's been drinking too much?" Epiphaneus muttered.

Ralla clapped his hands and the slaves brought forward another krater of wine (the second or third? Aculeo couldn't recall) while the flute girls played their aulos even louder, switching from soft, subtle melodies to a mad buzzing sound like a hive of angry hornets. Two lovely young women in diaphanous chitons came dancing and spinning into the centre of the room, moving to the music, their hair flying in their faces as they spun about, taking one anothers' hands as they came together, pressing their bodies against one another, their backs arching, then pushing away again.

Balbus and Camillus were clapping with the other guests as the girls danced, cheering as the girls suddenly paused to kiss one another on the lips then pushed away again. Slaves appeared carrying more platters of food. Aculeo watched as Hipparchus took a pomegranate from a passing slave.

"You appear deep in thought," Zeanthes said.

"I just remembered something," Aculeo said.

"Oh? What is it?"

"Yes, tell us," Hipparchus said as he bit into the fruit, the bright red juice running down his chin.

"Pomegranate seeds were found in Myrrhine's mouth when her body was pulled from the canal."

Hipparchus spat the seeds out on the floor in disgust. "Now you tell me?"

"I think it fascinating," Zeanthes said.

"You would," Hipparchus muttered as he flushed his mouth out with wine, spitting it on the floor. "What's this evening's conversation degrading into? Dead hetairai and pomegranates."

"The pomegranate has a special place in the lives of our most ancient Gods, since the time of Arcadia," Zeanthes said. "Perhaps even before that." He asked a slave to pass him one of the fruits and delicately tore open its thin waxy peel. He pressed the tip of his thumb into the fruit and scarlet juice dripped down his hands and arms. "The colour of blood, you see, and a symbol of death."

"Why did you have to get him started?" Hipparchus sighed.

"Demeter, goddess of the cornfields, had a daughter, Persephone, by her brother Zeus," Zeanthes began, settling back on his couch. "The young girl was gathering flowers with her friends in a meadow in Eleusis one day when she was spotted by Hades, who fell in love with her and stole her away to his kingdom in Tartarus. Demeter was grief-stricken, of course. She didn't know what had happened, only that her beloved daughter was missing. She searched across the world for nine days and nights for the girl, but to no avail. Finally, on the tenth day she met with a young swineherd who told her of an extraordinary occurrence. He had been in the fields of his father's land, feeding his animals, when there was a loud crack and the earth split open, swallowing his entire herd all at once. Even as he cried out in surprise, there was a pounding of hooves and a great black chariot appeared, drawn by four black horses. The chariots driver's face was a visage of fire, and in his arm he held a screaming girl. The chariot thundered along the land before finally disappearing into the chasm, which then closed behind them.

"Demeter was enraged, knowing at once that it was Hades who'd stolen her daughter. She demanded that Zeus help her get their daughter back, but he refused to go against his brother. This enraged Demeter even further, and while she has no dominion over the underworld, she has great power over ours. She cursed the earth, refusing to allow trees to bear fruit or crops to grow, and the race of man suffered and starved. Fearing that humankind would die out and there would then be nobody to make sacrifices to the gods, Zeus finally interceded and forced Hades to return Persephone to Demeter. On one condition. That she had not tasted the food of the dead while living in the underworld. She kept this promise until the very morning she was to return, when Hades tricked her into picking a pomegranate from his orchard and tasting six seeds.

"Thus she was condemned to return to Hades for six months of each year, one month for each seed. This always made Demeter grieve, and she would again cause all the plants in the world to die, only to be reborn again in springtime, with the return of Persephone to her mother's arms. The pomegranate seeds, then, are her taste of death. And as she tastes it, so do we all."

"So you propose now that Hades killed these women?" Hipparchus scoffed. "There's little chance of stopping him then."

"I would offer a libation to my dear guests," Ralla cried out drunkenly. "A good Roman wine, in Caesar's honour."

"I didn't know there was such a thing," Epiphaneus muttered.

"What, good Roman wine?" Hipparchus said.

"Yes, that, or Caesar's honour. It's like a Thracian virgin or a literate Gaul, the two terms are impossible to reconcile."

Hipparchus' eyes narrowed. "I'd watch your tongue if I were you, old man," he said softly. "The wine's stolen your senses."

"I don't need wine to speak the truth," Epiphaneus sniffed. Zeanthes climbed off the couch and stretched. The other sophist looked at him in surprise. "Leaving already?"

"I'm afraid so. A bite of food, a taste of wine, and a little talk with good friends and I'm done for the evening. What about you, Aculeo?"

"I think Capito and I will stay a little longer."

The Magistrate muttered incomprehensibly, his attention on the dancers.

"Of course, that's the way it's done," Hipparchus clapped. "See the night out. You could learn from this fellow, Zeanthes."

The elder sophist smiled. "I've no doubt I could. Have a wonderful evening, dear friends." He gave a small bow before going to pay his respects to their half-comatose host.

Calisto was standing still as a statue as she watched Ralla grab Tyche roughly around the waist, pulling her onto his couch. Aculeo noticed the scar that ran along Calisto's jawline had turned stark white against her olive skin. The banker kissed the back of the girl's neck, then shoved his hand beneath her chiton to molest her right there for all to see. Tyche's eyes met Aculeo's for the briefest of moments, a desperate, pleading expression haunting her face. Aculeo started to rise from his couch, ready to intervene. But Calisto was already moving towards the banker.

"Ralla, what do you think of the wine?" Calisto asked as she approached the man's couch, reaching for his cup.

"What?" Ralla asked in sluggish annoyance.

"It's too young, I think. Come, we'll find you a more suitable vintage." Aculeo smiled in admiration as Calisto graciously took the banker by the arm and helped him to stand, allowing Tyche to slip away. Ralla weaved on his feet as he was led from the andron, pausing only to vomit on the marble floor. A slave scurried forward to clean up the mess, mopping it into the swill channel that ran down the centre of the room.

"She treats him far better than he deserves," Hipparchus said.

"But no better than he pays for," Epiphaneus said. "Ah well, good to see Myrrhine's death hasn't rent his heart too deeply."

D.L. Johnstone

"Why would Myrrhine's death affect him?" Aculeo asked.

Hipparchus looked at him, eyebrows raised in amusement. "Ralla was Myrrhine's patron as well. Every fine stitch on her hired back, every jewel around her pretty neck, even the roof over her head, all of it paid for by Lucius Albius Ralla."

Aculeo's mind reeled. He turned away, trying to think, the wine doing little to clear his head. Ralla was patron to Calisto, Neaera, and now Myrrhine as well? And what of Posidippus who owed the banker fifteen thousand sesterces, went bankrupt then disappeared? Capito was staring at him, jaw clenched tight. Clearly he'd overheard. Say nothing, he mouthed, and turned back ostensibly to watch the dancers.

Slaves brought out fresh wine – it tasted different than the previous sort, infused with cinnamon and sweetened with honey, all masking a bitter undertaste. The music grew harsher as a handsome lyre boy entered the central area. He wore a satyr's costume, with a wooden phallus strapped about his waist and long donkey ears atop his head. The guests applauded as the two girls broke apart from one another and began dancing around the boy, who made thrusting grabs for them, his wooden phallus bouncing up and down. As the girls danced about on the floor, the satyr seized the chiton of one. She pulled away and her chiton tore and fell to the floor. The men all cheered as the girl's lithe, naked body was revealed. She was quite beautiful to be sure, but too young, her breasts as small as ripe figs, and still with the rounded belly of a child. The satyr then grabbed the other girl, who squealed and tried to pull away, her chiton tearing as well. The music rose to a high pitched frenzy.

"You see," Hipparchus said dreamily, "symposia favour all the senses. Beauty for the eyes, music for the ears, food and wine for the mouth, perfume for the nose, fine talk for the intellect and lovely dancers for the cock."

Ralla stumbled back into the triclinium by himself, then fell onto his couch and settle back to watch the show. Aculeo saw a flash of red and gold silks and caught Calisto's eye before she disappeared into the shadows towards the garden. He felt a hand trace along his hip and turned to see a pretty flute girl slide onto the couch beside him.

"Would you like company?" she asked, stroking her soft fingertips across his thigh.

Aculeo politely moved her hand away then climbed off his couch, slipping past Capito's couch as he made his way out of the triclinium. "Where are you going?" Capito hissed. Aculeo ignored him and headed towards the garden. The night air seemed to dance around him as he walked, his head spinning. The path was dark, with statues standing here and there like silent guests in the dim lantern light. Minerva with her sword and shield.

146

Venus, an arm covering her breasts, Cupid at her knee. Apollo with his bow at the ready. He found Calisto standing in a distant corner of the gardens near a fountain, the music of the falling water masking the sound of her crying. She looked up at him in surprise, then turned her head away.

"Are you alright?" Aculeo asked.

She looked at him then, tears streaming down her face. "What are you doing here? You don't belong in this place, with these people."

"Who belongs with them then?"

"You couldn't even begin to understand, Aculeo."

"The Magistrate arrested Myrrhine's killer yesterday."

"What?" she said, startled, wiping her tears away. "Who?"

"The recluse. He attacked a porne in Epsilon two nights ago. She led us to him. As we thought, he was a disciple of Sarapis."

"I ... I can't believe it. That's wonderful news."

"Is it?"

"What do you mean?" she asked.

"I don't think he did this on his own. I think he may have acted under someone else's orders."

"But whose?"

"Ralla's."

"Is this some kind of joke?"

"It's not meant to be. Ralla has connections to a number of people who've met unfortunate ends. Iovinus, Neaera, Myrrhine. Why didn't you tell me he was her patron?"

"Why would that matter?"

"You told me they argued at his symposium the night before she was murdered," Aculeo said.

"Yes, but ..."

"Then there's Posidippus of Cos."

"Who?"

"A merchant. He worked with us through Iovinus. His warehouse is empty, his accounting records showed he was heavily in debt. He was in no position to repay his lenders, which put his life in jeopardy. The moneylender, Gurculio, even offered me a bounty to find him."

"I don't understand."

"The Cosian's main lender was Albius Ralla. Is the image clearer now?" Calisto made no response, just pulled her arm from his grasp, not meeting his gaze. "You're protecting him."

"Why would I?" she cried, her eyes blazing. "I'm his whore, not his confidante! I get to live like a bird in his pretty cage only to serve him!"

"Why didn't you tell me about Myrrhine?"

"And what else should I have told you? What would you like to know? Should I tell you of the vile things I must let him do to me whenever the mood strikes him? Or the things he has me do to him? It's my place in life, and I keep my place! At least I can help keep him away from the things he shouldn't have!"

"What things?" Aculeo asked.

"Oh don't be such a blind fool!"

"Yes, I suppose I am a fool," he said. "Trying to grapple with everything falling down around me while Ralla sits at the heart of it all like a viper. My fortune stolen, my family torn from my breast."

"But, it's not true – it can't be."

"Now who's being the fool?" Aculeo took her hands in his, pulled her close. "Calisto, you need to let me help you. I don't want anything to happen to you." She lifted her face up towards his, so close he could taste her breath, warm and sweet as flowers. He felt the warmth of her thigh as she pressed against him, letting him take the small of her back in his hand and pull her close.

"Don't," she said, her head tipped back, her neck arched, her throat pale and perfect. He kissed it gently at first, then hard, tasting the perfume that suffused her skin, then kissed her on the mouth, her lips pressing hard against his. She pushed against him a little, biting his lip softly, and his hands reached up, brushing over her breasts beneath the fabric of her chiton, her nipples hardening beneath his fingers. He felt like he was going to explode.

"No," Calisto whispered, pushing him away. "We can't."

"Why not?"

She took his hand and pressed it to her lips, her dark eyes glistening by the light of the coloured lanterns. "You can't afford me."

Aculeo's face turned hard. "Is it only gold you want then?"

She gave him a stricken look. "I meant you can't afford to be with me. Nor I with you."

"Why not?"

"Our lives are marked out by the gods. I have to go back inside," Calisto said. "You should go. And please, Aculeo, I beg you, leave Ralla be. For your own sake if not for mine." With that, she turned and left.

The back hallways of the villa were dark and quiet, dimly lit with torches on the walls, the distant clatter of slaves cleaning in the backroom and strains of music and laughter from the triclinium. Calisto's probably right, Aculeo thought bitterly. I can't help her, even if she wanted me to. It's a different world, one I have no part in anymore. I can do nothing to affect it. Nothing of any import at least.

Down the hall, the sound of muffled shouts. He walked quietly through the shadows down the hall to the foot of a stairway.

"You dog-eyed porne, who do you think you are?" a man's voice cried. It came from upstairs, Ralla's private chambers. Aculeo listened carefully but the respondent spoke too softly for him to make out the reply. It sounded like a woman's voice. He took up a torch and was about to head upstairs when he heard soft footsteps moving quickly down the corridor just ahead. He followed them. The footsteps stilled.

He continued quietly down the corridor until he entered another foyer at the far end, lined with three doors. The first room was a pantry, containing amphorae filled with grain, cheese, beans, spices and oil. The second room held baskets of yarn, bolts of cloth and extra chairs. The third door was locked. Aculeo slid his knife blade into the lock and turned it, listening until the bolt snapped, then slipped into the room. It was empty, save for a pair of wooden chests bolted to the floor in the corner.

He lifted the lid of one of the chests, held the torch over it. Inside was a stack of brick-shaped objects. He picked one of them up. There was an odd wrapping around it – dried leaves and faded red flowers. He peeled the petals away. Within was a brown cake the consistency of beeswax, its surface slick with beads of dark oil and coated with tiny black seeds. He pinched a small piece off and tasted it. It was bitter and pungent, smelling overwhelmingly of the flowers. Persian opium.

He heard movement outside the room, soft, trying not to be heard. I'm being watched, he thought, holding still for several long, tense moments, listening. Nothing. As he stepped warily into the hallway, he sensed a blur of motion coming towards him. He stepped aside and ducked, instinctively swinging his arm up to protect himself. Something smashed down on his forearm in a sickening explosion of pain. He caught a brief glimpse of his attacker's face – Panthea's harelipped slave. Aculeo shoved his torch into the man's face, making him howl and stagger back, slapping his hands against his now burning beard, trying to douse the flames. Aculeo kicked the slave in the crotch, dropping him to the floor with a gasp. Someone else grabbed Aculeo's arms from behind, pinning him. He snapped his head back sharply, felt his skull crunch against something soft, then thrust his elbow back into his attacker's stomach and twisted around to face him. Someone struck him on to the side of his head and everything went dark.

By the time he regained consciousness and climbed to his feet, his head still swimming, his attackers had already fled. He staggered down the hallway into the garden and looked around ... nothing.

A figure approached from the triclinium. "Aculeo, there you are. I was ..." Capito stared at him in sudden dismay. "What in Hades' name have you been up to?"

"Your concern for my well-being is touching," Aculeo growled, blood dripping from his throbbing mouth down the front of his tunic. "Did you see two men run past here a moment ago?"

"What men?"

"Oh never mind."

"Wait! Where are you going?"

"Home. I hope our host forgives me for not thanking him for his hospitality in person," Aculeo said as he limped out through the gates of the villa into the street, wondering what in the names of all the gods had just taken place.

CHAPTER XVIII

THE 28TH DAY OF APRILIS

The strings of blue glass beads that hung in the bedroom window caught the first light of the day, casting a dazzling violet design that danced like flames on the red terracotta tiles as the beads clacked and twisted in the morning breeze.

Idaia stretched and yawned, then she threw off her blankets and climbed from the bed, enjoying the feeling of her bare feet against the cold tile. She stepped into her pretty sandals, the ones with all the colourful beads, and slipped out of the bedroom. She could hear a pleasant chatter from the kitchen as the cooks prepared breakfast, the wonderful smell of fresh bread with cinnamon and honey baking in the oven. A handful of slaves were whispering to one another in the courtyard as they swept and worked in the garden. A pair of white geese waddled down the pathway, flapping their wings and running awkwardly away when she chased them. The rooster crowed, trying to wake the household. A good idea, Idaia thought wistfully, wake them all!

She spotted the little slave, Scato, holding a reed basket filled with grain, feeding the birds as they gathered around him, flapping their wings, making a fuss. She drew closer to him. He glanced up at her, smiling. "Yes, Mistress?" he asked.

"Come play with me," Idaia said.

"But cook said I'm to feed the geese and peacocks and gather their eggs, Mistress."

"Put the basket down and play with me," she commanded.

"Yes, Mistress," the slave said, and placed the basket at his feet. The birds all rushed forward and attacked the grain, spilling it onto the tiles, pecking savagely at one another to get at it. The boy gave a worried look at the chaos.

Idaia laughed, grabbed his hand and pulled him towards the gate. There was a space on the side just wide enough for them to slip through, and soon they were out into the street without anyone noticing they were gone. She beamed at him triumphantly. Even Scato permitted himself a small smile.

The sun was lovely and warm, the air filled with the extravagant perfume of all the spring flowers coming into bloom. Slaves walked about the outer grounds of the neighbouring villas doing their chores. Idaia smiled and waved at them. The slaves waved back, smiling wearily at the two children as they walked down the street.

"Where are we going, Mistress?" Scato asked.

"Stop calling me that, it's bothersome," she said.

"Should I call you by your name then?"

"No, that wouldn't be proper. Don't call me anything. We'll go to the Agora, I think. I want to get some candied dates."

"We've pears in the kitchen, I saw them," he said.. Perhaps cook would let us ..."

Idaia gave an impatient flip of her head. "Don't talk so much. How fast can you run?"

"I don't know," he said.

She looked down at Scato's skinny legs, his bony knees and his mop of intensely curly brown hair. He didn't look all that fast. She slipped off her sandals and held them in her hands. "We'll race and then we'll see."

"Alright."

"But if my legs get tired, you'll have to carry me the rest of the way."

"Yes, Mistress."

Idaia made a face. "Go!" she cried, and then she ran, her bare feet pounding along the paving stones, her hair flying out behind her, the sun warming her cheeks. She could see the whole city laid out like a precious mosaic below her, thousands of gleaming white houses and buildings with their pretty red rooftops, elegant, even streets with horses and wagons all heading to market, the Pharos Lighthouse standing tall in the harbour above all the little ships, all of it wrapped in a crescent around the brilliant blue jewel of the Egyptian Sea. She felt like she was flying over it all.

She glanced back over her shoulder. Scato had almost caught up – he was faster than he looked! She squawked in surprise and picked up her pace, flying down the hill now, past the gates of the villas, the groves of towering palm trees, past the fountains and gardens.

Her toe struck something sharp and she tumbled to the ground.

Scato caught up to her then, trying to catch his breath. "Are you alright, Mistress?"

"I'm fine." The boy looked like he might burst into tears at any moment. "What's the matter with you?"

"Cook will beat me if she finds out you got hurt playing with me."

"Well stop it, I won't let anyone beat you. Come," Idaia said, then she put her hand out and let Scato help her up. "Ah, it hurts!"

"Let me see." She held up her foot. The big toe was bleeding, her knees were skinned, her tunic torn and soiled. "Shall I carry you now?"

"Not yet." Idaia paused a moment, sniffing the air. "Do you smell something?"

Scato lifted his nose and closed his eyes. "Something's burning."

"Look," she said, pointing to a black cloud of smoke that had spilled into the sky like a cloud of ink. They followed the winding streets of Olympia until they came to the source of the smoke, a villa that had burned down in the night. The fire seemed to have gone out, though citizens and slaves alike were still running back and forth along the path between the street and the house, bringing buckets of water from the fountains and wells. She could hear something yelping from somewhere within.

"Whose house is it?" Scato asked.

"Gurculio's," Idaia said, in awe of the smoke that seemed to fill the pale blue sky.

The air still hung with smoke and the stench of wet ashes as Aculeo and Calisto approached the burned out shell of Gurculio's villa. The roof was gone and shards of broken clay tiles were scattered on the ground. The scorched walls of the house lilted like frail black bones trying to stand upright. Aculeo thought he heard a small child crying from within.

Calisto wore a simple linen chiton, the makeup from last night's symposium washed away, her glossy black hair lay unpinned across her shoulders, yet she looked all the more lovely for being so unadorned. Aculeo held her hand, squeezing tight. He felt her tremble in return and smelled her hair, the perfume of her skin.

"What happened here?" she asked, clinging to him.

"I wish I knew."

The front door hung awry on its warped brass hinges. Remains of tapestries, now little more than burnt tatters, hung on the wall of the main entrance hall. They walked along the passageway of the main floor to the garden beyond. The whimpering sound was louder there, a desperate, haunting lament. The pathway that wound through the garden was smeared and speckled with dried blood stains. And there, dangling from a pine tree in the corner of the courtyard, hung Gurculio, quite dead. Little Felix danced on his hindlegs beneath his master, whimpering and yelping himself into a frenzy. Gurculio's hands were bound behind him, his head twisted to the side, facing them. Calisto let out a horrified sob.

Aculeo took her in his arms and held her tight as the dead moneylender's bulging eyes stared down at them in wordless wonder.

After Aculeo sent Calisto back home – there was little she could do here, after all – he wandered about the moneylender's ruined villa trying to gather his thoughts. The questions Gurculio's murder raised left little time to rejoice in his death. He searched the storage rooms on the main floor – they were littered with fine ceramics, marble statues, expensive furniture and other treasures tossed aside in what must have been a frantic search by Gurculio's murderers. He could find nothing that gave him any clue to what may have happened. Clearly this was no simple robbery. So what was the motive?

Aculeo returned to the main entrance hall and carefully climbed the burned-out stairs that led to the rooms on the second floor. Slaves' sleeping quarters, most of them, little more than small, windowless closets with simple wooden pallets for beds. All of them empty. Where are all the slaves? Escaped from the fire?

The last door opened into an enormous bedroom. In the dim light he saw a vast, scorched mural covering one wall. Jupiter, Heracles, Apollo and Mercury, engaged in salacious encounters with one another, young boys, centaurs and satyrs. The images of the gods all bore more than passing resemblances to Gurculio. The mattress had been stripped from the bed and slit lengthwise, the straw bled onto the floor. A large obsidian mirror, cracked from the heat, hung on the wall in front of the bed. Something had dripped in hardened rivulets down the wall beneath it, pooling on the floor. Aculeo scratched at it with a fingernail. Wax.

He heard a sound downstairs and returned to the inner courtyard. The healer, Sekhet, was already there in response to his summons and squatted next to Gurculio's body. Her assistants had cut down the noose and laid the Roman's body out on the ground. The healer's dark eyes narrowed in concentration as she conducted her examination. Felix sat patiently at her side, watching her every move. He started to growl at Aculeo's approach, but Sekhet cut him off with a sharp word.

She looked up at Aculeo and frowned. "Should I even ask what happened to you?"

"Not enough cucumber juice. What do you think happened here?"

"To start with, one of his ears and two of his fingers were removed," Sekhet said, pointing to the charred stumps on his blistered hand. "They were cut off using a very sharp instrument." Sekhet cut Gurculio's blood-stained tunic from the neck down to the hem and raised an eyebrow. "He was castrated just before he died."

"Like Iovinus. But why? Do you think he was tortured?" Aculeo asked, trying not to vomit at the sight of the moneylender's wound.

"A reasonable guess," she said.

What were they looking for? Aculeo mused. The doors of the store rooms were open. The bedroom had been looted as well, the bed slit open. Did they find anything?

"It wasn't your madman from the Sarapeion that did this, we know that at least," Sekhet said.

"Beyond that we know little else though," he said, rubbing his eyes with the heels of his hands in exhaustion. He felt nothing in the way of sympathy for Gurculio – he'd been a ruthless, loathsome man who'd ruined so many lives – Corvinus, Iovinus, Trogus, Pesach, not to mention his own. Even so, there was something deeper going on here, and a chance to understand what it was had disappeared like smoke. He recalled the argument he'd heard at Ralla's symposium the night before. Could the man have been Gurculio? What was it he cried out? Something about a dog-eyed porne?

Felix lay on the floor and put his head on his paws, looking completely miserable. "What shall we do with him?" Sekhet asked.

"Send him to the street," Aculeo said.

"He'd be a jackal's dinner by nightfall." She scratched him behind the ears and sighed. "I suppose I could take him in for a short time. What of you, where are you going?"

"To a brothel."

Sekhet snorted. "And you call the Egyptian death traditions odd."

A reed barge punted along the foul-smelling brown canal adjoining the Tannery district, heavily laden with stacks of animal hides, the bargeman watching Aculeo walk along the street with vague curiosity. Few pornes were walking about this time of day, Aculeo noticed, mostly just hungover-looking residents of the surrounding mishmash of dingy little flats, merchant seamen making the most of their leave ashore, and the occasional tourist who'd taken a very wrong turn.

He knocked at the faded blue doorway of the brothel. No answer. He noticed the placard of the blue bird was missing from the lintel. He pushed open the door. "Tyche?" he called. No sound but the creaking of the door and the echo of his footsteps as he walked down the hallway towards the little courtyard. The looms were gone, the little tables and chairs as well. The plaster statue of the nymph looked back at him with empty, silent eyes.

Aculeo cursed and kicked it over, feeling little satisfaction as the statue smashed to pieces on the stone floor.

CHAPTER XIX

THE 1ST DAY OF MAIUS

Through the shimmering heat lines over the water's surface, a stark pink line stretched like a deep wound on the horizon.

"Hoi," the bargeman cried, the clap of sound breaking the silence, echoing across the still dark waters. The line trembled, shuddered, then rose, spreading out, a great flock of flamingos, their pink bodies filling the morning sky. Aculeo watched uneasily, unsure if it was an omen, not wanting to speak of it in case it was.

Tell him your story, Sekhet had urged the porne Tisris after they'd shown up at his door first thing that morning. Go ahead and tell him. And like a fool I listened, he thought, eyeing the young woman huddled in the corner of the dusty barge. Tisris glanced back at Aculeo. She was shivering, though the mid-day heat off the water was enough to make him sweat. She was pretty enough, dusky-skinned, with sharp cheekbones and fine black hair that fell midway down her slender back. She had closed her dark-lidded eyes, as though she was trying to sleep. More likely trying hard not to think where they were going.

"You need to tell him what happened," Sekhet had said, gently urging the girl along.

"Sekhet, please, can we do this another time," Aculeo had grumbled. He'd been out drinking most of the night, unwilling to return to an empty bed, and had little patience for any more puzzles.

"It was party," Tisris whispered in a dense Iberian accent. "He said we'd make lot silver. We thought would be okay, I don't know, don't know." She licked her lips, her fingers combing back through her long, dirty hair. "She dead now I think."

"What's she talking about?" he asked. "Who's dead?"

The porne had taken a deep, trembling breath and started again. "Heraïs and me, three days ago we meet man. He invite us to big party, said he pay us three silver each, even show the money."

"Alright."

"I don't trust him, strange eyes, I say no, don't want to go, but Heraïs say it okay … she need silver." Tisris had stumbled on her final words, her shoulders shaking. "So we go with him," she continued at last. "Say we have to take boat there, not far, down to harbour, take his boat, smell like animals. He give us wine, long trip, too long, even for three silver. I say I want go back, but he not nice anymore, tell me shut up. When we get there, he put us in cage. We wait there for long time until dark. Then party start, we still in cage. Others come, men, women too, they have faces."

"Faces?" Aculeo asked, confused.

"Yes, faces, like …" the young woman made a motion as if to slip off her own face.

"You mean masks?" Sekhet said.

"Yes, masks, masks of animals," Tisris said, trembling at the memory. "Cats. Birds. Wolves. Man come back then, bring us wine, tell us to drink. I not drink it. Heraïs not listen to me, she drink. She get sick, sleeping. There are sounds, strange animal sounds, they getting closer, I try and try but cannot wake her up. I have to escape, leave her, leave her there." She was crying, tears rolling down her drawn, pretty face. "She dead, I know she dead."

"You don't know that for certain," Sekhet soothed.

"What did you do then?" Aculeo asked. "Did you see them kill her?"

"No, no, I get away, take boat across water in dark, find farm. I ask them help me, help Heraïs but …" She wept, her head held low, unable to face them.

"I was told of stories like that, of girls not returning," Aculeo said to Sekhet.

"Some stories turn out to be true," she said.

He threw up his hands in frustration. "Enough of this."

"Where are you going?"

"What would you have me do, old woman? I'm trying to recover what was stolen from me, not waste my time hunting for missing pornes.

Besides, the recluse Apollonios is already awaiting trial, remember?"

"What if Neaera was taken to this place?"

"So I should run off chasing every wild tale?"

"She's telling the truth, you know it," the healer snapped.

"Did you see any other women held captive there?" he asked the porne, who bit her lip and shook her head. "What do you want of me, Sekhet?"

Sekhet glared at him. "Only a fool ignores a viper at his breast for the sake of a scorpion at his heel."

And so Aculeo had reluctantly hired a flat-bottomed barge later that morning – the marshlands being virtually impossible to reach by land – and set out along the shoreline of the inland sea to take himself and the Iberian porne to find a farm on the far edge of the city. A place where apparently people ran about in animal masks and forced bitter wine on captive pornes.

According to Tisris' jumbled recollection, the place they sought lay below the marshlands near the salt pans on the shores of Lake Mareotis. The waters were dotted with barges large and small, all heading in the opposite direction to market, some piled high with great sacks of grain and beans, others stacked with amphorae of oil, wine, beer, rough cages filled with livestock. A pair of ivory-white cattle in one barge lowed mournfully as they passed by, looking quite displeased with being caged, much less out on the open water. Aculeo felt much the same. The shore curved inland, out of sight of the city, and led into the marshlands. The air here was muggy and heavy with the ancient, oppressive stench of rot. A haze of mosquitoes pocked the water surface, filling the air with their high-pitched drone. The bargeman punted through the shallows with a long pole, weaving through the maze-like channels cut through the verdant reed-beds. Fellahin fishermen looked up at them as they passed, living the same lives as their ancestors had done for thousands of years, no doubt, whatever went on in the rest of the world, dropping their fishing nets and dragging them through the shallows amidst the pale green seaweed fronds and white and pink lotus flowers.

Something splashed at the river's edge, and a flock of geese and ducks flapped up from their nests in the reeds, disturbing the water with their frantic wingbeats. The bargeman tossed a bent throwing stick, just missing one of the ducks, rattling into the reeds instead. The birds all protested noisily as they lifted higher in the warm winds, turning on the wing to climb over the tops of the trees until they disappeared.

Past the marshlands on the western shores, the lake's bottom was scalloped out into broad, shallow bowls, the waters here coloured pinkish-brown from the salt pans, the air laced with the sharp taste of wet iron. Tisris sat up then, her eyes wide, face pale, hugging her knees to her chest, watching. The shore opened up again into a broad channel dotted with islands containing small settlements and individual farms. Most of the farms in the area were owned by cleruchs, ex-soldiers whose services had been paid for by Caesar in plots of farmland upon their retirement. The cleruchs in turn typically leased the land back to the fellahin to run as tenant farmers.

"There," Tisris said, pointing towards the shore. A desolate looking property stood at the mouth of the channel, marked by a barren bay tree standing at the edge of the wild shore. Next to the tree stood a crude wooden altar, to Neptune most likely. A pair of weathered looking barges lay across the yellow sands. One of the barges had a large hole in the bottom. Aculeo told the bargeman to bring them closer to shore.

"Stay here," Aculeo told the girl. She shook her head, her eyes wide with fear. "It's alright, I won't be long." He climbed out when the water was knee deep, wading the rest of the way. There was a splashing sound behind him – Tisris had jumped into the water as well and was sloshing towards him. She clung to his arm as if she was drowning. They moved a little more awkwardly now towards the property.

It was a shoddy little place with a half-finished canal leading to the fields, all of which appeared to have been left to fallow. The bugs were appalling, nipping any exposed bit of flesh they could find, swarming around the ears, nose and eyes. The bargeman sensibly covered himself with a cloth shroud and settled into the floor of the barge for a nap. Aculeo swatted the bloodthirsty demons trying to devour the nape of his neck. Why in Hades' name would anyone live here, much less throw parties? And why would Neaera come to a place like this? It made little sense, even if ...

He sensed someone watching them, turned and spotted a dirty-faced slave with crudely chopped hair standing in the brush. "Hey, fetch your master," Aculeo said. "We want to speak with him." The slave's eyes widened and she turned and ran. Tisris clung to his arm even tighter. "Seen the wolf, I suppose. Let's go."

They followed the slave up a rough path to a small mud-brick hovel with a thatched roof. The air was rank with the stench of manure and rot. A pen of animals stood off to the side of the house. A pair of glum-looking, raw-boned cows, flicking their tails at the dark clouds of flies that swarmed over their open sores. An adjoining pen was stocked with a dozen or so pigs squealing, grunting and thrusting themselves up against the pen gates, rattling them. An enormous slave carried a bucket of slop out to their trough.

"Hoi – where's your master?" Aculeo called out. The slave stopped in his tracks, blinking down at the ground, a trickle of drool dripping down his great whiskered chin, making incomprehensible grunting noises that sounded eerily like his charges.

"Hey," a voice called. They turned and saw a fat, balding man in a filthy tunic standing at the doorway of the shack, rusted gladius in his hand.

Tisris gasped as she dug her nails painfully into Aculeo's arm. "That's him?" he asked softly. She nodded, trembling, her breathing rapid as she stared down at her feet. "Greetings," Aculeo said to the man, offering a wary smile. "You're owner of this place?"

"Ay," the man said guardedly, wiping the sleep from his eyes with the back of his hand.

"What's your name?"

"Callixenes."

"You're a cleruch then?"

"A freedman, if it's any of your business."

A freedman? Aculeo thought. And this festering dungheap is what he aspired to in his dreams of freedom?

"What the fuck d'you want here?" the man growled. A slave had appeared behind him, just barely managing to restrain a very large and fierce looking dark brown Molossian dog that was practically strangling itself on the rope tied around its neck as it tried to get at the trespassers.

"I've some questions for you."

The man's dark, furtive eyes glanced back and forth between Aculeo and Tisris as he scratched his huge, hairy belly. The pigs were still making their maddening, high-pitched squeals and the dog gave its strangled barks as it strained to get at them. Aculeo noticed the dirty-faced slave girl now huddling near the side of the house, her eyes wide with terror. What's the matter with her, he wondered, watching her from the corner of his eye.

"What sort of questions?" Callixenes asked.

"You hired some pornes to come here a few days ago?"

"So? What's it to you?"

"One of them's gone missing. A girl named Heraïs. Know where she might be?"

"I took her back to the city the other night like I promised."

"He lie, she here!" Tisris cried, her voice quavering.

The freedman glared at her. "And this one stole my boat, didn't you whore!"

"What you do to her?" she screamed.

"Enough," Aculeo said to the girl. "There's a hetaira named Neaera I'm looking for as well. She may have come here a few weeks ago."

"I don't think so."

"Mind if I look around a bit?" Aculeo asked.

"Why don't you just bend over instead and we'll see if my sword fits your sheath," the freedman growled, his eyes dark with anger. The dog was frothing at the mouth as it danced on its hind legs, its thick, muscular neck straining against the rope.

Aculeo watched him for a moment, considering the situation. Any confrontation would surely lead to bloodshed. With himself and a terrified porne against three of them and an enraged Molossian dog, the odds weren't particularly encouraging.

Callixenes carefully watched them walk back down the path towards the barge, stroking the grip on his rusted sword as they went.

"Where Heraïs?" the porne asked Aculeo, clutching at his arm.

"Not here."

"But … why we go now?"

"Because there's nothing more I can do here."

"We need look for her."

"No, we need to go home, understand? I've wasted enough of my damned time coming here in the first place."

"But Heraïs …"

"Heraïs probably returned to Alexandria as you did. Or if she was halfway clever, she ran as far away from all of this as fast as she could. All I know is she's not here." Tisris looked up at him, eyes filled with despair. "Let's go," he said.

The porne clung to him the whole way back to the barge, as did the bloodthirsty cloud of mosquitoes. And from the muddy bank, the strange slave girl crouched, watching them, moving her lips, though no sounds came out.

CHAPTER XX

It was near nightfall by the time Aculeo returned to the narrow Street of the Marble Workers, hungry, filthy, covered in maddening bug bites and too drained to want anything more than to crawl into his foul little bed and fall into unconsciousness. He limped towards his darkened doorway and stopped. Someone huddled there in the shadows. He took half a step back, wary now. He realized it was just a girl though, a threadbare cloak wrapped around her shoulders, her bare feet filthy from the street. Then he noticed her face.

"Tyche?"

The girl opened her eyes and looked up at him, startled. Relief flooded across her face and she fell to her knees, pressing her paper-dry lips to the back of his hand over and over again.

As she ate what little Xanthias could forage from the pantry, Tyche told Aculeo how the pornes had all been sent away from Gurculio's house the night of the symposium after the festivities wrapped up. Panthea and her harelipped slave, Geta, had finally turned up at the Blue Bird right before dawn. There'd been a mad rush to clear everything out and the pornes were told that whatever they couldn't carry on their backs would have to be abandoned. There was no word as to where they'd be going. Tyche had been terrified, given Neaera's disappearance and all the stories of the missing pornes. She managed to slip away in the midst of the confusion and had been living on the streets since then.

"I'm sorry to burden you," she said. "I didn't know where else to go."

D.L. Johnstone

"I'm just happy you're safe," Aculeo said. "Did Panthea or Geta ever speak of Gurculio's death?"

"Gurculio's dead?" the girl asked in surprise.

"He was murdered the night of the symposium."

"Oh." She looked so small, so vulnerable, with dark circles like bruises under her eyes. She looked like she was ready to collapse. Aculeo helped her to her feet and led her to his bedroom where she fell asleep almost instantly.

"Was Panthea involved in Gurculio's murder?" Xanthias asked, watching the sleeping girl.

"Yes."

"Why would she have done it?"

"I'm not sure," Aculeo said with a yawn. "But then, I'm not sure of anything these days."

"What shall we do with the girl?"

"Let her sleep for now, we'll worry about it later. I'll take your pallet. You take the floor."

"Of course, Master. The floor is so much more suitable than a bed for my frail old bones."

"Oh stop it."

"I almost forgot, a messenger left this for you." Xanthias held out a scrap of yellow papyrus.

"I don't want to know," Aculeo said. He hesitated before finally accepting the note and opening it. He recognized the spidery scrawl instantly.

'Come to Necropolis! <u>NOW</u>!'

"The Necropolis," Aculeo groaned, slumping against his bedroom doorway in utter exhaustion.

"Does this mean I shall have to sleep on my old pallet after all?" Xanthias said in mock disappointment.

"Sleep where you like, old man," Aculeo snapped, heading to the door again. Where else should I go on such a night as this but the City of the Dead, he thought miserably. I'll feel right at home.

"Sekhet?" Aculeo called, heading down the steep staircase within the smooth walls of the Necropolis' cave entrance.

There was no answer, just a scuttling sound. Rats most likely. Possibly jackals. A pleasant thought. At the bottom of the steps was a narrow passageway cut into the rock, heading off into the darkness. I remember that, Aculeo thought, taking a deep, shaky breath. The walls felt like they were ready to swallow him, steal his air, crush his lungs, bury him alive. He felt his chest grow tight, his breathing rapid, shallow, his head spinning. He closed his eyes, forced himself to breathe slowly, deeply.

He followed the long passageway, touching the dimly torchlit walls with his fingertips, feeling it twist this way and that. "Sekhet? Are you there?" Still no answer. Did I miss a turn somewhere? It seems to go on forever. Curse this place! And curse Sekhet, the old crone!

He walked another few minutes that felt like hours, until at last he saw a dim light up ahead. The passageway emptied into a large chamber with four doors facing one another, a crescent moon carved in the pediment above each of them. He could make out the rough cut walls, the high ceiling that had been roughly hewn into a vault. There was a hole carved in the ceiling through which a splash of moonlight spilled, though it had travelled from a very long way up. How deep into the ground have I gone, he wondered. How sturdy are these walls? If they were to suddenly give way I'd be crushed beneath all this rock, unable to breathe, unable to move … his chest was growing tight again. Breathe!

Three of the doors were partially ajar and seemed to dip down lower than the floor of the chamber, leading further down into the darkness. The fourth door was open and led down another long, dark corridor. "Sekhet?" he called at the doorway. Nothing but quiet.

He had gone just a few steps down the corridor when he heard a rustling overhead. He raised his free hand warily and felt something brush across his skin, followed by a cacophony of high pitched squeals. He ducked down, covering his head, feeling a thousand leathery creatures slap against his arms and back, their wings thrumming through the air, flapping against the back of his head. When it was over, he looked up at last, saw the last few bats disappear into the chamber behind him, spiralling overhead towards the high ceiling. He shuddered and moved on.

"Sekhet!" Aculeo called again, an unintended note of anxiety colouring his voice.

"In here," came the muffled reply from up ahead. Finally, he thought, more relieved than he cared to admit to hear the sound of her voice. There was a large room at the end of the corridor with several chambers leading off of it. Two of the chambers were lit up with yellow torchlight. And there was Sekhet, standing next to a short, squat man with a shaved scalp polished to a coppery sheen.

She looked at Aculeo, appraising him, not altogether impressed by what she saw. "You're pale. And sweating. What's wrong with you?"

"Nothing."

"Any pains in your chest? Your left arm?"

"I told you I'm fine."

"You'll end up in here yourself soon enough at the rate you're going," Sekhet said, nodding towards a number of cremation jars sitting in niches carved into the rock walls. Cremation, while considered a loathsome taboo among the fellahin, was nonetheless the preferred method among Romans and Greeks and was therefore still regularly performed at the Necropolis.

"This is my nephew, Paheri," she said, indicating the man standing next to her. "He's a Man of Anubis." The Men of Anubis, the Egyptian jackal-headed god that ruled over the journey into the afterlife, were the priests who dealt with embalming and mummification of the dead. Paheri nodded politely. "How did your journey go with Tisris?"

"A waste of time. A miserable freedman and his miserable slaves on his miserable farm."

"Ah? Well, a worthy try at least. Come, this should make up for it."

Behind them, a mummy had been laid out on a stone funerary table. The table had been carved in the form of two lions facing forward with the mummy's head fitting into a basin between the lions' tails, a drainage channel running down the centre and feeding into the basin.

"Who is it this time?" Aculeo asked.

"Just be patient," Sekhet snapped.

"This is most unusual," Paheri said uneasily. "It's bad enough to be doing this after the rituals have been completed, but outsiders are not supposed to observe our practices. It is against the word of Anubis. If anyone catches us…"

"There won't be anyone down here this time of night and you know it."

"Still…"

"Shall I have a talk with your wife? Or worse, with her mother?"

The priest shuddered and started to slowly and carefully cut away the rough linen bandages that had been wrapped around the body. Aculeo glanced around the chamber. A densely packed series of rectangular niches had been carved into the rock walls, at least nine across and five high on each wall of the chamber. Some of the niches had not yet been completed but had been marked off with red paint. Mummies had been placed in most of the completed ones, sealed in with thick stone slabs.

"A million or so," Sekhet said. She was standing just beside him.

"What?"

"There are at least a million people buried here. The caverns go forever under the city. Even I sometimes get lost down here, and I know the paths fairly well."

"All this effort to wrap a dead body in cloth and stick them in a hole in the ground," Aculeo said.

"It's the responsibility of the living to provide the dead with their path to the afterlife. When a person dies, their ka can only return to an undamaged body, assuming that Osiris judges them worthy when he weighs their heart. If a body is spoiled or allowed to rot, it destroys their chance for life in the hereafter. An eternal death."

The stone slabs that sealed the niches were marked with the occupants' names and decorated with winged sphinxes, lintels with winged suns and false double doors. Painted keys hung from some of the doors. A few small tokens had been set out in front of the painted doors – oil lamps, incense burners, bowls of wheat, cups of wine – offerings for the dead.

"Come," Sekhet said, "Paheri should be ready for us."

They returned to the stone funerary table. Paheri was just now starting to remove the rough linen wraps from the mummy's head. He hesitated a moment, muttered a prayer under his breath, then reluctantly pulled away the last wraps. Her body was desiccated, the dark, plump skin of her face now dry as leather, but her features were perfectly preserved, and all too recognizable.

"Neaera," Aculeo said in surprise.

"No, not Neaera," Sekhet said. "This one was mummified in the month of Thoth, over ninety days ago."

"Who is she then?"

"Show me the portrait you took from Neaera's flat."

Aculeo retrieved the portrait from his satchel and handed it to the healer. Sekhet unrolled it on the funerary table next to the mummified woman. Three women standing before the Pharos lighthouse. Calisto, Neaera and ... Aculeo felt his blood run cold. Her eyes were dark brown to Neaera's green, her nose slightly broader, her face thinner, and no birthmark on her upper lip.

"See the piercing on the side of this girl's nose," said Sekhet. "In the portrait she wears a jewelled stud there. Do you know her name?"

"Petras," Aculeo said. "She disappeared several months ago. Everyone thought she'd run away."

"What's taking you?" Sekhet snapped at Paheri. "Keep unwrapping!"

"This is so wrong," the priest muttered. At last, Petras' body was fully unwrapped. It had been perfectly preserved. Two lines of red wax traced along her naked abdomen and several smaller lines of wax across her breasts, shoulders and thighs.

"Is that the death wound?" Aculeo asked, pointing to the longest of the lines, which led along the pelvic crest diagonally to the navel, then turned sharply upwards to between the breasts.

"This was the incision to prepare her body for embalming," Sekhet said. "We remove all the entrails and inner organs and preserve them in the canopic jars of the four sons of Horus. Amset the man, Hapi the baboon, Qebehsenuf the falcon and Duamutef the jackal. The heart, which holds our intellect and our emotions, is replaced in the chest with a heart scarab that will stand before Osiris in the funerary tribunal of the afterworld."

"These cuts we did not make," Paheri said, tracing his fingertip along the other lines of wax that covered Petras' body. He touched one as long as his hand that ran beneath the left half of her ribcage. "This cut especially went very deep, I remember, penetrating her abdominal wall almost to her spine, then turned upwards to pierce her heart."

"And see here," Sekhet said, pointing to the girl's wrists and ankles. Pinkish-brown rope marks were still visible in the soft skin. "And around her neck, another rope mark."

"Her neck was broken, her windpipe crushed," Paheri recalled.

"She was likely hanged," said Sekhet. "Like the moneylender."

"There's another thing," Paheri said. He hesitated a moment, then retreated to his workroom and brought out a much smaller mummy which he laid beside the first.

"How far along was she when she died?" Sekhet asked, eyeing the lonely little figure.

"Four months, I would guess. Five at most."

"It would have been difficult to ignore at that stage."

"But why murder her?" Aculeo asked. "Why not have her abort the child instead?"

"It's not so difficult," Paheri agreed. "Just drink the wine used to smother a red mullet."

"There are less idiotic ways than that," Sekhet snapped.

"But nothing as foolproof as murder," Aculeo said. "How did she come to be here in the first place?"

"Where else would she go?" Paheri asked.

"Somebody brought her body here. Someone gave you instructions and paid for her to be embalmed. Who was it?"

"I can't tell you that," Paheri said, offended by the question. "It's bad enough that we have gone back and removed her wrapping after completing the rituals ..."

"We'll beg Anubis for forgiveness later, nephew," Sekhet said with a steely smile. "Now tell us who paid for it or we'll be embalming you next."

The Man of Anubis sighed. "Wait here a moment."

Aculeo and Sekhet walked to the other end of the long whitewashed chamber as they waited for the priest to return. Some of the niches had already been sealed with stone slabs. There were two scenes on one of them. The top scene was of a naked hunter holding a lance, pursuing an ibis, which was also being attacked by two hunting dogs, while satyrs and nymphs danced at the forest edge. In the bottom scene, someone was escorting a dark-haired young woman through a pair of black gates. Hermes Psychopompus most likely, Aculeo thought, conductor of souls to the underworld, taking the woman's soul into Hades. Mourners stood at the edge of the scene, saying their farewells. Nearby stood a white tree, with long, oddly shaped branches twisting towards the ground. Aculeo was about to take a closer look at the tree when he was startled by the sound of someone clearing their throat behind him. It was Paheri.

"The embalming was paid for by Sabazius," Paheri said reluctantly.

"Anything else?" Aculeo asked.

"No, just the name. But there is one more thing I noted in the records," Paheri said. "I found something unusual on the girl during the embalming process. I forgot to mention it." He held up a small bleached linen pouch, tapped the contents into his hand and held it up for the others to see.

A thin yellow cord, tied into a bracelet and stained with blood.

CHAPTER XXI

THE 2ND DAY OF MAIUS

Tyche walked half a dozen steps behind Aculeo, saying nothing as they walked through the Agora. He'd given her little information about where they were headed that morning, just abruptly told her to follow him as they were going to visit a friend then headed out the door of his little flat and into the street. They walked from the Street of the Marble Workers towards the Agora, past vendors carts selling fruit and fish and cloth towards the great central square, the slave-trade quarter.

Tyche felt a sick, familiar emptiness bloom inside her chest when she heard the sharp voices of the slave-traders rising above the din as they called out to prospective buyers. She couldn't help but look at the sullen faces of the slaves chained to one another, their naked skin covered with chalk dust to soak up their sweat and stink while disguising any unsightly scars or blemishes that might bring down their price.

And she remembered her sister Anchises' last tears.

Anchises had cried a great deal during their final days together. Tyche had wanted to go to her, to hold her, comfort her, but she knew the trader would likely beat them both. It made his customers uncomfortable to see slaves caring for one another. Some of the market-goers would stop to look at what he had in – they liked to squeeze the slaves like pieces of fruit, look into their mouths to count their teeth. It had happened so often she'd learned to simply tolerate it. Tyche had tried to make herself look smaller and more sickly when the customers examined her, even made small coughing noises. The trader had noticed and beaten her for that as well, but it had worked for a while at least.

On their last day together, she'd waited until the trader was distracted with a customer then tossed a pebble at Anchises, who'd looked up, tears streaking down her dirty cheeks. Tyche had stuck her tongue out and made a face. Anchises had smiled a little, sniffed, wiped her eyes, then stuck her tongue out as well. Tyche had muffled her laughter. The trader shot them both a threatening look, but it was worth it – it was good to see her sister laugh again, even if it meant being beaten for it later.

A couple had come along shortly after – a red-haired woman and her slave, a cruel looking man with a harelip and greasy, ill-cut hair. He'd spoken to the trader in their babbling tongue. Tyche could understand a little Greek, she'd been around them long enough, but they spoke so quickly it was difficult to follow. The trader pointed to the girls, his brown, leathery face split into a gap-toothed grin and walked them over, babbling in broken Greek to the couple, roughly caressing Tyche's cheek. She had been beaten enough times in the past two weeks to know not to resist. The customer looked at her critically, took her face between his fingers and squeezed painfully, turning it one way, then another. He forced her mouth open with his dirty thumb then peered into her mouth. Be strong, Tyche had thought, be strong for Anchises. Please don't buy me, please just leave me be …

Anchises had started shaking and blubbering like a child. The trader yelled at her to shut up. Tyche had bitten her lip to keep herself from crying as well. The red-haired woman intervened and shushed Anchises then offered her a boiled sweet. She stroked her head, petted her, wiped away her tears. Then she walked over to Tyche, offering her a sweet as well. Tyche had hesitated at first, then accepted it. It was the only food she'd had that day. She rolled it around in her mouth – she recalled its delicious taste, like fruit and honey.

The woman had cooed, smiling at her. She babbled something to her slave as she stroked Tyche's face, her smile hardening. Tyche coughed and tried to make herself look small. The woman put a finger to her lips, then reached her other hand beneath Tyche's peplos, slipped her skinny dry hand between her legs, poked her fingers inside of her. It was so horrid, Tyche had wanted to bite the woman, hurt her, do something, but she didn't dare. She closed her eyes, trying to think of something else, anything. Then it was over.

Anchises dared not even look at her sister, she could only stare at the ground, her face flushed, expressionless. We'll get away, Tyche had promised her silently, whatever happens, I'll find you, we'll get away and we'll find our way back home. Don't worry – everything will be alright. I give you my oath. She had listened vaguely as the woman haggled with the trader before they'd finally settled on a price, and Tyche went with their new owners. She hadn't seen Anchises since.

Aculeo led her out of the crowded Agora to the palace district along the northwestern shore of the city, up broad, winding lanes where the villas were set well back from the street, the air spiced with the perfumed smell of the lush pink flowers and ornamental trees that capped the tall garden walls. Why are we here? she wondered anxiously. She couldn't fight the feeling that Aculeo was planning to sell her. He had seemed like such a good, kind man, her only hope in this vast, terrifying city, but how could she be certain? Perhaps he's found a buyer for me already and is taking me to him now. She wanted to turn and run but her legs felt leaden and weak as she followed him helplessly along the winding streets.

Aculeo slowed as they neared a particularly lovely looking villa near the Shrine of Ares, where a pair of perfect plum trees grew on either side of the entrance, their branches bowing under the weight of the ripe violet fruit. They approached the gates and an enormous, black-skinned slave silently examined them before allowing them to enter.

They stepped into the gatehouse through the elegantly decorated fauces to the atrium. The compluvium in the centre was filled with pretty fish and bordered with carefully tended box hedges and ornamental figs and acacias. Beyond the atrium was a marble peristylium, with what appeared to be a garden behind that. The tapestries hanging on the walls undulated in the warm breeze that wended its way from the sea to the hilltop and through the broad hallways of the villa. Tyche was quite certain she had never seen a more beautiful house in her life.

A dark-haired little girl of perhaps eight years watched her from behind a column in the peristylium. The girl's eyes were wide with curiosity, a small smile dancing on her pretty lips. She reminded Tyche so much of Anchises she felt her heart catch in her throat.

She heard the sound of nearing footsteps and looked up to see a woman approaching the atrium. The woman was young and elegant, almost regal-looking with dark, unpinned hair that fell just past her shoulders and large, intelligent eyes, the sort that took everything in. She was dressed in a simple but expensive looking cream-coloured silk chiton elaborately knotted at the breast. The woman smiled when she saw Aculeo. She took him by the hands and let him kiss her cheek, lingering a few extra moments in his arms when they embraced, both of them reluctant to let go. Finally she pulled away.

"And who is this?" she asked as she looked at Tyche, her voice rich and exotic as her eyes.

"This is Tyche," Aculeo said, then briefly explained her story. Tyche stared down at the stark geometric patterns of the mosaic floor, only half-listening, not daring to let herself believe what might be happening. That Aculeo might not be selling her after all. That something else was taking place. Was it a dream?

After a few moments, Tyche felt someone touch her gently on the shoulder and glanced up. Calisto took her hands in her own soft, perfect ones, offering a warm, welcoming smile. She turned her head towards the peristylium and called out "Idaia."

The little girl appeared at her side within seconds, barefoot and breathless, beaming shyly up at Tyche. Calisto introduced them to one another.

"Would you like to stay here for a while with us?" Calisto asked Tyche in Phrygian.

Tyche could scarcely believe her ears – the most wondrous words, and spoken in a tongue she hadn't heard in far too long. She nodded desperately. Idaia squealed in delight, almost dancing on the spot she was so elated.

Calisto smiled and embraced the girl, kissing her on the cheek. "Welcome to your new home, Tyche."

The waves slapped against the sides of the boat as the oars swept through the calm waters of the bay. The day was fair, the light Etesian winds from the north-west smelling of the sea and distant shores. The sea was clear and deep indigo, with great schools of fish glittering in the sun like handfuls of silver coins scattered in its depths. The pilot steered the little dorry through the muddy shallows of the harbour basin where fronds of mauve anemone undulated in the waves, and rowed southwest from Cape Lochias around the reefs and the breakwaters, then headed out towards Pharos.

Aculeo had met with the sophist at the Museion to pick his brain. Zeanthes had suggested a small adventure was more in order. And so they'd walked to the eastern harbour and hired a small boat to taxi them out to Pharos, the island of the Lighthouse. Zeanthes closed his eyes as he sat back in the boat and seemed to be dozing. Aculeo sat back as well and let the sun warm his face, listening to the rhythmic creaking of the oars, the lap of the waves and the raw cries of the bone white herring gulls and pelicans as they wheeled through the clear blue skies, darting down to pluck up any fish that ventured too near the water's surface.

The slate blue waters were dotted with fishing vessels and trading ships almost as numerous as the fish themselves, for this bay in the mouth of the Egyptian Sea was by far the busiest in the world, surpassing even Athens at its peak. The bay at Pharos itself had historic fame, for its safe anchorage and favourable winds had been written about by Homer himself centuries before, long before there had even been an Alexandria. And what the Gods had provided, Ptolemy Soter, Alexander's successor in Egypt, had improved on by creating two distinct harbours.

To the southeast was the Great Harbour, which consisted of three inner ports, the Port of Augustus, the Port of Lochias, where most commercial vessels moored, and the Port of Poseidon, where several Roman warships were moored. To the northwest was the Eunostos Harbour from which the Heptastadion had been built, like a long, crooked finger pointing towards the island of Pharos. The seven-stade long quay had been commissioned at great cost to allow ships to move from one anchorage to another to provide the best protection in all weather and sea conditions, passing through channels split along its length.

"Such a lovely day," Zeanthes said with a gentle smile. "I'm so pleased you came to see me. You seem troubled, though. Is everything alright?"

"Gurculio was murdered a few days back."

"I heard as much."

"Did you know he was castrated and tortured before he died?"

The sophist turned pale. "Men like Gurculio have their enemies I suppose. But why would he have been tortured?"

"I don't know. And now there's yet another murder to investigate – another girl murdered in a similar manner to Myrrhine and the river slave."

"Ah?"

"This one was murdered three months ago though. Perhaps you knew her. Petras, she was Neaera's cousin."

Zeanthes closed his eyes and nodded. "Yes, yes of course, I remember her well. A lovely girl."

"Any idea who her patron was?"

"I really don't know."

"She was stabbed," Aculeo said. "A single killing wound to the abdomen, like Myrrhine."

"Our visit to Pharos should allow us to consider the matter from a different perspective," Zeanthes said.

The little dorry approached the wooden docks built out from the rough-hewn limestone blocks of sloping embankments on the shore. Aculeo followed Zeanthes ashore. Crowds of tourists and foreign sailors milled about the little island, with its sunbaked limestone shoreline edging the blue-green sea, sparse golden sea grass, warm winds and, of course, the Lighthouse itself, enormous and brilliant white in the midday sun. It was, he had to admit, an even more impressive sight up close than from the shore. Broad steps at the base led to a low platform, around which the gawking tourists gathered to pass through the entrance, housed within a square-shaped wall that surrounded the tower itself.

The tower was two hundred cubits high, the height of fifty men, and Aculeo's neck ached as he looked up towards its soaring peak. It had been commissioned almost three centuries ago by the Greek Pharaoh Ptolemy Philadelphus, constructed of native white limestone, but with enormous solid pink granite blocks, polished to a high sheen, themselves ten cubits high, interposed around the lintels, supporting the towering structure. The base tier was a square-shaped tower a hundred cubits high, with rectangular windows cut into its surface at regular intervals, atop of which stood the second tier, an octagonal-shaped tower that stood another fifty cubits. The third and final tier was a tall cylindrical tower which housed the beacon, capped with cupola. On the very peak was an enormous marble statue of Zeus Soter staring out to sea, welcoming all arriving ships. The beacon, which had remained lit every hour of every day for the past thirty decades, could be spotted ten leagues out to sea.

As they awaited their turn to pass through the entrance, Aculeo looked around at the enormous statues that stood atop the wall surrounding the lighthouse. Six soaring Aswan pink granite statues of three Ptolemies, Soter, Philadelphus and Euergetes, he dimly recalled, portrayed as ancient Egyptian Pharaohs, sat on their thrones alongside their loving sister-queens, facing out to the open sea, their vast shoulders brushed by the fronds of tall palm trees wafting in the winds. And alongside them were statues of Poseidon with his trident, and Isis Pharia holding a great sunbleached cloth sail that billowed and snapped in the wind, in honour of sailors seeking safe harbour.

"Lovely, isn't it," Zeanthes said. "The world is full of such great wonders of course. The Great Pyramids of Giza. The Hanging Gardens of Babylon. The Collossus Helios of Rhodes, a marvel even in ruin. Who knows how long before even this too crumbles to magnificent dust? Such is man's recurring folly. Look out there." Zeanthes pointed out to sea, where a number of ships sailed, like specks on the water. "What do you notice about the ships on the horizon?"

Aculeo looked at them, then back at Zeanthes. "What do you mean?"

"We lose sight of them as they grow more distant of course. But what do you notice about how they disappear?"

Aculeo looked carefully. "Their hulls disappear first, but their masts are still visible."

"Remember the ship with the red sails," Zeanthes said with a smile, then he led the way through the entrance into a great courtyard. The grounds within were lovely, filled with more statuary, sphinxes, towering columns of white marble shot through with rich grey veins and obelisks covered with hieroglyphs, remnants of ancient Egypt looted from Heliopolis to adorn this modern wonder.

In the centre of the tower itself was a spiralling stone staircase for visitors and pack animals to climb. Broad platforms had been built at various stages along its height inside the tower, with windows for visitors to pause and look out at the city or the sea. Alongside the staircase was an elaborate system of platforms, ropes and pulleys, a lift device to transport fuel for the beacon fire.

They began their ascent along with the other crowding, sweating tourists, a few of them riding up on donkeys. They paused to rest at the top of the first tier, where a platform had been set up like a small marketplace, with food and wine vendors, portrait painters, jugglers, musicians and merchants at their little booths selling souvenirs.

They continued their climb, finally reaching the top of the second tier where an observation deck had been constructed. The deck was thick with milling tourists, all craning to get a look at the city and the sea from the finest vantage point in the world. Graffiti adorned the walls, carved by countless visitors before them. Aculeo looked down on the city. The view was breathtaking. He could see everything – he spotted the Agora, then followed the lines of streets to his own humble neighbourhood, then along the Canopic Way to the Crossroads at the Street of the Soma, then east to the Museion. He could see the Harbour of the River and thought he could almost see to the farthest shores of the inland sea. The canals wrapped through the city like roots of a tree, out to Canopus in the east, Rhakotis in the west and Lake Mareotis in the south, all fed by the Nile, which seemed to stretch forever into the distance.

"Now, let's find the ship with the red sails," Zeanthes said, looking out at the horizon. "There, you see it?"

"Yes."

"What do you notice?"

"It's travelled further out, but I can see the hull now."

"Excellent. Why do you think that is?"

"Our height enables us to see the ships better, I imagine."

"But for that to be possible, the sea must be curved, such that the horizon is actually higher at ground level than from this vantage point. One might conclude, in fact, that the world must therefore be spherical in shape. The great Eratosthenes once calculated the arc of the world using his theory of shadows. If his calculations are correct, another seven-eighths of the world remains for us to discover and explore."

"Is that true?" Aculeo asked.

"Truth is another question entirely. A Skeptic can never truly know anything, not even the nature of truth. Right now, we are simply exploring what potential conclusions may be made from our observations. Yet as we untangle the thorniest questions, we come across even more difficult problems. For example, if the earth is spherical, how is it secured in the heavens? What forces keep men, the waters, the land, the sky affixed to the earth's surface? What of the nature of space and time? And what does it say of the heavenly bodies? According to Aristarchus, the only body in the heavens to move about the Earth is the moon. The Earth, Mars, Venus and the rest actually move about the Sun."

"But how could that be?"

"It is proposed in quite elegant treatises," Zeanthes said. "There's another explanation of course. That our perception of reality is imperfect. That the purity of the Divine cannot be grasped here in this world, but only in the heavens. That the heavens are not a cold universe of mathematics, measurements and Pythagorean formulae wherein planetary spheres shuffle about the skies in musical harmony, but are instead the thrones of the Gods, from which they watch our goings on. Why else might the universe have been created at all, if not for the Gods' divine pleasure?"

"If you call what they do pleasure, I suppose."

"Such are the reasons the Ptolemies first commissioned the Library, and why the Caesars continue to patronize so many great minds at the Museion. With knowledge comes power, especially if it is unique and self-owned knowledge. Now, how does all this relate to the questions that you seek to unravel? Let's explore the questions surrounding the murders."

"What, here?" Aculeo asked, looking around the crowded observatory.

"Why not?" the sophist said. "What do we know? A slave is murdered in the Sarapeion. Her killer seems obvious at first, like the ship on the horizon. A recluse was seen in the temple, his act of murder witnessed. And if he murdered that girl, he must have murdered Myrrhine and Petras as well, for their murders appear connected by design if not by time or circumstance. What could be clearer?

"Yet your former associate, Iovinus, was also murdered, the tablets he carried were stolen, his lover gone missing, and though we know not Neaera's fate, the coincidence makes one fear that she too may have suffered some terrible end.

D.L. Johnstone

"What else do we know? Some of the murder victims were hung, all were stabbed, some several times, tortured perhaps, while the slave in the Sarapeion was struck across the head. One girl was murdered three months ago. The others only in the past few weeks. And then there are the pomegranate seeds, of course. So we must accept there are differences – correct? The question is … why? What differed between them? Why were some of the victims hanged, tortured and butchered and others not?"

"Apollonios had less time in the Sarapeion with the river slave," Aculeo said. "The witness Cleon interrupted him. He altered his method, but not the result."

"But why were they murdered in the first place? And what of the three-month gap? Is there even a gap? Were there in fact other girls murdered during that time period? Or before? Or since? You only just discovered Petras, after all. How many others might there be?"

"I don't know," Aculeo allowed, feeling a sickening sense of despair at the thought.

"There's something different about the girls, the situation, or else the killer."

"Could there have been two killers?"

"A possibility," Zeanthes mused. "The way you describe this Apollonios, I find it difficult to understand how he could have committed any of these murders other than that of the slave."

"He's a lunatic. He scalded one of the men with boiling water when we tried to take him. It was like trapping a rabid beast."

"That's the point of my argument. Why would any sensible woman have gone with a man who is clearly mad? Yet we must presume that he was successful not only once, but over and over again, and in almost complete secrecy? And then there's Gurculio's murder."

"That's a different matter. The brothel-keeper Panthea did that."

"You base that on guesswork or some specific knowledge?"

"I heard them arguing at the symposium. I was attacked by her slave that night and her brothel was cleared out the next day."

"A false deduction," Zeanthes said. "You cannot assume Gurculio's murder is not connected to the murders of these women. Especially given that he had his manhood stripped from him at the end, did he not? Which implies it is part of the pattern. And if it is connected, where then does your recluse fit? He was in prison when Gurculio was murdered."

"You talk about it like it was some geometry problem you're trying to unravel," Aculeo said irritably.

"It is like that, yes, and why not?" Zeanthes said, holding Aculeo's gaze with his own placid eyes. "The murders follow a pattern designed by the

178

killer, or killers, choosing the victims, the time, the place, the means of their murder. He would have needed to have access to them, gaining their trust, their cooperation at least for the time it took him to take control of them. And after killing them, he needed to be able to escape unnoticed. Can you picture Apollonios doing all this?"

Aculeo stared back at him for a moment, then glanced back towards the city, towards Olympia. He thought for a moment that he could just make out the pink walls of Calisto's villa. "Not on his own, no. What do you know of Albius Ralla?"

"Ralla? Why do you ask?"

"He was Myrrhine's patron. They were together at Gurculio's symposium the night she was murdered. He was also Neaera's patron which links him to both Iovinus' and Neaera's fates. Posidippus of Cos also owed him money before he disappeared."

"Is your concern simply about Ralla, or about his relationship with Calisto?" the sophist asked gently.

"What if he's behind the murders? What if he used Apollonios as his instrument?"

"Even if you truly thought such a man as Albius Ralla is capable of such a thing, why would he rely on such an unreliable instrument?" Zeanthes asked.

"I don't know. I don't know anything anymore."

Zeanthes put a hand on his shoulder and they gazed at the waves crashing down below. "So much death, so much tragedy," he said. "And you are left with your own sense of culpability, trapped in this madness, incapable of stopping it, incapable of helping anyone in fact." Aculeo didn't answer. He couldn't have spoken, even if he wanted to. "Everyone plays a role in these things, you know. None of us are innocent."

"What do you mean?"

"I think you know my meaning. The real question you need to ask yourself is, are you a hero, a villain, or simply part of the chorus? Whatever your answer, be careful, my friend. Ralla is no fool, and he's not a good man to have as an enemy."

CHAPTER XXII

THE 3RD DAY OF MAIUS

"Don't you dare move," a quavering voice said. Aculeo opened one eye a crack and saw a filthy, bearded face inches from his own, the man's breath hot and fetid. He thought at first it must be some beggar who'd broken in to rob him. It took him a moment to recognize it was Gellius – the man looked wretched, his tunic torn and stained, his body odour enough to make a Carthaginian's eyes water. The knife he pressed against Aculeo's throat, however, left little doubt as to his intent.

"Alright," Aculeo said, as calmly as he could. "I'm not moving. Where've you been, Gellius? We've been worried about you."

"Liar!" Gellius hissed, pressing the blade close enough against the flesh to nick the flesh.

"Gellius, put the damned knife down before you kill me."

"That's the point though, isn't it?"

"I thought we were friends."

"So did I, but that was before you betrayed us. Trogus was right – I never should have trusted you again. More fool me. But I wasn't the one to pay for it, was I? He was!" Gellius' eyes welled with tears, his voice tremulous. "You won't get away with it though! Not this time!"

"I'm sorry about Trogus, but I swear I never betrayed anyone."

"Liar!" Gellius cried. "Sorio said he saw you at the Games sitting alongside your dear friend Gurculio, watching Trogus get cut down like a common slave! You were playing us all that time!" He gripped the knife in both hands and held it over his head, readying to plunge it into Aculeo's neck.

"Wait! It wasn't me that betrayed you, dammit, it was Bitucus!"

Gellius paused, an expression of doubt crossing his face as he lowered the knife an inch. "What are you talking about?"

"I went to the Little Eagle to find the two of you the night Trogus was taken. Bitucus was waiting there with the merchant Theopompus."

"The Icarian?"

"Yes. They wanted me to tell them your whereabouts, even offered me coin. I refused. I'd never have betrayed you, Gellius. You or Trogus."

"You're ... you're lying. Bitucus would never do such a thing. We took him in, put a roof over his head when he had nothing."

"He'd have sold his father's bones for soup to be with his family again," Aculeo said. "I was at the Games with Gurculio, I admit it, but I was forced to be there. He wanted me to witness Trogus' murder."

"But why?" Gellius asked, dumbfounded.

"Because he's a sick bastard. Or was. Someone murdered him last week."

"Wait. What? Gurculio's dead?"

"Yes. Someone tortured him and hung him in his own villa before setting fire to it."

"Oh," Gellius said, sitting back on his heels, lowering the knife. "Oh."

"Can I sit up without you stabbing me? Again?" Aculeo asked. He saw Xanthias watching from the doorway, eyebrows raised in puzzlement, and waved him off.

"What? Oh, yes, of course," Gellius said, lowering the knife.

Aculeo sat up in the bed, tentatively dabbed at the nicks on his throat, twinging at the touch and sting of sweat. "You've really got to stop trying to murder me."

"I'm sorry, Aculeo, truly. When Sorio mentioned he'd seen you at the Games, I thought for certain it was you who'd betrayed us."

"I understand," Aculeo said.

"Yes, I'm sure a number of people dream of murdering my Master," Xanthias offered helpfully from outside the bedroom. "Why even I ..."

"Enough, old goat," Aculeo growled.

"It's been so ... so challenging of late," said Gellius. "I thought I'd hit bottom already. Not as bad as Pesach perhaps, but still..."

Pesach, Aculeo recalled guiltily, I'd forgotten about him.

"But then to lose Trogus ..." Gellius looked up at Aculeo, his eyes hollow with grief. "I truly loved him."

"I know you did. He loved you too."

"I miss him so." Gellius buried his face in his hands, unable to utter another word.

"Stay here as long as you like. It's better than living in the street."

"Not by much," Xanthias muttered.

"You would offer me refuge?" Gellius said in astonishment, tears streaming down his cheeks. "I racked my soul for days plotting my revenge against you."

"You had good reason to, or thought you did," Aculeo said.

"And yet the day I come to kill you," Gellius said, "I learn you're still the dearest of friends, still a man of virtue!"

Aculeo stepped reluctantly into the fullery's taberna, eyes stinging from the ripe stench of the smoldering sulphur pits with little breeze to thin it. He walked through the stuffy little fauces and poked his head around the doorway to the atrium where he could see the slaves hard at work. And there was Pesach, carrying a yoke slung with two great slopping skins of aged urine. He looked even worse than he had before, just sticks and hide, his face raw and red as a radish boiled too long in a pot. His left shoulder and arm were discoloured with a sprawling, yellowish-purple bruise, remnant of a beating no doubt. He felt sick at the sight.

"Pesach," Aculeo called in a low voice, walking towards him.

The slave glanced up and one of the skins sloshed its odious contents onto the dusty ground. "Gah, look what you made me do!" he spat, then continued staggering towards the treading vats. "I told you last time to leave me be," he growled as two slaves helped him unhitch the skins from the yoke.

"Gurculio's dead."

Pesach scowled, taken aback. "What did you just say?"

"He was murdered in his villa a week ago."

The fuller's slave nodded slowly to himself, lips twisting into a half smile. "Who did it?"

"Panthea I think."

"That whore," Pesach said, then shrugged and dumped a foul smelling skin into the vat. "But it hardly helps me. The treacherous bastard already sold me off like some old plough-horse."

"What does that matter? Come on, let's go."

"Easy enough for you to say. Do you know the punishment for a runaway slave?" He nodded towards a thoroughly wretched looking young man limping painfully through the atrium, lugging a basket heaped with dripping wet clothes. "He tried to run away four months back. When he was finally captured, they cut the three middle toes off each foot. He won't be running far anymore. Thanks very much for your encouragement, Aculeo, but I happen to like my toes."

"Stay then," Aculeo said. "You'll likely be dead before the year is out."

"There is that," Pesach allowed grudgingly. "But where would I even go? I dare not face my family. I've no friends left. None that would admit to it at least."

"Stay with me then. We'll figure it out from there. I just took Gellius in as well."

"Gellius?"

"It's a long story."

Pesach considered him for a moment, then gave a bitter laugh. "No, I don't think so," he said, hoisting the second of the skins of stinking urine to empty into the treading vat.

"Why not?"

"You're up to something. What's in it for you?"

"What do you mean?" Aculeo asked.

"Why are you trying to help me?"

"Because this is no way for a Roman citizen to live. I feel responsible for you somehow. I can't bear to have your fate hanging like a millstone around my neck."

Pesach snorted. "See, it's always about you."

"Just put down that pisspot and let's go before the fuller catches us."

"But I'd be giving up all I accomplished here. I'm to be head velicus once Polus over there is dead. Which should happen soon enough. He's not looking well lately. It comes with an extra ration of bread per day, you know."

"I'll get you all the bread you can eat. Now come on!"

"I might as well, I suppose," Pesach said with a sigh. "What's the plan?"

"What do you mean?" Aculeo scowled. "We just ... go."

"So we're to simply traipse out the front gate? You really planned nothing better than that?"

"Well ..."

"I have to do everything I suppose. Alright then." Pesach grabbed a clean tunic from a drying rack and changed into it, tossing his old one onto a smouldering sulphur pit. A yellowish-grey stream of smoke spilled forth as the tunic ignited. "Come on, help me out," he snapped and they grabbed a few more tunics and piled them on the fire until a thick smoke reeking of rotten eggs filled the atrium.

Then came the first screams of panic from the other slaves.

"Now we can go," Pesach said, coughing and gagging from the smoke.

The master fuller stumbled through the atrium and looked around, florid-faced and confused. "What's going on here?" he cried. He grabbed a pair of frightened slaves by the shoulders. "Empty the vat on the fire you fools! Pesach, help them!"

"Why would I help them put out the fire, you pox-faced cunt? I'm the one who started it," Pesach said cheerfully.

The fuller gave him a bewildered look, then threw up his hands in exasperation and ran towards the exit. Pesach tripped him as he went past, sending him sprawling to the ground.

"Can we go now?" Aculeo demanded.

"With pleasure," Pesach said, leading the way to the posticum at the back of the atrium.

As they walked back along the city streets, Aculeo revealed what he knew about the murders of Gurculio, Myrrhine, Trogus and Iovinus and the search for Neaera and Posidippus of Cos.

"I'd have been safer staying in the fullery," Pesach said. "It sounds like a madhouse out here these days."

They came to the edge of the Agora, the smell of fine food and rich spices from all the merchants' carts and little shops like heavenly perfume. Pesach stopped, closed his eyes and sniffed the air, licking his cracked lips. "Ah, the smell of freedom! I've not eaten anything decent in months, unless you count maggoty bread. Which isn't all that bad, by the way, you rather get used to it, but still ..."

"Come on then, we'll get you some food."

"Not so fast," Pesach said. He was looking towards a tall limestone building with long blue glass windows and a pair of weathered statues of some old Egyptian gods dragged from some abandoned temple propped up on either side of the entrance. The Baths of Sabinus, the inscription over the lintel read.

"The baths? Now?" Aculeo asked irritably.

"Of course. What are we, barbarians? If I'm to return to some semblance of civilization, surely a visit to the baths is a requirement, is it not? Besides, we can get something to eat in there."

"Fine. Whatever, let's go."

A few minutes later they'd stripped off their chitons in the change area, walked barefoot down the mosaic-tiled corridor to the showers and stood next to one another as funnels of cool water poured from the stone lions' maws overhead, dousing them both head to foot. After the showers they headed into the vapour room, taking a bench well away from the braziers of hot coals. The steam smelled of sandalwood and enveloped them like a thick cocoon. Bath attendants came forward to apply oil to their skin.

"Make certain you use real Attican oil, not that cheap Syrian dreck," Pesach said haughtily. "And don't skimp on the myrrh." He leaned back against the wall and sighed as an attendant rubbed oil into his shoulders, arms and back and began to scrape it off with a strigil.

"I'll see you in the pools," Aculeo said irritably, and headed into a vast, crowded chamber with several large mosaic-tiled hot and cold pools. He plunged into a cold pool, the chilled water pumped up from the underground caverns prickling against his feverish skin, and tilted his head back so that only his mouth and nose broke the surface, letting the cool air fill his lungs in slow, deep breaths. Pesach entered the pool a few minutes later, looking almost meditative.

After a few minutes they moved to a steaming hot pool, sitting on one of the underwater ledges. Fresh, hot bath water gushed from the amphorae held by a pair of marble nymphs standing at the edge of the pool, both of them with generous curves and welcoming smiles. A food vendor carried his tray over to the side of the bath and met them with an eager grin. "Some food, gentlemen? I have spiced pork, wonderful fresh bread, luscious, plump olives, aged cheese, perhaps some chilled wine?"

"Mmm yes – I'll have everything," Pesach said, then settled back as the vendor began to set out some plates and cups at the pool's edge, humming happily as he worked. "Wretched baths, you must admit. Is this where you usually come these days?"

"When I can afford it, yes," Aculeo said, worrying what his generosity might cost him.

"They're nothing like the Baths of Vitus, are they? I wouldn't be surprised if they pump the bath water in from the latrines to save an as. Still, I suppose we all need to make accommodations in these trying times."

D.L. Johnstone

"I suppose." He was already beginning to question his wisdom in freeing Pesach – he'd forgotten how irritating the man could be!

"It's not like we're alone in this ignoble fate, I suppose. You'll never believe who I saw in the vapour room after you left. Bitucus! Remember him?"

Aculeo sat up suddenly, startling the food vendor. "Who did you say?"

"Bitucus. That pompous prick, I never liked him."

"We need to get out of here," Aculeo said, and started climbing from the bath. He spotted a fully clothed man emerging from the vapour room, scanning the crowded room. Bitucus. Theopompus and Viator the slave were right behind him. "Shit," he whispered, and sat back down, sliding down as low as he could in the water.

"What's the matter with …?" Pesach began, then spotted the men. He grabbed Aculeo's upper arm, digging his fingertips deep into the flesh. "What trap have you led me into now?" he hissed. "It's not enough to see me suffer in that pisshouse you induced me to escape and then this?"

"Shut up and hide, fool!"

Pesach scowled at him, then slid down in the water, watching, waiting. The four men finally turned around and left, not having seen them apparently.

"Come on," Aculeo said. They climbed out of the baths, walking naked back towards the vapour room.

"Wait, what about your feast?" the vendor cried.

Aculeo peered into the vapour room. No sign of Bitucus or the others. They had just made their way back into the shower room when someone called out, "There he is!" Theopompus! Pesach sprinted back into the vapour room, shoving past the other bathers.

Aculeo tried to follow but Viator caught his wrist in a vicious grip and slammed him face-first against hot, dripping wall of the vapor room, twisting his arm so far behind his back he feared his shoulder would tear out of the socket. Viator wrapped his powerful forearm around Aculeo's throat, almost choking him as he turned him about, then thrust his knee up hard between Aculeo's naked buttocks. The other bathers and the attendants quickly cleared out. A moment later, Bitucus appeared, barely managing to keep ahold of the spitting, cursing Pesach.

Theopompus was right behind them, and gave a predatory, brown-toothed smile. "Good to see you again, Aculeo. And you've got a friend with you? What are you doing out, Pesach?"

"Fuck you, Icarian," Pesach growled. "On my oath I'm going to kill you."

"You're not in much of a position to do that."

"Not you, ball-sucker. Him," he said, jerking his head towards Aculeo.

"You're moving up in the world, Bitucus," Aculeo gasped. "First working for a moneylender, now kissing his sycophant's ass."

"Shut your mouth, Aculeo," Bitucus snapped.

"Just tell us where you stashed them," said Theopompus.

"I don't know what you're talking about."

The Icarian stepped in and punched him hard in the stomach. Viator had to hold him upright for a moment as Aculeo doubled over in pain, trying to catch his breath. "Now, where did you put them?" Theopompus asked slowly, as if he were talking to a slow-witted child.

"He's not telling you a thing," Pesach snarled. Theopompus gave him a pleasant smile, then backhanded him across the face. Pesach shook it off, then grinned at the man, blood dripping from his split lip. "Ooh, that one tickled a bit. You'd better try harder than that, you Icarian shit."

"Shut up, Pesach," Aculeo said, trying to think, his head spinning.

"Tell me, Theopompus," Pesach gasped, "do Icarians really have cocks like radish sprouts? Your mother told me that's why your women prefer to be fucked by donkeys ..."

Theopompus struck him across the face again, then kneed him in the groin. Pesach cried out in pain, collapsing to the floor.

"Sorry, Pesach," Bitucus whispered.

"Fuck you ... up the ass ... with Vulcan's poxed cock," Pesach moaned.

Theopompus turned to Aculeo, considering him for a moment, then punched him in the stomach. Aculeo fell to his knees, crying out in agony when Theopompus kicked him in the back and kidneys. He curled in on himself, covering his head with his hands, trying not to vomit.

"Where ... are ... they?" Theopompus demanded, punctuating each word with another well-placed kick.

"You know, Theopompus," Pesach managed to gasp from where he lay. "I've been led to believe your mother likes it up the ass. Like mother, like son I suppose."

"Pluto's stinking hole, shut up, Pesach!" Aculeo groaned.

Theopompus had clearly had his fill. Aculeo closed his eyes and turned away as Theopompus proceeded to savagely beat the naked man. Pesach lay on the ground, unmoving, his blood staining the water that pooled beneath him.

"Do I have to ... beat you both ... to death?" Theopompus huffed, out of breath from the exertion. "Come on, Aculeo. I can't say I even blame you for killing Gurculio. I only want to know where they are."

"What … what are you talking … about?" Aculeo gasped, breath jagged and sharp in his chest. "I didn't kill Gurculio."

"I told you," Bitucus whispered.

"Shut up," Theopompus snapped, then turned to Aculeo. "Who did it then?"

"My guess is Panthea," Aculeo said. "The Blue Bird was abandoned the next day. She's long gone."

The Icarian licked his lips, thinking – it seemed he hadn't considered this. "Even if that's true, the whore's not clever enough to have done it on her own. She'd have needed help. I'm guessing it was you, Roman. Now where are they?"

"What are you talking about?"

"Flavianus' tablets, what else? It's a bit late in the game to play stupid, isn't it?"

"Flavianus' tablets? Are they the same ones Iovinus was murdered for?" Aculeo asked.

Theopompus stared at him, startled. "You mean you really don't know?" He started to laugh.

A shrill squeal of pain echoed through the chamber. Viator turned to see what was happening, his grip loosening just enough. Aculeo seized the slave's hand and bit it, feeling the bones and tendons crunch between his teeth, a warm gush of blood filling his mouth. Viator screeched in pain and Aculeo swung his fist up hard into the man's groin. He slumped to his knees, chirping little moans of pain. Pesach was standing nearby, battered but quite alive, a strigil in his hand, smeared with blood. Bitucus stumbled from the room, his face grey and pallid, holding onto a ghastly wound across his belly that threatened to unleash his innards.

"Shit," Theopompus said under his breath. Pesach started towards him and the Icarian squealed in terror and ran. Viator found his feet and limped after them.

"Should we follow them?" Pesach asked. One of his eyes was swollen shut, his nose looked broken and he was missing a tooth, but he managed to grin.

"We wouldn't get too far chasing them naked through the streets," Aculeo said. "Thanks, by the way."

"Fuck you and your thanks. I still need a place to sleep, don't I?" Pesach narrowed his eyes at him. "What was all this business about the tablets?"

"I'm really not sure," Aculeo said as they headed back towards the change room, holding his tongue for the moment.

"Hah, just like you," Pesach scoffed. "About to get yourself murdered and you've no idea why. Well, come on then, I might as well see the little hole you've crawled into."

That evening, after Pesach and Gellius had both passed out on the floor of Aculeo's little flat, their stomachs filled and the wine amphorae empty, Aculeo returned to the ruins of Gurculio's villa. It was raining steadily. He stepped into the ianua, protecting his torch from the drizzle. The place carried the stench of rot and wet ash. A steady stream of water dripped from the tiled roof through the impluvium and into the mossy green pool in the centre of the entrance hall. The villa had been well looted, stripped of tapestries, statues, vases and furniture down to its cracked tile floor and scorched walls. Not too thoroughly, Aculeo hoped as he climbed carefully up the skeletal stairs to Gurculio's cubiculum. And there it is, he thought, the obsidian mirror at the foot of where the moneylender's bed had been. It would have been worth a small fortune if it hadn't been cracked from the heat of the fire. It was all but worthless now.

Aculeo traced a finger along the line of hardened wax dripping down the smoke-stained wall below. He found a marble bust of Gurculio – a disturbingly good likeness not even the looters had wanted – and heaved it against the mirror. Shards of obsidian rained on the floor, along with three wooden frames. The type used to hold wax tablets.

Were they worth dying for, Iovinus? Aculeo wondered, crouching down to retrieve the frames. But what wax had once been there had melted in the heat of the fire, leaving nothing but bare wooden backboards. And whatever had been written there was now long gone.

The rain cast a damp chill on the evening. The smart thing would have been to return home and get some rest. Instead Aculeo found himself standing outside Calisto's villa. It seemed she already had a visitor, though, for a handful of slaves he didn't recognize lingered just outside the gates of her villa, standing guard. The rain spattered on the paving stones and tapped on the clay tile roof, but Aculeo stayed where he was. Thunder crackled overhead, rumbling across the sky like rocks through a hollow cavern. The air smelled sharp, earthy, and the rain began in earnest, but Aculeo simply closed his eyes and listened, the rain running down his face, soaking his robes. He thought he could hear Calisto's cries from beyond the walls. Whether they were of passion or pain he couldn't tell, but the ache that roiled up from the depths of his heart punished him nonetheless.

He watched the rain falling all around him in glistening sheets, washing down the rutted streets, spilling into the gutters and the canal. We all play a role in this life, Zeanthes had said. A hero, a villain, or just part of the chorus. He may well be right about that, but the question remains, do we even have a choice of what role we play?

The alley reeked of vomit, piss and unwashed, sweaty bodies as the gamblers gathered around, placing their wagers. I've nothing left, Aculeo thought as he threw down more silver then cast the dice against the wall, vaguely registering the roar and curses of those around him.

Whatever secrets Iovinus and Gurculio may have hidden have gone to Tartarus with them. It's all been for naught – and I've been a fool. There's nothing here for me. Calisto's not even within my reach. She's Ralla's hetaira. Bought and paid for. The crowd roared again as the dice landed. More silver fell, another call to place bets.

Silver, Aculeo thought miserably, putting down more coins. It always comes down to that, doesn't it? What happened to Titiana when the silver was gone? Back to Rome to marry Spurius Lartius Carnifex, no less. Let her. I can do nothing to stop her anyway. I've nothing left.

Calisto's no different. I can't afford her, not on any level, he thought, casting the dice into the dim shadows against the wall, the crowd aroused, pushing and shoving, roaring and scrabbling, straining to see them land. He downed his wine, harsh and sickeningly sweet, spiked with cheap perfume, spilling half of it down his chin. He emptied his purse on the ground to the glee of those around him then gathered up the dice again.

Albius Ralla. Friend of the Prefect, no less. What was his role in all of this? I suppose I'll never know. There's no one left to tell me – Iovinus is gone, Corvinus, Neaera, Myrrhine, Petras, Gurculio … That bastard's outplayed me on every turn. He must have laughed to see me at his symposium, blind fool that I am. Everything I touch has turned to shit.

Images of Titiana rose in his mind unbidden like smoke, the pain he'd seen in her eyes when she'd learned of how he'd lost their fortune, and their family honour with it. It was as though a cord tying them together had been severed, never to be repaired. And what of Atellus? My own son to be raised by another man, to call him father, to take his name. What will happen to mine? Atellus will lose it – he won't even remember it.

Aculeo threw the dice. The crowd roared again, a handful of sweaty silver was shoved into his hand as others pounded him on the back. A rare winning toss.

"Come on, darling, let's find some place quiet," a woman's voice whispered in his ear. He felt a soft hand taking him by the arm, pulling him away into the dark alley. He looked blearily at her, her dark hair tangled with curls and a sloppy, drunken grin on her face. "Let's help you spend some of that."

"Why not?" he said, slumping against the wall, his eyes unfocused as he gazed at her. So young, he thought, so sweet. "But another drink first. I'm so thirsty."

"Already flying with the birds, aren't you? Come here," she said, leaning down to kiss him on the mouth, her breath sour and dirty. He could hear the crowds still playing dice, roaring in the darkness as the next player tossed.

"What's your name?" Aculeo slurred as she fumbled with her chiton, helping his hands find her.

"Philomena," she said.

"Philomena … how do I know that name?"

Someone opened the back door of the kapeleion and dim yellow light flooded into the alley. He recognized her when he saw her face, the dark bruise under one eye, the swollen lip. She turned away self-consciously. Aculeo cupped her chin, touched her throat, a cold wave of sobriety flooding through his clouded head. The girl pulled away, frightened now, but Aculeo held her tight. "Wait."

"Let go of me," she whimpered. "Please!"

"I'm not going to hurt you. Just tell me where you got this?" Aculeo asked, holding up the necklace Philomena wore around her neck.

Neaera's cameo necklace.

CHAPTER XXIII

THE 4TH DAY OF MAIUS

The recluse lay curled up on a pile of straw on the floor, his breathing rough, laboured. Flies swarmed about his festering wounds, filling the hot, fetid air with their relentless buzzing. His skin was sallow, his wounds puffy with a greenish haze blooming beneath the flesh.

"Apollonios!" Aculeo growled. The recluse started, squinted up at him, his glassy eyes slowly coming into focus. Aculeo held out his fist. The man flinched, drawing away in fear. "Do you remember this?" Aculeo opened his hand, revealing the necklace he'd taken from Philomena.

Apollonios looked at it, blinking. "So pretty," he whispered, then resumed muttering to himself.

"You stole this from Neaera, didn't you?" Aculeo said.

"Such a pretty thing," the recluse whispered.

"Then you gave it as a gift to the porne Philomena. Your Eurydice."

A flash of recognition, touched with regret. "She loved me."

"She's a porne, fool. You paid her to love you. Not to let you almost kill her though."

"Eurydice..." Apollonios whispered, tears running down his filthy, wounded face.

"Yes, well, she's alive at least, not like the others, eh?" Aculeo weighed the necklace in his hand, looking down at the broken man before him, trying to piece the horrific pieces of the puzzle back together. How could I have gotten myself mixed up in all that madness about Ralla? Spinning twisted fantasies, trying to make sense of things when it was this filthy wretch behind the women's murders all along! "What did you do with Neaera? Did you toss her body in the canal as well?"

Apollonios hugged his knees to his chest, his eyes closed, rocking back and forth as he muttered nonsense to himself.

"How did you even take her in the first place? Did you lie in wait for her? Attack her when she was alone on the street then murder her and steal her necklace?"

The recluse looked at him in confusion. "I took the necklace from the slave. Sarapis provides ... gives me sanctuary. I must give sacrifice."

"You're tripping over your own lies now, fool," Aculeo growled. "The necklace belonged to Neaera, not the slave."

"I went to the temple of Sarapis to ... to seek forgiveness. To give worship. To pray. Please, I must give sacrifice ... sacrifice ... I must give sacrifice."

"Is that it then? You killed them in sacrifice to Sarapis?"

"Nonononononoooooo ..." Apollonios said as he covered his ears, closed his eyes and rocked back and forth.

"Their blood still stains your tunic. The supplicant Cleon saw you murder that slave."

"The necklace ... the necklace was the slave's. I ... I gave her my bracelet so that Sarapis would save her. Fair trade," Apollonios said weakly, then he seized Aculeo's hand with a frantic fury. "Do you know of the Great One's divine purpose in this world?"

"To Tartarus with your Great One! Tell me what you did!"

"The Furies," Apollonios cried, pointing a quivering finger over Aculeo's shoulder. "Do their eyes not drip with the sickness of their desire for vengeance?"

Aculeo glanced warily over his shoulder, then spat on the floor just in case. Pah, listen to him, getting me tangled again in his lunacy like some black foul muck. He grabbed the recluse by his grubby tunic and threw him up against the mud-brick wall. "Here I was thinking it couldn't possibly be a mad recluse like you who killed those women," he whispered hoarsely. "It had to be another. Gurculio, perhaps, or even Albius Ralla, no less, a Friend of the Prefect's!"

"Please ..." Apollonios gasped.

Aculeo could smell the man's foul breath, his flesh feverish to the touch. "Tell me what happened, damn you, before I feed you my knife and let your filthy blood drain into the dirt."

"Hail O Great One," Apollonios choked, tears running down his scarred face. "May others learn to worship you as I so humbly do."

Aculeo shoved his forearm against the man's throat, choking him. "Pray all you like, but your god has abandoned you. We're all alone here, just you and me, facing what you've done at last." Apollonios looked up at him, his confusion suddenly cleared like a passing storm, replaced by the oddest expression – a gentle smile. "What are you grinning about?"

The recluse snatched the knife from Aculeo's belt with startling speed.

"No!" Aculeo cried, breaking free of the lunatic.

"Hail Sarapis," Apollonios cried, his eyes now lit with a fervent glow, then turned the blade and shoved it into his own belly. A gush of blood spilled from his mouth and he slid down the wall, gasping for breath.

"What did you do?"

"I … I give … sacrifice!" Apollonios whispered.

Aculeo stumbled retching from the cell, stinking of blood and death, and called to the guards for help.

"There was nothing anyone could do," Sekhet said solemnly, closing Apollonios' eyes. "Even if I'd gotten here in time, he was too far gone to begin with."

Aculeo said nothing as he looked down at his trembling hands, the front of his tunic still sticky with the other man's blood.

"He was a soldier?" she asked, examining the heavy scarring on the man's wasted limbs.

"Many years ago," Aculeo said. "A hero in the Battle of Teutoburg, his brother claimed." The healer looked at him, puzzled – the battle's name clearly meant nothing to her.

Sekhet summoned the guards. "Take the body to the Necropolis, ask for the priest Paheri," she said. "And don't try to dodge this, it's not a good idea to deceive those in charge of guiding your journey into the afterlife, understand?" The guards grudgingly carried Apollonios' body from the cell. The healer looked at Aculeo and frowned. "When's the last time you had something solid to eat?"

"I can't remember. Yesterday sometime I think."

"Come. We can talk of these things while you eat."

Sekhet's home was a single story, mud-brick structure on the end of a row of similar houses built along the edge of the winding blue Draco River in Rhakotis. She led Aculeo through the anteroom into a large central room with a simple table and four mud-brick benches along the walls cushioned with reed mats. Behind that was another room with a low bench and two sets of stairs, one leading to the roof, the second down underground. She brought him a basin of water to wash up and a fresh tunic to change into.

When he was done he went out to the back of the house where an open garden looked over the river. Half a dozen women, young and old, sat in the courtyard beneath the shade of a sprawling acacia while an old man sipped beer slowly from his clay jar. Gurculio's little dog Felix sat on the old man's lap, growling when it spotted Aculeo. A number of children ran up from where they'd been playing alongside the canal and gathered excitedly around Sekhet. The adults offered Aculeo polite nods of greeting, though they seemed not to have a single word of Latin or Greek among them.

"My family," Sekhet explained. "Too many names. You'll never remember them." She spoke to them all quickly in Demotic. The other women laughed and chattered to one another, while the old man cast Aculeo a suspicious glare.

"This way," Sekhet said, and led Aculeo up the back stairs to the roof, where they sat beneath a sun-bleached canvas awning. They had a fine view of the river from there, a winding sapphire ribbon feeding out towards the dark Egyptian Sea.

Aculeo told her of the porne Philomena, Neaera's necklace and of his final interrogation of Apollonios. Sekhet listened quietly, the sun warming her lined, weary face as she gazed out towards the sea. When Aculeo was done, the healer remained silent, her eyes closed, as though she was sleeping. She looked up at him finally, staring at him with her dark, penetrating eyes. "Why should Apollonios have wanted to kill himself?"

"He feared prison, trial, execution ..."

She snorted. "I doubt whether he was even capable of committing these murders much less almost getting away with it," the healer said calmly.

"Oh? And what do you think happened then?"

"Let's define exactly what we know. First, the river slave's murder. The Temple of Sarapis is a destination for the ignorant who seek to be healed. We know for a fact she'd been mortally wounded days before she ever reached the temple. She may well have gone there on her own accord to pray to the god to mend her wounds. By the time she reached the sanctuary, she was almost dead."

"A witness saw Apollonios attack her there."

"Your so-called witness sounds confused at best," Sekhet said with a dismissive wave. "He was frightened, it was dark, and much time had passed when he finally spoke to you about what he saw. The mind often fills in details over time, changes them, trying to rearrange them to make sense of chaos."

"We know for a fact that Apollonios attacked the porne Philomena," Aculeo said. "He tried to murder her."

"Yet for that he had a motive. A deranged one, I admit, but a motive nonetheless. What motive did he have to murder a dying slave?"

"The same one he had for all the other murders!"

Sekhet shrugged. "Again, I question whether he murdered anyone."

"You say that so easily!"

"You may be a Roman but that doesn't give you the privilege to stop using your head. How many pornes do you know that would have gone with a man like him in the first place? None. They're not fools. Apollonios was clearly deranged, an unwashed, scar-faced beggar. Pornes learn early on to judge who to go or not go with, else they don't survive on the streets long."

"Philomena went with him, didn't she?"

"And when he turned on her she stabbed him in the throat," Sekhet said. "One of the first things pornes learn is how to defend themselves. They can still fall victim, clearly, but not at the hands of a man like Apollonios. It's inconceivable.

"And then there are the hetairai. Petras, and after her Neaera, then Myrrhine. Do you honestly think Apollonios could have seduced any of them, drawn them away from their world of symposia, sophists and song, made them vanish with barely a trace, even thinking to send and pay for one of them to be embalmed at the Necropolis?" She stared at him, her black eyes glittering and fierce.

Aculeo leaned back in his chair, hands covering his face, exhausted all of a sudden. "My head's spinning from it all."

"Think about it – a man like him wouldn't have been permitted near a hetaira. They're never alone when they're in the street – they have slaves and bodyguards protecting them at all times, guarding their owners' investment. No, it had to be someone closer to them instead. Someone who can move in their circles, not draw suspicion."

Two women arrived then, carrying platters of unleavened bread, lentils, pickled cucumbers, onions, and long strips of saltfish. The old man followed, truculently bearing a large jar of beer that he practically threw on the table, letting it slosh over the sides of the jar. He muttered something under his breath to Sekhet, who shot him a scowl, sending him scuttling back down the stairs after the women.

"What's wrong with him?" Aculeo asked.

"My brother's just not a big lover of Romans. Not an uncommon sentiment in this part of the city, I'm afraid. Still, I suppose if Egyptians can bear our conquerors' yoke for the past few centuries, those conquerors can bear the occasional display of resentment. Eat up – this should do wonders to restore your humours."

Aculeo dug into the food, surprised at how hungry he actually was. The plates were emptied in no time, and the cups refilled several times. At last he sighed and sat back in his chair. "So if Apollonios wasn't responsible, what do you think happened?"

"The answer starts with the river slave," Sekhet said. "Her path intersected with Neaera's, that much is clear, for she had her necklace. She most likely stole it and planned to sell it when she could. She was injured though. She managed to make her way to the Sarapeion, seeking to be healed. Apollonios came across her there, but it was too late for her, her injuries were too severe. She died there, and Apollonios stole the necklace. Eventually he gave it to Philomena. When you interrogated him, reminding him of what he'd done to her, his gift to her in your hands, it was more than he could bear. And so he offered himself as final sacrifice to his god."

"It's possible," Aculeo admitted.

"It's more than possible," Sekhet said sharply. "It's brilliant. What am I missing?"

Aculeo recalled another detail he'd almost forgotten. "I found a symbol drawn in blood on the Furies' shrine near the Sarapeion when the slave was murdered."

Sekhet narrowed her eyes and called out something to one of her cousins, who quickly brought some scraps of used papyrus, a brush and a block of ink. "Show me," she said.

Aculeo daubed the brush in the inkblock and drew the symbol he'd seen on the Furies' shrine.

She smiled, took the brush from him and drew the following symbol.

"This is Djew," she said. "The Egyptian hieroglyph for mountain, and the cosmic mountain range that holds up the heavens. Now this," she drew a circle between the two peaks, and two outstretched lines below it.

"This is Akhet. The circle is the sun, which rises and sets between the mountains, while lion deities sit upon each peak to guard it during its journey. The Nile flows from it, the source of all life." She lay the brush down. "It's a symbol of tombs where the Great Kings of ancient times were buried. A symbol of the afterlife. The slave likely drew it before she died."

Aculeo watched the children run laughing down to the canal to splash and play in the dark blue waters. "But what about Myrrhine? Or Petras? What about the yellow cords they wore on their wrists?"

"That I don't know yet, but it's a start," Sekhet said. "Learn where the river slave came from and you'll find where Neaera was taken."

"You think she could still be alive?" The thought was almost too much to hope for.

Sekhet looked dubious. "Anything's possible, I suppose. If the gods are less kind, you may at least learn who her killer is. Not to mention the killer of Petras and Myrrhine."

"Someone close to them," Aculeo said. "Someone who can move in their circles and not draw suspicion. Someone like Ralla." He shook his head bitterly, his eyes closed in exhaustion. "If I'm right, we haven't a chance."

"Why not?"

"It's not the way the world works, that's why. Ralla is much too powerful, too well connected."

Sekhet knitted her brows, narrowed her deep-set eyes at him, unsmiling now. "There are other women at risk as well you know. Your friend Calisto most of all. He's her patron, is he not?" Aculeo gave a reluctant nod. "And what of the girl you entrusted to Calisto. Tyche? How long before Ralla gets his hands on her? And the little one after her." They could hear the shouts and laughter of the children down at the canal ringing through the afternoon air.

"That can't happen," Aculeo said.

"Don't be naïve. Of course it can. In fact it will. Calisto can't stop him. She's his chattel."

"I won't let it happen."

"Oh? And what will you do about it then?" the healer scoffed. "Change the way the world works?"

"Just a small part of it. My part."

Sekhet laughed suddenly, patting his hand. "See, you're looking better already."

CHAPTER XXIV

THE 5TH DAY OF MAIUS

The monkey leapt off the man's shoulder onto the wagon of fruit, landing without a sound. The monkey's owner, an old man with dark skin like ancient, cracked leather, winked at Idaia and Tyche as his pet clambered noiselessly up the fruit, pausing every so often to sniff a piece or to scratch itself. The fruit merchant never noticed it, calling greetings to the patrons as they strolled past. Idaia admired the silver fur that covered the little creature from the tip of its long, curving tail to the top of its head, save for the patches of white and black fur that marked its little face like an actor's mask.

The monkey grinned at the girls from atop the mountain of gleaming fresh pears and figs, quite proud of itself. Idaia covered her mouth, trying not to laugh. Tyche smiled in spite of herself. Calisto was just up ahead, arm in arm with another woman dressed in yellow silks, as they examined a bolt of cloth, the litter bearers standing nearby paying little attention.

The monkey crept along the fruit until it found itself a choice banana and sat on its haunches, peeled it with its tiny black hands and popped a piece in its mouth, chewing with great gusto. The fruit merchant kept calling to passersby, waving flies off himself, still oblivious to the little thief sitting atop his wagon. The monkey's owner gave a little whistle and the monkey stuffed the rest of its banana into its already bulging cheeks and leaped back onto his shoulder.

Calisto and her friend were further up ahead now, not watching them at all. "Can we pet her?" Idaia asked the man.

He smiled – revealing his toothless purple gums – and had the monkey run down his arm and jump into a surprised Idaia's hands. She squealed in delight as it curled its tail around her wrist, rubbed its head against her chest, then jumped onto Tyche's shoulders, wrapping itself behind her neck, making her laugh as well. Idaia was so intensely happy at that moment, she felt like she would burst.

The monkey peeked up suddenly from beneath the girl's hair, its bright eyes wide, its black lips pursed in a small o shape, then bared its teeth and shrieked, startling them both. It jumped back into the man's arms, scuttling up his shoulders to safety.

"Look," Idaia said solemnly, looking over Tyche's shoulder.

The older girl turned her head. Four men were staring at them from across the way. One of them had a harelip, the other three were dishevelled looking with wild, greasy hair and unkempt, salt-caked beards, like sailors just come ashore. Idaia felt a cold shudder when she noticed the way the men stared at them. One of the men licked his wormy lips and they began their approach.

"Come," Tyche said, squeezing Idaia's hand tight in her own. As the girls made their way towards Calisto and her friend they spotted three other men armed with stout sticks advancing on her from the opposite direction. One of the litter bearers noticed as well and moved next to Calisto, protecting her. The men with the sticks made their move. The litter bearer knocked one of them to the ground but another attacker clubbed him across the head. Any nearby patrons and merchants scattered, unsure what to do except to save their own hides.

The three sailors pushed their way through the crowd from the rear, heading straight towards the children. Calisto noticed them then. "Run!" she cried, pushing her friend away. She started to move towards the girls but she was so far away and the crowds so heavy. Tyche seized Idaia's hand and they took off through the narrow laneways of the Agora, weaving their way through the dense bustling square of vendors' carts, countless shrines and temples in the crowded marketplace, past open stalls of salt vendors, unguent boilers, sellers of ebony, cosmetics, sandals and myrrh, finally turning down a side street. They immediately realized the trap – the street was abandoned, hidden in the shadows of tall, windowless warehouses, and at the end of the street was a dismal little section of the canal. The men were right behind them now.

Calisto reached them then but twisted her ankle on the uneven pavement and fell to her knees, crying out in pain.

D.L. Johnstone

"What's happening?" Idaia whispered.

"Just run!" Tyche cried.

"We can't just leave Calisto."

"We need to find help. Now run!"

The girls ran down the dark laneway, panicked, until they came to the end. There was a little dirt pathway that ran along the canal, littered with trash and broken mud-brick. And there almost hidden in a crop of tangled weeds was a forgotten shrine, its dedication hidden behind the tall yellow grass.

"Wait here," Tyche said, shoving Idaia behind the shrine. "Don't come out for anything, understand?" Idaia nodded, terrified, and watched, sick with fear, as Tyche kicked off her sandals and ran down the muddy path in her bare feet.

Idaia crouched behind the shrine, her heart pounding in her chest, her breath fast and painful in her throat until she couldn't bear it any longer. She peeked out from behind the shrine and watched as Calisto stood to face the men, her face pale, her expression a mixture of anger and fear. "Osti," the child whispered.

One of the men called something in a foreign tongue to the others, who laughed. They approached Calisto then, one from the front, two from the side. The fourth man, the harelip, hung back, watching.

The man in front grabbed Calisto's arm, pulled her in close against him, kissed her on the neck. She screamed, tried to push him away. He slapped her hard across the face then grabbed the front of her chiton, tore it open, baring her small, pale breasts, her necklace breaking, the jewels spilling on the broken street.

Calisto reached into her belt as the man approached, found her small knife, the blade flashing in the sun as she swung it and sliced the man's face open. He squealed in pain, stumbling backwards, hand pressed to his bleeding face. Two of the other men stepped back warily. Geta stepped in and grabbed Calisto's knife hand at the wrist, twisting her arm around until she dropped the knife. One of the other men picked it up, moved forwards as the harelip held her fast, pulling her by the hair to make her stand upright, her throat and chest exposed.

Idaia smothered a scream.

"Hoi, let her go!" The attackers looked up in surprise. Half a dozen Roman soldiers dressed in bright red capes had appeared, Tyche right behind them. The harelip shoved Calisto to the ground and the men all scattered, the soldiers chasing them into the marketplace.

Idaia ran from her hiding spot towards Calisto, sobbing in relief. Calisto sat up, her arms across her chest to cover her nakedness. Tyche helped her to stand. The litter arrived then. "Are you alright, Mistress?" one of the soldiers asked.

"I'm fine," Calisto said, trying to regain her composure. As he helped her to stand, though, she wavered, putting her hand against the side of the litter to catch herself. Her arm and hand were wet with blood.

"You're hurt!" Idaia cried.

Calisto glanced at her arm and shook her head, her face pale as paste. "It's not my blood."

"Tyche says..." Idaia began, but Tyche shook her head. "I mean..."

"What?" Calisto said, looking at the girl.

"Nothing," Tyche said. "I'm just glad you're alright."

Calisto stroked the girl's cheek thoughtfully then climbed into the litter. The girls followed her. Calisto pulled the curtain across the window, then bowed her head. They could see her shoulders were trembling. It sounded like she was crying.

Idaia and Tyche looked at one another but neither of them said a word.

"There are too many ships," Pesach announced.

Aculeo had tried in vain to ignore his interminable guests. Having settled rather comfortably into Aculeo's modest lodgings – a little too comfortably, Xanthias had mentioned on more than one occasion – and continuously emptying the pantry in record time, Pesach and Gellius had since taken to entertaining themselves by nosing about in Aculeo's private papers, including those in the chest of company documents Aculeo had inherited following Corvinus' suicide.

"What do you mean?" Aculeo said wearily.

"I mean as I say – there are too many ships. How much grain is shipped to Rome each year?" Pesach asked.

"How should I know?"

Gellius snorted. "Far be it from Aculeo to trouble himself with such minor details as the lifeblood of his belated company."

"Allow me to educate you then," Pesach said. "Fifteen million modii of grain are shipped to Rome each and every year. Two million for the annona that the government annually grants its citizens, the remainder sold to private hands."

"Fascinating," Aculeo said, stifling a yawn.

"Now, each ship can hold perhaps five thousand modii at most. So fifteen million divided by five thousand, that's three thousand grain ships to Rome per year thereabouts. Yet look here. According to Corvinus' records, the company chartered ships to carry three million modii last year just for the annona. That's half again what Rome even grants in toto."

Aculeo laid his head on the table and closed his eyes. The left side of his head had begun to throb – this sort of detail always made him ill. "The records must be wrong. The balance probably includes what was shipped to private merchants as well."

"It's little wonder he lost his fortune, he doesn't pay attention to the details," Gellius said.

"Anyway, it was a large enterprise," said Aculeo. "It's not so difficult to believe we shipped that much grain."

"Was it large?" Pesach asked, the corners of his mouth lifted in a mocking smile.

"Yes. What are you smirking about? Are you trying to make a specific point, Pesach?"

Pesach shrugged. "All I know is, there's not enough grain in the world to account for what's claimed in Corvinus' company records. The trouble is, we only have a partial record here."

"You kept no papers of your own?" asked Gellius.

"Corvinus held them all."

"Of course he did."

"And this was all you got from Corvinus' estate?" Pesach asked.

"Yes, that's it."

"Someone else must have taken the rest, then. Or destroyed them. Perhaps Gellius and I can find more information in the public records office, or at the Emporium." Pesach sighed and scratched his armpit, then his eyes fell across the scorched tablets that Aculeo had found in Gurculio's house now sitting in the corner of his tiny kitchen. He picked them up curiously. "What about Flavianus' tablets? Any idea what was on them?"

"Not a clue."

"Who is Flavianus exactly?" asked Gellius.

Aculeo shrugged. "Marcellus Flavianus is the only one I can think of. An associate of Corvinus'. I met him once years ago when he visited from Rome. I really know nothing about him though."

"Hm, well, whatever was on his tablets must have been important somehow. Jupiter himself knows enough people died for them," Pesach said, emptying the last amphora of wine into his cup.

Aculeo and Zeanthes found a quiet tavern near the crossroads just before dusk. The Palace District lay to the north, a majestic tapestry wrapped around the Great Harbour, bathed in the cool Etesian winds off the bay.

"This is quite lovely," Zeanthes said. He considered Aculeo for a moment. "You seem distracted though."

"An unrelated matter," Aculeo said with a rueful smile. "Apologies."

"Of course. It's such a pleasant surprise you called on me. I take it you have some news about the murders?"

Aculeo explained the events of the past few days – the discovery of Neaera's necklace, Apollonios' death in the prison and his own growing suspicion that Ralla himself was involved in Neaera's disappearance as well as the murders of Myrrhine and Petras.

"A disturbing conundrum," Zeanthes said solemnly, taking a sip of the cool black wine. "How certain are you of Ralla's involvement?"

"As certain as I can be without proof."

"Then we'll simply need to find our proof."

"Is that all?" Aculeo said with a bitter laugh.

"Trying took Troy, as they say. It's like Theseus and the ball of string. You have to follow it to find your way out of the labyrinth." Zeanthes signalled to the server to bring them more wine. "Tell me more about Petras. You seem to think her death is connected to this somehow?"

"Yes," Aculeo said. "She wore the same bracelet of yellow twine about her wrist as the others."

"Yellow twine?"

"Yes. It's worn by some worshippers of Sarapis."

"Did all the victims wear such a bracelet?" Zeanthes asked.

"Yes. Why?"

"First tell me what else you know about Petras' murder."

Aculeo shrugged. "I've little else to share. I know who paid for her embalming, the name at least, but little else."

"What's the name?"

"Sabazius."

"Sabazius?" Zeanthes smiled, swirling the wine around in his cup before he sipped. "Someone's playing a game, I think."

"What do you mean?"

"Sabazius is another name for Dionysos."

"The wine god?"

D.L. Johnstone

"Oh, he is far more than that, I assure you. And what's more, pomegranates also play a key role in his story. So," Zeanthes said, pushing his chair away from the table and taking a torch from its bracket on the tavern wall. "Let's make a visit to the underworld."

Aculeo followed the sophist along a narrow back alley towards a small, windowless mud-brick building with an unmarked door. "In here I believe," Zeanthes said. He opened the door and led him into the dark passageway within. A set of steps carved in the soft limestone led downwards. Zeanthes headed down the stairs, his footsteps echoing off the uneven rock walls, the torchlight flickering, the air stale and thin. Aculeo reluctantly followed.

The steps ended in another passageway, which led to a great cavern. Magnificent stone arches towered overhead, stretching endlessly into the dark void beyond like still and glittering waves in a cold, dead sea, linked to the towering columns rising out of the depths of the water down below. A maze of catacombs ran beneath the city to store autumn floodwater from the Nile and supply the city's residents through the year. Pipes fed from the cisterns to the many public fountains and pumps across the city, as well as to the palace and a select number of wealthier citizens' homes.

"A city beneath the city," Zeanthes said.

"Why have we come down to the cisterns?" Aculeo asked.

"Because this represents the katabasis – the descent into the underworld. The liminal boundaries where Dionysos is Lord," Zeanthes said, his torchlight dancing off the water, dappling across the cavernous, echoing walls. "Dionysos is a son of Zeus. His mother was Semele, a sea nymph. Zeus came unto her in human form, but after he laid with her she realized he was the great god himself and begged him to show himself as he truly was. After much initial resistance, he finally relented, allowing her to see him in his true god form. His brilliance was too much for her, of course, and she immediately turned to ash. The babe Dionysos was rescued from the cinders of her womb, born with horns and crowned with serpents. Hera was enraged when she learned of her husband's infidelity and ordered the Titans to murder the child. They tore him apart, then boiled the pieces and devoured most of him before Zeus destroyed them with a thunderbolt.

"The only part of Dionysos that was saved was his heart, which Zeus buried in a sacred grove. A pomegranate tree grew from the soil where his heart had been buried. The ripe pomegranate splits open like a wound, the red seeds spill forth like blood. It symbolizes death and the promise of resurrection, as when held in the hand of Persephone.

"Dionysos' grandmother, Rhea, sowed seeds from the fruit into the

206

leg of Zeus while he slept, from whence the child was re-born. He was then taken by Persephone and hidden in Heliconia until he grew to manhood. It was there that he invented wine, a most admirable gift to which we must all give thanks," Zeanthes said with a smile.

"But when Dionysos was recognized by Hera, she drove him mad. Attended by his wild army of Satyrs and Maenads, swords and serpents, the god wandered the earth, cutting a swath of war and murder across the land. Until at last he was purified by his grandmother Rhea, and released from his madness."

"What does this have to do with murdered hetairai?" Aculeo asked.

"You know of the Mysteries, I'm sure," Zeanthes said.

"What of them?"

"The Mysteries celebrate the life and rebirth of Dionysos, re-enacting them, including his sacrifice."

"A human sacrifice?"

"In ancient times, yes, but not anymore," Zeanthes said. "The sacrifices are usually of animals as manifestations of Dionysos. A bull, for example, from whose hollowed horns wine is drunk. Or a goat whose flesh provides wineskins. Wine itself is the embodiment of Dionysos, of course. Its production from the dismembered body of the grape, the intoxicating and uninhibiting effects of the drink itself, release man from his otherwise shallow vision of reality, opening his mind and soul to the hidden reality within and without. Wine is the fruit and blood of harvest. It inspires divine madness, brings communion with the Gods. Dionysos is the God of passion, of ecstasies and excesses. Of madness. He is the God who murders, as he himself was murdered."

"You think all this has something to do with the Mysteries then?" Aculeo asked.

"Perhaps. Perhaps. Let's return to the bracelets of yellow twine. You see, such bracelets are also worn by some worshippers of Dionysos."

"I thought it was Sarapis."

"One of the many features Sarapis borrowed from other gods," Zeanthes said. "Now, Dionysos is a god, of course, so any role he might play would be indirect. The question is who his agents on Earth might be."

"Ralla?" Aculeo said.

"Possibly. But as I said, first we need our proof. Taking on a man of Ralla's stature is not something to be done lightly."

"What is it?" Aculeo asked.

"Dionysos has a counterpart, you know. You see, it is the realm of Apollo, the God of Law and Wisdom to avenge the victim. It is Apollo's

D.L. Johnstone

law that murderers be purified through punishment. Blood for blood. As Apollo is a God, however, it must fall to a man to act as his agent." Zeanthes looked him in the eye, his gaze unrelenting, the sound of splashing water echoing through the catacombs. "That would be you, dear Aculeo."

CHAPTER XXV

THE 6TH DAY OF MAIUS

Morning lectures had always been one of Sostra of Nicaea's greatest joys. For any true lover of pure sophistry, sitting on the famed square porch of the Museion with one's peers listening to the scintillating, well-reasoned thoughts espoused by other great minds, with the dawn breaking over the bay, the gardens lush with blooms, the grounds filled with glorious architecture and outstanding works of art ... surely there was no better place on the face of the Earth to be!

This morning's lecture was from a Neo-Pythagorean, whose talk obviously prompted a great deal of lively debate amongst the Chryssipians and Posidonians! When at last it broke up into the usual smaller cliques to dissect into more finite theorems, Sostra decided it was at last time to find something of physical sustenance. He politely disengaged from the others and tottered off through the portico to the vast gardens, where clusters of scholars walked and talked and jibed with one another while others sat and read in peace.

Sostra passed through the Library itself, without question the greatest wonder of the world, a grandiose and carvernous joy with its countless hallways disappearing into the distance like intricate strands of a spider's web from the centre, each filled with stacks of shelves, every one of them filled with scrolls. It contained the greatest works known to man, from Aristotle's own personal library (including personal copies of the Iliad

D.L. Johnstone

and The Odyssey he'd annotated for Alexander the Great) bequeathed here by his estate, to Hippocrates' works in medicine, from Euclid's original essays in geometry to the poetry of Euripedes and the like. To have the time to peruse the true jewels that lie within, to simply read, a journey through the tide of ideas as great and profound as any travels on the physical earth.

He walked past the common dining area where he found a quiet shady spot and summoned a slave to whom he gave precise instructions on the proper preparation of five quails' eggs, a small loaf of barley bread and some of that delicious fermented Pompeiian fish sauce, of which he understood they had just received a new shipment.

Sostra sat back, gazing about at the gardens filled with delicate pale pink and yellow flowers, still damp from the early morning dew. Bees buzzed over the sweet smelling blossoms, dusted with pollen, drowsy with nectar. He closed his eyes and drifted off in thought.

A moment later, he heard an odd noise, rather like a rooting animal. He opened his eyes the smallest of cracks. Ah, he realized, it's that horrid bore Epiphaneus. What's the matter with him sitting on a bench all by himself? He looks completely miserable. Sostra seriously contemplated just ignoring the man, for did not Zeno himself write that friendship with one's fellow man should not be carried so far that another's misfortunes might destroy your own inner harmony?

Still …

Sostra sighed, stood and made his way as slowly as he could over to the bench where Epiphaneus sat slumped. The man looked disturbingly dishevelled up close, his thatch of bristly white hair sticking up at odd angles from his blocklike head, his eyes watery and bloodshot, his tunic stained with wine and bits of food, and oh! he stank like a Phoenician sailor right off the boat. What's more, he was muttering to himself like the beggars in the street, not even noticing that Sostra was standing only a foot away.

Sostra cleared his throat. "Epiphaneus, dear fellow, is, ah, everything alright?"

The other sophist gave a start, then winced in pain. "Ow … ah! This cursed skull of mine." He glared blearily up at Sostra. "What do you want?"

"You look quite dreadful, if you don't mind me saying so. Whatever's the matter with you?"

Epiphaneus gave a deep, tremulous sigh. "Look over there, Sostra. The Muses' shrine. And the garden that surrounds the cloister. What do you think of that?"

The other sophist looked over to the ornate shrine. "It's lovely."

"That's hardly the point," the other sophist roared. "Look at it – it's completely and utterly empty! Who among us gives dedication anymore to the Muses, the goddesses of music, dancing and letter? Or is that too an outdated custom? A quaint and archaic act? It's maddening!"

"Epiphaneus, dear friend, you should keep yourself above such worries," Sostra said jovially. "Acts of ignorance and injustice of others afford the sufferer the best opportunity to exercise his own virtue."

Epiphaneus glowered at him from beneath tangled white eyebrows. "Am I now such a dolt that fools like you must teach me how to piss in a pot?" the sophist cried. "Have I truly fallen this far?"

Epiphaneus' voice had gotten so frantic they were attracting attention from others. Sostra would have been perfectly happy right now if the earth were to open up and swallow him whole. No such luck. "Epiphaneus," he whispered urgently, "please calm yourself, I meant no offense."

The fire and fury quickly drained from the sophist's bloodshot eyes and he slumped back in his seat like a slackened sail on a windless sea. "Virtue, Sostra. Virtue is all that is good in the world. Health, happiness, possessions, they matter not. A poor man can live as a king if he lives with virtue, whether he resides in a prison or a palace. You believe that, don't you?"

"Well…"

"Oh yes, you're a Cynic. I quite forgot."

Epiphaneus spoke these last words with such hopeless resignation that the other scholar could think of nothing else to speak upon to help the poor man. "Well," Sostra said at last. "I'm afraid it's getting rather late. I suppose I should really be leaving."

"What? Why? Where are you going?" Epiphaneus demanded, his eyes tearing up. "Is something going on I haven't been told of? Oh, wouldn't it be just like the Chief Librarian to humiliate me in this fashion, pouring a ladle of salt into an already festering wound!"

"It's nothing, really!" Sostra stammered, backing away a few steps. "I'm merely going to look at the new scrolls."

Epiphaneus caught himself, looking at the other sophist in surprise. "What new scrolls?"

"The ones at the depot. There's a new batch arrived just last week, I thought I'd …"

"Ah, well then, fine," the sophist said, and suddenly stood up. "Let's go."

Sostra looked at the other man in surprise. "What? But I … you …

I'm sure there's nothing to even interest you there."

"How could you possibly know that? You haven't even seen them yet, have you?"

"Well, no, but … Not to mention I was going to eat something first."

"Don't be an idiot," Epiphaneus snapped. "You know it's unhealthy to eat anything more than a crust of bread or a cup of wine before sunset. Upsets the balance of one's humours. Besides," he said, prodding the other sophist's substantial belly, "you could stand to lose some weight. Come along, anything's better than waiting here in this ghastly place even a moment longer."

The Imperial Book Depot was a decidedly lengthy walk around the edge of the Great Harbour from the Library. The harbour was already full of activity, the waters thick with flax-sailed skiffs and barges sliding up to the jetties near the Emporion, loaded down with grain, amphorae of wine and other tradewares, the shouts of the sailors along the pier as they off-loaded their goods, their sails now snapping smartly in the morning breeze. Many of the ships had single, square white linen sails swinging on yards that ran their entire lengths, their cargoes in open holds, exposed to all the elements. Others had full decks protecting their precious cargoes and two square sails at mast. A few sat in the harbour, great two and three-masted, long-oared vessels that could carry enormous loads of wares across the open sea in a single journey, now bobbing helplessly, awaiting the little dorries to tow them to dock.

The book depot, a plain, nondescript warehouse just outside the bustling Emporion, was filled with stacks of scrolls, the unsorted overflow from Caesar's collection. There was said to be half a million scrolls housed already in the Library, in addition to another hundred thousand or so held in the sister library in the Sarapeion, making the total collection the largest in the world by far. And that in spite of the fire that Julius Caesar himself had caused some eighty years prior, which had apparently destroyed thousands of irreplaceable works of science and literature. The library in Pergamum was considered to be quite good as well, but still a distant second. Yet there were more books arriving all the time, culled from ships that came to port, or purchased abroad by Imperial agents. One never knew what other treasures might be found. It would have been such a treat for Sostra if he'd simply followed his initial instinct and let Epiphaneus wallow in his own misery.

"I suppose you heard about Gurculio's passing," Sostra said as they walked along the street.

"The moneylender?" the other sophist demanded, tightening his grip on the other man's arm, wary all of a sudden. "Why? What have you heard?"

"Well, very little actually," Sostra said. "Only that he was murdered after his symposium. What do you think happened to him?"

"Why are you asking me?"

Sostra gave the other man a puzzled look. "I was merely making conversation. It's natural to be curious about such things, is it not?"

"No, it's not. And it's no business of mine or yours."

"I suppose. Still, it's hardly a surprise. He was such a loathsome fellow."

"Oh, and you knew him quite well, did you?" Epiphaneus snapped.

Sostra blushed. "No, I'd never met him, but from all I'd heard ..."

"That's the problem with an empty head, Sostra. It's like a hole in the ground - all sorts of refuse may gather in it when you're not careful."

"Never mind then," Sostra muttered. They'd come to an unshaded section of the street. It was so blazingly hot out now, the white paving stones glaring and brilliant beneath the noonday sun, it was giving Sostra a blistering headache. It was either that or the conversation.

"Besides, even if he was wicked, what of it?" Epiphaneus said. "If a man be wicked, it's Nature which compels him to be so. The liberty which a virtuous life may afford other men mightn't be available to him."

"Yes, yes, as you say," Sostra said, exasperated. "Ah! Here we are." He disengaged his arm from the other man's and looked about at the great stacks of scrolls on the thick plank tables like a child at a sweetshop.

Epiphaneus, however, appeared almost disappointed. "Do you know if there are any libraries in Phaleron?" he asked gloomily.

"What?" asked Sostra. "Oh, I don't know. Why should we care about Phaleron?"

"No reason, really," the elderly sophist said as he lovingly stroked the vellum cases stacked on the table.

"Ah, look here," Sostra cried, holding up one of the cases in triumph. "A copy of Aristotle's Politics! Oh, it's in splendid condition! I'll wager it's worth a fortune."

"I despise Aristotle!"

"That's absurd."

"Why do you say that? Did you know that ..."

"Never mind then. Look, here's some Straton. I don't think we have this one. The Chief Librarian will be delighted!"

"The Chief Librarian can sit on the lighthouse for all I care!"

Sostra looked at the other sophist with alarm. "Are you sure you're well?"

Epiphaneus sighed, closing his eyes. "My head. It's the poor light in here – let's go."

"But we just arrived! No, there are hundreds more scrolls to read. Just sit down and relax. I won't be long."

Epiphaneus grudgingly sat down. "Gah, I'm sweating," he grumbled. "It's too damned hot in here. There's no air - I can hardly breathe."

"Oh, this is interesting," Sostra said, and passed a set of scrolls to Epiphaneus, who barely glanced at it before setting it aside.

"I've got pains in my chest, Sostra. I need to get out of here and find a physician, I ..."

Sostra held up a scroll in delight. "Well, well, just look at this! You know I was looking for this a few months back, but the librarians told me our only copy had been lost some time ago."

"Justifiably burned more likely," Epiphaneus said. "Just look who it's written by."

Sostra laughed. "Oh, that's terrible – listen to you." He waddled off towards another stack of scrolls. Driven more by boredom than curiosity, Epiphaneus reluctantly unrolled the scroll and began to read. His eyed widened. What in the Muses' divine names? The pains in his chest had suddenly vanished.

"Hah, look at this one!" Sostra proclaimed.

"Shut up you fat fool, I'm trying to read!"

The other sophist gave him a hurt look. "Alright then, fine." Honestly, Sostra thought, some people can be so hurtful.

CHAPTER XXVI

Idaia felt terribly restless. Neither she nor Tyche had wanted to walk in the Agora with Calisto and Aculeo at all – the attack the day prior had been terrifying – but Calisto had insisted that they should not change their routine, and the girls could hardly disobey. She glanced over at a filthy beggar boy, sitting on the walkway beside the puppet theatre, begging bowl in his lap. He was no more than five years old, with a withered left leg and the swollen, round belly of the truly hungry.

The child looked up at Idaia and smiled. "Are you a princess?" he asked, his eyes shining.

"No," she said.

"You look just like a princess, you're so pretty."

"I know. Are you a slave?"

"No."

"I wouldn't have you for a slave, you're far too dirty. Where are your parents?"

"I don't have any. Are those your parents?" he asked, pointing to Calisto and Aculeo, who were deep in conversation beside her.

"My parents were killed when I was little," she said. "Where do you live?" The boy nodded towards a dreary little corner behind the back doorway of a building. Idaia considered him for a moment. "Are you hungry?" The boy said nothing, just nodded.

"Come Idaia," Calisto said, taking the girl's hand.

"Can we get this boy some food first? He's terribly hungry," Idaia said.

"Poor thing," Calisto said, smiling down at the child. "How long since you last ate?" He stared up at her, speechless, flies buzzing about his dirty mop of chestnut curls.

"Please don't encourage him, mistress," a portly man standing next to her said gruffly.

"Don't encourage him to what? To eat perhaps?" Calisto said sharply. "Maybe you should be encouraged to skip a meal or two yourself. He could use it far more than you."

"I earn my bread at least, mistress," the man said, taken aback.

"He's a child, fool." The man turned away, muttering under his breath. Calisto smiled at the boy and dropped some coins in his bowl. A half dozen other ragged children swarmed her from nowhere, tugging at her robes and crying out how hungry they were. Aculeo threw a few coppers into the street and the children ran after them, the coins ringing along the paving stones, glinting in the sun.

They walked back into the main market area. People were walking with leashed baboons, child acrobats leapt and tumbled through the air, Andalusian dancing girls, flute players, snake eaters, actors and storytellers moved amongst them. The smells of the Agora, an exotic fusion of rich spices from Arabia, fragrant unguents, fresh flowers, and, overriding it all, the ripe smell of humanity all around them, were almost overwhelming.

Aculeo watched Calisto out of the corner of his eye as she weaved her way through the crowds, the girls close on her heels, matching her every step. Others were watching her as well, he noticed, unusual as it was to see women, other than slaves and fishwives, walking through the marketplace. Although Calisto had modestly veiled her head, her grace was obvious in the way she carried herself, in every step she took. Idaia and Tyche ran past her then, chasing one another in amongst the vendors' stalls.

"Tyche seems well settled into your household," Aculeo said.

"She's a lovely girl," Calisto said with a smile. "Idaia adores her."

They passed some farmers' stalls, pens of chickens, white lambs, goats and pigs. "Suitable for food or sacrifice!" proclaimed the vendors. They came upon a cart laden with fresh garlands, their lush perfume filling the air. Aculeo bought a garland of white hyacinths and presented it to Calisto.

"It's lovely," she said. She drew her veil back, her thick, black hair gleaming in the sun, her long neck pale as milk. The necklace she wore, an elegant gold filigree encrusted with dozens of sparkling jewels, was as fine as anything Titiana had ever worn – worth many times more than all Aculeo's remaining possessions combined. A gift from Ralla perhaps? he thought, with a stab of jealousy. It doesn't matter, she's here with me now. He placed the garland on her head like a crown, touching the skin on the back of her neck, soft and cool. She smiled and leaned forward to kiss him.

There was a sharp squealing sound behind them, cutting through the air, startling them both. They turned around and saw that one of the pigs at the drovers' stalls had fallen amongst its brethren, which had savagely responded by slashing at its belly with their razor-sharp tusks. The smell of blood was in the air, and the drover had to beat the other pigs off the injured one with a heavy stick.

"Foul creatures," Aculeo said. "They'd eat anything, even their own."

"Perhaps we could rest for a while," Calisto said, unsettled.

The four of them sat at a table beneath a shade tent next to the stall of a wine merchant, who served them a quick meal of sweet wine and bread dipped in herbed oil and opson. They watched the people walking through the Agora, Romans, Greeks and fellahin, merchants from China to the Indus to Persia, red-bearded Gauls, a colourful, bustling sea.

"I've something to tell you," Aculeo said gently. "About Neaera."

"Oh?" she said. "What is it?"

Aculeo lay the cameo necklace out on the table. Calisto stared at the tiny portrait, the finely carved ivory face against an indigo background, blinked rapidly, saying nothing. "I hesitated saying anything of this to you until now."

"Where did you find it?"

"It was given to a porne by Apollonios."

She closed her eyes. "It really was him that murdered Neaera then?" she asked, her voice weak and trembling.

"I thought so at first, but no, I don't think he did. I'm not even sure she's dead."

"I don't understand."

"Apollonios was deranged, no question of that, but I'm not sure he killed anyone. He claimed he'd found the cameo in the hands of the slave found murdered in the Sarapeion. Neaera was likely abducted. The slave stole her necklace before she escaped."

"Escaped? From where?"

"I don't know yet."

"You think it's possible Neaera's still alive somewhere?"

"There's still hope. But there's another thing I'm afraid. It's about Petras."

"Neaera's cousin? What of her?"

"We discovered her body as well," Aculeo said.

Calisto's eyes filled with sudden dread. "What?"

"Her body was sent to the Necropolis to be embalmed three months ago."

"You found her ... in the Necropolis?"

"Yes. She'd been murdered in much the same way as Myrrhine."

"Oh!"

"I'm sorry. We think they may have been sacrificed as part of a Dionysian ritual."

"What do you mean 'we think'? Who else thinks this?"

"Zeanthes," Aculeo said.

"Zeanthes?" Calisto's hands trembled as they held the cup, her face pale – she looked like she might faint any moment. "I don't understand. Why would anyone do such a thing?"

"Are you alright?"

"Yes," she said, unconvincingly.

"I'm sorry, I know it's a great deal to bear all at once."

"It's not just that."

"What is it then?"

"Some men tried to murder us in the Agora yesterday," Idaia announced. Tyche shot her a warning look.

"They what?" Aculeo demanded.

"It was just some thieves," Calisto said. "We're fine."

"Tell me exactly what happened."

"Some men, sailors I think, they jostled the litter, tried to steal my necklace. There were some soldiers nearby who chased them away. We're fine, really."

"They tore Calisto's dress," Idaia said. "She cut one of them with a knife. I hid behind a shrine, I was so scared!"

"Idaia, shush!" Tyche said sharply.

"You stabbed one of them?" Aculeo said in astonishment.

"The child exaggerates," Calisto said dismissively. "I was afraid you'd react this way."

"I thought they were going to kill us!" Idaia said.

"But who were they? You said they were sailors?" he asked.

"I think so," Calisto said. "I didn't understand their language."

"How many of them were there?"

"I'm not certain. Not many."

"They were six at least," Idaia said. "One of them had a twisted lip."

Aculeo looked at her in surprise. "Like this?" he asked, running his finger down across his upper lip. The child nodded. He glanced at Tyche. "Was it the slave Geta?"

Tyche bowed her head, making an almost imperceptible nod. The

218

poor girl was terrified. Aculeo smiled grimly and squeezed their hands. "You need to be more careful. Keep out of the Agora for a while, yes?"

"How is it you know the man?" Calisto asked.

"He's one of Panthea's slaves. Don't worry. Just promise me you'll not leave your villa on your own for a while."

"So we should hide away like bees in a hive?"

More like moths caught in Cob's web, Aculeo thought. He forced a smile. "What's wrong with being bees? Especially when you live in such a pretty hive?"

"I don't understand what's happening," Calisto said hollowly.

Aculeo leaned closer to her, took her soft chin between his fingers, tipped her face towards his and kissed her on the lips. She resisted at first, then kissed him back. Idaia giggled. "Let's enjoy this moment at least," he said.

They noticed an old man approaching them tapping his walking stick along the paving stones, a young slave at his elbow guiding him through the crowds. The man's robes were tattered, his eyes clouded white, but he gave a broad smile when he stopped next to them.

"Welcome in peace, in peace in peace," the old man said in a singsong voice. "A beautiful lady, a handsome gentleman, and two lovely little flowers, my boy tells me. How are you all this fine day?"

"We're well, and you?" Calisto said graciously, wiping away her tears, recovering her composure.

"Every day I can still feel the sun's warmth on my face is a gift, Miss. Come now, give me a brass coin, I'll spin you a golden tale."

"What sort of tale?"

"Anything you like, Miss. What shall it be? A tale of love or a tale of war?"

"One that has both," Calisto said, gazing at Aculeo, who pressed a coin into the man's outstretched hand.

The blind poet smiled. "Of course – the finest sort."

Aculeo opened his eyes, still half asleep, listening to the sound of the children playing in the garden, squealing with laughter. He felt the feathery touch of Calisto running her fingertips along his face, his jaw, then tracing the ropey scar that stretched from beneath his ribs to the breadth of his chest in a knotted pink line. He pulled her close, his hand against the small of her back, her skin soft and smooth as silk. She kissed him, her warm, sweet breath against his neck.

"Is it from a battle?" she asked, tracing her finger along the fibrous band, which wrapped around his right shoulder to his upper back.

"I never fought in any battles," he said with a smile.

"What's it from then?"

He sighed. "I was seventeen, training to be an officer in the army. One of the other trainees caught me during sword practice when I wasn't looking."

"You were a Roman officer?" Calisto said, surprised. "I had no idea."

"My father had a great deal of ambition for me. More than I had for myself. He thought some military experience would help advance my career. Anyway, this put an end to those dreams.

"He died soon after, leaving me a small inheritance. I got involved in business with one of his old friends, a man named Corvinus who ran a grain export company. Corvinus became like a second father to me. With his guidance I was able to turn my inheritance into a fortune." He paused, his expression darkened, brows knitted.

"What happened?" Calisto asked.

Aculeo shrugged. "I thought I knew once, but in truth I'm not entirely certain what happened anymore. Either way, what fortune I once had is long gone."

"Idaia told me you have a son," Calisto said. She paused for a moment. "And a wife?"

Aculeo lay his head back on his pillow. "Yes. She left me when I lost everything. They returned to Rome in Januarius. Titiana just remarried." He turned his head away.

She kissed him, held him tight. "You must have truly loved her."

Aculeo said nothing in reply, just lay in her arms. He pulled back a bit so he could see her, threaded his fingers through her dark hair, combing it off her face, tracing down her forehead, around her closed eyes, around her cheekbones, touching the white scar that ran along the line of her chin to her jaw. "Where did you get this?"

Calisto flinched and looked away, her eyes clouded. "I'm sorry," he said. "I only …"

"My husband sliced my face with a whip one night."

"Oh," Aculeo gasped.

"It was many years ago, and he was drunk. I left him that very night. I made my way to Alexandria. Then I met Ralla."

"And you became his hetaira?"

"Yes." They held one another close as they listened to the sound of the children playing in the garden.

"I think we should leave," he said.

"Let's stay here just a while longer."

Aculeo shook his head. "I meant we should leave Alexandria."

"But why?"

"It isn't safe."

"I have you here to protect me," she said, kissing his chest.

"It wasn't a random attack on you in the Agora yesterday. Panthea's slave Geta was behind your assault in the Agora. It was her men that attacked me at Ralla's symposium and likely murdered Gurculio that same night."

Calisto pulled away from him, looked up at him in surprise. "Why should they have wanted to do these things?"

"It has something to do with some tablets Iovinus had been carrying when he returned to Alexandria. Gurculio's men almost murdered me over them."

"What tablets?" Calisto asked.

"They belonged to a man named Marcellus Flavianus. It doesn't matter anymore, we'll never know what was on them. They were destroyed in the fire at Gurculio's villa."

"Why would he attack us though?"

"I wish I knew. It must be connected to the murders of Myrrhine, Iovinus and Petras somehow."

Calisto tucked her head against his neck. "I don't know what to do."

"Tell me something – who was Petras' patron before she disappeared?"

She paused a moment. "Petras was involved with a number of men."

"Who?"

"There was Gemellus. And Hirpinius I think. And Posidippus ..."

Aculeo looked at her in surprise. "Posdippus of Cos?"

"You know him?"

"Yes, I know him. What was his relationship with Petras?"

"They were quite close for a time," she said. "There was even talk of him buying her from Panthea, of emancipating and marrying her. That was until Ralla set his eyes on her as well."

"Ralla?"

"Yes. Posidippus sold off what properties he held and made Panthea an offer for her, but Panthea wouldn't go against Ralla."

"When was that?"

"I'm not sure, Februarius perhaps?"

"That was a month before Petras was murdered. Ralla's women don't survive for long, do they?" Aculeo said bitterly.

D.L. Johnstone

"Aculeo…"

"Did you know Petras was with child when she was murdered?" he asked.

Calisto gave a sharp intake of breath and closed her eyes. "Oh …"

"The priests mummified the child she carried as well, it was not three months along. So small I could have held it in the palm of my hand."

"Please, no more," she said weakly.

"Who's next? You? Then Tyche? Idaia even? Whatever madness that drives him, whatever reason he has to do these things, what makes you think he would stop now?" Calisto buried herself in his arms, crying, unable to speak for a while. "Come with me," Aculeo whispered. "We'll take the girls and run away."

"You say that so easily. Where would we go?"

"Anywhere but here."

"You have money?"

"A little. Enough for us to get away at least. After that …"

"After that we'll be paupers. I can't even sell my properties," she said. "It's all such a mess right now. Everything I have is held through Ralla."

"Ralla? Why?"

"Because I'm a woman. I can no more own property directly than if I were a slave or a freedman."

Aculeo stared at her a moment. "What did you say?"

"I'm not permitted to own property. I had to put the title in Ralla's name in order to …"

Aculeo bolted from the bed. "I have to go," he said, pulling on his tunic.

"Why? What's the matter?"

"I'll explain later. Pack your things. You need to be ready to leave at a moment's notice. Understand me?"

"No, I don't …"

"Then trust me."

CHAPTER XXVII

What was it Zeanthes said? Aculeo thought as he rushed along the street towards the Titles Office in the administrative district. Follow the string to find your way out of the labyrinth. The Titles Office, though, proved to be a dead end – they had no record of properties in Alexandria or the surrounding area under the freedman Callixenes' name. Little surprise – it would have been quite a long shot for that to have fallen through the administrative cracks, as only freeborn citizens of Rome and Alexandria were permitted to own any property. Freedmen could only act as tenants, yet Callixenes could clearly not afford rent – he raised no crops, only farmed a few foul pigs. That meant whoever did own it must have known exactly what it was used for. The problem was, without a specific lot number, no bribe could have enabled the clerks to find out who actually did own the farmland down on Lake Mareotis.

Aculeo headed home, frustrated by his lack of success. There must be a way, he thought, I can't have come this far only to hit a wall. He paused in the middle of the street, closed his eyes, thinking of the Iberian porne, Tisris, being taken to that ghastly little farm, her friend Heraïs, who never returned. Myrrhine, Neaera, the river slave, Petras … and Calisto will surely be next if I can't find a way to get her to leave with me. And what about the Cosian? What linked a man like Posidippus to all of this? What a mess. How am I to…?

The Cosian! Did Calisto not say he'd sold off his properties to buy Petras? Now what in Pluto's cursed name did Pesach and Gellius do with his documents?

Aculeo, Pesach and Gellius spent the next hours poring through all the papers documenting Posidippus' crumbling enterprise one more time, piece by piece, trying to make sense of the tangled mess of deeds and property records.

"The Cosian owned properties from here to Canopus," Gellius said at last.

"So what?" said Pesach, scratching himself. "I'm hungry and the pantry's empty. Let's get something to eat."

"Wait. What about this?" Aculeo said when he noticed a small square of parchment that had been stuck to the back of another.

"What's it say?" Gellius asked with a yawn.

Aculeo scanned it quickly, then stopped and read it word by word to himself before saying anything. "It's a receipt of the sale of twenty arouas of land on the shore of Lake Mareotis five months ago. Twelve hundred sesterces."

"What I wouldn't give for twelve hundred sesterces right now," Gellius said.

"Who was the purchaser?" Pesach asked.

"It doesn't say," said Aculeo. "The sale took place in October last year. Lot #384. No other details."

"What of it?"

"I'll tell you later. Come on."

"Where are we going?" Gellius asked in surprise.

"To get some food, I hope," Pesach said. "I'm thinking spiced pork and a jar or two of beer."

"We're going back to the Titles office," said Aculeo.

"Why would we go there? I doubt their pork is especially renowned."

The clerks back at the Titles Office found the title to lot #384 easily enough this time. The property was described in their documents as being twenty arouas of arable farmland, located on the southwestern shore of Lake Mareotis. It had been sold on a writ on the twenty second day of October. The purchaser was none other than the Concessionary Bank of Arsinoe the Consummator.

"Another dead end," Gellius grumbled. "The damned Cosian sold it to the bank, along with everything else. His business was a mess, he owed a small fortune. He likely just sold off everything he could and defaulted on his lenders. Satisfied?"

"Yes and no," Aculeo said. "The owner of the Concessionary Bank of Arsinoe the Consummator is Albius Ralla."

"Ah?" Pesach said with a harsh laugh. "Well, we're well fucked now, aren't we? Are we going to eat or not?"

THE 7TH DAY OF MAIUS

The rain fell in full force the following morning, pounding down from an iron-grey sky, pocking the water's surface from the moment they'd left harbour, casting up an oppressive shroud of mist across the inland sea. The shore lay at the edges, all in shadows, while the chilly dampness seemed to seep into every pore of their skin. They could hear the birds call out to one another along the water with their haunted, echoing cries.

"I don't know why I listened to you, coming all the way out here," Capito grumbled to Aculeo. The two Roman soldiers accompanying them looked similarly glum about their situation that morning as they huddled, shivering beneath the only bit of shelter on the barge.

"Forgive a simple fellahin woman from asking foolish questions," Sekhet said, "but is it not the duty of city officials like yourself to investigate crimes of this nature on behalf of your blessed Emperor?"

"We already arrested the madman Apollonios for the crimes."

"A crime he didn't commit," said Aculeo.

"That didn't stop you from murdering him in his cell," Capito shot back.

"He killed himself. We've been through all this," Aculeo said.

"You're lucky I didn't arrest you. All told, it gives me little confidence in your judgment, or my own for listening to you in the first place. What would a man like Posidippus of Cos even have to do with the murder of a hetaira?"

"That's what we're here to discover. Trust me, it'll be worth our while," Aculeo said.

D.L. Johnstone

"Let's hope so." As they reached the salt pans near the south-western shoreline, they saw a group of fellahin sitting in the rain, watching them. One of the young soldiers gave a friendly wave, but the natives simply stared back like ghosts from the shore.

"We're almost there," Aculeo said at last.

Capito sneezed. "And what do you expect us to discover in this cursed place exactly? Besides mosquitoes, mud and crocodiles that is."

"Answers."

"And I don't even know what the questions are."

They anchored the boat and slogged through the shallows, the rain still teeming, whining clouds of mosquitoes greeting them with shrill enthusiasm, burying their red-hot needles into any exposed bit of flesh they could find. And they seemed to find them all, behind ears, armpits, elbows, backs of knees, thighs. Capito and the soldiers were cursing before they even set foot to shore. They walked up the rough pathway, past the crude wooden shrine to Poseidon, past the abandoned barges that lay in the sand. Even Sekhet looked uneasy.

"What is it?" Aculeo said.

"I have the feeling someone's watching us," she said.

Aculeo peered into the dense brush, heavy drops dripping from the leaves, listened to the birds chippering all around them, but he could see nothing there. They carried up along the path, Capito and the officers keeping their short swords ready.

There was a rustling sound in the bushes next to them. One of the soldiers started in surprise, then charged in, emerging a minute later, dragging a skinny slave girl out with him. She struggled and hissed, making odd, guttural sounds like a wild animal.

"Gah, she stinks," the soldier named Machon gasped. "Grab her, Dryton, she's stronger than she looks!" The other officer grabbed her by the shoulder, but the girl quickly spun around and bit his hand. He cried out in pain and released her. Capito cursed, drew his sword, ready to strike her.

"Hold off!" Aculeo cried. It was the same slave girl he'd seen on his trip here before. He held up his hands, palms forward, showing her he was unarmed. She looked up at him, her eyes wide with terror, her thin face filthy with grease and ashes. "It's alright, don't be afraid."

She struggled again to free herself from the soldier's grip, kicking her

226

bare heels back into his shins, making her strange, barking sounds as she flung herself about. "Is she a halfwit?" Capito demanded.

Sekhet stepped forward then, spoke gently to the girl in Demotic. The girl calmed herself almost immediately, gazing at the healer in surprise. "Let her go," she said to the soldier, who looked to Capito for confirmation. Capito gave a reluctant nod and the soldier released her. The girl simply stood there, watching Sekhet.

"Look at her legs," the healer said.

Aculeo looked down at the slave's legs, which were streaked with the same reddish clay they'd seen on the river slave. And there, running the length of her left calf, the telltale whitish ridge of a guinea worm. She came from this place then, Aculeo thought, his blood running cold. Neaera too. Could she still be here somewhere?

"Ask her about Neaera," he said. Sekhet said a few words to the slave, but the girl shook her head. The healer reached her hand out gently, stroked her cheek, spoke to her again, her voice soft and soothing.

"What is it?" Capito asked.

The girl reluctantly opened her mouth. Sekhet peered inside her mouth, then nodded. "Someone stole her tongue."

"Perhaps she's not a fool, then. Ask if there's a cage somewhere."

"What cage?" Capito said irritably.

Sekhet talked to the girl, who grunted in reply, then turned and ran into the brush. They followed her along a rough, broken path, winding and twisting through the thick underbrush, slipping on the slick wet mud, tripping over tangled tree roots, trying to keep up with the slave.

It stood in a clearing, a rough, empty wooden cage about the height of a man. The door hung agape. Two stout wooden posts had been pounded into the dirt inside the structure, links of rusted chains secured to them. Thunder crackled through the morning sky, the rain fell heavier now, the rainwater streaming down the slope of the cage's dirt floor, the runoff tinged pink from the clay, like the stain of old blood. Aculeo felt his stomach turn at the sight. Sekhet spotted something at the edge of the clearing, bent down, brushed aside the debris and held it up to show Aculeo – it was a broken mask of a snarling panther.

They made their way back down the path to the farmhouse. The pigs grunted hungrily from their pen. The door of the farmhouse hung open on its leather hinges, like a mouth agape. There was no sign of Callixenes or his Molossian dog. "Ask her what happened to her master," Aculeo said.

Sekhet spoke to the girl, who looked back at her, puzzled. Sekhet talked to her again, but the slave merely shook her head. Aculeo led the way into the house, taking care with every step, certain that the freedman

would be waiting for them. The house was filthy, strewn with rubbish on the table and floor. No sign of Neaera or Callixenes. There was what passed for a bed in the corner of the shack, barely more than a wooden box with a jumble of tattered flea-bitten hides on it. Beneath the bed, three baskets. One was filled with potshards. Another held a stinking, filthy looking tunic. The third was filled with fine silk chitons – brightly coloured, beautifully embroidered – half a dozen at least, some of them stained with blood. A clump of long dark human hair was caught in a crack in the bed's frame, a crusty scab of dried flesh holding the clump together – from whatever scalp it had been torn from.

He shuddered and pulled the bed away from the wall. There was a small, finely carved wooden chest with enamel inlay, tucked into the corner against the wall. The box was filled with jewellery, most of it cheap gilded terracotta, but there were some fine engraved ivory hair combs and a few silver fibula pins as well. And an earring, encrusted with pearls, lapis lazuli, and caked with red-brown blood about the filigree.

Sekhet patted his arm. "Look." He turned his gaze to where she was pointing. Something had been scratched into the mud brick wall over the bed, barely visible in the dim light. Aculeo held the torch closer, squinting for a better look.

He caught his breath, then passed the lamp over more bricks, then the rest of the wall. More, more, a dozen more, all the same thing.

"One for each woman brought here," Sekhet said, her voice low, bristling with anger.

"What happened to them all?" Aculeo whispered darkly. Sekhet talked to the girl, who merely looked away, fidgeting. "Ask her where Callixenes took all the women."

Sekhet asked her, and the girl took her by the hand and pulled her back outside along the path toward the pigs. They were great, fat stinking beasts, a dozen in total, spattered with mud and waste, blinking at them in the rain, squealing and grunting. The slave led them to the pen's gate where the huge slave they'd seen here last time stood in the pouring rain, watching the pigs. He glanced up at the intruders, his tiny eyes anxiously darting about, his face red, and began grunting like a pig himself, flexing his great fists.

"Ready yourselves," Capito cautioned.

The girl put a hand on the other slave's huge, meaty arm, stroked it, touched his red-blotched cheek. The man gazed down at her, his grunting stopped, he calmed down, stood aside for them to pass.

"There are no more cages," Capito said uneasily, looking about. "Where are the women?"

"Come," Sekhet said. She and Aculeo walked toward the abattoir.

"Where are you going?"

"Wait here in case Callixenes returns," Aculeo said. They stepped inside the crooked little shack, rain dripping through the leaky roof, a thin grey light seeping through a rough hole cut near the ceiling. A heavy cleaver, greasy with blood, lay atop the wooden block table, a large salting tub next to it. The fetid air was filled with the drone of flies, drawn to the hot, gagging stench of the rotting hogsheads and sides of meat hanging from the rafters. Aculeo glanced up at them anxiously.

Sekhet shook her head. "Not human."

"Where are they then?" She shrugged. They stepped outside again. The pigs were slashing at one another now, squealing in desperate hunger. The giant slave seemed to wake up from his reverie, walked to the trough and emptied his dripping bucket into it. The pigs squealed in delight, burying their faces into the slop.

Sekhet watched them feeding, her eyes narrowed. "Move them back."

"What, and lose a hand? Are you mad?" Capito snapped.

She glared at him in irritation, then grabbed a heavy sword from one of the officers and banged it against the trough, crying out at the pigs in Demotic. The pigs backed off from the trough in surprise, jostling one another in their attempt to get away. Sekhet thrust her hand into the slop. The pigs immediately charged, squealing in eager anticipation, throwing themselves up against the pen gates, rattling them. Sekhet almost fell through the rails of the pen had Capito not grabbed her just in time.

"What was so important that you had to do such a stupid thing as

D.L. Johnstone

that?" he demanded. Sekhet held up her hand. And there in her open palm, amidst the pasty grey gruel and vegetable peelings, was a human toe, the toenail painted a pretty shade of coral. The others cried out in horror.

Aculeo put his hands over his eyes and shook his head. She's truly dead, he thought miserably. It's all over. He felt like he would be sick.

A roar of anger sounded from the brush up near the shack, then a shrill whistling sound cut through the air. An arrow struck the soldier Dryton in his midsection. He cursed, staggering back. A second arrow thwacked against the wall of the abattoir next to Aculeo's head. The others scattered for cover. The Molossian hound tore out of the brush and pounded along the dirt straight at them, teeth bared. Capito managed to strike the beast across the head with the flat of his sword, sending it twisting and yelping into the mud. It rolled to a stop, then dragged itself whimpering back into the brush.

Aculeo grabbed the fallen soldier's sword and followed the dog, slipping in the mud along the path, hoping it would lead to its master. He heard a rustling just up ahead and braced himself, heart pounding in his chest, sword at the ready. There was a blurring motion beside him – Callixenes charging him from the side, catching him by surprise, sword raised high. Aculeo stepped out of his path, barely managing to block the freedman's deadly swing with his own sword, then turned and hacked at the backs of the man's thighs as he passed. Callixenes cried out in rage and pain, falling to his knees in the mud. Aculeo managed to dodge out of the way, then cracked his sword pommel down hard on the man's elbow. Callixenes bellowed like a hobbled mule, then head-butted Aculeo to the face. Aculeo felt his nose break, blood gushed from it, filling his mouth. Callixenes shoved him to the ground, then limped into the dense scrub. Aculeo staggered to his feet, dizzy with pain.

Capito arrived, looking about, rain drizzling down his face. "Where is he?"

"This way," Aculeo said, heading into the scrub. They followed a tangled trail of broken branches leading up a steep bank of loose limestone and rubble towards a partially cultivated, level area. No sign of Callixenes. Capito pointed to a bloodstain smeared on the grey wet shale. There was another stain further down, and another leading towards a rocky crevice near a muddy grove of date palms. They moved quietly towards the crevice. Callixenes lay inside like a viper in its nest, his face twisted in pain.

"Either we take you out in pieces and feed you to your pigs or you crawl out on your hands and knees," Capito said. "Five seconds to decide."

Callixenes considered his severely limited options and finally crawled out towards him, head down. Aculeo shoved him to the ground with his foot and Capito tied his wrists tight behind his back, looping part of the rope around the man's throat to keep him from trying to work the bonds free. They were back at the property in a few minutes. The slave girl watched from near the animal pen, trembling in fear as Callixenes was led towards her. Sekhet looked up from her work on the wounded soldier, her eyes filled with a cold rage as she gazed at the freedman.

"What in Pluto's name did you do with those women?" Aculeo asked.

"What women?" Callixenes asked, his face twisted in a maddening smirk.

Machon cracked the man across the skull. The freedman fell face first into the mud, out cold. "That's for Dryton, prick," the soldier said.

Capito gave Aculeo a grudging nod. "Have we finally discovered your cursed answers?"

"Some at least. We know Neaera was murdered, but not why."

"You've the murderer at least."

"Callixenes? He's only the tool. There's another we want," Aculeo said.

"Who?"

"Albius Ralla. He stole this property from Posidippus six months ago. He's behind the whole thing. Whatever it is."

The Magistrate stared at him for a moment, then smiled. "Ah, I thought you were serious for a moment." Aculeo turned and walked away. "Aculeo? Don't tell me you're ..." Capito looked down at the unconscious freedman in dawning horror. "Oh."

CHAPTER XXVIII

When the rain finally ended, they gathered what dry wood and reeds they could find, built a pyre down on the dismal shore and set it ablaze. Even soaked in pitch, the pyre produced little more than an acrid black smoke at first that curled into the sky. Until the fat from the slaughtered pigs caught fire, that is, then the flames popped and sizzled and swelled until the fire seemed to fill half the beach and the air was thick with the sickly tantalizing smell of the animals' roasting flesh. Aculeo could feel the greasy, roaring heat of the fire lick his face and closed his eyes against it, his skin aglow with crackling yellow-orange light.

"I wonder if we should have sacrificed them to the gods instead," Capito said uneasily.

"To what god would you make sacrifice of these foul creatures?" Sekhet asked. "Whatever gods have dominion over this place, I doubt they'd covet such an offering."

"We can only hope as much."

Aculeo watched as a dozen fellahin workers crawled on their hands and knees, side by side through the dark mud of the farm. They had commandeered them from farms up along the western shores, as workers from neighbouring properties had been unwilling to come to the farm at any price or threat; having heard the tortured cries of the victims that had come from this wretched place, they considered it to be a place of demons. The searchers focused on a quadrant Sekhet had marked out with twine, in and around the clearing where the farmhouse, abattoir and pig pen were located, sifting through the filth, looking for bones, hair, clothes, jewellery, anything that could give them a link, a clue.

Every now and then one of the workers would let out a cry, holding up their find for Sekhet to come and examine. They'd found a large number of bones so far, mostly in the great stinking piles of pig waste that sat out behind the pen, thick with clouds of voracious flies. Tangled lengths of hair, partially digested fragments of vertebrae and other bones, along with several teeth. One worker had spotted what he thought to be a piece of skull buried in a huge ant heap. When the workers tried to dig there, the fiery red ants had swarmed, stinging them, and so the workers drenched the ant heap in pitch and set fire to it as well. Eventually they were able to retrieve four blackened human skulls from the smouldering heap.

"What kind of nightmare is this place?" Capito growled, sweat dripping down his face.

"Maybe the fellahin are right," Aculeo said. "It's a place of demons."

"Worse than demons," Sekhet said darkly. "To be murdered is crime enough, but for their bodies to then be desecrated this way, consumed by these miserable beasts ... they're cursed to eternal death, their kas wandering aimlessly with no way to find their khets."

"We can make sure it stops here at least."

"Albius Ralla is linked to this – you're certain?" Capito said, all too willing to be told otherwise.

"Certain enough."

"If he catches wind of what we've done before we're ready, we're both dead men."

Aculeo looked down at the injured officer, whose face was deathly pale and drenched with sweat. "How is he?" he asked Sekhet.

"He's stabilized at least," she allowed. "Still, he's suffered heavy bleeding and is already running a fever. We need to get back to the city as soon as we can."

Capito watched the black, stinking smoke spiral up into the sky. "We should just set fire to the whole cursed place."

"I'd like nothing better," said Aculeo. "Right now we need to head back to Alexandria."

Capito shook his head. "I'd be much better off hiring a boat and heading to Thrace. I could hide out there for a while, start a new career, change my name of course ."

Aculeo smiled grimly and clapped him on the back. "We have him, Capito. We just need to finish the job."

"Easily said. Let's go back," Capito said with a sigh.

They noticed too late that some sparks from the blazing pyre had fallen on the crude wooden shrine to Poseidon that stood on the beach, setting it ablaze as well. By the time they managed to finally douse the flames the shrine was little more than a charred stump. The omen couldn't possibly have been worse. They looked at one another helplessly, none of them wanting to speak. Aculeo gazed out to the sea, hoping the Gods wouldn't be too vengeful this time when they claimed their retribution.

Lycarion the Harbour Master gazed through the window of his dockside offices, watching the little two-sailed merchant's ship tack neatly around the Bull's Horn, an enormous craggy white rock that jutted from the water's surface near the entrance of the Great Harbour of Alexandria. It was a fine, deep harbour, highly favoured among merchant ship masters. One just had to be careful near the treacherous Hog's Back Rocks and the Arm of Lochias on the left, then ease the prow to the right around the tawny-coloured breakwater. There she goes – nicely done. Now swing in towards the Poseidium, pinched between the island of Antirrhodus and the Imperial Galley Port, with its twin triemes and various round boats, beyond which was a swell of elegant dove-grey limestone and Aswan granite buildings, the inner palaces and the ostentatious Caesarium, almost hidden by a copse of palm trees and sacred groves.

I wonder what she brings, Lycarion mused, absently tapping his walking stick on the floor. Saltfish from Lycia? Hymettian honey? Or some fine woollens from Miletos? Some decent wines I hope. Countless ships from all the known world were lined up at dock in the slips of the inner harbour, lines of square, white linen sails snapping in the breeze. A few stood at anchor further out in the harbour, great two and three-masted vessels with larger holds that could carry great loads of grain and other wares across the open sea in a single journey. And the Harbour Master controlled the entrance and exit of every last one of them – an enormous responsibility, but not without its rewards – a piece of this, a bit of that, it all added up quite nicely. Gulls and pelicans flapped overhead in the morning sky, just as curious as he was to what the new ships might bring.

"Excuse me," said a voice. The Harbour Master turned about, startled – he'd not heard anyone enter his offices.

Look what we have here, he thought, taking in the two men's tattered tunics, broken sandals and messy mops of hair. Both of them unshaven and unbathed in the gods knew how long. They were likely crawling with fleas. A dozen of their sort poked about the harbour every day, runaway slaves, army deserters fleeing some distant war, or ordinary beggars looking for handouts. It didn't matter, Lycarion thought irritably, everyone has their own problems to worry about.

"Who do you think you are sneaking up on me like that?" he snapped.

"Oh, apologies, sir," the grey-haired fellow said solicitously. "My name is Marcus Augendus Gellius, this is my associate Gaius Durio Pesach. You must be the Harbour Master."

Lycarion didn't bother to reply. He didn't believe the Roman names for a minute. Everyone wants to be Roman these days. He looked askance at the other man, the one named Pesach, a rusty-haired little fellow, skinny as a plucked rooster with knobby knees and arms covered in red patchy skin that he kept scratching at. He had an altogether scurrilous look in his pink-rimmed eyes that made Lycarion grip his cane a little tighter.

"We were hoping you could help us," Gellius said, offering a tentative smile. "We're looking for some ships records."

"Oh are you?" This Gellius fellow was certainly well-spoken for a slave. Probably a Greek. "And why's that?"

"We're gathering information on behalf of the Magistrate Capito."

The skinny fellow, Pesach, actually walked over to the wall of shelves where he kept the ship's logs and started nosing about. "Hey you, keep out of those!" The man shot him a scowl but put the scroll down all the same. "I assume you have a letter from the Magistrate then, do you?"

Gellius grinned and bobbed his head, preparing to spin another transparent lie. "Not exactly. It's a simple task though, really. There are some ships we need the records of. We have questions of when they may have left port, what they were carrying. That sort of thing."

"And I have all that information, of course. But why should I let you see it?"

"Oh, but it's quite important, I assure you," the fellow said. "Magistrate's orders."

Pompous little prick, Lycarion thought. He smiled. "Fine. Without a letter, though, it'll cost you ten sesterces."

The skinny one actually hawked and spat on the floor, then looked him right in the eye, daring him. Insolent wretch – he could use a good hit upside that pointed head of his! "You should get control of that friend of yours," Lycarion seethed.

Gellius looked mortified. "Please, Pesach, this is not the time. Sir, this is a matter of public record. We beseech you as citizens of Rome …"

"Oh, well then, since you're citizens of Rome …"

Gellius looked rather pleased with himself. The fool even moved towards the shelves to start digging through the records. Lycarion struck

D.L. Johnstone

the floor in front of him with his cane, and laughed to see Gellius jump back. The man nearly pissed himself! "For a citizen of Rome the price is only thirty sesterces." Gellius' eyes went wide. "And you can take me in your mouth out back."

"I ... I don't understand."

"Then why don't you come back when you have things figured out."

"I could use your little thing to pick my teeth if I wasn't afraid it would get lost in there," the skinny fellow said with a sneer.

"Let's start with you then," Lycarion said, running the tip of his tongue across his lips, tightening his grip on his cane.

"You should watch that tongue of yours before I rip it out of your mouth."

"Pesach, please, now is not the time," his friend whispered.

"You're going to let him talk to us like that?" Pesach demanded.

"Talk to you like that?" the Harbour Master roared. "Who do you think you are speaking to me that way? Get out of here the both of you before I knock you into the harbour and let the fish feed on you!"

"Sir, calm yourself," Gellius pleaded. "We must have got off on the wrong foot somehow. We only want to look at some old shipping records you might ..."

"You're speaking to Roman citizens, you fat stupid swine!" Pesach yelled, his face red as a boiled beet, spittle flying from his mouth.

"Pesach, let me handle this. Don't mind my friend, sir, he means no harm."

"Maybe you should tie him to a post somewhere and beat him then!" Lycarion growled. "He's like some sort of mad dog!"

Gellius winced. "Oh. You really shouldn't have said that."

The Harbour Master barely had a chance to react as Pesach wrenched the cane from his hand and jammed the end of it hard into the man's stomach. Lycarion doubled over in pain, gasping for breath, and could only watch as Pesach swung it across his head with a sharp thwack. He crumpled to the floor in a broken heap.

"What have you done?" Gellius sighed.

Pesach casually kicked the Harbour Master in the head. "Let's just look at the damned records, alright?"

The sun had climbed high into the hazy spring sky, the clouds rolling back to reveal great swaths of blue, the sweltering air drenched with the smell of fertile mud as the barge headed through the dark channels cut between the high green walls of reeds. Dryton moaned and twisted in agony on the floor of the barge, the front of his chiton dark with blood, his face grey, greasy with sweat. Sekhet talked to him in soothing tones, but she looked worried. Callixenes lay trussed up in the bottom of the boat, silently watching the healer as she worked.

"You work for Ralla then," Capito asked Callixenes. The freedman met him with a cold stare and returned his attention to Sekhet. "You want to be tried for murder yourself? Executed?"

"They should sew him into a sack of scorpions and toss him in the Nile," the soldier Machon growled.

"It doesn't have to be that way," Aculeo offered. "Not if you help us. We know it wasn't you who arranged all these killings." The freedman glanced back at him, a smirk on his pocked face, then looked back at the healer, licking his lips. "Who else came to the rituals?"

"He'll die, you know," Callixenes said.

"Who'll die?"

"Your soldier there. He's a dead man."

"Shut your damned mouth," Machon said. Callixenes met him with a grey-toothed grin.

"Don't listen to him," said Sekhet. "He'll be fine."

"I doubt that. I dipped the arrowheads in pigshit," the freedman said. "The poisons have seeped into him already – he'll be dead in a day or two if he's lucky. A week or more if he's not." He laughed so hard he began to cough.

The soldier grabbed the freedman by the throat, punched him in the face over and over, sending the boat rocking wildly. "Shut your cursed mouth, or I'll shut it for you!"

"Enough!" Sekhet barked. "You'll tip the boat!"

Capito grabbed the soldier from behind in a bear hug, pulling him off. "Machon, stop, we need him! We'll deal with it later."

Machon sat there, straddling Callixenes, his breathing ragged, angry, before finally climbing off. The freedman gave a wheezing laugh, his nose gushing with blood, his left eye swollen and pink, his lip split. He spat a thick wad of bloody phlegm at their feet. Aculeo and Capito gagged him tightly, blindfolding him as well to prevent him from infecting others with his murderous gaze.

Sekhet dipped a length of cloth over the side of the boat, wrung it out and laid it on Dryton's forehead to try and cool his fever. He'd fallen asleep at least, as had Machon and Capito. Aculeo sat in silence, watched as fellahin fishermen along the shore swept their nets through the water.

Sekhet slid over then to examine Aculeo. "Your nose is broken."

"Is it?"

"Hold still," she said, kneeling before him, positioning her thumbs on either side of his nose.

"Watch it, what are you …? Gah!"

"Your gratitude overwhelms," she said, sitting wearily next to him. "So the one behind all this, Ralla. He's a man of wealth and influence?"

"Yes. A great deal of both."

Sekhet sighed, quietly watching the fishermen at work as they took care not to tangle their nets in the reed thickets. "And you think you can stop him?"

"We have Callixenes. He was linked to four of the victims at least. We have the remains we found at the farm. And I have the documents proving he owns the land where the murders took place that I can provide the Magistrate. He has everything he needs to go after Ralla. Though he doesn't seem so pleased with the prospect."

Sekhet looked him in the eye, unsmiling now. "Nor should he be. Egyptians have a saying about such things, you know. When you hook too big a fish you should start worrying who's caught who."

Aculeo returned home, exhausted and apprehensive at the same time. Sekhet's right, he thought. A man like Ralla likely has a thousand ears and eyes about the city – if he learns what we have on him, he'll try to crush us before we can act on it. This is not my battle anymore, it never truly was. I've done what I can. It's for men like Capito to finish it. I need to gather Calisto and the girls so we can flee the city while we still can.

As he stepped through the door of his lodgings, Pesach practically attacked him. "Where've you been?" the man demanded.

"It's a long story." Pesach's stay had become increasingly difficult to tolerate of late. He never ventured outside, never bathed, spent most of his time drinking Aculeo's wine, eating his food and sleeping and had become as clinging and wheedling as an old woman. "Where's Gellius?"

"How should I know? He got himself drunk and stormed out of here." Pesach scowled and slumped back into the slingback chair that had become his permanent headquarters of late. He belched and scratched absentmindedly at his crotch. "Tell me again what happened between you and Corvinus."

"I don't have time for this," Aculeo said irritably. He tried to walk past him but Pesach stood up suddenly, blocking his way.

"Tell me again about you and Corvinus," he slurred, his breath stinking of fermented fish paste and sour wine.

"Pesach, I'm tired, and I've many things to do, so if it's all the same to you ..." Aculeo pushed his way past the other man. "Xanthias," he called.

"Yes, Master?" Xanthias replied, emerging from Aculeo's cubiculum, rubbing his eyes.

"Were you sleeping in my bed again?"

"Master, I would never even consider such a thing!" the slave said, visibly shocked.

"Pack our things. We're leaving."

"Of course, Master. An easier task each time we do it, might I say, given how dramatically our possessions have diminished. Where are we running off to this time?"

"As far as we can go," Aculeo said. "Oh, and set aside Posidippus' documents. I'll need you to take them to Capito before we go." Xanthias grumbled vague complaints but set to work all the same.

"And what of Gellius and me?" Pesach demanded. "Where shall we go?"

"Stay here if you like," Aculeo said. "Or go. I've done what I can for the both of you. I need to care of myself now."

"I see. That's a new thing, then, is it?" Aculeo ignored him, heading towards his cubiculum. "You know I used to think you were just a fool," Pesach called after him as Aculeo changed into some fresh clothes.

"Oh did you?" Aculeo said, weary of the game.

"Yes. The way you lived. You were always such a rich, pompous prick. All the parties you threw, your ostentatious villa, and that fine wife of yours, Titiana. She really was lovely by the way, such a fine ass, and those beautiful milky tits."

"Shut your mouth, Pesach."

The other man ignored him, just closed his eyes, lost in his recollections. "Yes, you were a very lucky man. The way you spent your fortune, throwing money away like flower petals cast upon the water. You must have thought yourself a god."

Aculeo glanced around at his shabby little flat. "There's not much casting of flower petals now, is there."

"No indeed," Pesach cackled. "Then, when it all fell apart and the money started to disappear, and we all lost our fortunes while you continued to live your life in that fine villa of yours, I assumed you must have been a thief. That you stole it from us. It was the only explanation I could think of."

"My Master's no thief!" Xanthias cried indignantly.

"He's a poor one if he is," Pesach acknowledged. "Now just today, I've come to realize I was right in the first place. You're just a simple fool," he said, his bleary eyes blinking, his words so slurred they were barely intelligible. Xanthias offered no defense this time.

"I've things to do," Aculeo said, bristling.

"Yes, Aculeo, you're just an idiot. It wasn't you who was the thief – it was Corvinus."

Aculeo's irritation suddenly boiled over into a red hot fury. All the hurts, fears, insults and resentments that had formed his life of late congealed at once. Corvinus, a good, kindly and generous man who had been like a father to him, to be called a thief by this stinking drunk? He moved in fast, his fist raised to strike the man.

Xanthias leaped in, holding him back. "No, Master! Stop!"

Pesach merely laughed. "Why not? Let him come! I don't care anymore. You can't do anything to me I haven't endured a dozen times or more these past few wretched months."

"Corvinus was my dearest friend and an honourable man!" Aculeo cried.

"He was a thief and a coward!"

"He can hardly speak for himself now, can he?"

"No, but these can," Pesach said, shoving the scorched remains of Flavianus' tablets across the table towards him.

"What are you talking about?"

"I read what was on the tablets."

"How? The wax was completely melted."

"Yes, but the wax inscriptions left impressions in the back wooden panel. I was able to reveal them with powdered charcoal pressed on papyrus. I admit I wasn't able to read all of it mind you, but still ..." Pesach started giggling like a child.

"And what did you find?" Aculeo demanded.

"There were details of the company's financial obligations to Marcellus Flavianus dated the 14th Day of Augustus last year."

"So what? I have records of the company's obligations already, not to mention what I have from the documents Corvinus left behind."

"I know, I know," Pesach said dismissively. "I've already been through those in great detail. The problem is the numbers don't match those recorded on the tablets. According to my calculations, the actual assets of the company could never have been more than two million sesterces, and that was at its peak over four years ago. As of the 14th Day of Augustus, the company's debts were close to seven million sesterces."

Aculeo looked at the man in disbelief. "You must be wrong. The first shipwrecks didn't occur until the month of October, two months later. The company's finances had been fine until then."

"A fair point," Pesach said, waggling his index finger in the air. "And so Gellius and I followed up with the Harbour Master's logs this morning. There was no record of any ship belonging to or chartered by the company shipping so much as a turnip past last Maius, and that was a single freighter called the Winged Bull headed to Puteoli, bearing 2,000 amphorae of ordinary wine, 1,500 amphorae of oil and 2,300 modii of barley. It was barely half-full, the records said. The company's only recorded shipment prior to that last year was two months before, the month of Martius, involving a similar load."

"But that makes no sense at all," Aculeo said. "We lost ten ships enroute to Puteoli in October, a dozen more in December."

"You lost the money you provided Corvinus certainly, but my bet is the company's ships didn't exist outside of whatever papers he showed you. He stole it from you."

Aculeo felt a chill stretch its talons out from the pit of his stomach. "But I saw them with my own eyes," he said. "I watched them being loaded in the harbour."

"I've no doubt you saw some ships being loaded. You can see that any day you wander down to the harbour. Their provenance, however, is another question entirely. Remember what I said before? There were too many ships in your records by far. There aren't enough ships or grain in the world to hold what they said. Flavianus' records confirm the lie. The company's ships never sank enroute to Puteoli. There never were any ships to sink. Iovinus didn't survive a shipwreck – he simply fled the city with the only thing of any value that remained in the company – the tablets linking Flavianus to this scheme."

Aculeo felt the room spinning around. Could it be true? he wondered. How could it be? I lost everything over this, my family, my fortune. "It's not possible," he whispered hoarsely. "Corvinus was my dearest friend, he was like a second father. He couldn't have lied to me all along, knowing full well it would ruin me. I don't believe it."

"You were already ruined, Aculeo," Pesach scoffed. "You simply didn't realize it yet."

"But he convinced me to invest everything I had left in the final weeks to support ... what?"

"To keep the lies afloat a little longer. Perhaps he truly did think there was a way to still keep things going." Pesach narrowed his eyes as he

241

looked at Aculeo. "You don't look well. Xanthias, fetch him some wine."

"You and Gellius already drank it all," the slave said sourly.

"Oh, right. Sorry."

Aculeo stood up abruptly and headed towards the door. "Master? Where are you going?" Xanthias asked.

"To find Calisto."

"Ah yes, don't forget your whore," Pesach said.

"She's not a whore," Aculeo growled. "She's a hetaira."

"It's as a chariot to a wagon, isn't it?" Pesach said. "It may look prettier and cost you more but it's used for much the same purpose."

Aculeo lunged across the table, turning it over, striking the man across the face once, and again. Pesach didn't even bother to defend himself, he just gave his maddening laugh.

Xanthias seized his master around the chest, pulling him off. "Stop it, you'll kill him!"

"Let him, what do I care?" Pesach cackled and coughed, blood dripping onto his tunic from his nose and mouth.

"Maybe you're right – maybe I am a fool," Aculeo said, trembling with anger. "What does it matter in the end? Whatever happened to Corvinus and Iovinus and the company is over and done. I've lost Titiana and Atellus, my fortune, my honour and everything else I held dear. It's all gone. There's nothing I can do to get it back. But I've got something worth living for again, and I won't lose it as well. I can't. So I'll get Calisto and the girls to safety. And I'll finish what I've started."

Aculeo was still shaking when he went to the Baths of Sabinus four blocks over. He couldn't go to Calisto like this, still filthy from the journey to the wretched farm. He entered the showers, stood gratefully beneath a funnel of cold water which doused him head to foot, wincing at the stinging sensation where the water washed across his face and scalp. The water swirled pink with blood and red clay around his bare feet, trickling down the drain.

He headed into the vapour baths and found a bench well away from the braziers of hot coals, the steam enveloping him like a thick cocoon. His head was ringing with insane thoughts. Could Corvinus have actually been a thief all these years? Building an empty empire on lies? How could he have allowed me to do the same? How could I have been such a fool to follow him blindly, sacrificing everything ... Fuck!

Enough! he thought, I can't let it distract me now. I have to get Calisto and the girls away from this damned city, tonight if possible before Ralla has a chance to respond. Capito will have the documents he needs to make the arrest as long as he can get the advocates on our side as well. No matter how powerful Ralla might be, he's still just a man, isn't he? Still, he'll be no less dangerous once he's arrested. He'll be like a cornered animal, and prison walls will likely do little to hinder him.

Aculeo closed his eyes for a moment, but found rest elusive. He couldn't get the nightmarish images of the farm out of his head, the cries of the pigs as they'd been slaughtered, the sensation of the scorching, oily heat of the fire on his face, Corvinus' smiling, liar's face and Pesach's maddening laugh …

Slaves stood outside Calisto's villa. Ralla's men, Aculeo realized. He waited until dark, hiding in the shadows, but the guards gave no indication they'd be leaving anytime soon. The lamps in the villa finally dimmed for the night. It devoured him, the thought of Ralla being there with Calisto and the children now like a viper in the nest. They couldn't wait any longer. He decided to return home, gather his things then return for them.

He made his way along the dark winding streets to his flat. He realized before he even set foot across the doorstep that something was amiss. The door hung limply from its hinges. Inside, the furniture had been overturned, the chairs smashed and broken against the plastered mud-brick walls. Did Pesach throw another tantrum, he wondered. There was no sign of him or Xanthias though. What then? Ralla? Theopompus? He could only hope Xanthias, Gellius and Pesach had managed to escape in time.

The door to his cubiculum was open. His storage chests had been dumped out on the floor, the funeral masks of his ancestors lay scattered, the waxen faces staring at him accusingly with their empty eyes. A few of them had been stepped on, destroyed. It was a senseless, sickening loss. He searched frantically through the flat but Posdippus' documents were all gone. That's what they were after. How could they have even … ah, someone at the Titles Office must have told them, he realized wretchedly. Which means the records there have likely been stolen as well. Capito will be left with no evidence to go on.

Something sounded in the street outside, the sound of many pairs of boots marching against the paving stones. They're back. Aculeo slipped down the stairs, his back against the wall, heart pounding in his chest. He could hear them outside the door now. He slipped out the posticum into the tiny courtyard, his heart pulsing in his chest. As he clambered over the wall then slipped into the alley, he wondered desperately whether it wasn't already too late.

CHAPTER XXIX

THE 8TH DAY OF MAIUS

Aculeo slumped on a hard bench in the backroom of the healer's shop and gazed out the window, the early morning sky stained the colour of an old, forgotten bruise. He closed his eyes, leaning his head against the wall, but his mind still raced in circles. After escaping his house he'd tried calling on Capito but the Magistrate's slaves claimed their master had never returned home from the trip to the farm, nor was there any sign of him at his offices in Beta. Meanwhile Ralla's slaves maintained their post outside Calisto's villa. Aculeo had waited out the night in a back alley tavern before making his way to Rhakotis when the Night Guard finished their rounds.

He'd finally drifted off into a sort of sleep when Sekhet appeared. "You've had me running about so much of late my patients are quite distraught," she announced as she dropped wearily into a chair, her eyes underscored with dark circles. "Fortunately they save up all their illnesses for me to take care of upon my return."

"How's Dryton?" Aculeo asked.

"No better. I was up with him most of the night – the arrow seems to have done its job too well I'm afraid."

"Poor fellow," he sighed, shaking his head. "Ralla's done his job also. Capito never returned home – he must have been taken. Ralla's guards watch Calisto's villa like a hawk. Xanthias, Gellius and Pesach are also

245

missing."

"Ah."

"The documents I had linking Ralla to the farm were stolen. Likely the Titles Office deeds as well. I wouldn't be surprised if he hasn't already had Callixenes murdered."

"Clever man," Sekhet mused. "He's slipped the net quite neatly."

"I should have gotten everyone out of Alexandria days ago when I had the chance," Aculeo said bitterly. "We'll never be able to leave safely now – the city gates and harbours are surely being watched."

"There are always ways. You just need to clear your head."

"I need to talk to Calisto."

"And how exactly do you intend to do that?" Sekhet snapped. "If what you say is true, Ralla's simply sitting back, waiting for you to try such a foolish thing."

"What else can I do? I've nothing left!"

"There's something else that might interest you." She took out a leather pouch and tipped it onto the scarred wooden table, spilling out half a dozen oily dark spheres, their potent incense smell filling the little room.

"More opium," he said, looking at her in surprise. "Where did you get it?"

"Dryton was suffering terribly last night. He was unresponsive to anything else I had. So I went to the Agora and found a Cosian merchant who had a substantial inventory on hand. I inquired where I might get more, he mentioned a supplier in Canopus. A fellow Cosian it turns out."

"Posidippus?"

"That's the name he gave, yes," Sekhet said with a smile. "It seems your old colleague has risen from the dead."

"I need to get to Canopus."

"One of my nephews can take you as far as Demanhur on his fishing barge. A thirty stade walk to Canopus from there, but the harbour in Demanhur is small and unguarded which should give you one less thing to worry about. But you'll need to leave right away."

"You're brilliant," Aculeo said, embracing the old woman.

"So many wondrous revelations in one morning," Sekhet said.

Aculeo started towards the door, then turned around. "Promise me something."

"I'm too old to make rash promises."

"Watch out for Calisto and the girls while I'm gone," he said. "I need to know they're safe."

"I'll do what I can." Sekhet was silent for a moment. "Have you given thought to what you and Calisto might do when all this is over? Assuming you're still alive, of course."

"We'll leave Alexandria, live out our lives in peace somewhere, far away from all this madness."

"A pleasant dream," she acknowledged. "And Calisto shares it, does she?"

Aculeo narrowed his eyes in irritation. "Sekhet, please, just watch out for them, will you?"

The healer considered him for a moment, then gave a reluctant nod.

Dusk was falling when the barge finally reached Demanhur, the last vestiges of daylight draining from the sky. Sekhet's nephew steered towards the makeshift harbour, a rough wooden dock at the end of a dirt road.

"May the gods be with you," the young man said as Aculeo stepped onto the dock.

I'd feel safer if they kept to themselves for a change, Aculeo thought and looked about the dusty looking palm grove where a small settlement of Egyptian-style buildings seemed to have risen whole from the muddy banks of the broad canal. The only signs of civilization were the priapic wooden Hermes posts that lined the road to Canopus. He set out down the road.

He heard the raucous sounds of nightlife from town well before he stepped foot on its streets an hour or so later, the strains of flute and lyre and the drunken voices of the revellers echoing across the dark, sloshing waters of the canal that bordered the dusty road. Canopus was essentially a playground for wealthy Alexandrians, soldiers on leave and tourists looking for a fun night out on the town. Aculeo could see the lights from countless taverns that had been built out over the murky-smelling lagoon. Musicians played from barges well-stocked with food and wine to serenade and serve their boisterous patrons, whose little round boats drifted about the lagoon through tangled islands of lotus.

Aculeo rented himself a room at a dingy little inn at the edge of town, then visited a dozen taverns along the waterfront over the next several hours, asking for information on Posidippus of Cos. While a number of people were willing to sell him virtually anything else he might be looking for, no one seemed to know anything about the Cosian. Or would admit to it at least. He left them each with a promise of reward for the information and the name of the inn where he could be found. He was taking his chances being so open, he knew, but desperation won out over caution. Time was running out.

Exhausted and out of options, Aculeo returned to the inn and fell into bed. He'd just drifted off, having learned to ignore the stench of dry-rot that pervaded the room, when a knock came at the door. He slid out of bed, listening at the door for a moment. The knock came again, more urgent this time. He opened the door – a plump, furtive little fellow he'd talked with in a tavern that night quickly pushed his way into the room.

"Close the door, will you," the man said, nervously eyeing about the room. "I know where you can find Posidippus of Cos."

"Why didn't you tell me when we spoke earlier?" Aculeo asked.

The man snorted. "You can wander about Canopus all day and night blabbing about the damned Cosian to anyone who might care to listen, but I'd like to keep my head attached to my neck, thank you. Ten silver sesterces, right?" he said, touching Aculeo's travelling satchel with an appraising eye.

"Put that down. I said five."

"Let's call it eight."

"Six. Now where is he?"

"Pay me first."

"I don't think so," Aculeo said.

"Then never mind," the little man said, and turned to go.

"Wait," Aculeo said, taking some coins out of his purse. "I'll pay you three now. The other three after you take me to him."

The man considered it for a moment, licking his lips. And finally, "Alright, then, let's go."

They headed out into the street, the street torches burning low by now, the songs and cries more raucous then ever as the night unwound. The town never slept – its stinking streets churning with drunks, gamblers, government workers and pornes spilling out of the taverns to find their next drink. Aculeo's erstwhile guide led him down some back streets where eventually the rough crowds thinned to a scattered few.

They made their way down to the main harbour district, then to the docklands. The jetties were filled with boats of all shapes and sizes, rocking in the waves, past dark warehouses, pens of livestock, the beggars and riffraff that made their beds there watching them warily as they passed.

"Posidippus lives here?" Aculeo said dubiously, keeping his hand on his knife.

"Just hurry up," the man said.

They came at last to a deserted-looking building at the edge of the docklands, the sound of rats scuttling into the darkness, the only light coming from the flickering torchlight and the stars overhead.

"This is it then," the man said. "Pay me the balance now."

"Where's Posidippus?"

"He'll be here soon."

"So will your payment then," Aculeo said, moving towards the edge of the dock, gazing into the darkness, the sound of the waves slapping against the jetty. He looked back towards the west. He could see the fire from Pharos even from here, like a golden eye glittering against the blackness of the night. You can't escape it easily. He thought of Calisto and the girls, wondering whether they'd make it out of this ghastly mess safely, out of Ralla's clutches.

"So when is Posidippus coming?" he asked finally as he turned around. The little man was gone – he was alone. He heard something to his left, a creak of the boards of the jetty, a blur of movement towards him … the back of his head exploded in pain and everything crashed into a sea of blackness.

CHAPTER XXX

Aculeo choked and gagged as cold, brackish water filled his mouth and seeped into his lungs. He struggled to move but something was pinning his arms and legs. Dark starbursts exploded in his head. He thrashed and twisted, trying desperately to free himself as it all began to slip away ...

Rough hands dragged him from the water and dropped him on the muddy shore. Aculeo crouched on his hands and knees, coughing and retching but alive at least. Someone kicked him hard in the ribs, once, then again until he rolled onto his back. He blinked up at them, trying to make out the features of the three figures looming over him in the darkness.

"Why are you here?" a man's voice growled.

"Depends," Aculeo said, still coughing. "Who are you?" One man nodded to the others, who seized Aculeo and dragged him back into the water. "No!" he cried. "No, wait!"

He managed to gasp a single breath as they forced him under. He clung to it desperately until his lungs felt like they'd burst. He roared in impotent rage when they hauled him back up and threw him in the stinking mud.

"Still want to play games?" the man asked.

"Fuck you ... up the ass," Aculeo gasped.

The man knelt down in the mud beside him, grabbed him by the hair and yanked his head up – his axe-thin face cold, merciless, considering Aculeo with detached puzzlement. "Old Corvinus always said your tongue was faster than your wits, Aculeo. You've come to kill me, haven't you?"

"Posidippus … I didn't come to kill you. I came to ask your help!"

Posidippus gave a gap-toothed grin, then struck him sharply across the face. "You lie more than a Persian porne, Roman."

"I'm just looking for answers." The Cosian struck him again, his gold rings cutting Aculeo's cheek open, the warm coppery tang of blood trickling across his lips. "Will you stop doing that."

"How'd you even find me?"

"You did a poor job covering your tracks. The opium dealers in Alexandria knew where you were."

"You're a lying son of a poxed cunt whore," the Cosian said, then drew a knife from his belt and placed the cold blade casually alongside Aculeo's throat, sending a shiver of fear coursing down his spine. "Last chance, Roman – Gurculio sent you after me, didn't he?"

"Gurculio's dead," Aculeo gasped. "He was murdered last week."

"You don't like to make it easy for yourself, do you?" Posidippus said, slowly tracing the tip of the razor-sharp blade across Aculeo's naked neck, like a thread of liquid fire across his flesh.

"No, wait! Wait. I know who killed Petras."

The Cosian stared at him, his eyes cold, expression blank. "What did you say?"

"Petras," Aculeo said. "I know who murdered her."

"Petras … she's dead?" Posidippus asked, his voice thick with emotion, disbelieving. Aculeo nodded, not sure how the man would react. The Cosian said nothing for a moment, just stared at him. Then he dropped the knife, covered his face with his hands and began to weep like a child.

They sat on the loading bay of an abandoned warehouse near the docks. "Tell me what happened," Posidippus said in a hoarse whisper. "Leave nothing out Roman or on my oath I'll gut you like a tunny."

Aculeo told him most of what he knew, about the murders of Iovinus, Myrrhine and Gurculio, the discovery of Neaera's necklace, the freedman's wretched farm where likely a dozen more women had been murdered and disposed of.

"You're sure of this?" the Cosian asked.

"As sure as I can be. We found no bodies."

"What's that supposed to mean?"

"The killers fed the victims' remains to the pigs."

D.L. Johnstone

"Gah. Throw me that skin, will you?" the Cosian said to one of his men, who tossed him a wineskin. Finally he asked, hesitantly, "And what of Petras? Was ... was she among them?"

"No. We discovered her body in the Necropolis. She was buried anonymously as a fellahin. She was murdered three months ago."

"Three months, by the gods. Februarius then?"

"Yes. Why? What's so ...?"

"Shut up, Roman. What else d'you know?"

"Her wounds were similar to those found on Myrrhine. They were likely murdered by the same person. Her burial was paid for by someone named Sabazius."

"Who?"

"It's a false name. Sabazius is another name for Dionysos."

"Dionysos," the Cosian said, and spat on the ground. "Filthy peasant god that he is, him and his Symposium of Gallus."

"What happened, Posidippus? Tell me what you know."

The Cosian raked his fingers back through his lank, greasy hair and sighed. "Petras was a part of Panthea's brothel. I fell in love with her the moment I laid my eyes on her – so lovely, witty, bright, beautiful, and her voice like honey in my ears. I had to have her. I'd had enough dealings with that foul bitch Panthea to know it wouldn't be easy to buy Petras from her. And when she figured out I'd fallen for her, that multiplied the price tenfold – and she played me for all it was worth. Gurculio agreed to loan me the money. Like a fool, I agreed, not caring about the price or the interest. It gave us no way out, though. I'd leveraged myself far too much already. Then Ralla bought her out from under me. I wanted to murder the man but I couldn't even get close to him. I'd lost Petras, yet my debts remained. I paid back what I could but the interest that had already gathered hobbled me. Then Gurculio began to squeeze. He wanted to take over my trade routes, my ships, everything. Everything was closing in. I made plans for Petras and I to escape. We'd go to Assyria, make our way from there," the Cosian said bleakly, taking another draw on the wineskin.

"The night before we were to leave, Petras was told to attend a special symposium. The Symposium of Gallus. She couldn't say no, it would have raised too many suspicions. We planned to make our escape the next day. Except ... she never returned. I held onto my hope, but feared for the worst. I knew the people I was up against were far too powerful. I was no match."

"Ralla?"

"Him, yes, but there were a dozen others as well. Gurculio, Avilius Balbus ..."

"The Prefect's son?"

"The same. Petras had no chance against them. Nor did I."

"And what of Iovinus?" Aculeo asked. "Was he involved in this as well?"

"Iovinus?" Posidippus said with a bitter laugh. "He's just the mouse that fell in the pitch when he stood on the edge of the pot for a sniff. He went up against too many powerful men, with even more powerful friends. You should have learned from his mistake, Aculeo."

"I've lost too much already to give up now."

"Have you? We'll see about that, I suppose." Posidippus stared into the distance. "Iovinus was living right here in Canopus all the time, did you know that?"

"No."

"He came here to hide right after the second fleet was supposed to have sailed to Porteus. I learned he was here soon after I arrived. I had him brought to me. He told me all about Corvinus' treachery. Did you know of this?" he demanded.

"Only recently. Corvinus betrayed me as much as anyone."

"So you say," Posidippus said dubiously. "I should have cut Iovinus' balls off the moment I saw him."

"I wish I'd done the same. Did he have some tablets with him?"

"Ah, so you know about Flavianus' tablets do you?"

"Why did Iovinus have them?"

"Blackmail, why else? He stole them from Corvinus to use against Ralla and Flavianus. He got cold feet though. He tried to sell them to me but I wanted no part of it. Far too dangerous, even for me. He thought Gurculio might give him a good price." The Cosian looked warily at Aculeo, evaluating him. "You said the moneylender was murdered."

"Yes, a week ago."

"Who did it?"

"Panthea."

"The whore finally made her move then," the Cosian said. "She wants it all, that one. Pah, fuck them all. It's all over."

"No it's not," Aculeo said. "We still need to stop them."

"To what end? They've already won, and I've cut my losses."

"You won't avenge Petras?"

"You really are the worst kind of fool – an earnest one. You go after these people you'll accomplish nothing more than getting yourself caught, which will bring them that much closer to finding me."

"What of Petras?" Aculeo demanded. "You were ready to give up everything to be with her. Ralla and the others stole from you, from her, just to feed their sick desires. They murdered her, and others like her, using them and throwing them away like trash."

"It's over damn you!"

"Is it? And what will you tell Petras at the end of your days, Posidippus, when you find her shade still wandering on the banks of the Styx, her murder unavenged?" The Cosian looked away for a moment, lost in his misery. "We've a chance to stop them."

"We've no chance at all!" the Cosian roared, hurling the wineskin into the darkness.

"So we should just turn our backs and run away?"

Posidippus glowered at Aculeo for a long while, looking as though he might murder him on the spot. Finally, he held out an open hand. Aculeo took it, relieved, and the Cosian grasped it tight, pulling him close. "Fine. I'll give you passage, Roman. But let's be clear about something. You haven't seen me. You don't know where I am. As far as you're concerned or anyone asks, I'm already dead. Understand me?"

"Yes, of course."

Posidippus stared him hard in the eye, unblinking, not releasing his hand. "I'm not sure you do. Not fully." He signalled his men who grabbed Aculeo and forced him face-first to the ground. The Cosian knelt on his right forearm, pinning the hand flat on the ground, splaying the fingers out. "I won't make the same mistake I made with Iovinus. Try not to move," he said calmly, then put his knife to the base of Aculeo's little finger.

"No!" Aculeo cried. The Cosian chopped the knife down quick. Aculeo screamed, the pain excruciating, hot blood pumped from the stump where his finger had been only seconds before.

"Now you understand, eh?" Posidippus said, his voice cutting through the searing pain. "Every time you eat, drink, wipe your arse or stick your hand up a woman's box, you'll remember. And the thing I want you to remember most of all is that if I ever see your face again, Roman, I swear to all the gods it won't just be your finger I take."

CHAPTER XXXI

THE 10TH DAY OF MAIUS

Zeanthes of Araethyrea took little notice of the man walking towards him along the crushed red gravel pathway of the Museion grounds, a broad-brimmed straw sun hat obscuring his face. The sophist, lost in meditation, tried to veer around him, but the man shot towards him suddenly, seized him roughly by the wrist and clapped a hand roughly over his mouth. Zeanthes tried to break free but the man held him fast, shoving him back against a marble column. They were quite alone. His attacker looked up at him then from beneath the brim of his hat, wary, watching, and slowly took his hand from the sophist's mouth.

"Aculeo!" Zeanthes said in relief. "By the gods, you startled me. But I thought you'd left the city."

"I just got back this morning," Aculeo said, eyeing him still.

"Why did you come back? It isn't safe."

"I could hardly have stayed away. It's time I did something right in my life."

Zeanthes smiled. "The Skeptics contend one can never truly tell right from wrong. In fact …"

"Enough with your cursed sophistry," Aculeo snapped. The scholar's smile faltered. "Where's Calisto? She's not in her villa – it looked abandoned."

"I don't know," Zeanthes said. "I understand Ralla moved her."

"Of course," Aculeo said wearily, dropping onto a nearby bench.

Zeanthes sat next to him, then stared at Aculeo's hand. "You're injured!" he gasped. "What happened to you?"

"Nothing I want to discuss now," Aculeo said. "What do you know about the Symposium of Gallus."

"Ah," Zeanthes said, looking across the grounds at a shallow meditation pond, where a snow-white ibis waded stilt-legged through the water lilies, spearing fish with its sharp beak. The bird stared back at them for a moment, its bright yellow eyes cold, unblinking. "I take it you found Posidippus."

"You knew?" Aculeo cried and grabbed him by the neck of his chiton, wrapping his other hand around the man's throat.

"Aculeo, please!" the sophist gagged.

Aculeo squeezed his fingers into the soft flesh of Zeanthes' throat. "No more lies old man. Tell me, damn you, or I'll break your neck."

"Please, please stop, I beg you!" the sophist gasped, his fleshy face turning from red to purple. Aculeo loosened his grip and Zeanthes slumped back on the marble bench, coughing, rubbing his throat. Another sophist walked by then, giving them an odd look before moving on.

"Let's find a more private place to talk," Zeanthes said. They followed the maze of pathways through the lush, exotic gardens to a private meditation area near a plane tree and a shrine to the Muses. The sophist found another shaded marble bench and sighed. "It's not what you think."

"How would you know what I think?"

"I know what I would think were I in your place. I give you my oath, Aculeo, on all I hold dear, I never took part in these terrible events. I know only what others spoke of to me."

"Did you know women were murdered?" Aculeo demanded. "Did you know they were sacrificed like goats to the Gods?"

"I suspected as much, but you have to understand ..."

"Understand? Why didn't you just tell me?"

"But don't you see?" Zeanthes pleaded. "I tried to help you to discover the truth for yourself. When we talked at Ralla's symposium that night, I introduced you to them all."

Aculeo glowered at the other man, incredulous. "How many women were murdered?"

"I don't really know," the sophist said weakly.

"You don't know, or you don't care?"

"Oh, Aculeo, I care more than you can possibly imagine," Zeanthes said. He looked like a feeble old man all of a sudden, shoulders bowed, eyes clouded with fear. "My dear, dear friend, how can I make you believe me?"

"Who's at the centre of this?"

"I'm not certain."

"Then who do you suspect?"

"Ralla," Zeanthes said. It was practically a whisper, but the name was like a roar in Aculeo's ears.

"Who else?"

"Gurculio when he was alive. And Asinius Camillus. And Avilius Balbus."

"When did it start?"

The sophist was quiet for a moment, looking meditatively towards the Museion buildings. "Six months ago perhaps."

"They've been murdering girls for the past six months, and you said nothing?" Aculeo demanded, his fury barely in check. "You did nothing?"

"I couldn't be certain. It was all just talk."

"Of course, all you do is talk! What are the lives of a few women worth to you compared to your beloved patronage, another bowl of wine and an evening of pointless talk!"

"I told you what I could," Zeanthes cried fervently, clutching at Aculeo's tunic. "I taught you about Persephone, of the pomegranates, of Dionysos. I guided you, helped reveal the true nature of the killer."

"What help was that to the girls who were murdered while you spun your tales, you old fool?"

"I was afraid."

"I thought as much."

"No, don't misunderstand me," Zeanthes wept, tears streaming down his cheeks. "I wasn't afraid for myself, but for you, Aculeo. For Calisto. For the love you share with one another. After all you've been through, with your wife and son ..."

"Don't dare speak of them to me!"

"I'm sorry, it's just that I didn't want to see you come to ruin out of misplaced pride." Zeanthes covered his face with his trembling hands. "Oh why did you have to return? Why didn't you just flee the city?"

"Why didn't you just tell me the truth?"

"What good would that have done? A simple sophist and a bankrupt Roman merchant against these powerful men? If I'd spoken out, they would have murdered us both, and then who would stop them?"

"So you said nothing in order to stop them?"

"I hoped to convince them to change their ways through discourse," Zeanthes said desperately, tears running down his cheeks.

"More talk. Yet instead of saving them, more girls were murdered."

"I know," the sophist said, weeping now. "I know, you're right. Oh what have I done?"

"When's the next symposium?" Aculeo asked.

"Tonight, at Ralla's villa."

"Calisto's life is in danger."

"Oh surely not. I know he cares deeply for her!"

"That didn't stop him from murdering the others, did it?"

"I can only pray you're wrong. Ralla, he's far more powerful than you might realize."

"He's just a man, like you and me," Aculeo said. "He thinks he's something more, and others believe him. So he murders, steals, attempts to crush the rest of us. And cowards like you stand idly by as he tries to take from us everything that's meaningful in this world. But in the end, he's only a flesh and blood." With that, Aculeo stood up and walked away.

Zeanthes watched him leave, then simply sat there, quiet for a moment, his eyes closed. The only sounds were the song of birds in the fruit trees of the Museion orchards and the distant drums of the festival.

Aculeo could see the gleaming white shoreline of the Harbour of Kiobotos where a great number of cows, goats and donkeys had been gathered and crowned with garlands, for the festival, all the beasts of burden were celebrated for the contributions their ancestors had made carrying the loads to build the city. Thin streams of smoke threaded like white ribbons into the blue sky overhead, as even ordinary citizens were encouraged to make a sacrifice to the health and salvation of the divine Caesar. They did so in front of their houses, on rooftops and in the street along which the litter passed, sacrificing whatever they could afford, a goat, a duck, or a handful of grain.

Vendors had parked their wagons at the side of the street, having been given special dispensation on festival day to do so, and the air was rich with the smell of spiced meats, roasted beans, bread baked with honey, and chilled black wine. The streets were alive with the sound of drums and flutes and plucking lyres as entertainers wove through the crowds, dancing and singing as they went. One wagon was festooned with linen flags and banners that snapped in the breeze, another stacked with portraits of Caesar Tiberius and Augustus on clay plaques, bracelets and rolls of papyrus, another selling wind chimes, their hollow songs like half-remembered dreams.

Aculeo watched the oarsmen sweep their long oars through the slate blue waters in steady, practised rhythm, and the great barge, a hundred cubits in length, with gilt prows and scarlet awnings stretched across its teakwood decks, swept to the front of the procession. The short journey across the bay from the palace past the Caesareum to the Harbour of Kiobotos had begun, thus formally initiating the Festival of the Founders, which had been celebrated every year in the city since its founding over three centuries before.

The buildings and houses were all freshly whitewashed for the festival, their red clay roofs pretty as pebbles on the beach against the bright blue sky. The street leading up to the Soma, where the dedication would be made, was hung with yellow and green awnings which flapped gently in the sweet morning breeze off the sea. The Prefect's barge slowed to a crawl as it approached the pier where the priests and worshippers had gathered, waiting for them to disembark. The crowds cheered as the barge pulled alongside the pier, the sailors threw long, stout jute ropes to tie it off and an ornate ramp was lowered to the deck.

Aculeo watched as the wealthy citizens and their families emerged from their litters into the sunlight and joined the procession, walking the rest of the way like common folk. He recalled the times he and Titiana along with Corvinus with his family had walked alongside them, so far removed from this time and place, another lifetime. Attendance of such families in the procession was considered both an honour and an expectation. It could be his only chance to get to the man before the symposium that evening.

And there he saw a balding, middle-aged man emerge from a gaudy-looking litter, his watery brown eyes blinking in the bright sunshine. Lucius Albius Ralla. He was followed by his family, a shrewish, dark-haired woman and a girl of perhaps eight years, a pair of muscular slaves a few steps behind them. Soldiers held back the masses as the procession made its way along the Street of the Soma, which had been laid with fresh-cut palm fronds. Priests robed in white led the procession, followed by priestesses bearing sacred objects for the festival – the Basket-Bearer, the Prize-Bearer, the Crown-Bearer and the Light-Bearer. The streets were filled with the sound of music, flutes, lyres and drums, as the procession slowly moved towards the golden dome. The many statues of the Caesars that lined the street were all adorned with double-horned cornucopias, flowing with fragrant white flowers, in honor of the Festival.

The procession finally made its way up to the Soma where the tombs of the Ptolemies were housed. At the front entrance stood a towering statue of Alexander the Great himself, so young and handsome, a sword in one hand, a set of scrolls in the other. A grand pavilion built of beams of fragrant wood had been constructed for the sacrifice, hung with Phoenician curtains, purple rugs, military cloaks and rich tapestries embroidered with mythological scenes. Great, twisted logs of dried olive-wood had been piled high at Alexander's feet while a pair of steers with ivory white hides and frightened pinkish eyes stood to the side, uncertain why they should have been brought to this place.

Aculeo had a good view of Ralla and his family standing near the Prefect Vitrasius Pollio, not fifty cubits away, watching the prayers being given. The priests laid a burning branch on the olive-wood, which quickly snapped and crackled with fire. A grey-bearded pontiff dressed in magnificent gold and murex-purple robes led the prayer, a very long, tedious honorific to the Founders, the Caesars and virtually every god in the Roman and, for good measure, the Egyptian panoply as well. At the end of the prayer, the pontiff cast a handful of barley meal onto the now blazing fire, making it pop and hiss. The white-robed priests then led the suspicious steers forward. The pontiff gave a signal, and a tall, powerful looking priest stepped back from the fray, then swung a gleaming bronze axe into the first steer's broad neck, slicing through its thick muscles and ropey white sinews. It dropped almost instantly, falling prone on both its horns.

The second steer was dragged forward, lowing in fear, scraping its hooves against the dusty ground, trying to escape. The priest swung his axe again and that steer too fell to the ground. The priests quickly cut the steers' throats and hot blood gushed from the animals' wounds, splashed upon the altar floor, washed around the worshippers' feet, the ripe, heady stench of death filling the air. Some drops of blood had splashed on Ralla's daughter's pretty white robes – she let out a cry, a high pitched wail that echoed through the temple. Ralla gave the child a look of irritation and whispered something to his wife, who nodded obediently and led her away, escorted by one of their slaves. The priests flayed the steers' hides, then cut out the sacred thigh bones, covered them with thick pink-white slabs of sundered fat and laid them spattering on the fire.

Aculeo glanced up at the statue of Alexander, his serene marble face wreathed in the smoke of sacrifice, which climbed in good omen in a dark spiralling column to the Soma's vaulted ceiling. The ceiling was adorned with the carved images of the Caesars and the ancient kings.

He almost missed seeing Ralla and his remaining slave head out of the pavilion, slipping past the other worshippers and down the broad marble steps. He crossed the Street of the Soma and turned down a side street. Aculeo crossed the street and followed as close as he could behind the men, afraid he might lose them as they weaved their way through the teeming multitudes. They turned down another street just ahead. Someone cried out, a pair of wagons bumped across the cobbled street, blocking Aculeo's path. A gaggle of merchants loading fresh goods from their wagons into their stalls, laughing, yawning, scratching at themselves. Aculeo shoved his way past them, ignored their cries of protest, and turned down the street. No sign of Ralla or the bodyguard. Where did he go? He turned down another side street up ahead – still nothing. They were gone.

There were a number of taverns and shops lining the street, they could have stepped into any one of them. Damn it, Aculeo thought, looking about, where could they have gone? He turned back and tried another side street where he spotted the banker deep in conversation with another man beneath a covered walkway. The slave glanced over at Aculeo, then looked away, unconcerned. Ralla had his back turned. The crowd had thinned to only a handful of people.

Aculeo felt his heart pound in his chest as he drew his knife, the blade tucked back against the flat of his wrist, and moved closer to the man, only ten cubits away now. How shall I do it? he wondered, his knees like water. Move in from behind, take him by the throat, end it fast before his slave can act, then run.

This is madness, he thought. I'm no killer, am I?

Yes, yes I can be, I must be if the alternative's too much to bear.

And if I succeed, what then? This street leads the wrong way, down to the harbour. I'll need to double back then, head towards the Agora, try to lose any pursuers there. His heart was in his throat now, his breathing shallow, harsh, his hands trembling as sweat trickled down his back. Only a few steps away now.

He could smell the man's oiled hair scented with dense, expensive perfume. He could see the soft roll of pale skin on the back of his neck, the collar of his fine tunic dark with sweat. Aculeo lifted the knife, his other hand ready to grab the hair on the back of the man's head, to pull it back, expose the throat, then cut. He took a deep, shaky breath and started to move in.

The sound of a child's laughter. A boy no more than three years old emerged from one of the shops with his nursemaid. Aculeo hesitated as he locked eyes with the child who smiled at him, a beautiful, innocent smile
...

Things seemed to move too slowly after that. Aculeo stayed his hand, turned awkwardly away, slipping on the paving stones, dropping his knife. Someone let out a warning cry and Ralla looked up, eyes lit with fear. The banker snatched the boy from the nursemaid's arms and fell back against the wall of a shop, shielding himself with the now wailing child.

Aculeo tried to escape but someone grabbed his tunic, holding him back. He felt a sudden electric jolt in his side, his mouth filling with blood as the pain radiated through him like a brushfire. He saw the slave sweep the knife towards him for a second strike and managed to block it just in time, then punched him in the throat. The slave dropped his weapon and fell to his knees, gasping for breath. Ralla scuttled to safety into an oblivious group of tourists just emerged from the shops, still clutching the bawling child in his arms.

Aculeo staggered away, hand to his side, his tunic slick with blood, trying to breathe, a wet sucking sound emanating from his chest. He made it out into the main street, fell into the anonymous evening crowds around the Agora. He stumbled off into the night, everything spinning around, knowing he'd just lost the only chance he'd get.

CHAPTER XXXII

Epiphaneus grimaced as he limped towards the rail of the Pharos balustrade, looking down upon the city. Dusk was falling, visitors had thinned to a few scattered tourists. The sophist pulled his himation tight around his round, sloping shoulders. "A cold, lonely place to meet, Zeanthes."

"Apologies, my dear friend," Zeanthes said. "You told me you wanted to meet somewhere private away from the Museion. I should have been more respectful of your age."

"I'm but three years older than you," Epiphaneus snapped. "It's not frailty on my part – it's this wretched place. There's nothing to cut the sea wind."

Zeanthes looked down at the waves that crashed across the island's white sands, the winds off the sea blowing stray hairs across his face. "I do enjoy spending time up here. It gives one a unique perspective of the city and the world, as the gods must look upon such things."

Epiphaneus snorted. "You're just a man, though, standing with another man at the end of the day upon a tower still other men have built."

"Yet here we can bear witness to what great things the gods have inspired us to dream, create, achieve."

"The gods are for children and fools."

Zeanthes put a hand on the man's shoulder. "You haven't been yourself of late, Epiphaneus. What ails you?"

The sophist said nothing for a while, just gripped the rail, looking down at the grey-white tower wall to the rugged shore far below. "I came here some years ago to conduct an experiment. I took two projectiles of similar dimensions but of different weights, and dropped them from this very balustrade at precisely the same time. I had a slave stand below, measuring the time and distance they fell from the starting point. And what do you think happened?"

"Tell me."

"They reached the earth at exactly the same time, exactly the same distance from the starting point. This force that draws us to the earth is fundamentally the same for all things. All bodies might thus be connected. The sun is drawn to the earth as the earth is to the sun. We in turn are drawn to the earth, hence we do not fall from its face, and we are similarly drawn to one another, collecting in cities where we bridge our relationships with our fellow man."

"So the world, the cosmos, even our perception of reality itself are purely mathematical?" Zeanthes asked.

"As Pythagoras taught us, yes."

"Still, you must also accept that none of the things that are known by us could have come into being without the handiwork of the divine artisans."

"I accept nothing of the sort. Our lack of understanding of our own existence is hardly proof of existence of higher powers."

"Nor is our inability to see these higher powers any proof of their non-existence."

"Rubbish. We've nothing else to measure but our own reality."

"But what most men interpret as reality, our day-to-day lives, are just poor reflections, imperfect emanations from our eternal souls."

"If reality is nothing, then what is death?" Epiphaneus demanded, scowling at the other sophist from beneath his bushy white eyebrows.

"Merely a transmigration, a phase," Zeanthes replied. "Human souls are divine and immortal but they are doomed to follow a grievous circle of successive lives. Between our lives, a void exists, which separates and distinguishes our natures as do the spaces between numbers."

"More rubbish," Epiphaneus said irritably. "You speak of Anaximander's theory of metempsychosis. A minor work, unworthy of our consideration."

"Yet consider the consequences. If our true reality is within the void, not in our day-to-day experience of reality, then whatever we do on this earth to bring us closer to the Godhead must therefore be virtuous."

"So that lends credence to our actions against others? Even immoral actions?"

"You speak of morals, as though they are akin to rules of nature guiding heavenly bodies," Zeanthes said with a strained smile.

"Morals at least provide a set of rules for man, for civilization such that we might live in some degree of mutual content."

"So you espouse not divination but determinism, such that man's only way forward is driven by the result of previous causes?"

"Determinism is a just approach," Epiphaneus said.

"But there is a higher reality. If we act of free will, by definition we act with virtue, for it is that part of ourselves that is divine."

"I repeat my original question: even if the actions we take are wicked?"

"Come, Epiphaneus. The wickedness of one man does no harm to another. Man's soul is eternal. Aristotle himself said whatever steps we must take along the path to reach the end do not matter, only the end itself."

"Yes? Well as far as I'm concerned the end is a decidedly loathsome place and hardly worth the bother," the other sophist said bitterly.

"But the end is the nature of the thing."

"Do you mock me now?"

"I meant no offense," Zeanthes said.

Epiphaneus considered him for a moment, then turned away. The platform was empty now save for the two men, their silhouettes aglow in the light of Pharos, the silence between them bridged by the rhythmic crash of the waves below.

Zeanthes laid his hand on the other man's shoulder, squeezed it gently. "Epiphaneus, something clearly troubles you. You asked me to meet with you for a reason. How can I help you, my friend?"

Epiphaneus sighed. "The Chief Librarian has decided not to extend my patronage."

The other sophist looked at him in surprise. "But why?"

"Why else? To make room for younger, lesser minds. After twenty-three years in this place, I've now been relegated as redundant."

"But that's appalling! Whatever will you do?"

"I've struggled with that same question for some time. Then I realized the answer was obvious. I will simply speak with him about you."

"About me?" Zeanthes asked, caught off guard.

"Yes. I will speak to him about how well noble Zeanthes espouses in such dulcet tones the words of Pythagoras, Anaximander, even Aristotle as his own, while he seems so blissfully unaware of his own. I'm sure he will find it quite illuminating."

"I don't understand."

Epiphaneus reached into his satchel and took out a soft vellum case. He opened it, and from it slid a scroll. "Do you recognize this?"

Zeanthes took the scroll from the other man and scanned it. He smiled and shook his head. "So this is what you wanted to speak to me about in such secrecy."

"Would you have preferred I'd raised the question on the square porch in front of an audience of our peers?"

"Where did you find this?"

"It matters not. It's your work and in your own handwriting, is it not? A rare and unusual document for that and other reasons. Not the least being that you make within it a quite eloquent argument that man must trust reality, and that all else is subservient. You come across as a true and well-considered Stoic, in fact."

"A youthful exercise in thought," Zeanthes said with a shrug, though his gaze never left the other sophist.

"Youthful? It was written but five years ago. It should be noted, however, that no copy of it exists in the Library. Which brings me to another interesting observation. The Library holds original copies of virtually every book known to man, as has been its purpose from the beginning. Yet original copies of your works are not to be found, much to the surprise of the Librarians themselves, for they claim they used to have a complete collection. All of them are now gone, it seems. This scroll, however, was taken from a Persian merchant ship just this week."

"I don't know what you're getting at, Epiphaneus, but my views have changed since that was written," Zeanthes said dismissively.

"Such things happen of course. A ship may change course with the winds. A rider may change a tired horse. But tell me please, how does a well-spoken Stoic develop into a muddle-headed Skeptic like yourself? And even if I could grudgingly accept such a thing, what am I to make of the fact that when I compare your work to other documents I recently obtained from the desk in your room, it is apparent that your handwriting has changed as markedly as your philosophy."

"So we have at last arrived at the root of the matter then," Zeanthes said, watching the seagulls kite through the dimming sky.

"I suppose we have," Epiphaneus said, smiling in triumph. "You admit you are not Zeanthes of Araethyrea?"

"What does it matter now?"

"What does it matter?" the sophist asked, dumbfounded. "It matters a great deal!"

"Why?"

"Because I have lived my life, done my work, advanced the field of human knowledge and understanding, yet I am ridiculed, despised, called redundant. You, meanwhile, have somehow latched onto your acclaimed career like a parasite, plastering over it with muddled lies. You should be despised and scourged as a fraud but instead you are respected and honoured."

"I'm sorry, Epiphaneus," Zeanthes sighed.

"You're sorry?" Epiphaneus spat, pulling his himation tight around himself against the cold wind off the sea. "Well, it's far too late for half-hearted apologies, Zeanthes, or whomever you are. I'm certain that the Chief Librarian will be most interested in hearing ..."

Zeanthes moved with surprising speed, shoving Epiphaneus hard against the platform's ballustrade, making it creak against the sudden force.

"What do you think you're doing, you fool?" Epiphaneus cried out. "You nearly made me..." A flicker of sudden realization sparked in his eyes. "Oh, of course."

Zeanthes seized the sophist by the ankles and tipped him over the ballustrade. As Epiphaneus tumbled, screaming in terror and rage against the injustice of it all, another part of him couldn't help but notice his sandal slip from his foot and fall at precisely the same velocity as his own, despite its obvious lesser weight. He did not have the opportunity to observe that his head and the sandal both struck against the tapering Lighthouse wall halfway down at exactly the same time before both of them cartwheeled to the rocks below. A passing tourist screamed as the old man's head splattered against the rocks like an overripe melon, spilling forth on the pale sands all the pink-grey matter that had produced such grand thoughts. Other tourists gathered in shock about the sophist's broken, lifeless body. One of them looked up to the ballustrade, but Zeanthes was already gone.

The moon had edged its way onto the horizon, the fire raged in the beacon overhead, casting its light across the darkening sea. The waves crashed against the shore, and the red crabs scuttled across the sand, their shelter swept away by the rising tide.

Tyche walked through the central atrium, past the lush, fragrant flowers and ornamental shrubs within the peristylium, hardly noticing the little birds that hopped and fluttered along the pathway before her, trying to get out of her way. She stood in the shadows of the gatehouse, watching Calisto approach the litter. Tyche was about to pass through the gate when someone grabbed her arm.

"Where are you going?" Idaia whispered.

"With Calisto," Tyche said.

"But I thought you said she shouldn't go to the symposium tonight! That something bad might happen, like what happened to Myrrhine!"

"She has no choice – Ralla insisted."

"But ... but why are you going then?"

"To watch out for her."

"But why is she letting you? Who'll watch out for you?" Tyche said nothing. Idaia felt her heart sink when she noticed the fear in her eyes. If she leaves now, I'll never see her again, she thought. I know it! "I'm coming too!"

"No you're not."

"But ..."

"No!" Tyche said, too sharply. Idaia's lower lip started to tremble and she began to sob.

"Please, Tyche, please don't go. Osti ..."

Tyche knelt down and wrapped her arms around the child. "No, it isn't that, don't worry."

"But what if it is?" Idaia wept. "What if it is and you and Calisto never come back?"

"I will, I promise," she said, kissing Idaia's left cheek, then her right, squeezing her tight. After a moment she held her at arm's length. "You shouldn't stay here, though. Who else do you know in the city?"

"A... Aculeo," the child sniffled, wiping her eyes with the back of her hand.

"That won't do," Tyche said. "He's gone now."

"Wh ... where did he g ... go?"

"I don't know. Who else do you know? Think! You must know someone."

Idaia closed her eyes, thinking hard. Then she thought of that terrible morning in Rhakotis when she'd witnessed poor Myrrhine's savaged remains. "There's an old healer woman," she said dubiously. "She's a friend of Aculeo's. She lives where all the Egyptian people live."

"Good!" Tyche said. "Do you think you can find her house again? It's important."

"I ... I think so," Idaia said uncertainly. But it's so far away, she thought, I'll have to walk across the whole city all by myself. And it's so dark – I hate the dark!

"Go then. Go now! She'll make sure you're safe until we get back, alright?"

"Come be safe with me! Please!"

"I can't. Now promise me you'll do what I said, okay?" Tyche held the girl firmly, lifting up her chin when she tried to look away.

"Okay," Idaia whispered at last.

Tyche hugged her again, painfully tight this time, kissed the top of her head, then pulled her cloak over her head and slipped into the mounting darkness.

CHAPTER XXXIII

The streets were almost empty save for a few wandering groups of drunken revellers looking for yet another tavern. Aculeo approached the outer gates of Lagos, the exclusive deme in Gamma where Ralla lived high up on the hill. He could see the Western Harbour cupped below like a hand around the shore of Lake Mareotis where ships bobbed gently at anchor, cast in a silvery wash from the moon and stars in the deep black sky.

He paused to rest a moment, the wound in his side throbbing, pain shooting through his body as though red-hot coals were embedded in his side. The side of his tunic was wet with blood. He'd rested in a tavern until it got dark, not wanting to risk walking to Sekhet's to have his wound tended – he doubted he could have handled the exertion or the old woman's remonstrations.

Half a dozen revellers walked just ahead of him, all of them dressed in black, travelling on foot and by litter. Aculeo followed a short distance behind them up the winding streets, past the villas hidden like secret jewels behind high stone walls. They came at last to a large fountain in the centre of a boulevard, just outside of an elaborate pair of iron gates. The sculpture within the fountain appeared to be of Jupiter straddling a naked nymph from behind, holding her head down in the pounding water, obscuring her face as he mounted her. The Rape of Eurynome, he thought. That would be Ralla's idea of high culture.

He could hear the steady rhythm of music from behind the compound's walls, the soft buzzing song of aulos, the sound of lyres and high-pitched, drunken laughter filling the night. Slaves wearing peacock masks, tall feathers fanning up from the backs of their heads, met arriving guests at the gates. Guards stood like statues near the gates, the guests presented their invitation tiles to gain admission. A very private affair. Slave girls dressed in translucent robes stood at the edge of the garden path and handed each guest a cup of wine and bowed before leading them through the gardens towards the villa, lit only with coloured lanterns and smoky torchlight. A large cage sat in a corner of the courtyard, inside of which paced a gaunt, tattered looking panther, which snarled and swiped at any guests who dared to poke at it with a stick between the bars of its cage. The guests roared in laughter at the poor animal's indignant fury.

Aculeo felt weak, his wound throbbing, the music emanating from beyond the gates a mad, wild thrill of flute, drum and lyre that seemed to echo all around. He could hardly walk unopposed through the gates. He turned about and followed the winding street past the pretty villas. He spotted some thorn bushes at the side of the road next to a cluster of large mud-brick storage crofts. He pushed through the bushes, the thorns catching at his tunic, tearing at the flesh of his arms and legs. And there, in behind one of the crofts, a square opening cut in the ground.

There were several entrances to the cisterns about the city – from the palaces, public buildings and the street, for the cisterns fed the city's many public fountains and water pumps. A few villas, those belonging to the wealthiest citizens, had private access to the cistern network. Including, he hoped, Ralla's villa. A pair of grooves had been carved into the rock slab as handholds. Aculeo set his torch down and slipped his fingers into the grooves to test it. He gasped at the weight – it barely budged. He reset his grip, took a deep breath and heaved, trying to ignore the pain. At last the slab lifted high enough that he was able to drag it off the opening, letting it fall with a heavy thump on the ground. He fell next to it, laying there for a minute, head spinning, trying to catch his breath. At last he rolled to his hands and knees.

He dropped his torch into the opening, listening to it clatter down the rock wall, revealing an open area perhaps five or ten cubits down before the flame sputtered and extinguished. I won't be dropping into an endless pit at least, he thought. He slipped his feet into the hole and slowly lowered himself in, twisting around, scrabbling his feet against the rock wall, searching for a toehold. He found one finally, shallow but acceptable, and began to ease his way down. His hand slipped and he lost his toehold, falling the rest of the way into the dark hole, twisting his ankle, sprawling painfully on the rough ground. He eased himself up to a sitting position, the sound of water sloshing around below.

When his eyes had finally adjusted to the darkness, he saw that he was on a raised area near a set of steps carved into the rock leading down

D.L. Johnstone

into the cisterns. Stone arches towered overhead, stretching endlessly into the dark void beyond like still waves in a cold, dead sea. A city beneath the city. Faint light danced off the water, reflections dappling across the cavernous walls.

Aculeo eased himself to his feet and tested his ankle. Painful but manageable. He limped down the steps to the narrow walkway that lined the cistern walls and moved towards the light up ahead. Random strains of music lilted in the air, a lyre, some pipes, a mournful flute. He kept moving towards it until he came at last to the end of the darkness, where shadows gave way to light. He held back, slipping into a shallow recess in the rock wall.

A broad platform had been built in a great open area overhanging the cistern, lit with torches, hung with tapestries, garlands and grapevine cuttings. A tree, its twisted branches barren and white, stood beside an elaborate gilt wood throne. At the base of the barren tree a woman wearing a goat mask crouched inside a cage, her skinny arms wrapped tightly around her knees, shivering despite the rank heat of the place. The sacrifice, Aculeo thought starkly.

A dozen black-robed people wearing masks were gathered about the base of the platform, crying 'Euoi!' as they danced wildly to the pounding of the drums, throwing their heads back and forth in a rage. A bellowing, rhythmic thrum of bullroarers echoed through the catacombs, the pounding of the drums, the shriek of the pipes, and the revellers all swayed in ecstasy around Aculeo, pushing against him, the heat of their bodies rank and thick, trying to draw him into their wild dance. He spotted Avilius Balbus standing with his friend Camullus at the edge of the crowd, their masks lifted so they could drink freely, their eyes lit in the drunken fire of worship as they swayed rhythmically with the others.

From the crowd emerged a man in a satyr's mask and clad in goat skins, a headpiece of pronged horns set upon his head amidst a wig of dark curls. The worshippers parted to let him through and ascend the platform steps. Ralla, Aculeo thought coldly. At his side atop the platform stood a woman dressed as a nymph, suckling a baby goat to her naked breast. A man in a horse mask stood at the foot of the platform steps plucking notes on a lyre while two slaves knelt at his feet filling a large krater with an amphora of wine.

The crush of masked, sweaty revellers pressed towards the platform, writhing to the pounding drums and cacophonic music. Two slaves in dragon masks led a snow-white goat towards the platform, garlands draped over its horned head. It bleated in confusion and fear, kicking and bucking, trying to escape, but its handlers prodded it forward with pine cone-tipped staffs until its white coat was stained with blood. The goat was hauled up onto the platform, bleating in terror at the blood-crazed fury of the worshippers, sensing what was to come.

"The first wine is offered to the immortal Dionysos," the high priest Ralla cried, his voice echoing through the catacombs as he took up a cup and forced its contents down the poor beast's throat. "God of the ancients, God of Arcadia, horned child crowned with serpents, you who take raw flesh." The goat twisted and tried to turn its head away, eyes wide with panic, but Ralla held it fast, pouring until the cup was empty.

The undulating chants of the worshippers echoed all around, mixed with the pounding drums and the bleating of the goat as it was tied to the barren tree. "Dionysos, killer of the vine, fulfilled at last by his red and bleeding feasts, as we now fulfill ours," Ralla proclaimed. He raised his arms, his hands spread wide, the revellers roared when the first stone struck the goat in the head. It bleated in pain and confusion as another stone struck it, then another, until its eerie cries of terror were drowned out by the drunken cheers of the worshippers as the stones rained down. Aculeo watched in revulsion as they descended on the wretched goat, screaming as they tore at its flesh. In a moment, it fell silent, a bloody, lifeless pulp on the ground. The revellers all stood and pressed forward, their faces and hands wet with the beast's blood, their eyes alight with lust.

"As the vine is taken at harvest," Ralla cried, "so Dionysos was devoured by the Titans, who gained his spark of divinity."

I need to find Calisto, Aculeo thought, scanning the crowd, the wound in his side a dull, aching throb. We need to get out of here. He noticed a woman standing off to the side dressed in a bright red peplos and a bee mask, an ornate gold and topaz necklace around her fleshy neck, a fringe of scarlet hair sticking out from the edge of her mask. Panthea, he thought. He slipped through the surging revellers until he stood behind her, feeling the sour heat from her body as she swayed back and forth. He felt for his knife, readying himself to grab her, drag her into the shadows, force her to tell him where Calisto was.

"The initiate," Panthea cried. A figure clad in purple robes, a myrtle crown and a dove mask was dragged onto the platform by the dragon-masked slaves. Aculeo's heart stopped when he saw her – the way she held herself, the shape of her hands bound before her, the slenderness of her ivory neck, the curve of her hip ... Calisto!

"In madness, we are released," Ralla cried from his giltwood throne. "We start to comprehend the majesty of the universe revealed, the joy as our souls are freed from the shackles of this life!"

D.L. Johnstone

"Take her, take her, take her," Panthea chanted drunkenly, rending her own robes as she writhed to the mad, grating music. "Take her!"

"Murderous whore," Aculeo hissed, knocking Panthea to the ground. She looked around in shock, her mask askew, as she struggled to her feet. Aculeo shoved past the swaying, inebriated worshippers clustered about the platform. Two slaves noticed him then and made their way towards him as he continued towards the platform, towards Calisto.

The dragon-masked slaves dragged Calisto towards the barren tree. Aculeo was steps from the platform's edge now. One of the guards seized him by the shoulder, trying to restrain him.

"Dionysos enters his worshippers through their eyes, their ears, their blood," Ralla cried.

Aculeo swung his elbow against the guard's head, grabbing the man's short sword from his belt as he fell. The other guard ran at him, sword raised to attack. Aculeo stabbed him in the neck and the man went down, blood spouting like a fountain onto the platform as he collapsed. Avilius Balbus, his flushed face suddenly sprayed with the dying slave's blood, looked about in horror like a child awoken from a nightmare and began to bawl, a sound few noticed over the screams of mad revelry. Other slaves noticed, though, and moved to protect the Prefect's son.

The girl in the goat mask was dragged from the cage and now stood next to Calisto. She was terribly slight, with thin arms, child's ankles – Tyche! Aculeo realized desperately. Ralla threw a pair of ropes over the highest branch of the barren tree, then slipped one of them in a noose about Tyche's slender neck, the other about Calisto's.

"We know true joy as our souls are freed from the shackles of this life and we become one with him!" cried Ralla, then he pulled Tyche's rope taut, the noose squeezing against her pale throat as she lifted into the air.

The crowd cried out "Euoi!" in delight, their blood-lust rising to a feverous pitch.

"No!" Calisto screamed, struggling in vain against her captors.

More slaves were coming, too many now. There was no time. Aculeo grabbed a blazing torch from a sconce in the rock wall and threw it on Ralla's throne, the bone-dry wood immediately catching fire. The tapestries draped about it ignited seconds later, orangey-yellow flames that crackled and leapt to set fire to several branches of the barren tree, inches from where Calisto stood. Tyche kicked her feet frantically, twisting in the empty air as she choked to death.

Someone screamed, then the revellers paused their mad dance, their bloodlust suddenly doused, twisting instead into blind panic as smoke filled the cavern. They pushed and shoved at one another as they tried frantically to escape, knocking Ralla to the ground. The rope released, Tyche dropped to the rock floor in a heap. Aculeo climbed onto the platform and knelt beside the girl, releasing the noose, slipping it off her head. Her lips were blue, her cheeks pale and lifeless. He laid her on her back and breathed into her mouth until at last the girl coughed and gasped for breath.

"Aculeo, how did you...? Oh, I didn't think I'd ever see you again," Calisto cried, wrapping her arms about him from behind, kissing his neck as she wept. "Is Tyche alright?"

"I think so. Tyche, are you okay?" The girl felt her throat, blinking, and nodded, slowly climbing to her feet, disoriented.

The High Priest Ralla tried to stand as well, his mask askew, his worshippers gone. He seemed unaware that everything had just fallen apart around him. "We call ... call upon Dionysos and beg you look on us ... with favour," the man said, his voice faltering.

Aculeo grabbed him by the tunic and tore his mask off. He looked at Zeanthes' face in disbelief.

"No!" the sophist snarled, his face twisted in rage as he tore himself free, disappearing into the shadows of the catacombs.

"Let him go!" Calisto cried, coughing from the smoke. "We have to get out of here while we still can."

They were caught up in the crowd of panicked, coughing revellers swarming up a stairway carved into the rock wall, fleeing the smoke-filled cavern to the villa above. They came to the top of the steps and through the doorway into the villa. Fresh, sweet air filled their lungs at last. They stood in a small ala at the edge of the atrium, the walls still decorated with olive branches and lit with torches. It was virtually abandoned, the revellers had all fled.

"What happened here?" Aculeo asked Calisto, weak from exertion and pain.

"I'm not sure," Calisto said as she clung to him. "Ralla told me to come here tonight. I thought it was just another symposium but they seized me as soon as I arrived, bound me, drugged me ..."

"You're lucky to be alive. But where's Ralla?"

"I don't know, I didn't see him," she said.

"Wait," Aculeo said, looking around. "Where's Tyche?"

"She came up from the cisterns with us, didn't she?" Calisto asked. Her eyes widened with sudden alarm. "Didn't she?"

Aculeo looked back towards the stairway leading down into the cisterns. Down to the underworld, where Dionysos was still Lord.

CHAPTER XXXIV

Aculeo grabbed a torch and he and Calisto descended the stairway into the dark catacombs, the torchlight reflecting off the uneven rock walls. They could find no sign of Tyche. The smoke was still thick enough to burn their eyes and make them cough. Aculeo's entire left side was throbbing in pain. He made his way to the walkways overlooking the great cistern.

"Tyche?" he called, his voice echoing off the cold stone walls. "Tyche?"

"Where is she?" Calisto asked desperately.

Aculeo spotted a dim light deep in the catacombs, moving away from them. His heart sank. "There," he said.

"But she wouldn't go there on her own," Calisto said. "She'd have no reason."

"Zeanthes must have taken her," Aculeo said. "I have to stop him."

"But look at you, you can barely stand!" She looked down at his tunic and gasped. "You're bleeding."

"I'm fine," he said, his left side throbbing with agony.

"Don't lie to me! What happened?"

"It doesn't matter now. Just go home and gather Idaia. We have to leave tonight before Ralla comes after us."

"But what if...?" She trailed off, not daring to utter the words.

"If we're not back by dawn you're to leave without us."

"Aculeo, no!"

"Promise me," he demanded.

Calisto hesitated a moment, then held him close, kissed his cheeks, tears streaming down her face. "Be careful." She headed back up the stone steps.

Aculeo moved as quickly as he could along the narrow pathways through the darkness, the only sounds the sloshing of water in the cisterns below and the echoes of his own footsteps. The catacombs were practically endless, a shadowy web beneath the city. Still, Zeanthes appeared to know its routes well enough, for even with Tyche in tow the distance between them never seemed to close. He was like a firefly always flitting just out of ...

The ground suddenly disappeared beneath Aculeo's feet. He twisted around and was barely able to catch the edge of the walkway before he fell into the water below. He gasped in anguish, his left side radiating with pain, soaked with blood. He managed to haul himself back up onto the pathway. It was completely, utterly dark. His torch must have fallen into the water. He lay there, trying to catch his breath, pain washing over him in aching, nauseating waves, afraid he might black out. Focus, he thought. Remember Tyche, the way she'd followed me into the alley from the Blue Bird that day so long ago, risking herself to help me find Neaera. She came to me, trusted me, and I let her fall into Zeanthes' hands. He forced himself to sit up, then to stand, ignoring the dizziness and the pain.

Aculeo looked around. There was no sign of Zeanthes – the beacon of his torchlight had disappeared. He made his way tentatively along the pathways again, running his hands along the cool, dripping cavern walls until he came to a narrow opening in the rock wall. It was a fissure of some sort, the height of his shoulders, barely as wide. He could see a dim light emanating from within. Zeanthes, he thought. They must have gone in here.

He crouched down and reluctantly squeezed inside, the walls tight, pressing against him, the air stale and chalky with dust. The fissure's ceiling dropped lower and lower the deeper he went, the passage tightening around him until he feared he'd become stuck if he went any further. He dropped to his hands and knees and crawled, following the fissure as it cut deeper and deeper into the earth. And what if I'm wrong? he thought bleakly. What if I've taken the wrong path, a path that leads to nowhere? What if I get stuck in here beneath the earth? Tyche is murdered, Zeanthes escapes, all of this in vain? I can't breathe, the walls are so tight, pressing on me, what happened to the air? Enough! he thought, forcing himself to keep moving, to stop thinking, to just move!

At last the fissure widened and his lungs filled with fresh air. He climbed to his feet and looked around, blinking in the sudden gleam of light, trying to orient himself. On the ground glowed a small, gleaming silver disc. The moon, he realized, or its reflection in a pool of water at

D.L. Johnstone

least, the ground surrounding it littered with shards of shattered rock. The night sky stood suspended between two craggy walls. He was standing at the bottom of a crevice deep in the earth. Is this the light I followed, he thought wretchedly. A mere reflection of the moon?

"Apollo has emerged," a man's voice proclaimed.

Zeanthes stood perhaps ten cubits away in a patch of moonlight. He was almost unrecognizable, his eyes gleaming and wild, his robes soiled with dirt and soot. Tyche knelt trembling before him, wrists bound before her. The sophist held a knife to her throat. She looked up at Aculeo, not daring to speak, her eyes pleading with him silently.

"Zeanthes, she's just a child," Aculeo said. "Let her go."

"Have you learned nothing in our time together, Aculeo?" the sophist asked with a desperate smile. "I taught you of Persephone, of Dionysos. I guided you, gave you my Ariadne."

Ariadne? Aculeo wondered. Wasn't she Dionysos' wife or something? What the hell is he talking about?

"Don't pretend you cannot see the splendour of it all," Zeanthes cried.

"The splendour of what?" Aculeo demanded. "Of kidnapping and murdering innocent women? All to satisfy some sick fantasy of yours?"

"Fantasy? No, it's an exploration, a journey to reality, a voyage to the greater truth!"

"What truth?"

"All of it of course. Do you not see that?"

"No. Nor do I care. It doesn't matter anymore, Zeanthes. It's over."

"O dear Apollo, there is no such ending," the sophist said. "There is only this life and the divine."

"You want to speak to me of this? You want me to understand? Fine," Aculeo said, stepping closer to Zeanthes, his hands held up, clearly empty. "Let the girl go and we'll talk of it all you like."

"Stay where you are," the sophist warned, pressing his knife against Tyche's throat. She gasped in pain.

"Zeanthes, please don't hurt her."

"I can do no real harm to her. Human souls are immortal."

Aculeo looked at the girl, so young, so terrified, pleading with him with her eyes. "But why cause her suffering?"

"The Gods require their sacrifice."

"Then take me instead."

Zeanthes looked at him in surprise. He licked his lips, thinking. "Apollo as the sacrifice?"

"Yes."

"A beautiful construct. But foolish."

278

"How is it foolish to save your own life? Your own soul?"

Zeanthes yanked the girl's head back sharply, making her cry out. "It's not my life that rests on the edge of a knife, dear friend."

Aculeo removed his knife from his belt and laid it on the ground between them. "I give you my oath, Zeanthes. Release Tyche and my life is in your hands to do with as you will. Hurt her and I'll cut you down, piss on your scattered ashes and give sacrifice to every god there is that your divine, immortal soul be cursed for all eternity. Your choice."

"No," Tyche whispered, shaking her head at Aculeo. "Don't ..."

"It's alright," Aculeo said, smiling at the girl, tears stinging his eyes.

The sophist stared at him for a moment, licked his lips, considering the offer. He slowly nodded. "Kneel before me, then."

"Let Tyche go first."

"Oh? And trust you to simply keep your word?"

"I come to you alone and unarmed," Aculeo said. "My only wish now is to save the girl. After that I'm yours."

The sophist glared at him, his breathing heavy and uneven. He cut the ropes binding Tyche and shoved her to the ground. She climbed unsteadily to her feet, looking at Aculeo, her eyes filled with dread.

"Don't worry," Aculeo said. "Just get yourself to safety." He watched her take a hesitant step away, then another before she finally slipped into the shadows.

"On your knees, hands out before you," Zeanthes demanded, his face pale in the reflected moonlight, his eyes like empty holes cut in the sky. Aculeo complied, the sharp rock on the ground cutting the fragile flesh of his knees, as his wrists were bound behind him. "Embrace Dionysos, the beast god within," the sophist whispered hoarsely, stepping behind Aculeo, pressing the knife to his throat. "Become one with the primal herd, be as one with him, the twice-born." Aculeo could smell the man's sour sweat, felt the edge of the cold blade against his flesh, a sick shock of pain rippling through him. He closed his eyes, ready to die.

A shriek of fury pierced the darkness. He opened his eyes just as a demon flew from the shadows and launched itself at Zeanthes. The man cried out in surprise, spun around to confront his assailant, knocking Aculeo to the ground. Aculeo twisted his head around in time to see Tyche step away from Zeanthes, a razor sharp rock clutched in her trembling hand, the edge of it stained with blood, her eyes filled with loathing. The sophist's right bicep was gouting dark blood where the girl had cut him. He looked down at it in astonishment.

"Tyche, please, just get away," Aculeo cried.

Zeanthes lunged at the girl. Tyche took half a step sideways, then slashed him again. The sophist dropped his own knife, looking down in bewilderment at the blood gushing like a fountain down his arm. His hand had been sliced open at the base of the thumb, almost severing it, exposing a web of pink-white bones and tendons. Aculeo struggled to his feet, trying desperately to free himself. Zeanthes grabbed the girl by the neck with his good hand and pulled her close. She swung the rock up in a short arc, cutting his stomach open. The sophist bellowed in shock and staggered back. Tyche thrust the razor-like rock into the side of his neck again and again. Zeanthes gave a strangled cry, fell to his knees, blood spouting from the gaping wounds. He held out his bloody hands in desperation, squealing like a beast in a slaughterhouse as the girl hacked at his face, his cheeks, his neck, his eyes. He curled in a ball on the ground, trying frantically to protect himself. Tyche plunged the rock into his back and neck over and over, crying "Osti! Osti! Osti! Osti!" until Aculeo finally managed to pull her off.

Tyche looked up at him, her face and robes soaked in the slaughtered sophist's blood, trembling, eyes lit with waning fury. "Osti," she whispered, then collapsed into Aculeo's arms.

CHAPTER XXXV

The moon was shining into the open atrium as Aculeo and Tyche entered Calisto's villa. There were no lamps lit and the furniture was covered with sheets, which snapped and rippled like restless spirits in the breeze scattering sand blown in from the street. Peacocks ran wild through the empty halls, filling the darkness with their eerie cries, pecking occasionally at the handfuls of seed left for them on the marble floors which were spattered with the birds' waste.

Aculeo heard the sound of footsteps and looked up to see Calisto hurrying towards them. "You found her," she said. "You're alive!"

Aculeo collapsed on a nearby couch, his face slick with sweat. "Where's Idaia?" he asked.

"I've no idea, she's not here!"

"I sent her away," Tyche said simply. "She's safe."

"Gods be praised," Calisto said.

"We need to gather her and leave tonight, understand?" Aculeo said. "Ralla will come after us. It's not safe to stay any longer." He groaned, grinding his teeth against another sickening wave of pain that washed over him.

"We're almost ready," she said, forcing a smile as she stroked the damp hair off his forehead. "Here, let me tend your wounds." He closed his eyes and let her lift his tunic. He heard her gasp. "Ah, my love. You must have lost so much blood."

"I'll be fine, just get me some water," Aculeo panted.

Tyche gave Calisto a worried look. "He needs a healer," she said.

"Fetch Kushu – hurry!" Calisto said to the girl, who nodded and ran from the atrium. Aculeo could still see the walls of the catacombs when he closed his eyes, the sound of waves slapping against the walls of the cistern, the pinpoint of Zeanthes' torchlight as he tried to escape into the darkness.

He woke up with Calisto stroking his face, gazing down at him, her eyes glistening with tears. "Where are we?"

"Still here – come," she said, helping him to sit up. He grunted in pain, his face covered in sweat. "I'm so sorry, I know it hurts my love. You've been so brave. Drink this," she said, holding a cup to his mouth. The wine was strong and sweet, infused with myrrh and cinnamon.

Aculeo shook his head. "Just water."

"In a moment, I promise. Drink this first."

He drank it down in small sips. A warm sensation spread through his stomach, seeping tendrils throughout his body. The room was spinning. He closed his eyes again, leaning back in her arms. "We need to go."

"We will. Just rest a bit first," she said, her voice soft, soothing. "Where shall we go to?"

"Somewhere far away from here, anywhere you like," he said. "Neapolis perhaps, or Knossos. We could have a farm."

"Yes," she said, stroking his head. "Tell me about our farm."

"It sits on top of a tall hill overlooking a grove of olive trees," he said. "Fat goats run about in the pasture. A path leads from the house down to the sea, a beach of white sand, the sea blue as azure. We have vineyards, and the wine we make is so sweet the bees envy us."

"Do we have children?" she asked, pressing his hand to her cool, soft lips.

"Of course," he said, drifting off again. "As many as you like, all of them beautiful like their mother. They run out across the sand to play in the sea, their faces brown as acorns." He looked up at her suddenly. "We should go now, Calisto."

"Rest a little longer. How long will it take us to get there?"

"I don't know, two days, maybe three depending on the winds."

"Then we shall give sacrifice and pray to the gods for favourable winds."

"Yes, favourable winds," Aculeo said. He listened to the sounds of slaves stacking wooden chests and furniture in the fauces, waiting to be ported down to the harbour for the journey. "You've packed too much, it will only slow us down. Just bring the clothes on your backs, what money you have. We'll buy passage on the first ship ready to leave."

"Alright."

"You need to gather Idaia. And Tyche. Where is she?" he asked, looking around in a panic.

"My love, stop worrying so much."

He lay back in her arms again. "Zeanthes would have murdered me down there if not for Tyche."

"She's very brave," Calisto said.

"I can scarcely believe Zeanthes was behind this madness."

"He wore his mask well," she said, stroking his head. "Never mind, it's over now. Try to rest."

A fragment of memory came to him then, unbidden. "When we were in the catacombs, Zeanthes said something about how he gave me his Ariadne. What could he have meant?"

Calisto bent her head and kissed him gently on the cheek. "He meant me, my love."

"What?"

She sighed and drew her hand gently from his grasp, holding it to her breast. "He meant that he gave me to you."

"You? But ..." A sudden chill coursed through him like a river of ice. "You knew?"

"Yes, I knew. Zeanthes and I have been together for a very long time," she said. "He trained me since I was a child. As I've been training Idaia."

"No," he gasped. "No ..."

Calisto gazed down at him, her lovely violet eyes dark as midnight, the scar along her jaw stark white against her face. "When you first appeared asking about Neaera, claiming to be a friend of Iovinus', I was terrified. It felt like all the other places we had to run from. I thought for certain we'd be discovered. I wanted to leave that very night. But Zeanthes wasn't afraid at all. He wanted to meet with you. To understand why you were delivered into our lives. It was Zeanthes who saw you for what you truly are. Our Apollo."

"Apollo?" Aculeo said. His head was pounding now, his chest on fire. "This was all just some sick fantasy to you as well?"

"No, not a fantasy," she said. "We needed to fall in love, and we did. You can't tell me our love wasn't real."

"But what of Ralla? Was he even involved?"

"He played a role of course," she said.

"A role? You make it sound like he was an actor in a play! You let me think he was at the centre of it all. I tried to murder him!"

"My Apollo," she said and tried to take his hand again. He pulled it from her grasp. He felt like he was going to vomit. She gave him a wounded look. "Oh Aculeo – what choice did we have? We could hardly have left Ralla alive knowing all that he did. He couldn't possibly have

D.L. Johnstone

understood – he would have made so much trouble. When he turned up just before the symposium began, he was completely unhinged from your attempt on his life. We had to deal with him or it would have ruined everything."

Aculeo felt a numb sensation seeping through his body. He clutched his stomach – it felt suddenly as though he'd swallowed a fistful of white-hot potshards. He tried to stand, fell to his knees, then dropped on his hands, cold sweat pouring down his face. He looked up at her in anguish.

"Aculeo, my love, forgive me. You would have realized the truth eventually."

He tried to grab onto her, to take hold of something real, but his hands wouldn't move. He tried to speak, but his tongue lay like a piece of dead meat stuck in his mouth. He lay there on the floor, unable to stand, his body started to convulse.

Calisto stood there, looking down at him, watching him die. "I'll always love you, Aculeo. That's real, I promise you." She bent over and kissed him then, a long slow kiss. Then all he could hear was the sound of her footsteps as she walked away.

Aculeo dreamed of Titiana, her lovely face, reaching out her hands to him. He dreamed of Atellus running down the hallway of their villa, laughing his beautiful laugh, always just out of reach. He dreamed of a crowded, bustling marketplace, of a mad, drunken symposium where the guests feasted on flesh, of dark, endless tunnels that wound through cisterns of blood. He dreamed of the sea. He dreamed of Sekhet standing over him, rolling him onto his back, her hands burning cold as she pressed her fingertips against the side of his neck, gazed intently into his eyes.

"Can you speak, Roman?" she asked, her voice echoing from an eternity ago. He just looked back at her, wondering why she was here. The vision of her slipped into darkness as she walked away.

Sekhet took a small pouch from her satchel, forced Aculeo's mouth open and pressed a pinch of powdered medicine under his tongue. His tongue and lips were tinged with blue, his eyes glassy and unfocused. He had little time left. He lay there for a moment, not responding, then he groaned and writhed in pain before vomiting up a mouthful of pink-white froth.

"What are you doing?" a woman's voice demanded from the edge of the courtyard.

Sekhet didn't bother to look up. Aculeo's breathing was rough and uneven, his pulse was thin as a thread being drawn out of a tapestry, beating far too fast to count. The poison had already worked its way into his system, so the lotus emetic had done little for him. "What did you give him? Rock flower?"

"How dare you! Get out of my house this instant! Kushu!"

The healer dug into her satchel again, searching. There, foxglove to slow his heart, she thought, putting a pinch of the dried flower under his tongue. Aculeo gagged, coughed half of it up, moaned and twisted on the ground, sweat running down his pallid grey face. It wasn't looking good, not good at all.

"Idaia told me everything," Sekhet said. "She even told me all about how you turned her into a little murderer as well, luring your victims to your depraved parties to serve as your osti. Your sacrifices."

"She's Phrygian. She understands sacrifice."

"She's a child!" the healer snapped. "Ah, it doesn't matter anymore. I sent word to the Public Order officers. Everyone will finally know you for the murderous bitch you are."

Calisto gave a cutting laugh. "You actually believe anyone would arrest me? That my friends would permit it? Why? For you? For justice?"

"You forget that whatever patrons you had are dead," Sekhet said.

"You've no idea of how Alexandria works," Calisto said. "I've a hundred others in high places ready to help me at a moment's notice."

"And what of Aculeo? Who'll help him?"

"He's already dead." With that, the hetaira turned to go.

Sekhet grabbed Calisto suddenly by the chiton. "You're not leaving here tonight."

Calisto spun around on her, slapping the healer across the face. "Know your place, fellahin witch!" she hissed.

Sekhet smiled grimly. "And what's your place, Phrygian whore? On your back with your well-worked legs wrapped around whatever lovestruck fool that's fallen for your poisonous charms?" Calisto's face went pale with rage. She lashed out at her again but Sekhet caught her by the wrist this time and twisted it painfully behind her back.

"Let go of me!" Calisto squealed, but the healer held fast, pulling her back tight against her own chest. She pressed her mouth against Calisto's cheek like a lover wanting to whisper in her delicate ear.

"It's true, we're quite different people, you and I," Sekhet said. "No

D.L. Johnstone

doubt the fools that run this city would sooner listen to your charming lies than hear the truth from the likes of me. But don't forget, from commonest slave to Phrygian whore, we all have one thing in common."

"What's that?" Calisto hissed.

"We all bleed." Sekhet put her hand to the shoulder of Calisto's chiton and drew out her fibula pin, long and sharp as any dagger, then stabbed it beneath the hetaira's left breast.

Calisto cried out, tried to pull away, but the healer locked her in a tight embrace, pulled her in closer, pushing the fibula in hard and deep until it would go no further, then gave a sharp twist. Calisto gasped, arching backwards in the healer's arms. Sekhet released her and she fell to the floor, blood spilling on her fine silks, pooling beneath her on the marble floor, the heady smell of death filling the dark atrium. Calisto looked up at Sekhet, her face white, unable to speak.

"Do you hear them whispering to you?" Sekhet asked. "All your victims, they're calling for you now, aren't they? Ah, so many I can almost hear them myself. They've been looking forward to this day, I think. Lingering on the shores of Abydos all this time, ready to escort you to your tribunal."

"Please ...no ... "

"Save your pleas for the gods you murderous bitch. Our gods this time. Just remember that when Osiris weighs your twisted, black heart, it won't matter how charming you are, how much money you have, how many important friends you've gathered. No, the only thing that will matter there will be the wicked deeds you've done."

Sekhet watched as the last light faded from her lovely violet eyes, then went to Aculeo and knelt beside him. "How are you now Roman, ah?" she said, examining his pupils, checking his pulse, trying to smile. "A little better I think. Come on, stay with me. You don't want to join that bitch anytime soon. I hope you'd be sick of her company by now."

CHAPTER XXXVI

THE 30TH DAY OF JUNIUS

The children laughed in delight as they played in the rushes at the side of the canal, splashing in the warm, slow-moving water while Felix ran along at their feet, barking and chasing the seabirds into the amber-coloured evening sky. Even Gellius and old Xanthias appeared to be enjoying themselves as they sat on the bank of the canal, watching the children at play.

"They seem to be having fun," Aculeo said, watching Tyche chase a delirious Idaia along the muddy bank.

"It's good to see them being actual children for once," Sekhet said. The smell and clatter of the evening meal being prepared filled the air. Fine loaves of bread, jars of beer, platters of asparagus, lentils, eel, it all smelled quite delicious. "And what of you?"

"Me? I'm fine," Aculeo said dismissively.

The healer cocked her head suspiciously, considering him. Over a month since the ordeal ended and he still looks ill, she thought. He continued to recover of course, and his wounds had healed with minimal infection, a miracle in itself. But the damage Calisto's poison had done to his heart might well be permanent – the effects of rock flower tended to linger for years. And there was something in his eyes as well … as though he'd been dragged to the underworld and back again, leaving something important behind on the journey. "Are you?"

"Better than some others at least." Ralla's body had been found in a store room of his villa, his wrists cut open. His apparent suicide had engendered whispers around the corridors of power about some sexual imbroglio possibly involving Mysteries worship. Officials had found it most expedient to blame the murders of Gurculio, Zeanthes and Calisto on Ralla's obvious madness and decadence. In the end, no one had the political will to conduct any investigation, official or otherwise, into the involvement the Prefect's son and his friends might have had in the scandal. Least of all Magistrate Capito, after finally being released from his thankfully short-lived incarceration.

Aculeo and Sekhet watched the children charge up from the canal, dripping wet and laughing, running through the back gate into the courtyard, Gellius and Xanthias well behind them. Pesach awoke from his nap as the children thundered past his bench. He grumbled and grouched at the sudden intrusion, but gave a rueful smile. The three men had finally turned up several days after the murders, a little worse for wear from living on the streets but alive at least. The girls sat on the ground near Pesach's bench and started up a game of Mehen.

"I'm grateful you took the girls in," Aculeo told Sekhet.

"They deserve to finally have a normal life."

"Do they ever talk about what happened?"

"Not a word since that night. Idaia still refuses to sleep alone. Tyche often awakes with bad dreams. It will take more time for them to heal. What about you?" she asked, listening to the rattle of plates and cups being set at the table.

He shrugged. "I'm alive, the murders have ended. I'll move on."

"And what of Corvinus?" Pesach asked, eavesdropping from his place on the bench. "Do you move on from his betrayal too?"

"Pesach, let the dead be," Aculeo said wearily. "I just want to live my life for a change."

"As does Flavianus and all his ilk," Pesach snorted. "Back in Neapolis or Capria or Pompeii, no doubt, living quite comfortably off the gold they stole from us and countless other fools."

"Perhaps you could let the poor man recover before you hound him for vengeance," the healer snapped.

Pesach muttered something under his breath but had learned from experience there was much to be lost and little to be gained by arguing with Sekhet.

Aculeo looked out at the sunset, the breadth and depth of the coloured sky, the seagulls catching their wingtips on invisible currents of wind to sail towards the light of Pharos glowing in the distance. "I still have trouble wrapping my head around how Calisto stayed with Zeanthes, helping him. Like Dionysos and Ariadne, Zeanthes claimed."

Sekhet smiled. "Yes, well, those two didn't have such a nice ending either."

"What do you mean?"

"Don't you remember your own mythology?" she asked in surprise. "Mad Dionysos, the god who was murdered, the god who murders. He travelled from one land to the next, killing as he went. Yet Ariadne loved him anyway, worshipped him. You know how Dionysos finally rewarded Ariadne for her loyalty? By ordering her to hang herself. He could have used his power to help his lover, yet he chose instead to use it to destroy her and all those who'd loved her as well."

"But Zeanthes didn't try to actually hang her. Her life was never truly in danger."

"Only symbolically. They used others in her stead for that role as they tried to do with Tyche. But Calisto was Phrygian. The Phrygians worship Cybele, the Mother-Goddess, who rules over all the other gods. Dionysos included. Her devoted male worshippers castrate themselves, then hang themselves in her honour. Like Iovinus and Gurculio. Her sacrifices – her osti. Be grateful you escaped with both your life and your manhood intact. You really should be more careful with the friends you choose."

They watched Idaia and Tyche, quiet now, hunched over their board game. "What shall we do with Idaia?" Aculeo asked quietly. "She helped Calisto lead countless women to their deaths."

Sekhet sighed. "That poor child lived through a great deal of evil not of her making. She comes from a place where human sacrifice is normal practice. She was torn away from her family, forced into slavery, then raised by that evil pair. Can she truly be at fault for the role that was forced upon her?"

"I don't fault her, only fear for her. For both of them," Aculeo said as he watched Idaia move her ivory game piece around the little maze, until at last it entered the snake's mouth. The end of the game – the afterlife. The children laughed in delight and clapped their hands. "What will become of them?"

"That's for the Gods to decide, as for us all."

THE END

Enjoy an Excerpt
from

CHALK VALLEY

by
D.L. JOHNSTONE

September 25th, 2005

Chapter 1

Chalk Valley, British Columbia – 19:00h

Phil Lindsay sat back in his seat, eyes half closed, trying to calm down. He took another hit, held it, then slowly exhaled, watching the smoke slip away. He gazed into Chalk Valley, its cracked white walls like broken shoulders sloping unevenly into the dense pine forest below. The sun was dipping below the horizon, bleeding away the day's warmth and colour, leaving behind a lifeless grey sky. The keening of cicadas echoed through the valley, a lonely, wordless song against the coming darkness. Then, like an eye winking shut, the sun was gone and all that remained was its scarlet stain like an angry welt across the end of the day. The toke had burned down so close to the tip that Lindsay could feel the heat singeing his fingers. He took a final hit before tossing it out the window.

He shook himself from his daydream and checked the glowing green numbers of the dashboard clock. Shit. Where'd the day go? He felt spent, tired and hungry. He ate a half-melted candy bar he'd found stashed in the glove compartment, washing it down with a few mouthfuls of warm beer. Now what? Go home?

Fuck that. Just fuck it.

He started up the car, threw it into gear and gunned it up the dirt road, brown dust clouds boiling up from the wheel wells as he made a sharp turn onto the main road, the tires squealing. The road ran downhill fast and dark and empty, the early evening air rushing through the open windows of the car, smelling of damp, rotted cedar and faded summer. He followed West Gimly back to Highway 1 and headed back to Vancouver, an hour and a half away.

Time enough to think …

* ◆ ◆ ◆

Sundale Mall, East Vancouver - 20:25h

Lindsay stared at his reflection in the chipped metal mirror that hung over the bathroom sink. He hadn't bothered to shave that morning, his dark hair was stuck up at the sides and his face and hands were caked with mud from the valley. He washed up with pink liquid soap from the dispenser, the filthy black water swirling around the bowl of the sink, then wet his hair with his hands and combed it carefully back off of his forehead. He splashed some water on his face and shaved as best he could with a plastic razor. Only a few nicks.

He took a couple of red and black capsules from a ziplock bag in his pocket and washed them down his throat with a cupped handful of tapwater. He checked himself out in the mirror one last time, pointed at his reflection, cocked his finger and fired.

A girl in a denim jacket was just coming out of the women's bathroom. Her hair was short, dirty blonde. Her head was down, oblivious. Lindsay looked around. All alone. Two bathrooms, utility room off to the side, emergency exit down the hall. He could feel his heart pounding against his ribs. Total rush. He moved quickly towards the glass door that led back into the main mall and stepped in front of the doorway, blocking the girl's way. She looked up at him, confused. Lindsay smiled and stared down at her breasts pushing against her tight black T-shirt, bare at the midriff, too perfectly tanned and the gold belly button ring that glinted above her low slung jeans.

"Hey, Tricia," he said. Too fast, too anxious, he thought, take a deep breath, relax. The girl moved away, wary. Nobody to hear you, all alone, bitch. Lindsay smiled, reaching out a hand to grab her wrist.

A teenage boy came up from behind him, shoving the door open into his back. Lindsay turned around, startled. "What the hell's going on," the boy asked, scowling at Lindsay.

"Just some freak," the girl said, taking the boy's arm. "C'mon."

He watched them leave, then walked past the store fronts to the food court, ordered a cheeseburger, onion rings and a coke and glanced around for a place to sit. Most of the tables were occupied by low-lifes, old people, losers. A handful of teenage girls sat at a table in the corner, chattering with one another, their haunted eyes like bruises in the pale shadows of their faces. Lindsay felt deeply depressed all of a sudden. Look at them for God's sake, they're like empty shells, there's no feeling there. What's this world coming to anyway? Why did I even come—

Oh.

His heart skipped a beat when he saw the girl. Her face was delicate, pale as bone china, her eyes, pale green like spring leaves unfolding beneath the pink rose petal eye shadow and too-thick mascara. Her long, strawberry-blonde hair was parted straight down the middle, held out of her face by two plastic barrettes pinned just above her ears. Lindsay sat on one of the orange plastic mushroom-shaped seats just three tables away from her and watched her out of the corner of his eye. She wore silver rings on several fingers and half a dozen earrings in her ears. Her sneakers were a little tattered, her blue jeans frayed at the pant cuffs – nothing lasts these days. It's a disposable society.

The thing that impressed him most wasn't so much that she sat by herself, but the way she sat by herself. She doesn't check her watch, no half-expectant glances around the food court. No friends are coming to join her. Look at the way she's dressed, she's not on a break from her job at one of the stores. Sitting there all alone and lonely at that sad little plastic table, eating french fries and drinking a pop. Virtually invisible to everyone else in the food court, a vaguely pretty, forgettable face in a sea of forgettable faces.

She glanced up at him. He gave her a friendly nod, pulled out his cellphone and pretended to talk into it. She looked away again. He began to daydream about Chalk Valley, only an hour and a half away, a hundred and fifty klicks, with its dense scrub forest, secret paths and deep rushing river, washing over the round grey stones ... In his mind, the thing was already done, played out in countless permutations.

Lindsay shook himself awake. She's getting ready to go, stacking her tray, gathering her things. He pushed his tray away, the burger half-eaten, and stood up. He staggered a bit, unsteady on his feet. The pills are kicking in. Hurry up. He walked past the few tables towards her. The tiles of the floor seemed to swell and sway beneath his shoes like puzzle pieces rearranging themselves on a board. Birds twittered in the trees that grew in the center of the court, little dark shadows that darted after one another against the backdrop of the skylights far overhead. He could see it all unfold before him, knew exactly what to say, how to say it, what would happen and how, he could feel the roaring in his ears like waves of a dark, inner sea, he felt like he was going to explode.

Do it. Do it now.

Alright.

20:40h

Lindsay walked in quick, short steps, the girl had to almost run to keep up with him as he moved along the sidewalk that adjoined the parking lot. He kept looking over his shoulder, not to look at the girl

D.L. Johnstone

directly, though, but to see if anyone was watching them. Nobody was.

"I can't believe my luck, I mean, running into you, getting an amazing job like this," she said breathlessly.

"Yeah, must be fate, huh?" Lindsay smiled. "I can tell a lot about people when I first meet them, Robbie, and I think you'll be perfect for this job."

"I know I will. You won't be sorry."

The car was parked at the far end of the parking lot in an all but deserted section, no other cars were around, the streetlight had burnt out so that the vehicle sat in shadows. He noticed the girl's moment of hesitation, but he kept walking towards the blue sedan, totally confident she would follow.

"Looks like an old shitbox, doesn't it?" He smiled at her, a broad, confident smile. He could taste a hot, electric snap in the air between them. We're alone, all alone, I could just take her now, but ... "I keep my good cars at home," he said breezily. "I just take this to the mall and stuff because I don't want anyone ripping me off. Know what I mean?"

She was right beside him now as he unlocked the door. Lindsay just barely restrained the urge to put his hand on her face and squeeze it. He bent into his car for a second instead, pretending to look around. Robbie moved a little closer, trying to see inside. "Shit. I can't believe it," he said. "I must have left the forms at the office. Can you believe this? Well, come on, we might as well go get them." He could see in the back of her eyes a coil of fear, a deep, ancient sense of the predator, subconsciously drawing together the words, the tone of his voice, the place, the smells, the utter quiet that surrounded them.

"No ... um ... I don't ... maybe I could come tomorrow, in the daytime."

Just get her in the car, nothing else matters except getting her into the car, just calm her down and get her in the goddamned car. "Tomorrow? No, that wouldn't work, see, I leave for Hong Kong tomorrow, then I'm in Zurich, right, so I won't even be back for like three or four weeks, know what I mean?"

She looked pale, the light in her eyes flattened and she hugged her arms more tightly around herself. "Oh I totally understand, I mean, Hong Kong and everything, it's just that I gotta meet my friend here and it's getting late —"

Just throw her in the car, motherfucker, nobody's around, nobody will see. No. No. Just calm her down, it'll be okay. "You still want the job, don't you, Robbie?"

"Of course, it's just —"

"Just what? You're wasting my time here. Do you want the job or not?"

"Oh yeah, no, like I totally do."

"Well you say you do, and I'm offering you the job, but you don't want to fill out an application form. You seem very indecisive."

"No, I'm not, I want the job. Honest."

"Okay then. My office is only three minutes from here. Let's go." Lindsay smiled at her, still holding the door open for her. Get in the fucking goddamned car you stupid cunt.

"I ... I don't know —"

"Robbie, if you want to get anywhere in life, you gotta take some chances. It's only three minutes away. Now. Are you ready to do something with your life?"

Watch the eyes, he thought, pale green spring ponds, see how they widen with fear of losing out, watch the mouth, see how it makes a little round "O" with her lips, and she bites the hook deeply, forces a smile, a beautiful smile, she wants me to like her so badly, and I do.

"Oh, okay, sure. Sorry." She climbed into the car and Lindsay slammed the door shut.

Chalk Valley, 22:05h

John McCarty and Kate Morris stepped out of the Glass Tavern into the cool night air, their ears still ringing from the loud music the band had been playing in the bar. The only sound outside was a muted thrum of music through the windows, chirping crickets and the occasional car whistling by on the highway that lay on the other side of the grassy bank from the tavern. A full moon hung midway in the sky against an ocean of stars, flooding the land in a soft, silvery glow.

"Why do we have to leave now?" Kate pouted, wavering on her feet, holding onto McCarty's arm for support as they walked towards the line of cars in the parking lot.

"It's late, that's why."

"But we were just starting to have fun."

"Then you stay. I have to get home," McCarty said.

"Oh of course," she sighed. "You have to be home for the wife and kids, right?"

"Right." They reached the unmarked cruiser and he unlocked the door.

"Okay then, go," she sulked.

"Come on, Kate, don't be like that."

"Like what?" She pulled away from him slightly, swatting his hand away when he tried to touch her. She turned around and started back towards the bar.

"Kate, where are you going?"

"Wherever I want to go, Mac. You can go to hell for all I care."

"Kate. Kate!" McCarty grabbed her by the shoulders and turned her around to face him, pushing her up against the unmarked cruiser.

"Let go of me," she snapped, avoiding his gaze.

"I need to talk to you first."

"Fine. So talk."

McCarty put his finger under her chin and gently lifted her face up to him. Her pretty face was flushed, her cheeks tinged with pink, her short hair lit in gold from the parking lot lights. Her mouth was still turned down in an irresistible pout, her blue eyes welled with tears. He traced his hand along her cheek to wipe away the tears, then slipped his hand around the small of her back and pulled her close, feeling her resist at first, then melt into his arms. She smelled of night-time and wild autumn flowers. He kissed her on the lips, gently at first, but she returned it with wild passion, her lips soft and warm, the tip of her tongue dancing against his like velvet.

"So I'm forgiven?" he finally said.

"Maybe. For tonight at least."

McCarty bent to kiss her again when he heard a car racing down the highway behind them, the roar of its engine splitting the night. He looked up and saw a dark car speeding past the entrance to the tavern. It was washed with yellow light for a millisecond as it passed beneath the streetlights, blue sedan, two passengers. Then it rocketed past, its red tail lights trailing off into the darkness. "Asshole."

"He's gotta be doing a buck eighty easy," Kate said. "Maybe we should go pull him over."

McCarty considered it for a second, then shook his head. "Screw it. He's headed out of town at least." He stroked the back of Kate's head, letting his fingers trace down her white neck, kissed the soft skin, listening to her moan.

"I thought you had to get home to your family," she whispered.

"Don't confuse me with details," McCarty said.

Chalk Valley, 22:15h

Robbie King woke up with an incredible pounding in her head, a heavy, nauseating pain that crashed like waves of broken glass through her aching body. What happened? Why does everything hurt so much, my head, my mouth, I taste blood. Her eyes fluttered open. It was dark, the night was rushing past. I'm driving somewhere. Where am I going? She felt somebody move beside her. She looked over, wincing at the pain in her neck, the strain of keeping her eyes open. A man was sitting in the driver's seat. His face was deep in shadows. "Who … who are you?" she asked, her voice slurring.

"A friend," he said. "Just sit back and relax, everything will be okay."

"Why does my head hurt?"

"You were in an accident."

"An accident? I should go to a hospital. Where's my Dad?"

"He's not here. I'm taking you to him. We'll be there soon."

"Oh. Who are you?"

"My name's Phil. Now shush, we're almost there."

The pain in her head was horrible. She felt like she was going to puke. She closed her eyes for a moment, just to block out the pain. Fractured images rushed through her brain. None of them made any sense. She wanted to ask her parents what they meant, she looked everywhere for them but everything was moving so fast …

When she woke up again, the car had stopped. Everything was dark. The shadow man was gone. What was his name again? Phil. She reached for the door handle, but there was only an empty cavity where the handle should have been. She felt herself slipping away again. The door opened. Phil was standing there, a harsh white light swept over her face.

"Hey," she groaned, holding a hand over her eyes.

"Sorry," he said, lowering the flashlight. "Come on, we need to go. Can you walk?"

"Of course I can walk," she slurred.

He helped her climb out of the car. Everything was so quiet and dark. Trees everywhere. We're in a forest. Why are we in a forest? He put his arm around her, his hand gripped painfully under her armpit while the other hand held the flashlight. They walked carefully along the dark path, deeper into the forest, but everything was spinning around, her head was aching. "I don't feel good. Where's my parents?"

D.L. Johnstone

"We're going to see them right now. Just keep walking, you're doing great." After a dozen steps, the ground seemed to swirl around her, she felt her legs give way. Phil stumbled as he caught her, almost dropping the flashlight. "Shit." He bent down and hoisted her over his shoulder.

She felt chilled now, her head was aching, her mouth was throbbing. Why do we keep moving? I just want to lie down and go to sleep. His shoulder was digging into her stomach, thrusting into it with every step as he walked through the darkness. Somebody said something about a hospital. Did I have an accident? It all felt like a bad dream, images flickering through her throbbing head. I was at the mall. I was talking to somebody in the food court. He said something about a job. He had to get some papers out of his car. Then ... suddenly the grey veil lifted, and everything became terribly clear. "Oh God, where am I?"

"Just shut up, do what I say and you'll be okay."

Robbie listened, terrified. The smell of him was sickening, sour sweat mixed with alcohol, and something else, something ghastly, like rotted meat, like death. He kidnapped me, oh God, he's going to rape me, or murder me. I have to get away, just punch him, kick him, run away, go back to the road, or deeper into the forest. It's dark, he couldn't find me, I could hide there until morning, then I could get away, flag down a car, call my parents ...

They stopped moving. Lindsay's breathing was heavy, gasping.

"Please let me go," she whimpered, "I don't want to ..." She felt herself falling, felt the earth blindly rushing up at her, she cried out, tried to reach out her hands to slow herself but she wasn't fast enough. A thick wall of pain exploded through her, shattering against the most painful parts of her body, her head, her mouth, casting her back into the numb darkness.

Robbie awoke again. It felt like hours had passed, it might only have been minutes. Where am I? She smelled the sharp deadness of the earth, like worms and rotting leaves. She saw that she was in a hollow of a dense, dark forest. The moon was high, lighting up the tree line that lined the broken hills climbing up into the cold black sky. Where is he? Where's Phil? I can't hear him anywhere. Maybe he's gone, maybe now I can get away, just crawl into the forest and hide, he'll never find me, not out there.

She tried to sit up, but the pain was so intense, worse than before, she felt like she was going to pass out again. Oh God, what should I do? All thoughts of running away now seemed hopeless. She was shivering so badly her teeth chattered, her whole body shook. "Please," she called. "Somebody please help me." There was no answer. Please, I don't want to die. Please God, help me ...

Robbie awoke to the sound of something moving next to her. She turned her head towards it, her head ringing, the roar of blood in her ears. Two eyes looked back at her from only a few feet away. A mirror. I'm looking at a mirror. But why ... the girl in the mirror had short, dark hair. It isn't me at all, it's someone else, another girl, her eyes are so dark, and the look in those eyes, so filled with despair, with fear, with pain. The other girl closed her eyes, a tear coursing down her cheek.

And Robbie started to scream.

D.L. Johnstone

October 21st, 2005

Chapter 2

Chalk Valley – 20:00h

The brief rainstorm had dissipated, the thunder had rumbled to an end, the fat, dark smears of storm clouds curled back like a bruised lip across the moonlit horizon. The rain had left the yellow field grass damp and flattened against the ground. Bluebottle flies stirred from the blades of grass, drawn to the sound of the boys' footsteps and the traces of rank perfume of what lay in the valley below. The beams of their flashlights bobbed in front of them as they walked, sweeping over the brush alongside the path as they searched for firewood. Any wood sitting out in the open was now too damp to burn, so the boys moved deeper into the forest. The flies had been bad enough in the open, but in the thick of the forest they were bloodthirsty, swarming in from all around and descending on the new arrivals.

The teenagers were already partly stoned from the drive up, so they just laughed and swatted the flies away. One boy stepped off the path where the ground was soft and slick and his foot slipped. The second boy laughed as his friend skidded down the muddy slope of the ridge towards the river before he came to a crashing halt at the bottom of the ridge after finally managing to grab onto a tree root. He was covered in black mud and was laughing almost as hard as his friend.

He smelled something that stopped him, a putrid, rotted stench that made him catch his breath. Goddamn, what is that …? He heard the high pitched whine of a deerfly dive-bombing in behind his ear, then two more as they attacked the back of his neck. He turned to run up the slope, then saw his flashlight lying on the ground a few feet away, its beam weak and flickering. He bent to pick it up, nearly gagging from the stench. The flashlight died. Damn, c'mon bitch! He shook it. Nothing. He smacked it hard against the heel of his hand. It flickered to life again, its beam casting a white pool of light on the ground. There was something odd there - like a white chalk drawing of a person on the black mud. The white line was moving. No. It was churning. When he took a closer look, he realized that the line was actually hundreds, maybe thousands of glistening white maggots, each one the size of his baby finger tip, all squirming and wriggling beneath the light around what appeared to be the remains of a human body. Its ravaged, leathery skin was alive with flies that rose in a dark buzzing cloud as the boy stumbled backwards, before they settled back down again. The body was face down, the skull turned partly to the side, the single exposed eye socket was empty and dark, crawling with small red ants, its mouth wide open in a silent shriek.

The boy screamed out loud.

Highway 1, Blind River, BC - 20:30h

The twin beams of Dave Kreaver's headlights converged before him, cutting a broad white swath through the darkness of the road ahead. The air was filled with the sweet, slightly rancid wet cedar smell from the lumber mills that lined the river's edge. A pair of headlights appeared in his rear-view mirror as tiny pinpricks of light. Eighteen wheelers ground past him in the oncoming lanes, gearing down in lumbering echoes as they descended the hill, their loads swaying across the orange dividing line as they rushed along the highway just slightly out of control. The headlights in his rear-view mirror were now the size of dimes. The little towns along the Fraser all seem the same these days, Kreaver thought. Whatever unique characters and charm they once possessed had eroded over the past decade, diluted into an amorphous sameness of neon signs for the Costcos, Futureshops, Save-On-Foods, Tim Hortons and Subways that now lit the edges of every town that mushroomed along the highway.

The headlights in his mirror had swelled to the size of quarters. Slow it down, buddy, he thought. The lights quickly flooded the mirror, making Kreaver squint. It appeared to be a truck or van. He watched in the mirror as the vehicle swerved over the median behind him as though to pass, then back onto the gravel shoulder, spewing up a cloud of dust, before swaying back onto the asphalt and straddling the median. Kreaver checked his brakes as the light coloured van then moved up alongside him clocking at what had to be a hundred and fifty klicks an hour. The van's windows were dark, making it impossible for Kreaver to see the driver's face until it was lit by the headlights of an oncoming truck. The driver wasn't even watching the road, he was looking down at something beside him, a map, or more likely reaching for another six-pack of Molson's. Kreaver didn't care what the other driver was doing at the moment, he just wanted to be clear of this van, all of his senses were on full alert like mini alarm bells going off inside of him. The van swayed towards him again.

"Fuck you," Kreaver growled, checking his brakes. The van shot in front of him and rode off the asphalt up onto the shoulder again, tossing up another cloud of dust. The truck in the oncoming lane roared past them, blaring its horn. Kreaver gritted his jaw, pressed hard on the brakes, the tires squealed underneath him and his car shimmied but held. The van kept moving onto the shoulder then off the road, sending up a shower of yellow-orange sparks as its bottom scraped up over the gravel. Only then did the driver seem to realize what was happening and try to slow down, but the van's backend swept out to the side. It would have rolled over if its tail end hadn't clipped a stand of poplars first. The van's inertia made it spin out on the gravel, until it finally shuddered and stalled.

"Goddamn." Kreaver pulled over onto the side of the road about twenty feet behind the van. His heart pounding, he flicked on his hazard lights and climbed out of the car. He hesitated for a second, then decided to leave his gun behind. He left his headlights on, the car alarm pinging in protest as he shut the door. No movement from anyone in the van ahead. He called 9-1-1 on his cellphone. The operator promised to send someone out within ten minutes. Kreaver sniffed the cool evening air, no smell of gasoline yet, a good sign. He was within six feet of the van when he heard the engine trying to turn over, resulting in nothing but a dying series of metallic groans and clicks. The driver's door opened with a sharp creak and a man staggered out, his hand held to his head, and kicked the side of the van.

"Hey. Hey! Just what in hell were you trying to do?" Kreaver asked.

The other man just stood there in the white banner of light cast by the headlights, wavering on his feet, his expression blank as he stared at Kreaver. Probably in shock. Or drunk. Or both. He was average height and weight, with dark hair and a lean, pale face. His eyes were unusual, however, almost black, and wide with rage. Kreaver instinctively stepped back, half-thinking that the man was going to try something, and found himself wishing he'd brought his gun afterall. The man blinked, the anger lifting like a veil. "Oh sweet Jesus. What happened?"

"You had a little accident. Are you alright?"

The man paused, still blinking. "Yeah, yeah thank God. I ... I can't start my car."

"No kidding. I think what we need is a tow truck, and maybe an ambulance for you."

The man shook his head, stepping closer to Kreaver. "No, I'm okay, thanks though, I appreciate your concern." He smiled and offered his hand. "My name's Phil." Kreaver shook his hand and took a closer look at him. The man's eyes were rimmed with red, his breath was sour. No question he'd been drinking.

"I'm Dave Kreaver." He noticed something in the shadows within the van. "You got a passenger in the vehicle?"

Phil smiled. "Yeah, my niece. She's okay, she was asleep."

"She slept through that? Let's see how she's doing, okay?"

"You know, really, she's okay. If you can just help me get the van started, or —"

Kreaver walked over to the van and peered through the tinted window. A young girl maybe fifteen, sixteen, pretty face, short brown hair, sat in the passenger seat. She looked unconscious. He tried the passenger side door, but it wouldn't budge. Locked. "I think she might be injured."

"Oh Jeez, really? Maybe I better get her to a hospital."

Kreaver went around to the driver's side door, wishing he had his flashlight. Another car approached, slowing as it came near them. Then the roof lights came on, spinning like circus tops, a cop car. "Fuck," Phil said under his breath. He put his hands in his pockets, pulled out some cigarettes, offered the package to Kreaver, who shook his head.

"Not a good idea right now. Your gas tank might have ruptured."

"Yeah, okay." Phil's hands trembled as he put the cigarettes away. He seemed nervous all of a sudden.

The police got out of their cruiser. One of them, a woman, shone her flashlight on the scene. "Hi. Everybody okay?"

Phil smiled. "Yeah, we just had a little accident, Officer, nobody's hurt thank God. We'll let the insurance companies settle things. I just need a boost if you could —"

The policewoman shone her flashlight first in Phil's face, then in Kreaver's. "Hey Sarge."

Kreaver held up his hand to block the harsh light. "Hey Kimberly, come here and help me, there's a girl in the van who may injured. Fred, can you call for an ambulance and a tow truck. And keep an eye on our friend here."

"You're a cop?" Phil said under his breath.

Kimberly Lee came over to help Kreaver while her partner, Fred Andersun, returned to the cruiser. Kreaver opened the driver's side door. The car smelled rank with beer and cigarettes. Empty cans littered the floor. The girl sat back in her seat, unmoving, her mouth open. Her blouse was partially unbuttoned, her bra was showing, and the white skin of her belly. Her jeans were undone, pulled partly down, exposing the top part of her pink panties. Kreaver reached in and tapped her arm.

"Wake up. Miss, wake up now. Come on, honey, wake up." He touched her small, pale hand, picked it up and waggled it. No muscle tone, no reaction whatsoever. "Shine the light in her face please," he told the patrolwoman. She did so as Kreaver held the girl's eye open. The pupil contracted in the bright light to a black pinpoint in a round circle of blue, but the girl herself didn't flinch. He checked her breathing, shallow but regular, then took her wrist to check her pulse, rapid, thready. Kreaver climbed out of the van.

Lee was looking at him, worried. "Is she okay?"

"She's alive. You keep an eye on her while I talk to my new friend Phil about his niece." Kreaver felt a hot coal of rage burning in his gut as he walked back towards the cruiser.

Andersun got out of the cruiser. "The ambulance will be here any minute. Everything okay, Sarge?"

Kreaver shrugged. "Not sure. Where's Phil?"

The patrolman looked puzzled. "You mean that guy?"

"Yeah. Where is he?"

The patrolman bit his lip. "I don't know. He can't have gone far."

Kreaver looked down the dark stretch of road in both directions, then into the darkness at the side of the road. Phil could have taken a dozen steps into the brush and disappeared if he'd wanted to. And apparently he had done just that. "Dammit."

"Why the heck would he run?" Andersun asked.

"I don't know. I need to use your radio." Kreaver called dispatch and had them send out another cruiser. They would need to run a search on the van, on the girl, on everything they could. Andersun's question was a good one. At most Phil could be charged with drunk driving, maybe reckless endangerment, corrupting a minor, but why add on evading a police investigation and fleeing the scene of an accident?

The patrolman had no luck in finding Phil on foot. "Sorry, Sarge, I guess I should have been watching him. I just never thought he'd take off like that."

"It's okay. Kimberly's going to take care of the girl. I need you to do a search on motels and hotels within a ten kilometre radius. Stop any hitchhikers and taxis you see with passengers inside."

"Okay. What did the guy do anyway?"

Kreaver stared off in the darkness. "I'm not sure yet, but it can't be good."

Chapter 3

Chalk Valley - 21:45h

Detectives John McCarty and Tony Laupacsis drove along Highway 1 in an unmarked navy blue Caprice. Just before crossing the Causewell Bridge that led into Hell's Gate Canyon they came to West Gimly Highway, a narrow two lane of faded asphalt pocked with potholes that followed the U-shaped bend of Chalk River. It sloped sharply uphill, following the line of the valley ridge. Three kilometres further along, a small white sign hanging under a low overhang of tall firs indicated Concession 48. McCarty pulled the cruiser over to the side of the road in front of a line of parked patrol cars. A rough dirt road extended from the upper ridge of the highway to a small meadow, where it continued as a beaten down trail through a field of knee-high grass towards the valley ridge where half a dozen uniformed cops were gathered. The moon was high in the sky, casting everything in a cold, silvery glow.

"The body's about five hundred feet or so down the pathway over there, Mac," said one of the cops, waving his flashlight towards a clearing on the ridge, where a length of yellow tape had been strung across the black mud path that led down below.

"Did you call the coroner?" asked McCarty.

The other cop nodded. "I kept everyone away from the body site." The patrolmen had made the teenagers wait on the rock and told them to not touch anything. The kids were scared enough to do the unthinkable for teenagers – they did exactly as they were told without question. They had also realized too late that they had never even bothered to hide their party accoutrements, although they were all clearly underage. A case of beer, a bottle of white Bacardi, some bags of Doritos and a ziplock containing half a dozen joints sat out in the open. McCarty and Laupacsis talked to the teenagers for a few minutes. McCarty sensed they weren't they weren't hiding anything, they were just a frightened bunch of kids, so he took down their names and let them go home. All except for Peter Caiden, the boy who had found the body in the first place. Peter was a tall, gangly seventeen year old with a swath of angry red pimples across his forehead and a wispy blonde beard and mustache. His clothes and face were caked with dry grey mud.

"You guys party here a lot?" McCarty asked the boy.

"No?" he replied, uncertain what he should say.

McCarty smiled. "Listen, Pete, I don't give a rat's ass if you get out with your buddies for some pops or a few spliffs, understand? I'm just trying to figure out why there's a dead body in the woods."

The boy nodded. "Well, we came here maybe a couple of other times, like two, three weeks ago, but that's it. We didn't even know about this place before."

McCarty looked at the ground, noted a few crumpled beer cans, scattered cigarette butts and the circle of scorched rocks that marked an old campfire. "Who found it?"

"We all did. I mean, we were headed to our usual spot down near the bridge and found this place kind of by accident."

Cuthbert and Morris arrived just then. Cuthbert had a black duffle bag slung over his shoulder. "We got some company," he said, jerking a thumb up towards the night sky. Helicopters.

"News crews already?" McCarty asked. At this early phase of the investigation, he wanted to allow himself and the team to get oriented to the crime scene without spotlights, noise, cameras and questions they weren't ready to answer yet. McCarty took a couple of flashlights from the duffle bag. "You two stay up here and sort things out," he told the detectives. "Set up the base camp right here. Tape it off. We can get the trailer down, right?"

"I guess," Cuthbert shrugged.

"Okay," Laupacsis said to the boy. "Can you show us to the body?"

A black dirt path cut from the grassy field to feed deep into the valley forest. The detectives carried the flashlights as they followed the boy, walking down the slope along the path, like a children's game, pushing aside the tangles of bushes, stepping over the naked roots that jutted from the ground, the sound of their footsteps smothered as they moved deeper into the forest. The deerflies were biting at their arms, neck, face, every inch of exposed skin they could find. The detectives kept swatting at them, but almost instantly more arrived to replace their fallen comrades, swarming in it seemed from everywhere. "How much closer are we?" McCarty asked the boy.

"It's just down here." The first officers on the scene obviously didn't have a chance to mark things off yet. "We'll be there any second now. Just keep to the left."

McCarty lingered behind the others. The tiny branches that tore at his face and clothes seemed to grow denser every minute. He stared up at the trees for a moment. The leaves and branches hanging high overhead were so thick they choked off any remnants of the dying daylight that tried to reach the ground, making the forest dark and silent as a tomb, except for the incessant whine of the deerflies and occasional chirruping of birds. Laupacsis and the boy were just up ahead, standing with another patrolman who had been assigned to protect the scene. Yellow tape had been strung up around a small square in the forest.

At their feet, lying in a pool of yellow-white light from Laupacsis' flashlight, was what was clearly a human skull, face down, turned slightly sideways as though it was looking up at them. A single clump of long, reddish-blonde hair remained on the skull, tangled with dirt and leaves. The knobbled ridge of vertebrae was covered with a thin skein of brown parchment-like skin, while a fingerless arm stretched out before it, reaching into limbo. A thin white line of maggots surrounded the remains, wriggling in the black dirt, trying to escape the beams of the flashlights.

McCarty knelt down beside the body. The stench was nauseating. He shone the flashlight on the exposed part of the face. The decayed flesh appeared to be covered with tiny bite marks. Laupacsis narrowed his eyes. "What is that?"

"Animal depredation probably."

"Think it's a murder?"

McCarty shrugged. There were maybe eight to ten homicides a year in the entire region; most of them domestics, a couple of drug-related murders over the years, but murder victims rarely turned up in the forest in Chalk Valley. McCarty stood up and stretched. The Coroner's Investigators would have to do their work before the detectives could examine the remains. He looked at the boy, whose face had turned a pale shade of green beneath the streaks of dried mud.

"Why don't we have somebody take you home." The boy gratefully agreed and the patrolman escorted him back up the path.

Not even a buzz of traffic could be heard from here; they could have been in a primeval forest a thousand years ago and it would have felt no different. McCarty noticed the small pathways that led from this clearing and disappeared under the bushes, so low you'd have to crawl under them on your hands and knees. The little predators were watching their every move, their bright eyes gleaming from the darkness of the forest. They weren't used to visitors.

"Okay, get a few other guys down here and set up the perimeter," McCarty told Laupacsis. "Give me five hundred paces out and around, all directions. No one has access but the investigation team. We'll grid search it in the morning."

The coroner's investigation team arrived a few minutes later. McCarty knew the CI well, Sally Donovan, a straight forward, fortyish

D.L. Johnstone

woman whom he respected. The CI team quickly set up a bank of floodlights around the area. The silence suddenly exploded all around them with the loud chugging sound of a diesel generator churning to life. In a few seconds, the clearing was filled with artificial daylight. The body, hidden so long in the shadows of the deep forest, now lay brutally exposed, luminescent in a bath of stark white light. Donovan removed the crime scene tape that had been put in place by the first patrol officers and had a technician pound a three foot long metal stake into the ground near the victim's head. She followed that with three smaller wooden stakes, one near each side of the body and one at the feet, then tied lengths of yellow tape to the stakes, forming a perfect square around the body. The metal stake would serve as their point of reference for all evidence they discovered around the site, like the centre point of a compass.

Other policemen officers had arrived and were busy combing the area with flashlights. Black jokes flew like charms in the falling night. Donovan took photographs of the body in situ from several different angles. McCarty pointed out specific areas of interest for her as she took closer shots of sections of the body before she knelt down, pulled on latex gloves and started to carefully sweep layers of leaves and detritus off the body. The body was shirtless, wore jeans but no shoes or socks. McCarty had the CI techies place the leaves into clear garbage bags so they could be sifted through later at the lab for evidence.

"From the size and shape of the body, and from the clumps of long hair, I'm assuming the victim was a female," Donovan said. "The state of decay makes it difficult to confirm until the autopsy."

"What's that around her neck?" Laupacsis asked. The body had what looked like a dirty rag wrapped around her neck. Donovan raised her eyebrows and shook her head. She and one of her tech's laid out a body bag on the ground and carefully rolled the body over into it. Clusters of insects scurried from the sudden wash of white light, pale maggots squirmed helplessly while flat, gleaming checker beetles scrambled for cover. Patches of flesh had decayed or been predated from the victim's face, leaving the bare skull only, stripped of its fragile humanity. The bone over the right orbital crest had been crushed, a spider web fracture the size of a silver dollar. The cheekbone was also fractured. The blows that could have caused such damage could have been death blows, delivered savagely, mercilessly.

Donovan took photos of the rag tied around the victim's neck. A short, broken-off stick was twisted up in it. "Ligature," she said of the rag. Shit, McCarty thought, his stomach lurching. It was easily the most brutal body find he'd ever come across. The coroner's team worked methodically under the floodlights, occasionally swatting at the bloodthirsty flies that buzzed around their heads, but otherwise oblivious as they worked. The human tragedy of what lay before them had been put aside, compartmentalized. Now, they had a job to do.

Donovan reached into the body's jeans pocket with her gloved hands and dropped the contents into a plastic baggie. A few dollars, some coins, some dirt which she also bagged, hoping it could provide a clue as to where the girl had come from. No ID was found, unfortunately. "Okay, I'm finished," she said. "Are we good to go?"

"Yeah, we're good," McCarty said. The two detectives escorted Donovan and her techs as they carried the body up the hill towards their van. The uniforms had cleared the pathway of branches, making their journey up a little easier than it had been coming down. A crowd had formed up top along the highway to see what was happening in this normally quiet little patch of nowhere in the night. "Have one of the uniforms stand guard down here for the night," McCarty told Cuthbert.

The other detective nodded. Laupacsis lingered back with Cuthbert and Morris and chatted as McCarty walked towards his cruiser. The air smelled crisp with ozone. Raindrops spattered on the windshield as McCarty got into the car. A downpour would start soon. A woman strangled, he thought, her shattered body left to rot in this dark, lonely forest. Christ. I hope we catch this guy fast. He fished his silver flask out from under his seat, looked around to make sure nobody was watching, and took a long drink.

CHALK VALLEY
Available at Amazon.com
In both paperback and ebook formats

About the Author

D.L.Johnstone lives in the Toronto area with his wife, four kids and a half-dog/half-sasquatch named Charlie. He is also the author of the contemporary thriller CHALK VALLEY.

FURIES is his second novel.

If you'd like to contact him, please drop him an email at: dljohnstonewriter@gmail.com.

Or follow him on Twitter @DLJohnstone1.

He comments on thrillers, "indie" publishing and other miscellany at his blog: www.dljohnstone.com.

Acknowledgements

I am deeply indebted to the following individuals. Books may have a single author listed in the byline but they are rarely a solitary effort:

- My Mom, Bette, my first reader ever!

- My Dad, Lorne, and my brother, Tom – it never gets easier

- My meticulous and generous proof editor, Karen Gold

- My A-Team: Linda Boulanger, Jeroen ten Berge and Ryan Mason, for helping me pull together an amazing package. Where would this book be without first-class formatting, a fantastic cover and an outstanding map I wished I'd had when I started writing this book

- My beta readers: Laura Johnstone, Lisa Arbuckle, Martin Cho, J.P. Gagnon, Glenn Miller, Donna Spafford and Uri Gorodzinsky

- Helen Heller – this journey took a bit longer than I'd intended

- Robert (Sensei) Bidinotto, Theresa Ragan, D.B.Henson and Drew Kaufman, four tremendous authors who took the time to encourage and support a fellow traveller

- My four amazing kids – Emma Lee, Aaron, Liam and Megan, who inspire me everyday more than they will ever know

- And especially Cathy, who, after all these years, still manages to put up with me.

Made in the USA
Lexington, KY
14 June 2013